The Rose Beyond

The Rose Beyond

A Novel

S H A R O N   A L L E N   G I L D E R

warren press

M a r y l a n d

Warren Press, June 2014

The Rose Beyond is a work of fiction. Names, characters, organizations, places, and incidents either are the product of the author's imagination or are used fictitiously. Any resemblance to actual persons, living or dead, business establishments, events, or locales is entirely coincidental.

Library of Congress Control Number: 2014940201

ISBN – 13: 978-0692214695
ISBN – 10: 0692214690

Printed in the United States of America

For Mark
with love

And Jackie, Reid, Tom, Nate, Sam & Luke

Acknowledgments

Here goes is an apt way to begin about a debut novel. There are so many family and friends who continue to inspire and encourage me it is impossible to list everyone…you know who you are and I thank you immensely. Thank you to Sylvia Kerr Koren for sharing her beloved Nantymoel with me, and Gary Ulmer for his amazing library of vintage volumes about Washington, D.C. Many thanks to my earliest readers: Mark, Mom, Jackie, Aunt Jo, and Sue Thorpe. Special remembrances and thanks to my late father, Warren Collins Allen and my late uncle, James Elbert Allen, Senior for their love of horses and helping me imagine and give life to my dreams.

There are standout artists and fellow authors who continually re-light the fire on my procrastination: Ellen Gordon Gordon, Paul Grimshaw, James V. Murfin, Ted Gup, Suzanne Brue, Cissy Grant, Mark Brodsky, and Tom and Alexandra Clancy. In fact, Tom's words, "Just write the damn book," spurred me forward to complete what is before you today.

Much gratitude goes to the editors who publish my work including Alex Scofield, Steven Mauren, Ashley Halsey, Sharon Dan, Kathy Carey, Judy Hruz, Diane Dorney, Pam Schipper, Tim Seldin, Doug Tallman, and Comfort Dorn.

The words of teachers who said, "Keep writing" echo in my mind today, so I say a big thank you to several of them -- my fifth and sixth grade teacher, Mrs. Crowe, my senior English teacher, Mr. Vartoukian, and my college professors, Dr. Eileen B. Karpeles and the late Dr. Lucille Bowie.

But most of all, I thank my wonderful husband, Mark, for everything.

Special credit and thanks to these talented individuals
Author's photo: Stone Photography, Bethesda, Maryland
Publisher's logo: Mark Brodsky dba Graphic Squirrel

The Rose Still Grows Beyond The Wall

by A.L. Fink

Near a shady wall a rose once grew,
Budded and blossomed in God's free light;
Watered and fed by morning dew,
Shedding its sweetness day and night.
As it grew and blossomed fair and tall,
Slowly rising to loftier height;
It came to a crevice in the wall,
Through which there shone a beam of light.
Onward it crept with added strength,
With never a thought of fear or pride;
It followed the light through the crevice-length,
And unfolded itself on the other side.
The light, the dew, the broadening view,
Were found the same as they were before;
And it lost itself in beauties new,
Breathing its fragrance more and more.
Shall claim of death cause us to grieve,
And make our courage faint or fall?
Nay, let us faith and hope receive,
The rose still grows beyond the wall,
Scattering fragrance far and wide,
Just as it did in days of yore;
Just as it did on the other side,
Just as it will forevermore.

Prologue

July 7, 1877
Nantymoel, Wales
In South Cymru

Melting wax gently slid along the full length of a solitary candle on a nearby table. The candle's flame cast a wandering glow about the otherwise dark bedchamber. Each drip found a different stopping point, as though the wax was mimicking the cadence of a metronome methodically marking time. As Annie observed the process of the candle losing itself in a slow decline, a wish for more time floated like a vaporous cloud through her confused mind.

For nine months, Anna Hollingsworth had envisioned the day she would hold her newborn babe, caress it, and promise it protection within a loving home. For nine months, she had also been urgently consumed with the shame she endured for the tiny life growing within her womb without the fence of matrimony. Yet, even with the shame ever present in her mind, she eagerly anticipated the birth of her first child. The child would provide a constant memory of the one whose virile seed and charming ways had brought her to this day.

She lay on her mattress of goose feathers covered in gray cotton ticking. Its soft cushion lent little comfort from the distress pulsating deep in her belly. She found herself unable to retreat from her thoughts. Unceasing pain made its prickly journey throughout her torso to the caverns of her soul. She reasoned she was getting her due, being brought to account for having gone astray. *I must suffer.* There would be no one to clean her by marriage. No mate, no first words, no first steps. She writhed with pain as the list of never to be's marched across her brain.

"Just take a wee drop o' tonic 'cross yer lips, Annie gel. 'Twill sooth ye and help ye rest yer eyes a bit," urged Maggie Galligan as she tended her dear friend. "I won't be losin' ye gel, ye best be knowin' that. I love ye too much."

Several hours had lapsed since Dr. Smithfield departed Annie's cottage with his sister, Olivia, a midwife who lent assistance whenever her brother became overly burdened with patients, which of late was more frequent than not. Nantymoel was prolific with new life. Though a small village, it readily replenished itself with young boys to learn the trade and work the coalpit located at the peak of the valley. Many of the young girls were reared to work as servants at the Big House, the name locals gave to the residence of the colliery owner.

For nearly half her score and two years, Annie worked as a pit brow girl in the coal mines of Hargrove Colliery, though her greatest wish was to be a mother. She had seen other girls die without issue and she did not want that to be her fate. Her thoughts had never strayed to the possibility of complications. Pain once again gripped her sides. She squeezed Maggie's hand. It provided a lifeline, a sense of remaining connected and loved in her final hour of need.

Sweet girl. Newborn cries echoed in her brain as she labored to draw a breath. An evening breeze carried a fragrant rose petal from the garden beyond her room to the open window beside her bed. The petal delicately brushed against the windowsill and came to its final rest upon her nightstand. With another gentle gust, the candle faltered as its flame and Annie's body succumbed to a force greater than themselves. All was at once dark and quiet. The room filled with a bouquet of reverence as Annie slumbered into eternal sleep.

The Rose Beyond

Maggie softly clutched her friend's hand and buried her tear-drenched face into the folds of the cotton coverlet caressing Annie's mortal remains.

"Oh, no, no, no. It cannot be. God bless yer soul, Annie Hollingsworth," Maggie cried, lifting her head, giving a gentle squeeze, a final loving touch, to Annie's lifeless hand.

The stillness in Annie's fingers awakened Maggie's senses, confirming the reality she had tried to cast aside by shaking her head in denial. Her dear friend was gone and her lingering would not make that fact any less so.

"I must gather meself and see to arrangements for Annie fach," Maggie sobbed as she slowly rose to her feet and lifted the corner of her apron to dab away her tears.

She recalled Annie's softly spoken words issued forth in her delirium, 'Be me safekeeper.'

"An oak box," Maggie said aloud as she recited the words Annie had repeated over and over. "That lies below me. Safekeeper ye must be. Promise me."

Curiosity, and the need to honor her friend's request prompted Maggie to drop to her knees. She reached her hand beneath the bedframe and began blindly searching the space for the keepsake Annie so insistently wanted in her care. Darkness and emptiness were all that came to her hands.

"Annie must 'ave been mistaken. The delirium must 'ave got the best of 'er. I best be tryin' one last time jest ta be sure."

Maggie lay with her chest flat against the bare wood floor and slithered on her belly until she rested halfway under the bed. Again, her fingers searched the open undercarriage of the bedframe finding no obstacles in their path. She gave herself another scoot, finding herself almost completely ensconced in the shallow chasm beneath the bed. Choking away a cluster of roving dust balls, she continued her probe of the space when all of a sudden the very tips of her fingers seemed guided to a firm object.

"One more shimmy forward will do the trick," Maggie encouraged herself as she inched her way closer to her destination.

The object felt like a box, a wooden box with some hardware on one side. Slowly, to avoid bruising her head against the bed-frame, she made her way from under the bed, coaxing the box along with her. She pulled herself up, came to a sitting position, and reached under the edge of the bed to retrieve her find. She ran her hand about the wooden box. Moonlight cast through the bedside window allowed her to see that the box was oak indeed, widely grained and sturdy, with a brass keyhole latch on its front side.

Satisfied that her search had met success, Maggie lifted herself up, brushed herself off, and secured the box in her arms. She then turned and faced the sad truth before her as the reality of Annie's death hit her full force. Her dear Annie had been gathered into eternal rest and the time had come to say a final goodbye. Maggie cringed. 'Goodbye' was such a final word.

"The poor gel has gone to meet 'er God before her time. God rest yer soul, Annie fach. Mind me last words to ye, Annie gel," Maggie spoke with a tremble in her voice, "Ye can count on me gel ta take good care 'o this 'ere box fer ye. I'm honored to, I am."

Maggie turned away, walked slowly to the door and paused. She felt drained and suddenly chilled to the bone. The burden of sorrow weighed heavy on her chest. She attempted a full breath and gave a glance back at Annie whose body was stoically still and at peace. For her the world had ceased. Maggie found it so hard to leave, so hard to give a parting gaze. She caressed the box and held it close. It was a way to keep a part of Annie's life with her.

"Annie's taken her last breath and it has taken her," Maggie sighed with choked back tears. "Oh, gel, we 'ave the pain because we 'ave so much love. And, Annie fach, we all know it does not end at the grave."

She paused once more. Tugged by the urge to honor her friend, she began to sing a haunting Welsh lullaby learned at her own mother's knee:

Cariwach medd Dafydd
Fe nelyn I mi
Ceisiaf cyn maro
Roi tone arni i.

Bring to me
Said dying David,
My harp,
That I may play another tune
Before I die.

She moved to the doorway and closed her eyes tight. Her mind filled with images of Annie singing lullabies to her wee one.

"I hope the wee babe's heart is filled with its mother's music," Maggie reflected as she looked skyward and cast a silent prayer. *But, what of the child?* The last hours of distress had so consumed her mind there had been no room to question the smallest detail.

Chapter One

March 1897
Washington, District of Columbia

Arielle raced ahead as though her very existence depended upon it. As she fled, she tried as she might to have her feet keep pace with the thoughts rallying round and round in her head. Hateful words and epithets railed against her father spun in her head, becoming magnified by her outrage. *How could I have been so shortsighted? Why did I not see through his mask of deceit, his armour of intent, so smoothly soldered and firmly welded with years of manipulation and misdeed?*

Vibrant flashes of lightning lit the heavens as the endless void of evening sky became filled with the roll of ascending thunder. Ever so discreetly, droplets of rain eased upon the pavement in the pervading darkness. Their force became more insistent as the elements engulfed the turf below. Arielle gathered the skirt of her satin gown and lifted it just enough to insure her feet freedom of movement as the intensity of the ensuing storm strengthened. She tried most fiercely to drive pounding thoughts and images from her mind.

It had been only moments since she fled the manse of Sir Ian Hargrove. She dared not let her mind dwell upon the night's events but, how could she escape them? It would be folly for her to think that anything experienced could truly be forgotten. *No, my encounter with my father will not be cleansed on this foreboding night.* She wondered how she would find comfort, trust and peace again.

Blinded by the steady, persistent rainfall, she repeatedly opened and closed her eyes and swiped her gloved right hand across her face to clear her saturated raven lashes. All of a sudden, her solo flight was brought to an abrupt halt by a very tall, darkly cloaked figure. Arielle's heart leapt.

"I beg your pardon," he said as he perused the young woman before him.

Arielle took a wary step back. From the glow of the gas lit street lamp she saw a most handsome face. His eyes were deep blue, as though washed by the ocean's waves and his jaw was firm, with a cleft in his chin. His dark brown hair was thick with a moderate wave and his clothing was nearly dry despite the unrelenting storm.

"I beg your pardon," he repeated, noting her fine features as his eyes studied her troubled expression.

The hour was late, quite late for a young woman to be alone and making such a fast run through the streets. He noted her reaction to his presence, her pace and attire, all suggesting a hasty, impromptu retreat with no pre-calculated destination. Her long tresses were as saturated as her gown. He had seen freshly whelped pups drier from the laps of their mother's tongue, and certainly in less distress with their surroundings than this lovely lass.

"May I be of some assistance? My coach awaits. It seems wherever you are bound might be reached with some dispatch by covered coach rather than by foot."

Arielle welcomed the momentary pause in her motion his offer allowed, yet her anxiety was keen. She clearly could not trust this handsome stranger who had happened upon her path. *Trust.*

The word held little meaning for her. What did she know of trust? Her father's drinking, his outbursts, and his disregard for her mother left her with a very weak foundation for trust. She had spent too many years doubting his motives and his feeble explanations for his behavior.

"Do not concern yourself with our lack of formal introduction, milady. You may trust in my good judgment this evening. I am William Clay, at your service and, so I do not find myself in the same dilemma as yourself, I suggest we move quickly to the sanctuary of my coach."

"But, sir," Arielle said as she drew back, surprised that any sound was emitted from her voice box considering her alarm.

"There is no time for hesitation, milady. On a night such as this, even my horses become impatient with the elements. Come along before they find cause to step away and we are left to our own devices. My umbrella, I assure you, will do little to spare us in this downpour."

Arielle was consumed with confusion and ready to flee, though she found some comfort from the man's voice. As she hesitated, his very capable arms suddenly caught her up. In a single motion, William Clay reached around her waist, took her close to his cloak and under the security of his umbrella. She felt her feet leave the pavement as he lifted her up, her head dipped slightly to clear the ribs of his umbrella, and that motion forced her cheek to rub against his jaw. There was no time to cry out and, strangely, she chose not to do so.

Swiftly, he turned and stepped quickly toward his coach. Arielle observed a sudden flurry of activity as the footman jumped from his perch, made ready the steps, and opened the coach door for their entry. He handed Arielle forward to the footman's steady hands as she made her way into the dry surrounds and onto the tufted leather seat of the coach. William stepped in behind her and at once she saw they were not alone. Visible only by the wavering flicker of flames from the coach's lanterns, Arielle could see a female form sitting on the opposite seat.

"Well, William. What have we here? It appears, from the looks of this creature, that you have chosen to take-in the less fortunate. Oh, William, do entertain me with the details of this trollop."

"Alexandra, I would advise you to refrain from any indignities you might cast upon our guest and allow us, at the very least, a moment to feel as though we have not entered yet another storm, possibly more severe than the one wreaking havoc beyond the walls of this coach."

As William took his seat next to Alexandra, she placed her hand on his left knee and, patting it gently, she cut a wayward glance toward the sodden intruder as she continued her inquiry.

"I am merely curious about our guest and await an introduction. Do be a dear now and tell me all about her before another puddle from her gown collects at my feet."

"Introductions will have to be made by the lady herself, if she so desires," William responded with a pleasant nod toward Arielle.

"My goodness, William. Are you saying you don't even know her name? A woman, alone on the streets at this hour -- I can only imagine the services she has to offer. What will people think of us harboring a woman of such questionable virtue?"

"Alexandra, it would be best if silence overtook your tongue before you find *yourself* without shelter," he gently, but firmly warned.

William was quite familiar with Alexandra's erratic, willful and disobedient behavior. He knew it required a tight tug on the reins to harness her outbursts. The moment she felt threatened, her back ceremoniously arched and drew her into a fighting stance much like a feral cat scared out of its wits.

Arielle watched William's face. His speech belied a steady composure only betrayed by the recurring pulsation of a muscle in his left cheek. She gathered that William Clay was a man with little concern for the expectations of others. He appeared to be a man of his own mind which made Arielle wonder why he kept company with such a contemptible, tenacious woman who persisted even though thwarted by his reprimands. Whomever this woman was, Arielle was in no mood for her repartee and, feeling quite weak, had not the strength to engage in an unpleasant verbal exchange. It seemed that Alexandra was as persistent as the rainfall that pelted the roof and slid down the sides of the coach. What remained to be seen was which would outlive the other -- nature's fury or Alexandra's. She clearly was ruffled by Arielle's presence and was as curious as a feline on the prowl for prey.

"Perhaps I have gotten off to a poor beginning. I have never been fond of the rain or the inconvenience it delivers. I am Alexandra Whitaker, and whom, dear, may I ask, are you?"

Arielle looked the flaxen-haired inquisitor in the eye with an intimidating stare as a sudden chill overtook her and she shuddered from her shoulders to the tips of her limbs. William took note and reached for a carriage blanket that he unfolded and prepared to place around her when Alexandra retrieved it in mid-air.

"William, let me. Our guest is obviously scared and uncomfortable in your presence. In fact, I am afraid you have frightened her to silence since it appears she has lost the ability to exercise her tongue!"

Arielle could take no more. She had endured enough for one night. *How could I have succumbed to this unknown man and allowed him to seize me from the street placing me in a confined space with such unpleasant raillery? Out! I must exit now while any of my wits are left about me and before this vile creature called Alexandra prompts me to carry out every unladylike response I have ever envisioned.* As Arielle began to rise from her seat, William reached out and halted her departure with a light touch to her forearm -- a bold move he administered cautiously.

"My intent has not been to frighten you or hold you against your will, but merely to offer you safe harbor and transportation which I had hoped would be welcomed," William clarified, while keeping a close guard on Alexandra as he continued.

"You have only to give me the word and I will instruct my driver to deliver you to the destination you desire posthaste."

"Spare the horses an unnecessary journey and let her go on her merry way. You would be wise to save your chivalry for someone who appreciates it such as myself. Here, let me assist you by opening the door."

Alexandra's words became a faint ramble as Arielle's mind drifted away and the very thoughts she hoped to escape vividly raced to the foreground of her mind.

H ow could her father have done such a thing? The evening had begun like so many others. Upon his return to the manse from committee meetings at the Capitol, Arielle observed him pass by the parlor where she sat reading. He entered the library where she heard him lay down his leather valise and begin opening the day's correspondence. She heard him mutter to himself, slam his fist down upon his mahogany desk and move across the room.

Inevitability. The word resounded in Ian's head. The sound of a crystal carafe being unstopped and the clang of glassware made Arielle take pause as she braced herself to incur his wrath. A glass or two of scotch would slow his pace but never mellow his disposition. It seemed the drink stirred his ire and launched him on a grand crusade to verbally diminish everyone around him. How she wished she could slip away upstairs and remain indisposed for the night. But, it was too late. The library doors remained open and it was simply a matter of time before his crusade began.

Where is Mum? Arielle thought to herself. *Fiona must have announced Father's arrival. It is not like Mum to delay her presence.*

"Elsbeth!" Ian's voice resounded off the walnut paneled library walls and echoed off the ceiling becoming absorbed into the thick pile of the Bristol carpet.

"Elsbeth! Damn! Where is the woman?"

"Lady Elsbeth 'es stepped out fer a bit, sir, an' asked that ye not wait fer 'er return fer yer supper sir," Fiona answered in a nervous bow with her hands twisting the edges of her freshly starched apron.

"Stepped out, you say? Where has she gone and when does she plan to return?"

"Aye, that she did not say, sir. Only sir that I was to serve ye supper as soon as ye demanded. Oh, I mean, as soon as ye were ready, sir."

"Stop that blasted fidgeting and get on with it!"

Fiona dipped into an off-balance, half curtsy and scurried off to alert the kitchen staff that the master had spoken and they need waste no time in getting the meal on the table -- not that their expediency would assuage his temper.

"Blasted woman! Dine alone? I think not! Arielle! Answer me, girl! I know you are about somewhere!" Ian ranted as he paced the plush pile of the library carpet.

Arielle's concentration on the passage she held before her had long since waned. One blast from her father's voice was enough to drive the good from any mood and put one's senses on guard that retreat might be the only road to protection.

"Arielle!"

The latest issue of Godey's would have to wait. Arielle took great pleasure in studying the journal's pages, some with copper engraved illustrations and hand-colored plates featuring the latest trends in ladies' fashions. The household hints, poetry, and original writings filled her leisure time with great pleasure, but her father's arrival had put an abrupt end to her calm. She put the journal down, drew in her breath, and rose to speak.

"I am here, Father." Arielle announced as she stepped from the sanctity of the parlor into the foyer where he stood wavering in an unsteady stance, thrusting his right arm up into the air like a swordsman ready to lead the charge.

"Why have you not spoken up sooner? Here I am, looking for company, only to be answered by that poor excuse for hired help, Fiona, who was in the wrong room when the brains were being distributed!"

"I meant no discourtesy, Father. Please forgive me. I was quite engaged in an article from my Lady's Book and hoped to finish its reading before dinner commenced. However, now that you are home, my attentions, of course, are fully focused on our evening together."

Ian maintained a modestly healthy physique for his five foot ten inch height, having thus far spared himself the portly stature ever present among many of the successful businessmen and politicos with whom he consorted. It seemed, for some, their measure of success grew directly proportionate to the distance their abdomens held from the dinner table's edge. Uncharacteristically as well, in contrast to many of his peers, his face was essentially free of growth, laying his handsome features out for full view, except for a well-conforming mustache that added a complimentary infusion of salt and pepper gray to his upper lip, a perfect match for the distinguished color his hair had acquired over time. His unruly brows with their wayward follicles lent the only unkempt contribution to his face. He carried himself with the confidence and conviction of a much taller man. His charm was in balanced rhythm with his visage, which found him at times in uncompromising positions that, on occasion, and for wont of his better judgment, would come back to rankle and haunt his existence. He had an eye for women and they for him. Regardless of his looks and charisma, his position of power insured he was a magnet for the attentions of the opposite sex. Elsbeth, rather than live without, set her mind to living *with* her husband's ways. She accepted him, she loved him, and knew in her heart of hearts that he held her in a high place in his life. High in his mind and in his heart. Their bond was ever set.

He looked upon the young woman of no more than a score of years that stood before him. A beauty with her raven hair upswept and delicately caught in place with a pearl-edged tortoise shell comb. Several locks from her tresses drew his eyes nearer still as they fell upon the nape of her neck and sent his eyes cascading down her full form. Arielle drew in another breath that lifted her torso, giving her a remote sense of security as she tried to find comfort in a most uncomfortable moment. Her father's glare was disconcerting at the very least. She wondered what was troubling him, yet dared not ask. What she did know was that his manner was making her feel very awkward. She wished to proceed to the dining room, consume her meal and retire for the evening.

"Don't just stand there, my dear. Here, take my arm and join me. It appears that we have been abandoned and fate is our companion this eve. We must serve as escort for one another," he proclaimed as he extended his arm forth to Arielle's reluctant acceptance and the two walked arm-in-arm across the foyer to the dining room.

Opulence was the force de rigueur for the Hargrove manse on any occasion and it was no less so this night as the staff knew fully well the expectations of their employer and the ramifications to be administered for performance beneath his standards. The dining room was a brilliant profusion of crystal and silverware. The chandelier was lit with all fifteen of its candelabras fully aglow, casting light upon crystal prisms that danced delicately to and fro as the natural movement of the air caught them in its stride.

Overhead, light reflecting off the chandelier's plaster medallion illuminated its ornate design. The expansive surface of the mahogany table was free of cloth, each place setting distinguished by a fine Irish linen mat set with Elsbeth's mother's china, crystal stemware, and sterling flatware engraved with an Old English "H" that Ian had given to Elsbeth as a wedding gift. The dining room chairs were upholstered in tapestry fabric intricately woven in jewel tones. The rich blend of threads added warmth and grace to the setting. Arielle observed that the table was set for three which gave her hope that her mother would soon join them, knowing her welcomed presence would temper her father's mood.

Ian escorted Arielle to the buffet where a large sterling salver held several crystal decanters amply refreshed with scotch, sherry, cognac, and wine.

"What is your pleasure?" he inquired as he released Arielle's arm and selected two glasses placing one before himself and one before her.

"You will join me in a toast will you not?"

Her father was at times imperious and found it difficult to escape his role as patrician host. He often lent an aristocratic air, even in the sanctity of his home. His overbearing ways tried Arielle's patience.

"A toast? You puzzle me Father. What is the occasion?"

"Ah, the occasion. The necessity that brings us to raise a glass. That would be inevitability, my dear," he decreed, pouring himself a hearty portion of scotch from which he drew a hefty swig, throwing his head back, closing his eyelids, savoring every intoxicating drop.

As his eyelids lifted, his eyes rolled in an induced stupor as he filled his lungs with a deep breath of air. He exhaled and put his lips to the glass to resume quenching what appeared to be more complex than the mere desire to placate thirst.

"Pardon me Father, but I am a bit too fatigued for riddles. What do you mean by inevitability?" Arielle queried realizing she was treading on unstable ground by questioning him.

She had not meant to challenge him, but something in her tone had an irreversible effect. Abruptly, he turned and glared at her, his teeth clenched and his jaw firm. Placing his drink upon the table and gripping the back of the chair beside him with his left hand for support, he waived his right hand before him and, with a look of acquiescence, cast his hand to the right as though to signal a fait accompli -- an inescapable truth that was being ushered in by the devil's own disciples with no hope for reversal.

Arielle was alarmed by his display. Though she had many times witnessed her father's tirades, she had never seen him so unraveled. *What could have propelled him into such an unstable state? He usually has the emotional fortitude to withstand the most difficult situations his business dealings in the coal industry offer, as well as the*

challenges the Trade Council provides, yet, of late, his need for potent for-
tification finds him in constant consort with 'the drink.'

"Do you not see it, girl? Why, it is right before us. Staring at us straight away. Come closer," her father said, raising his glass to his mouth, consuming the remaining measure of scotch as he stepped toward Arielle.

His brain was not performing in its usual nimble manner. His movement was unsteady and, as he came forward, he fell into her path and steadied his hands about her waist. Looking directly into her eyes, he stared so intently that she felt the sear of his gaze as a heat came over her. His hands moved deftly from her waist to her bodice and as he groped her breasts, she became frozen in time, emitting no sound lest the servants be put on alert. His hands traveled up the creamy fullness of her breasts. He stroked the full length of her neck from her chest to her chin. His fingers came to rest at the nape of her neck where he took the liberty of releasing the tortoise shell comb holding her locks. Her silken tresses cascaded about her shoulders, fell on her décolletage, and became entwined in his clutches.

Arielle felt trapped, yet within her, a sincere desire to flee scurried forth. She backed away only to be retrieved by his grip. She turned and twisted from his grasp in an attempt to make her way clear. Her father lurched forward, reaching out for her. His fingers were unable to secure their target, having lost the nimbleness of their grasp as the drink overpowered his senses.

Arielle gasped as she took flight to the foyer determined to reach the front entrance and exit into the evening air. Nightfall had a way of twisting the familiar and making it appear darkly distant and unknown. To her, her father had become like the night.

"Arielle. Stop. You misunderstand," he slurred as he hastily pursued her path.

Arielle could not find it within her being to respond. Her heart was racing as she reached the foyer. From the glow cast by the gasolier wall sconces, she could see her father's form in the shadow thrown against the deep relief of the Lincrusta walls making his visage loom large and sinister. She had been uncomfortable in her father's presence before but never like this. His commanding nature and perfectionism usually left a fallen victim in their wake, but his attentions had never been so directed at her.

As she pursued her path to the front door and was about to place her hand upon the brass door handle, he caught her by the shoulder and spun her around ever so slightly to face him. Arielle reached for the hall rack to steady her stance and her hand rested upon her leather gloves she had deposited there after returning from an afternoon outing. She picked up the pair and gripped them tightly in her hand. The intensity of the moment overcame her. She raised her arm, drew it back, and in full throttle, swatted him across the left side of his face with such force that the gloves cracked against his cheek throwing him off balance. He stepped back, stunned by the assault to his face and fell into the large palm nestled in the corner of the foyer. He swiped the leaves from his face as he began flailing his arms, trying to restore himself to an upright position. Arielle, with a shaking hand, turned the latchkey and released the lock. Her first attempt to turn the door handle failed her as her nervous fingers slipped from the slick brass knob. She again grabbed the shiny hardware that would enable her escape and opened the door wide. She quickly stepped into the vestibule and raced down the flight of stairs that aided her escape to the street.

William reached for Alexandra's arm and pulled the coach door closed to protect the occupants from the rain. The driving force of the precipitation had found its way into the open portal and appeared as relentless as Alexandra's stormy rage.

"Alexandra, you must cease this behavior this instant. I shall not ask again," William cautioned as he turned to observe the fragile one across from him who had become so pensive.

He felt they had lost her to a catatonic state when momentarily she lifted her eyelids and looked directly into William's deep blue eyes. She found solace there and an honesty in his face that gave her pause. She collected her thoughts. Although it was difficult for her to stray from the scenes that remained so fresh in her mind, she shook off a chill that passed over her body and, feeling a renewed strength, she addressed her companions.

"Please forgive my behavior, sir. Mr. Clay, I am most grateful to you for the care you have extended to me. I am afraid that I find myself in an awkward position among strangers who wish me well," Arielle stated while casting a wary glance Alexandra's direction. "And yet, I have no lodging to which I may return this eve. I would be most grateful if your coachman would provide me transport to a boarding house. I believe there is one nearby on 16th street. My name is Arielle Hargrove and I thank you Mr. Clay -- and Miss Whitaker -- for your generosity."

Alexandra kept a keen eye on their charge as she delivered her dictum. "My, my, William. Listen. Hear her voice? My goodness, she is not of our shores. It is time to rein in the night as you would the restraints that hold back your team."

William was wont to ignore Alexandra as he watched the very gentle, pendulated motion of Arielle's densely green eyes. As Arielle spoke, his eyes studied her face. He observed a worried expression that seemed to go deeper than a reaction to the company within the brougham.

"I will dispatch my coachman at once. If I may suggest, there is a home known well to me near 16th Street and Florida Avenue that is operated by a relative of mine. I am confident that she will be able to accommodate you and you will find the surrounds to your liking, Miss Hargrove," William assured with a tilt of his head as he signaled the coachman and gave him orders to drive at once to 2460 16th Street, Northwest.

Within a flash, the team of finely bred Morgans took the coachman's command and with a jolt, had their charges headed on their way along the streets that had fallen victim to uncompleted road repair. As the rain continued to pour upon the clay paved street base, the road became more cumbersome to maneuver. In unison, the horses' hooves stepped in and out of the muddy mix creating a slippery path.

Arielle became fixed on the cadence of their shoes as they made contact with the saturated road and still kept their steady pace. *Surely the storm will soon subside and everything will be made clear.* Her thoughts circled around as the carriage came to a complete halt. Her evening was drawing to a close, but she harbored the unsettled feeling that her quest for clarity was only beginning.

A large gasolier fitted with numerous glass globes lit the entry of their destination. She glanced out of the coach door's window and was able to distinguish the numerals that marked her haven for the night, 2460 16th Street, her home away from home. She wondered what she would find on the other side.

Chapter Two

Washington, District of Columbia

E mma Clay Willard intended to remain at her 16th Street residence until she took her last breath. When she moved into the manse, she was newly wed to the not so comely Horace Willard, who was noted more for his ability to make friends and money than his looks. Emma adored Horace. His adoration for her was expressed many times over taking its most ostentatious form in Chestnut Heights, the mansion he commissioned renowned architect, Alexander Jackson Davis to create for her. Celebrated for his skillful design and use of the Gothic Revival and Italianate styles, Davis designed a magnificent Italianate residence for the wealthy Horace to present to his revered Emma on the occasion of their marriage. For Horace, the construction of the 16th Street mansion signified his deep regard for his new bride and his commitment to her that she could always take great comfort within the walls of their home.

As their prosperity continued, life at Chestnut Heights brought them years of happiness. 'CEAD MILE FAILTE' read a stone plaque over the front portal. The Irish greeting, 'A hundred thousand welcomes' characterized the kindness and generosity between husband and wife that was extended to family, friends and acquaintances who were the fortunate recipients of their graciousness. Horace was ever attracted to Emma's contagious enthusiasm and radiant outlook. She always projected the best in herself while focusing on and drawing out the best qualities in others.

Lavish parties with an enviable guest list comprised of politicians, entertainers, artists and business associates, were hosted at Chestnut Heights year-round. The Willards were devoted patrons of the arts and drew the foremost notables and celebrities to their home for dinners that were as lively as their personalities. Philanthropy abounded. Receipt of an invitation was an honor, to attend was a memorable event. Emma was a hostess extraordinaire and, with her sizeable household staff, created a grand, yet tasteful, atmosphere for gaiety, offering the finest in food and drink with healthy doses of lively conversation. One needed only to open a daily edition of the Washington Star and turn to its society pages to read of the latest soiree given by the Willards. That was until Horace was stricken with influenza, causing the weakening of his heart and untimely passing.

Upon his death, Chestnut Heights lost its lord and master and for Emma the pulse of the mansion lost its steady beat. Returning from his funeral, she darkened the main rooms of the manse by releasing the heavy folds of the room's brocade draperies from their tasseled tiebacks causing them to fall across the panes, obscuring the entrance of light that normally radiated through the long, beveled windows. The rooms were now the perfect match for Emma's spirit, darkened and secluded. She was alone in her thoughts, feeling that all the good had been drained from her and she would never regain her sameness again. With Horace gone, her world was askew. She tried to fight against the grief, but ultimately embraced it. She maintained her commitment to don widow's weeds by keeping herself outfitted daily in black attire so all who crossed her threshold could bear witness to her despair.

Emma received numerous visitors who wished to maintain their friendship with the fine mistress of Chestnut Heights, but, mostly, her days were spent with all the business of the aftermath of death. She plodded through papers, clothing, all the things that were her life with Horace. She spent many hours responding to letters from well-traveled friends and acquaintances who sent correspondence from the states and abroad, all delivering a general courtesy of concern.

Each letter was answered in kind on a note card of heavy cream-colored stock engraved with Emma's monogram and banded with a wide border of black. Each letter began with the identical phrasing, "If words could only speak what this heart of mine so deeply feels, I would speak them, but, there are no words in this world to properly convey the sincere thanks and gratitude I hold for your love, care and sympathy. I am truly blessed to have you in my life."

As the calendar rolled ahead to the progressing month, her stationery's charcoal border was reduced in size, acknowledging the coming closure to her official period of mourning. She stared at the calendar's heading, 'March,' and shook her head. *How could the mere flip of a page bring me full circle to one year of loss and command my emotions to be grief free?* It seemed impossible that a year had elapsed since his passing, yet the calendar, her instrument of time, could not be challenged. It was on a similarly overcast March morn that she had had to say her final goodbyes to her beloved Horace. She knew she would always be profoundly affected as much for having lost him as she was for having known him.

She recalled the words of her clergyman at the close of Horace's graveside service, "We have lost one among us from our everyday life and there will forever be a void. We must fill that void with sweet memories and an eternal hope that will sustain us these days forward until we meet again."

At the close of his words, he presented the spade that would transfer the excavated mound of dirt back from whence it came. She relived the repeated hollow sound of the first dampened lumps of clay as their weight pounded against the top and sides of the simple pine box holding her cherished Horace for the rest of eternity.

Emma steadied herself to read the declamation she prepared to recite at his service. She prayed for strength of voice to carry her through each well-sought word as she followed her clergyman's blessing:

> *Peace be with you gentle friend and child of God, so dear,*
> *As you enter heaven's home from too brief a visit here.*
> *'Til we gather at the steps of God's eternal door,*
> *When farewell tears now shed, will need flow from us no more.*

Alone in the parlor, as she glanced through a family album of photographs she kept on display on a side table, she had an epiphany. She ran the fingertips of her left hand across a daguerreotype of Horace and herself taken just before they boarded a train at the B & O Depot to begin their honeymoon in New York. Horace made all the arrangements with deluxe accommodations at the Metropolitan Hotel. The lovely brownstone was the beginning of their married life that spanned nearly forty years before he took ill. Tears welled in her eyes. The hotel met its demise the year before she lost Horace. When they learned of its demolition, they reminisced about their time in the city and the abundant upscale shops at their disposal that he insisted she frequent to buy whatever her heart desired. Teardrops began cascading from the corner of her eye down the length of her cheekbone as the joy of that day and their week in New York filled her with melancholy.

With her right hand, she brushed the tears from her cheek as her eyes settled upon the golden band gracing the ring finger of her left hand. Horace's words, spoken at the altar so many years before, came to her as clearly as if he were in her very presence at this very moment. She could sense him caressing her shoulder, as he was so wont to do, as he leaned forward to give her a reassuring peck on the cheek. *With this mind, body and soul, I thee embrace and, if by act of fate, destiny finds us parted, I give you this ring as our bond and symbol of eternal love. My vow and pledge come to you with all my heart and devotion. I grant you my undying love and wish you joy, hope and fulfillment all the days of your life.*

Reliving Horace's decades old pledge as he held her left hand and gazed into her eyes, struck a new chord in Emma's being. She felt the load of despair that had consumed her lighten. The words joy, hope, and fulfillment co-mingled in a protective bond giving her renewed courage and strength. Horace would want nothing less for her yet, it was most difficult for her to move on when she was embracing her mourning. She would accept destiny's fate and God's will, doing her utmost to live as he always wished her to live.

Copious amounts of prayer, and empathy expressed by friends and family had kept her strong. The reality that Horace had gone from her forever, and that she must let him go, floated upon her like an airborne kiss. She gave herself permission to be cleansed of the grief that for twelve months held her in a tomb of sadness.

Emma evaluated her circumstances, thinking of conversations with widowed friends whose husband's predeceased Horace. *Ah, we widows, though saddened with grief, are fortunate to be left behind for a time with the anticipation of tomorrow's sunrise.* Emma knew this was not the way she would have planned it. Just before closing her eyes each night, as she lay alone in her bed, she recited Shakespeare's Horatio's famous words, "Good night sweet prince and flights of angels sing thee to thy rest." The words provided an unsung lullaby to comfort and carry her into the quiet of night.

As Arielle directed her attention to the dwelling before her, she saw the form of a stately manse, only dimly visible in the mist created by the rain drenched night. Massive exterior lamps illuminated its portico.

"It would seem that we have reached your journey's end for this eve, Miss Hargrove," William's voice reassured as he looked Arielle's way and readied himself to exit the coach.

"William, take your seat. Surely Miss Hargrove can find her way beyond the door of the coach without further assistance," Alexandra announced as she virtually seethed with every word she emitted.

"Miss Whitaker is quite right, Mr. Clay. I shan't take another moment of your time or patience. The generosity you have bestowed upon me is something for which I am most grateful," Arielle responded as she shifted her glance from William to Alexandra with definite ire toward the latter.

"If you will allow me, Miss Hargrove, I would prefer to see you inside and, considering the hour, assure that the mistress of the house is not caused undo alarm by our knock to her door."

"As you wish, Mr. Clay," Arielle said as she leaned forward to rise and exit the coach.

"William, shall I," Alexandra chimed in only to be stopped in mid-sentence as she was met by William's immediate stare.

"I won't be but a minute, Alexandra. Certainly you can amuse yourself for that period of time."

William looked to Arielle and with a dip of his head toward the door made ready his exit as the footman took his position. He held the door making the way clear for his charges to take their leave. As William stepped to the ground, he turned promptly toward the coach's open portal extending his hand to Arielle. He found himself engaged by her beauty. The moment found her radiant face highlighted by the emanation of light from fixtures adorning the mansion whose walls would be her respite for the night.

Arielle cast her concentration to the exit steps, then shifted her gaze to William. Her brilliant green orbs met his eyes. He scanned her porcelain skin marred only by a faint crusting of tears that journeyed down her cheeks. Luscious curls, falling loose about her shoulders, framed her face. As she made her way down the coach steps, her raven locks teased the ruffled edge of her gown as they touched, then fell gently away. Hesitantly, she took William's hand, becoming transfixed by his deep blue eyes. A sensation she could not trace pierced her being, as his comforting power overcame her, causing her to freely give over her hand to accept his proffer of assistance. William felt the softness of her as their palms engaged, his hand enveloping hers as her long, delicate fingers united with his strong, assuring grasp to lead her to sound footing on the pavement below.

The footman's close of the coach door harkened the concentration of the two, breaking the spell to which they had succumbed. They made their way beyond the refuge of the carriage, across the curb and up the stairs to face the wide double doors that protected the vestibule of the mansion from the world's elements.

William opened the door, standing back to let Arielle proceed. The two stood within the vestibule collecting their composure as William raised his right hand to the brass doorknocker to announce their presence. In very short order, a tall, lanky fellow with a wry grin greeted the two. He motioned them forward.

"Good evenin', Master Clay. Well, sure is good ta see you, sir. Miz Willard's just gwain up ta retire for the evenin' but I'm sure as I am 'bout my own name that she'll want ta know you're here ta see her, yas, I sure am sure 'bout that!"

"Thank you, Thomas. It is my pleasure to see you as well. It has been a while. Please inform my aunt that I am in the company of a guest who desires lodging for the eve," William explained with a pleasant smile as he gave a glance toward Arielle.

"Yas, sir. Youse can gwain the parlor and I'll goes 'n fetch Miz Willard. Yas sir," Thomas confirmed as he ushered William and Arielle into the parlor, then drifted off to let the mistress of the manse know there were guests to be received.

Arielle looked about the parlor as she took a seat on the edge of a nearby needlepoint-covered settee positioned just opposite the fireplace. The capacious room evoked a sense of things having been collected over time. The room was grand, one of the grandest she had seen since her arrival in Washington. The walls were painted a most daring shade of crimson that showed itself again in the expansive carpet that nearly covered the hardwood floors. Arielle recognized the carpet as a William Morris design, his work having recently been featured in an article in Godey's.

Though sizeable, the space was designed to inspire conviviality. The double parlor held several groupings of individual settees and lush slipper chairs indicating its great resourcefulness for accommodating large numbers of guests who could be guaranteed the opportunity for intimate conversation despite the room's grandeur. Columns with gilded capitals were the only structures dividing the room. Their ornate top pieces were ornamented with large acanthus leaves.

Remnants of the day's fire lingered as random embers went through their paces, casually cracking and popping, spitting themselves about the confines of the firebox, ultimately finding themselves spent. William remained standing, looking about the space, turning his attention away from Arielle toward the foyer where the sound of approaching footsteps could be heard.

Within moments, a woman appeared and approached William with the excitement shown when one receives an unexpected visit from someone held dear.

"William, when Thomas told me you were here, oh, I just cannot tell you how happy I am to see you, I had not been informed of your return and must say, I am most pleased. I was just thinking about you. Oh, you look so wonderful, as always, of course, dear and..." Emma could hardly catch her breath with her excitement as she turned from William and caught a glimpse of the beautiful young woman who sat perched at the edge of her settee.

"Oh, you must pardon me, my dear. Thomas did say that a guest accompanied you and I fear I am rambling on so that there has been no opportunity for a proper introduction. William, I would be delighted to meet your guest," Emma continued with much enthusiasm as she looked toward the lovely one with raven hair.

"Aunt Emma, let me introduce you to Miss Arielle Hargrove. Miss Hargrove, this is my aunt, the charming Mrs. Emma Willard, who is notorious for the inexplicable hospitality she bestows upon all who enter. Aunt Emma, Miss Hargrove is in need of lodging for the night and I assured her that she would find your accommodations most suitable to her needs," William explained as he turned from Emma to Arielle with his hand outstretched in a welcoming gesture.

"Oh, William. You bring sunshine to what has been a most dreary day! Miss Hargrove, one needs no more than William's good word for me to find your presence a most welcomed addition to my home," Emma assured as she approached Arielle with an abbreviated nod to bid her welcome.

Arielle responded with a shallow smile, the most she could muster considering the foregoing circumstances. She greeted the woman of the manse with a somewhat brisk, but sincere response.

"Mrs. Willard, it is most kind of you to welcome me into your home on such limited notice."

"My dear, you may feel totally at home here. Chestnut Heights knows no strangers. All who cross the threshold and linger, no matter how short the while, comprise a family of sorts and, quite frankly, I would have it no other way. Through the years, so many have traversed the risers to the rooms above that if it were plausible, the staircase could provide a wealth of stories about those who have tread the same path with a diversity of missions. How do the Italians say it? *Chi entra come amico, parte come famiglia. Those who enter as friends, leave as family.* Enough of my chatter, come, let me get you settled, Miss Hargrove, and ensure that your creature comforts are amply satisfied for the duration of your stay."

"William?" Emma queried as she turned to face her handsome nephew. "You must promise to return very soon so we may have a nice, long visit. I want to hear all about your travels and be brought current about your social life! You know it keeps me young to hear of your, dare I say, exploits!"

"Aunt Emma, it will be my pleasure to accept your invitation. There is some business to which I must attend tomorrow, but I assure you, I will call again very shortly," William answered as he reached for his aunt's hand which he brought to his lips. Placing a soft kiss on Emma's right hand, he bowed and turned to Arielle.

"You are in the best of hands, Miss Hargrove. I trust your nights stay will bring you comfort and that the 'morrow will provide clarity. Until next time, I bid you both a good evening."

William's words were sincere and comforting. Arielle responded with a 'thank you' as William walked toward the foyer, bid Thomas adieu, and stepped through the portal descending the steps to the street level. He heard the door to Chestnut Heights latch behind him as the footman took his post to assist him. He reached forth, hastening the opening of the coach's door which caught William full face with Alexandra's glare.

Nature's fury may have ridden its course for the night, but the same could not be spoken for Alexandra. Her serpent green eyes seethed, nearly emitting smoke. She drew in a deep breath expelling it slowly, setting the pace for the oratory that began to spill from her lips.

"William, I am aghast and dismayed that you, one of such fine stead and judgment that is visible on most occasions, would allow your exposure, much less mine, to the likes of that woman. Why, there is no telling what trouble or misrepresentation may come of it and, leaving me in the chilly confines of this carriage while you pay a social call with that loose woman, why, I had the mind to order Hap to take leave of this place so I might retreat to the sanity of my father's manse."

"Alexandra, the evening has held more than either of us might have anticipated. And, I hope you do not refer to my Aunt Emma as that 'loose woman.' I am afraid that your imagination does not serve you well this evening. We simply performed a kind service to one in need. There is no more to it than that. Come, let's savor the time we have remaining before we call this night to a close less we diminish the earlier hours spent together," William responded as his deep blue eyes converged directly on her face and she became transfixed.

This was neither the first nor the last occasion he would endure the rigors of time with Alexandra. She felt the bristle leave her skin. Her shoulders fell at ease and a delicate, fawn-like quality overtook her. The threat had left her midst. She was no longer on guard and, she was once again alone with *her* William.

Chapter Three

Washington, District of Columbia

The walls and ornately carved domed ceiling in the staircase at Chestnut Heights were fitted with lavishly woven Old World scenes of castles nestled among broad landscapes in subtle blues and greens. Arielle looked up and around at the scenes that were deeply embodied with rivers and glens. The pieces appeared faded, as though woven from medieval times. Sunlight that flooded the uppermost space of the staircase lent its part to further age the fabric adding a rich, pretentious appearance. The weighty tapestries were as snugly affixed to the walls as the stairwell's wainscoting and friezes. Each section had been notched and edited to fit perfectly about the turns in the carved wood of the door surrounds.

Arielle became keenly aware of her need for air. She did not feel faint, but she was feeling the residual, spinning effect of last eve. Looking up at the decorative ceiling while standing on the staircase was also contributing to her sense of vertigo. She realized she was holding her breath, taking in only enough air to sustain her. She drew in a hefty gale to chase the vertigo aside. Her chest expanded as her lungs took in the welcomed oxygen and her body immediately released some of its rigidity as a natural rhythm was restored to her heart, mind and lungs.

She gazed again at the walls about her. The tapestries lent an aristocratic air to the mansion, one from which Arielle drew comfort. She was a child of privilege and no stranger to upper class accoutrements. *This home was clearly built as a place to remain for life. I will find Mrs. Willard, thank her for my nights stay and be on my way.* Arielle condensed her thoughts and, feeling much more herself, moved along the landing to the next flight of stairs taking her to a point of pause on the final landing. It was at that moment that she saw him.

Simon Peabody was a curious fellow with a penchant for detail. A notebook and pen kept in his vest pocket made a ready appearance the moment conversation commenced that supplied the opportunity for him to extrapolate on a topic upon which he felt particularly well versed -- there seemed to be more rather than fewer of such topics. His knowledge base more than made up for his physical stature. The good Lord had provided him with an enormous brain yet a body that was inordinately small, but well formed. He walked at such a fast clip that he appeared to be scurrying as his short legs made every effort to keep up with the rapid placement of his feet to the floor.

Arielle observed the sprite man from the landing, giggling to herself as she watched the orchestration of his movements from the library where he exited with a book and scurried through the foyer into the parlor, all the while muttering to himself as he flipped among the pages of the book.

"Infernal vision," Simon said with irritation as he adjusted the wire-rimmed spectacles that rested a slipped distance from the bridge of his nose.

"This has to be the proper journal -- yes, has to be, has to be." Simon continued muttering and flipping pages.

Arielle resumed her descent of the staircase. She paused for a moment with her hand resting on the highly polished balustrade, then walked to the entrance of the parlor. Her presence was unknown to Simon as she stood behind the portière made of rich brocade embellished with golden bullion fringe, held back in a swag by a hefty, tasseled silk cord.

Simon's muttering parlayed into a conversation where he was the sole participant, asking himself questions, then responding predominantly in the negative until he came upon the answers to his quest.

Lifting a looking glass from a nearby table and placing it over his selection, Simon emphatically exclaimed, "Exactly as I expected. Heliotropic is correct. Helio, from the Greek for sun, and tropic, from tropos, meaning turn. Not autotrophic, which, let me see, is here defined as capable of self-nourishment. Nothing about the flower or stem turning toward the sun as in heliotrophe. Oh, and autotrophic is opposed to heterotrophic which is from the Greek, one that feeds or obtains nourishment from outside sources. I see, as it were, the human race is full of heterotrophes! I must tell Miss Emma. I'll make a note of it. In just a few short months the trees and flowers will have an abundance of sun to stretch their limbs skyward. Heliotropic, heliotropic, heliotropic. Say it three times, remember it three-fold." Simon lectured himself as he took pen to hand making notations in his notebook.

Closing the large reference book, Simon swiveled toward the parlor's doorway resuming his quickstep to leave the room. Arielle stepped back, hoping to remain obscure when she heard footsteps coming from the hallway behind her. She hoped no one had observed the watchful stance she had been keeping, and found herself a bit flustered as the footsteps behind her gained proximity to her heels while the impish man moved with great speed into the threshold of the foyer. Not to be distracted from his agenda, Simon continued on his way to the library caught in mid-stream by Emma's greeting.

"Why, good morning, Simon. I see last night's storm has not dampened your thirst for the written word," Emma teased as she pointed to the book Simon cradled with both hands.

Somewhat befuddled by being thrown off course, Simon stammered his retort, "Oh, oh, oh, Miss, Miss Emma, good morning to you. Yes, yes, yes, today promises to be a sight drier than yesterday's standards. Needed the rain though, needed the rain, yes, needed the rain. Pardon me though. I must see to it that this book finds its proper housing. Best to know it is back and secure on the chance anyone needs to avail themselves of its contents in the future. Pardon me, pardon me, yes, pardon me," Simon repeated with a tilt of his head, lifting one hand away from the book to realign his eyeglasses. The motion became a parting salute as he hastened forward into the library.

Arielle turned to face Emma and a broad smile lit up the elder one's face. Emma had had little opportunity to focus on her guest the night before with the lateness of hour and Arielle's disheveled state. She had not seen the full extent of her guest's beauty. The raven tresses, which last night had so carelessly fallen about her shoulders, were swept up in a lovely twist with softly spiraling tendrils accenting the sides of her face. Her features were crisp and she held herself in fine stature as one would who has been well prepared for social proficiency. Emma was delighted to see that the dress she laid out for Arielle was a perfect fit, its bodice not too snug about her ample breasts. The mid-section below the bodice was in excellent proportion to Arielle's slender waistline. The girl appeared renewed by her night's rest yet, Emma sensed an air of disquiet in her lovely emerald eyes.

"Forgive me, Mrs. Willard if I appear too bold. I suffered a moment of distraction, finding myself drawn toward the activities of your guest. I am quite ashamed to have been viewed observing him so," Arielle explained as she cast her eyes toward the library feeling less than at ease.

"Give it not a second thought, dear. Simon has a way of engaging one's curiosity, particularly upon first meeting. He is quite an innocuous soul though and keeps all of us amused and enlightened with his daily liturgy, engrossing himself in a self-directed study of people, places and things. He is enormously brilliant, which may explain his eccentricities and..." Emma stopped in mid-sentence as Simon came into the foyer.

"Simon, if I may take a moment of your time, I wish to introduce you to Miss Hargrove. Miss Hargrove, I would like you to know Mr. Simon Peabody, who, as I was about to say, is to be applauded for the astute contributions he has made in recommending various plantings for my gardens. Each year they bring me more pleasure than the preceding. The trees and shrubs have matured over the years as faithful old friends. You must see the gardens in June, Miss Hargrove, for they are full burst with color and, in the shade of the chestnuts, one can take tea and make most bearable a humid Washington afternoon." Emma beamed as she spoke of her sanctuary beyond the walls of her home.

"I shall look forward to that Mrs. Willard. It is most kind of you to extend such invitation to me." Turning to Simon, Arielle continued, "Mr. Peabody, I am pleased to make your acquaintance, sir."

Simon squinted as he studied the girl, moving his closed mouth to the left then to the right, scrunching and wiggling his nose negligibly, contorting his face like a half-hearted hare. Arielle wondered if his indifference was a sign of his preoccupation with his earlier quest or perhaps resulted from some lack of social discourse.

"Very rare, very rare, yes, very rare indeed," Simon announced as he leaned toward Arielle, maintaining his squinting fix on her face.

Arielle found herself feeling somewhat self-conscious as the moments surrounding Simon's scrutiny increased. She felt the heat of embarrassment swelling on her chest and face.

"Simon, I must take it upon myself to ask you to explain your observations, which I am sure, of course, are to the benefit of Miss Hargrove, lest you leave unresolved the curiosity of us both." Emma requested pleasantly with a firm look at Simon, letting the odd little man know that an immediate explanation from him was due and she would accept no less.

"As I watch your attempt to focus on Miss Hargrove's eyes, I am reminded of one of Horace's observations that it is a convenient phenomenon that as our appearance fades with age, so does our vision. It is the good Lord's way of protecting us from the truth of a mirror, I suppose."

"Miss Emma, I am merely noting that Miss, Miss Hargrove's eyes are most out of the ordinary indeed. Emerald, like fine gems with freckles I believe, freckles, yes, iris freckles is what they are called. One does not see this every day to be sure! Miss Hargrove, do not think me too forward when I say, your eyes are st-stunning! What exquisite specimens of iris freckles. Yes, st-stunning. Those little bits of pigmentation manifesting themselves in fine flecks of gold radiating beyond your pupils, why the illuminating effect is quite captivating and a pleasure to behold indeed, indeed, indeed. St-stunning," Simon reiterated as he stepped back, with a broad confirming smile, feeling pleasingly sated by his engrossment with Arielle's distinctive eyes.

He left the two, walking the length of the foyer and ascended the broad mahogany staircase to its first landing where he took firm hold of the spiral carved newel post that acted as his springboard to turn and continue to his room.

"Miss Hargrove, Simon's remarks are by no means meant to make you feel uncomfortable. He finds fascination in all that is about and, I fear, this morn finds your eyes objects of his interest," Emma assured as she hastened to move her guest to the dining room while breakfast service remained underway.

Arielle appreciated the subtle transition Mrs. Willard tactfully accomplished although she was somewhat unnerved by Mr. Peabody's attention and was not directly sure how she felt about the man. His coarse and abrupt manner was not easily dismissed, yet she was not so sure the quirky little imp deserved to consume much of her thought. However, Mrs. Willard tolerated his manner with resolve and seemed most forgiving of his approach. She, having known him longer, would be her compass at this juncture and she would therefore defer to the elder's judgment regarding his conduct as they proceeded to breakfast.

The dining room at Chestnut Heights was most impressive. Frequently the scene of fine food, spirits, and gaiety, the space had entertained an eclectic palette of individuals from the local art community to Washington's elite. The walls were richly appointed with ornately carved woodwork that extended the full width and height of the walls starting from just above the intricate, two-tone parquet floorboards and rising fifteen feet to the embossed coffered ceiling.

A highly polished banquet-length table centered the room over which hung a beautifully embossed silver chandelier, the most beautiful Arielle had ever seen. It was dazzling, with a bounty of clear crystal pendants with light catching facets. She gained a sense of the enormity of the parties hosted by the Willard's as she admired a large mahogany sideboard, its china cabinet fitted with silver sconces. Soaring nearly to the ceiling, the large piece held a stunning array of gleaming china, crystal, and silver.

Arielle looked to the far corner of the room where a charming feature caught her attention. An octagonal, turret-like space held a table covered by a cloth of English Cluny lace. Benches, upholstered in a thick tapestry melding the colors of forest green, gold and aubergine into a lively floral and leaf pattern, provided ample seating. The windows were dressed with an eggplant-hued velvet swag and jabot treatment trimmed in gold and green tassel fringe. Above the draperies, each window was topped with a leaded glass panel in the style of Louis Comfort Tiffany. Arielle had every reason to believe that with Emma's impeccable taste, and the funds that were obviously at her disposal, the transoms were most likely a product of the Tiffany studios.

"Miss Hargrove, come and enjoy your breakfast in what I champion to be the best seat in the house. As I mentioned, my gardens bring me great pleasure. The view of the gardens from this nook can be breathtaking, especially when the blooming season finds its greatest force. Make yourself comfortable and I will notify Cook that you are ready to receive your morning sustenance," Emma invited.

"Thank you, Mrs. Willard. Though I would be most grateful if you would join me. Perhaps in a cup of tea if you have already partaken of your morning meal," Arielle requested as she took a seat in the nook, which gave her a clear view of the grounds.

"Why, my dear, I would take much pleasure from that. I shall return in just a moment," Emma replied as she walked to the passageway leading to the kitchen.

Arielle turned to look through the windowpanes that were void of both glass curtains and lace panels. *Ah*, Arielle thought, *Mrs. Willard took every consideration into account when planning the view of her gardens.* The openness of the window treatment provided immediate sight access to the plantings about the grounds.

The Willard property was swathed in a lush cloak of green. Towering chestnut trees with calipers exceeding one foot were prolific and lined the perimeter of the property like a privacy belt protecting the chastity of the space. Spread about rather than clustered, their branches were laden with buds waiting for the first signal of spring to open their natural gifts of foliage. She envisioned returning to Chestnut Heights during summer's heat to seek the coolness of the trees and sit below their canopies. *What a colorful sight this must be when all is in bloom. Spring. Will the new season bring clarity?* Arielle looked to the sky. Any glimmer of sunlight was shrouded in clouds, as opaque as the thoughts she pondered. Her mind spun to the matters at hand. *I must return home. Mum will be worried and Father, heaven only knows, will be furious. With any luck, he will have begun his day with an early rise and be well settled in his office. I will have only Mum with whom to respond.* The thought was no relief to Arielle. *What ever shall I tell her? If I cannot understand, how am I to make her understand?*

Arielle became aware of a rustling sound and movement in the garden. She looked to find what proved to be the garden fairy himself, Simon Peabody, flitting from shrub to shrub like an elusive butterfly taking notes all the while. The morning breeze wrecked havoc with the limited tufts of silver gray hair remaining on his balding pate. His hair follicles whipped to and fro, signaling the wind's direction, making him a human weathervane of sorts. He tweaked dead blossoms from their hosts, first visually making his way about each plant before physically completing his editing process. Emma returned to the dining room. As she approached the nook, she saw the scene that captured Arielle's attention.

"Simon is about his daily ritual. He has an insatiable desire to keep my gardens in perfect balance. He maintains a log, recording each plant and all the details of its growing season," Emma remarked as she took a place in the cozy nook. "His great success comes from not allowing any part of the garden to deteriorate. Simon is consumed by details and forever finding new ways to transform areas so they appear to naturally evolve. I am reminded of our great statesman and president, Thomas Jefferson, with whom Simon feels a kinship. Jefferson said, 'There is not a sprig of grass that shoots uninteresting to me.' Simon, in his own way, has adopted Jefferson's dogma for there is nary anything growing that escapes his attention or observation."

"If I may ask, how did he come to live at Chestnut Heights?" Arielle inquired hoping to be enlightened about Emma's association with Simon.

"By all means you may ask and I shall answer, my dear. Simon evokes inquiry by his very nature. When my late husband, Horace, and I first married and moved to Chestnut Heights we secured a horticulturalist to design the grounds. Unfortunately, he departed this dear earth before many of the plantings were in place. We were made aware of Simon who at the time was a professor at Georgetown University and quite instrumental in the creation of the botanical society there. He was a follower of the work of Frederick Law Olmstead, the New York landscape gardener who created the beautiful plans for the Capitol grounds and is so noted for his admirable ornamentation of Central Park. Simon has also studied the work of L'Enfant, thus he delights in grids and corridors, finding them very effective in English garden designs. Horace and I invited Simon to review the plans for our grounds. His ideas were met with such enthusiasm that we hired him to complete the scheme for our gardens that are noted for their resemblance to the city itself. It is as though Chestnut Heights is the hub of a wheel laid on a gridiron with streets and avenues of shrubs and flowers radiating from it. Simon has no family so, upon his retirement from Georgetown, I suggested that he take up permanent residence at Chestnut Heights. In return, he monitors the conditions of the grounds," Emma explained.

"He is your groundskeeper?" Arielle queried.

"So it would seem. However, I prefer to consider him part of my Chestnut Heights family and a managing officer since there are others who perform the necessary physical tasks associated with the grounds maintenance," Emma further informed.

"Your point is well taken," Arielle stated, thinking Emma Willard was one of the most gracious women she had ever met, who despite, or was it, in addition to, her great wealth, was a humble humanitarian.

She was a rare breed. Arielle reflected how frequently she was dismayed to encounter ostentatious folk at the parties her parents hosted who held the news of their events and material acquisitions to be of much higher importance than any interest they could take in another human being. Emma Willard was the perfect antithesis of such sorts. She was a keen listener with a genuine regard for the thoughts and feelings of others. As Arielle spoke, Emma kept her eyes fixed on the younger one's face, allowing no distractions as she listened intently to what was said. Arielle had a good feeling when she was in her company and felt fortunate to have been brought to her doorstep.

"Simon designed my gardens with an equinox of public and private places, each given the proper measure of dense and airy plantings. You must visit again soon for I would enjoy your company and we will have ample time to tour Simon's complete masterpiece."

"You have a grand, stunning home which shows much care and planning within and without. You have been most kind to welcome me on a moment's notice and for that I shall be forever grateful. After breakfast I shall need to take leave for my return home. I am sure it will not be difficult to secure a cab within a block of your home," Arielle stated, as Emma promptly noted an expression of worry that shadowed her lovely face.

"My dear, you are most welcome to join me here at anytime and I shall hear of no such thing as a cab ride home. Thomas will summon my driver to ready the carriage for your departure. You need only state your destination and he will have you home in short order, if you are certain that is what you wish," Emma responded as she studied Arielle's face to see if the latter part of her statement evoked any reaction from the girl.

Arielle kept a fixed watch on Emma's face as the sincerity of the elder one blanketed her with soothing comfort. *'Certain that is what you wish.'* Arielle repeated Emma's words to herself knowing that of which she was most certain. If she did not return home forthwith, she would most certainly be in the unenviable position of having to explain last eve's flight from home and her whereabouts to an audience of some size greater than her parents. She could be assured that the minute her mother became aware of her disappearance panic would ensue, prompting her to engage the services of law enforcement officials. Arielle wished to avoid such a scene. She garnered the hope that Fiona had made no notice, as of yet, of her absence. That would provide her the time necessary to return without the fear that a flurry of inquisitions would greet her -- be they civilian in the form of her parents, or uniformed in an official capacity.

Emma observed Arielle's pensiveness. Her every instinct encouraged her to envelope the girl and offer some relief from the burden she so obviously kept cloistered within. Rather than open her arms to embrace her, Emma reached out her hand and gently rested her fingers on top of Arielle's hand.

"My dear, we have known each other for a very short while, yet, even though we are of recent acquaintance, I feel compelled to offer any assistance I may to you. Horace always accused me of wearing my heart on my sleeve. He was forever suggesting that it would serve me well to toughen up a bit. Dear man. He protected me from all he could, feeling that if I only had a tougher core I would not fall susceptible to the foibles of others. Yet, he mused that one of the traits he found most admirable in me was my ability to sense the needs of others and respond accordingly. He would take my hand as we walked about the grounds and say, *'Emma you are destined to feel every pebble under your foot as vigorously as you take pleasure from every flower that thrives under your watchful care.'* Oh my goodness, it appears upon reflection that I am absorbed in conversation of myself when my intent is to reassure you that *your* well-being is my primary concern. You may confide in me with utmost confidence."

Arielle was so moved by Emma's words and the delicacy of her delivery that her emerald orbs became glazed with moisture as tears welled in her eyes. A confidant such as Emma would be of great benefit Arielle thought as she forced herself to regain her composure, trying to suppress her tears. Now was not the hour to impose details of last night's ordeal on Emma even though it preyed heavily on Arielle's mind. There would be a proper time for such revelations. If her father's actions, his intent, could be explained to her satisfaction, she could move beyond their last encounter and rinse it from her consciousness. Perhaps her return to Chestnut Heights would be no more than a simple visit with Emma, free of explanation -- if all boded well at home. *No, until I know more, I will neither burden Mrs. Willard nor reveal details too private to relate.*

Arielle looked out the window to the spot where Simon had been collecting data. The little man was no longer in sight. She was refreshed with the promise she saw before her of a new spring. The shrubs were ready to spread new growth. Sprouts from bulbs planted below the branches of the evergreens were visible, having forced their way through the well-cultivated earth. They had found their proper time clock on their earthly calendar, striking a chord that all was well in the garden. She turned back toward Emma, slightly renewed with hope, and began to partake of the lovely continental breakfast Cook had prepared. Emma lifted the English chintzware teapot pouring cupfuls for herself and Arielle. The citrus aroma of the Earl Grey, its warmth and the very atmosphere of Emma's dining nook, further soothed Arielle. She felt more herself than she had in hours and had Emma to thank for that.

"Mrs. Willard, you have been most gracious to me, extending lodging, food and now, an artful ear. I am blessed to be in your company yet there is a pressing matter to which I must attend and it would be best for me to take leave. Your offer to return to Chestnut Heights is one I shall accept with great pleasure upon the prospect that our next meeting will offer a forum for us to know one another better."

"That will be lovely. Yes, you must come calling soon. Talking is always good. You come to know all things better."

"About your dress."

"There is no hurry about the dress, dear. Thomas has gathered your belongings. The gown you wore last evening is still quite damp so it is wise, of course, for you to travel home as you are."

Arielle finished breakfast, drinking her tea just shy of its last drop. Emma escorted her to the foyer where Thomas opened the massive front door leading to the vestibule filled with healthy green palms in urn-like jardinières. The morning air and gentle breeze swept a cool temperature under the overcast March skies. Simon had predicted a day much brighter than the one before. As Arielle stepped from the curb into Emma's coach, she prayed that the accuracy of his prediction would show itself and cast rays of healing sunlight over the home to which she would soon return -- the manse of Sir Ian Hargrove.

Chapter Four

Washington, District of Columbia

Fiona welcomed the commencement of the new day into the stately Hargrove manse as she pulled back one panel of the cranberry-hued brocade draperies adorning one of the three windows in Ian's study. Gathering together the folds of the weighty drape, she secured it to one side with a matching tieback adorned with ball fringe. The window's undulating glass captured the hint of sun attempting to make its way through the overcast sky. Refractions of light began to bounce about the rich wood paneled walls of the room. Flashes of intermittent sunlight danced about Fiona's strawberry blonde hair and across the freckles scattered in a random fleck all about her face. She dallied with the drapery, going over the same portions of cloth again and again, as though such repetition would improve upon the mediocre manner in which she performed her task. If Ian were present he would rail her, for his fuse was generally snipped short where she was concerned. He repeatedly reprimanded her pace, suggesting a tortoise without benefit of a head start could surpass her. Ian would shout, *'Moss grows under your feet as I speak, girl. Get a move on!'*

Fiona went to the companion section of drapery and prepared to pull it into place when her blue-green eyes caught sight
of a spectacular carriage. Formed of Honduras mahogany, the
park drag virtually glistened as a shaft of sunlight worked its way
through a passing cloud and took direct aim on the carriage's
highly lacquered panels. Outfitted with elaborately detailed fittings burnished to a brilliant finish, the hardware gleamed as the
Morgan mares stepped in choreographed unison, moving the ve-
hicle along with barely a sway from the cab of the coach. Its large
wheels were detailed with a deep burgundy stripe that beautifully
accented the rich, rifle green paint of the highly lustered wood.
The traces and harness were deluxe and of the hardiest leather.
Large brass lamps with beveled glass and mirrored backs adorned
each side of the exquisite turnout. Fiona observed the monogram
'W' on a plate on the carriage's side.

As the immaculate carriage approached the manse, the pace
of the four-in-hand slowed. The driver sat regally on his perch
as though posting on horseback. He drew back the reins, bringing the horses to a full halt at the Hargrove doorstep. Fiona was
so enraptured by the pageantry and lovely spectacle before her
that she was deaf to Elsbeth's entrance into the study and her
inquiry.

"Fiona!" Elsbeth raised her voice ever so slightly to garner the
girl's attention.

Fiona was all of a sudden jarred from her trance and turned
to acknowledge her mistress.

"Aye, mum. Sorry I am fer not seein' ya come inta the room."

"I asked, Fiona, if you have seen Miss Arielle this morning?"

"I was jest about to say I had not seen her mum, but Lordy
Almighty, if it's not Miss Arielle 'erself steppin' out 'o that fine
carriage!"

"Fiona, what are you talking about?"

"Come 'ere mum, to this 'ere window an 'ave a look fer yerself.
Oh mum, why it's one 'o the fanciest, grandest carriages I 'ave
ever put me smilin' Irish eyes to!"

40

Fiona's eyes were wide with excitement as she made room in the window for the mistress of the manse to stand beside her. It took a moment for Elsbeth to focus on the curbside scene and, once she did, she saw that the girl was not exaggerating in her description of the conveyance nor its cargo. To her surprise it was indeed Arielle who exited the coach with a small tapestry satchel in her hand.

Elsbeth was consumed with curiosity, wondering how her daughter came to be associated with the elegant coach-and-four, and how she had left the house without the awareness of herself or the household staff, particularly Fiona. She was not sure if Fiona was daft or merely caught up in her own little world. Her work was sufficient and she was a sweet girl who would not harm the most persistent of flies. Elsbeth kept her in her employ hoping she could be properly trained. She also wanted to provide the home she lacked ever since she was shipped to the states by her aunt and uncle.

Fiona's relatives reasoned they would pad their Irish coffers with the money she earned abroad. They required her to send the greatest portion of her wages to their attention, leaving a meager sum for her subsistence. They additionally hoped she would land herself a wealthy husband in the states, which would relieve them of their duties, further scheming that the grateful Fiona would still be duty bound to provide them some monetary gratification. Regardless of her aunt and uncle's intentions, Fiona had nested herself with the Hargroves and was content to be placed in domestic service.

"Do ye see mum, do ye see? It's Miss Arielle as sure as I'm standin' 'ere and right smart she looks in that gown, the likes of which I 'ave never laid me eyes to!" Fiona virtually squealed with excitement, swishing her apron side-to-side in a syncopated dance.

"Fiona, be still. My mind is spinning about enough. There is no need to draw attention to ourselves with your commotion."

"Aye, mum. I'm sorry mum, I just..."

"Fiona, please hush. Miss Arielle is on her way in, please see to the door."

Fiona hustled across the plush carpet that partially covered the dark stained oak floors of the study. She approached the front door as Arielle stepped onto the brick covered veranda outside the portal to the manse. Trying to stifle her excitement, but unable to rein in her youthful enthusiasm, Fiona began skipping her last few steps, barely pausing to grasp the door knob. As she opened the door, she continued her skip in a backward hop bending at the waist into a bow as an enormous grin formed on her face. As Arielle stepped into the foyer, Fiona greeted her with the same unabashed energy.

"Why, Miss Arielle! Just look at ya in that new gown all gussied up and ridin' in that fine carriage! What a sight fer me ta witness, why rest my stirrin' heart, I thought royalty was comin' fer a visit at Lady Hargrove's door!"

"Fiona," Elsbeth's voice was clear and humorless as she entered the foyer and faced Arielle. "You may leave us now and go about your other duties."

With a look of disappointed acquiescence, Fiona left the two, retreating to her chores on the upper level of the house. Arielle stood silent, wanting to bide more time before explanations were due, hoping her mother's barometer for details was at its lowest ebb this morn.

She knew her mother was unlikely to disregard the scene she just witnessed. She had always been attentive yet, she balanced her parental role by being neither too aloof nor overbearing. However, as the moments of silence became compounded, Arielle grew more uncomfortable, electing to break the soundlessness before her nerves got the best of her.

"Good morning, Mum. I guess it would be best for me to put these things in my room for Fiona to attend to," Arielle said with little conviction as she began to take steps to retreat upstairs, knowing her mother would thwart such motion.

"Arielle. It would be best if you joined me in the parlor. It seems we need to have an audience with one another for enlightenment, so to speak."

"As you wish, Mum." Arielle complied, entering the parlor and taking a seat in her favorite tufted back chair covered in a swirl-cut green velvet.

"Arielle, I must say that you have piqued my curiosity. You are wearing a beautiful dress I have never before seen and present yourself from the cab of a most exquisite carriage, unfamiliar to our home, at an hour that would scarcely have seen you up and about our manse on any given day. Unless this is a mere apparition, an explanation is in order."

"There is very little to explain, Mum. I have simply borrowed a dress from a friend who was additionally so kind to provide a ride home."

"I see. And, this 'friend.' Is there a name attached?"

"Her name is Emma and she is very kind. There is really no more to it than that."

"Emma. And how did you come to cross one another's paths?"

"It was just inevitable I guess that we would meet. One of those instances when things just happen with no particular explanation."

"Arielle, tell me. Does this Emma have a last name?"

"Yes, I am certain that she does."

"And what would it be?"

"Willard."

"Willard?"

"Yes, Willard."

"Emma Willard?"

"Yes, Emma Willard."

"_The_ Emma Willard?"

"I am aware of no others by the same name."

"My goodness, Arielle. How did you come into the company of Emma Willard? What is she like? Were you in her home? What is it like? How does she live?" Elsbeth pelted Arielle with questions that, for a fleeting while, gave her the false impression that the very idea of Emma Willard lent distraction to her mother's inquiries.

"We met by introduction of her nephew. She is a generous woman with a lovely home."

"*You* have been to Chestnut Heights then?"

"Yes."

"And, is it as grand as I have read, with enormous rooms richly appointed with imported pieces and lush fabrics?"

"Yes, it is quite so."

Arielle wished in the strongest way that she could slip from the room or perhaps just melt into a little puddle and evaporate away. If she were nonexistent then Elsbeth's need for explanations would be too. Such would not be her lot today as Elsbeth realized she had gotten herself off course. Rather than ascertain the full particulars at this time regarding Emma Willard, her tenor returned to its initial state, finding her focus aimed squarely at the matter of Arielle's absence.

"Enough, for now, about Mrs. Willard. The fact remains Arielle that your bed may have remained undisturbed last eve but my wit on this morn is not of the same fetish. I am quite disturbed and concerned that you have been away without notifying anyone. This is unacceptable and very much unlike you."

"It was all quite unexpected I assure you, and disturbing for me as well. To the best of my recollection, for I was quite confused, I ventured upon the veranda and lost my footing at the top of the staircase. In an attempt to save myself from the spill I reached for the railing but it too was slick from the rain and offered me no support, so I continued on my impromptu descent to the pavement. I must have hit my head and been rendered unconscious for my next memory is that of myself walking quite briskly in the storm seeking shelter."

"Why would you not have righted yourself and returned to the safety of our home?"

"I believe I was disoriented and lost my direction. That can happen when one has had a blow of sorts."

"My good gracious, Arielle. This is so alarming! You might have been seriously injured, and for all I know you are still out of your head! I would think that evidence of a head injury would show itself, yet I see not a mark on your person other than the hint of a bruise on your right wrist."

"I am as amazed as you are, Mum, that I escaped from last night's ordeal physically unscathed beyond the black and blue image on my wrist which must have occurred as my hand searched for assistance from the railing."

"When I arrived home last night, the hour was late, and the household was quiet and dark except for the lamp Fiona kept lit for my return. I made the false assumption that you were bedded down and decided not to chance awakening you by opening the door to your room. However, when I awoke this morning and entered your room, you can imagine my alarm to find your bed barren and unmussed! For a brief moment, I thought you had risen early and Fiona had uncharacteristically performed her housekeeping tasks with great speed. Realizing the unlikeliness of that scenario, I searched out Fiona hoping she could answer to your whereabouts. You can imagine my surprise finding that you have been *without* rather than *within* our home."

"I apologize for any worry I have caused," Arielle sheepishly responded, feeling guilty for the less than forthright explanation she offered regarding her departure. Her conscience was somewhat elevated from her fog of deception since she felt it was clearly the right decision to contrive a story to protect her mother from the truth of her father's actions. *Whew*, Arielle nearly shuttered, shaking her head as she thought about her father. *How would she cope in his presence when he returned from work?* She had several hours to ferret out a plan and hoped her good senses would prevail.

"Arielle, what is it? You started to tremble," Elsbeth said with motherly concern as she moved closer to Arielle and took her hand to ease her apprehension.

"It has just been an enormously unusual series of events. When do you think father will be home?"

"Your father and I hardly spoke this morning. He was rather out of sorts at the breakfast table, leaving most of his meal untouched. He rather hurriedly announced that not having slept well, he was going to forego eating and go directly to the office to prepare for a meeting. I gathered he would end his workday at a reasonable hour rather than render himself wearier with an extended workday. Do you need to speak with him?"

Speak with him? The thought of her next encounter with her father made Arielle seethe. She could not imagine being comfortable in his presence, yet, for her mother's benefit, she had to maintain a familial cordiality lest her mother question a change in their relationship. Elsbeth had always been very intuitive, especially where her only daughter was concerned, and Arielle could envision her being no less so now.

"Not particularly," came Arielle's delayed response. "I know he is sometimes kept late and, with the rapid changes taking place in industry, Father says the effect is especially felt by himself and the other members of the Trade Council."

Arielle was always more fascinated with the conversations that ensued with the gentlemen guests her parents entertained than the perspicuous prattle that consumed the gatherings of the ladies present. She found it of interest to make herself privy to the male point of view whether it be business, politics, or daily affairs at the top of their discussion roster.

She always regretted the traditional migration of the men to her father's study for their smoking cartel of cigars sided by crystal glasses filled with amber shots of bourbon. She could only imagine the male camaraderie and discourse she was missing as loud guffaws erupted in response to a bold tale well told or a sarcastic gibe well placed.

The pride and perils of management and labor drew Arielle's attention. Her appetite was always whet for designing solutions to ensure management was disposed to hearing the peel of its laborers. Keeping the workers in force, productive, and happy was the most efficient way of averting the threat of strikes. She had overheard her father's conversations with Trade Council members about the coal mine collapse two years prior near Almy,

Wyoming. An explosion at the Red Canyon Mine killed sixty-one miners, heightening fears among workers and their families, and weakening the security they felt for the only livelihood they knew. If conditions were not soon improved, both employer and laborer would be hard set to avoid a strike. Both sides would suffer from the inevitable losses that would be incurred by such action.

Arielle had heard the resounding speeches of her father on this very topic and knew his success in the coal industry came from his keen ability to govern matched with his untiring energy and perseverance. He excelled under adversity in the business place and expected nothing less than first-class work. His appointment to the Trade Council was well deserved. Years of owning a highly profitable colliery in Wales thrust him at the top of his league in the coal industry and made him an excellent candidate for the rigors of lobbying and policy-making in the nation's capital.

He was proud to be knighted for his numerous contributions to business in the United Kingdom and gladly added the moniker of 'Sir' to his name. He drew no hesitation one year ago hence at the thought of moving his family across the Atlantic to join the Council. Ian was confident the colliery would be well managed by Paul Nesbitt, his trusted foreman who had been with him for a score of years. Nesbitt, as he called him, knew the operations from the inside out, from the pit brow workers who knew him as Paul the Overman, to the dirty, dangerous tunnels heady with coal that provided them all their life's wages.

Arielle knew her father was a powerful man with notable influence among his peers. What she could not on occasion fathom was her mother's tolerance of his escapades that spun about the ever-present rumor mill keeping many a dowagers tongue wagging. His companionship with alcohol was known to inflict abrupt changes in his personality. Arielle had seen her mother brought to tears by his slurred, demeaning ramblings.

Despite her father's indiscretions, and poor rapport with drink, her mother maintained a quiet reserve, always providing 'a light in the hearth' so that no matter what the hour, her father was welcomed into a loving haven where his motives were never challenged by his spouse. Arielle was not sure she could muster the courage to challenge his motives either. He was her father. She loved him and was not inclined to render him any disrespect. Her head was heavy with reprimands directed toward him. After remaining for so many years restrained in her speech, Arielle prayed her thoughts would not betray her in a moment of supreme anger and find her suddenly speaking all she had held in silence.

"Arielle, I seem to have lost you deep in thought. I asked about the nephew, Mrs. Willard's nephew that you mentioned early on. You said you were introduced to her by him and I wonder how you met," Elsbeth queried, trying her best to make sense of her daughter's experience of late.

"After falling, I began walking in the rain in a direction that took me away from our home. It was very dark and the rain became increasingly severe. Mrs. Willard's nephew, Mr. Clay, happened upon my path and so kindly offered passage to his aunt's."

"My goodness. Oh, my, my. You were alone with him, a man you have never met and with no proper introduction?"

"Mum, propriety must sometimes be discarded when better judgment rules it so. Mr. Clay was concerned for my safety."

"Why then, did he not escort you to your own home?"

"As I explained, I was disoriented and did not express our address to him so he took me to Mrs. Willard's."

"You rode alone in a carriage with a man to whom you have never been introduced?" Elsbeth shuddered to think how news of Arielle's 'outing' would occupy many a teatime tête-à-tête if Mr. Clay were so bold as to make any mention of last night's event. *Surely, the man was higher bred and would consider the virtues of her daughter's good name.*

"Mum, you may rest renewed that we were not alone. Mr. Clay was in the company of a female companion and made great haste in assuring my arrival at his aunt's. Absolutely nothing improper took place."

Arielle knew her mother might reflect differently on the situation if she were a witness to its reenactment. Soothing warmth came over Arielle as she revisited her first introduction to William Clay and recalled the penetrating blue of his eyes. She felt his arms about her and the clean smell of him as their cheeks engaged. *What a handsome face, strong and well defined with the touch of a cleft in his chin. The wave of his thick brown hair begged to be tussled.* She nearly cooed as thoughts of him floated through her mind. The glow subsided as Arielle caught herself. *What am I thinking? I barely know this man and the way he took me up from the street without a thread of permission was bold indeed! I should have slapped him and insisted he put me down immediately!* She had allowed herself to be treated like a common street urchin with neither the good sense nor the fortitude to prevent such poor form. *How can I ever face him again? And, if I do, I will have to give him a piece of my mind. No, it would be best if we were never again at the same crossroads.*

"You have improved my comfort level, my dear Arielle. I will pray most diligently that you have neither sullied your reputation nor the Hargrove name. You must be weary. Let me see to it that a bath is drawn and your room readied for you to rest," Elsbeth offered as she walked to her daughter, took her hand in hers, and leaned forward placing a delicate kiss on her forehead.

Arielle could indeed use the restorative powers a good soak in the tub would provide. Her mother was wise, and having sated her inquiry at present, Arielle collected herself and made her way to her bedroom. It would remain her sanctuary until the footfalls of the master of the manse returned. She prayed he would not again tread the alarming path that had so shaken her solace.

Chapter Five

Washington, District of Columbia

Late afternoon spread over the Hargrove manse like a whisper. The silence of the household was startled to notice on the half hour by numerous timepieces appointed to each room. Ian was a collector of clocks and, though try as he might to have them all synchronized to sound their chimes at the very same stroke, there were several that persistently deviated from the rhythm he tried to impose. Nonconforming timepieces could be heard a full series of strikes after the others, forming a harmonic round of tolling tintinnabulation.

Arielle was so accustomed to the knell created by the clocks that their chimes were generally benign, rarely garnering her attention. Today was in sharp contrast to all others. As she lay under the multiple folds of comforting cotton and down comprising her bed covers, the clocks were like harmony gone awry or notes off key, arousing her to the reality that even her bed was not a safe haven from outside forces.

Having taken her midday meal in the sanctum of her room, leaving more of the fare untasted than consumed, she felt ready to don her attire and prepare herself for supper. Her bath had provided the much-needed respite from her meeting with her mother. In very short measure, her father's arrival would set in motion the plan that would move her forward and protect her from the events of the previous eve.

The final blow of the hammer from the mantel clock made it clear that five o'clock was but now a passing memory. A knock on her door brought the voice of her mother informing her that Fiona would soon be at hand to assist her in dressing for the evening meal. Her mother added that after dressing, she would meet Arielle in the dining room. She took comfort knowing her mother would not be the persona non grata she had been last eve so she would not be left in the *sole* company of her father. *But, oh,* she thought. *I will still be in his company.*

With all the fortitude she could muster from her empty spirit, Arielle turned the crystal knob of her bedroom door. The vacuum of sanctity that lay within was in sharp contrast to the uncertainty that formed a dwelling place in the public domain beyond. She turned and took a last, fleeting look at herself in the cheval mirror holding her reflection. *Yes, this will do.* With Fiona's assistance, Arielle's hair had been swept into a very conservative chignon, twisted, she thought, like the nervous knots that tormented her abdomen. Her skirt was dark and plain, enhanced by nothing more than several covered buttons that made their way down and along the seams on either side of the skirt's front panel. Her crisply pressed white blouse with its collar high to her chin fit her plan perfectly. Indeed, if her décolletage and wandering wisps of hair had encouraged her father to feel entitled to dally with her, then her ensemble for this eve would provide little flesh for the tempting or the taking. Her plan to dress modestly and remain reserved with no reference to his advances would indicate to him that she had no intention of revealing last night's episode to her mother. She would be obliged in her father's presence to act as though no awkward exchange had occurred between them. Now, it was her fervent wish that she could as formidably pluck the menacing memories forever from her muddled mind. She assumed she had obviously done something to provoke her father. However, though professing herself to blame, she assured herself she would not fall victim to a recurring series of events at his hands.

As Arielle walked the course of the hallway from her bedroom doorway to the crest of the staircase, the rustle of her crinoline was all that interfered with the sounds of a household whose pulse was kept on an even beat by the steady movement of established routines. The footsteps of household staff from kitchen to dining room, and the occasional clang of tableware as it found its placement at each setting, filled the air with an aura of order, of complacency.

Arielle stopped abruptly when the sound of the large brass doorknocker caught her attention. She heard Fiona announce her intention to '*see to the door*,' which she did with apparent gusto, for within moments the door opened and Arielle heard the muffled sound of voices. She proceeded to move slowly down the staircase to the landing which kept her from full view but put her within earshot of any conversation.

Fiona was so taken with the sight that engulfed her as she pulled back the door that she stood speechless, her jaw locked in a dropped position, opened just wide enough to become the perfect receptacle for a frisky fly if one where about.

"Forgive me if I have come at an inopportune time," the visitor repeated finding some amusement in the girl's dumbfounded greeting.

"Aye, aye, sir. Oh, I mean no, sir. Oh, please won't ye come in sir," Fiona babbled as she stood firmly centered in the doorway blocking the visitor's path.

"If you would be so kind," the visitor remarked as he politely motioned with his hand for the girl who bade him enter to step back.

"Aye. Sorry, sorry I am, sir," Fiona continued to stumble on her words as she stepped back, still mesmerized by the gentleman caller.

"I am looking for Miss Hargrove and hope I have come to the proper place," the visitor continued as he handed his card over to the girl whose face was covered in a nervous blush.

Arielle recognized the strong, soothing voice she heard coming from the foyer below. It had called to her and comforted her before and its effect was no different now. *William Clay. How did he find me? I left him no details of my place of residence. Why is he here? Why is his voice having such an intoxicating effect over me? No,* she thought. *I must be strong and I must be stern, for this man gave me no choice but to go with him last eve. I will not be taken advantage of again.* Her stubborn self told her to remain unavailable when Fiona came to announce his visit, yet something tugged most feverishly at her to go to him.

"'Ave a seat 'ere in the foyer sir an' let me see if Miss Hargrove says she is here. I mean, let me see if...please pay me no mind, sir, I'll be but a minute."

Fiona dipped and scooted through the foyer and up the staircase turning in such a rush onto the landing that Arielle threw herself against the wall rather than risk being run down by the girl. A flicker of reality caught Fiona as she realized she was not alone on the staircase. She stopped herself in mid-flight to the next step and, grabbing the handrail, turned quite out of breath to face Arielle.

"Oh, Miss Arielle," Fiona puffed as she continued, "There is the most gorgeously handsome man, oh, so handsome, waitin' ta see ye in the foyer, and if ye want me ta I can visit with 'im while ye decide if ye think yer in or yer not."

"Fiona, take a breath and hush before he hears you and thinks you are nothing but a half-witted twit!"

"Sorry I am, Miss Arielle. 'Ere's the card he gave me fer ye. Should I retrieve Lady Hargrove as well?"

"Thank you, Fiona. No, it will not be necessary to find my mum. Our visitor's stay will be quite brief. Please go see to the dinner preparations and I will see to our guest."

Fiona swept down the stairs nearly as rapidly as she had ascended them, passing quickly by the visitor and snatching a parting glance of his form before she exited to the back hall.

Arielle drew in her breath. Using the calling card as a calming prop, she held it in her fingers, quietly flicking at one corner as she completed her descent of the stairs. Her footsteps were soft and graceful yet they drew William's attention. He stood as her feet tread the last stair, enamored by the vision that cast itself before him. He knew there was something about her that caught his regard the night before, but that memory was minute in contrast to the response he felt within his being at the sight of her entering the foyer. Radiant beyond bounds, her jet-black hair was silken in an upswept coif. Her unblemished, alabaster skin had a pinch of rose tint across her high cheekbones, and her eyes were dazzling as they searched his posture for a clue to the reason for his call. The vision overcame him and, for the moment, the need to speak was of no consequence. He collected his thoughts, regained his composure, and bowed holding his hat against his abdomen, then he rose to his full height and greeted her.

"Miss Hargrove, I hope you do not mind that I took the liberty of locating your address from my aunt's coachman."

Mind. How could she mind? Or, had she lost her mind? She was allowing herself to be overcome by a transient trance. What was this effect he held over her that likened itself to the fixation one placed on a pendulum swinging back and forth before ones eyes? He seemed to have a hold on her very soul. Look at him. Tall, dark, handsome, everything she read about in her Lady's Book and dreamed of coming true. And look. He was here, in the flesh, not some words laying upon parchment. No page needed to be turned to smell the smell of him, taste the taste of him, feel the touch of him, or to hear the sound of him. This man, this William Clay, could fulfill all of her senses here, now. She shook her head ever so slightly to clear the cobwebs that spun about and prayed he had not read her mind. *He thinks nothing of me, that is clear. It is obvious from his stare. He is here on business, maybe to retrieve his aunt's gown, but certainly not to come in company with me for any other purpose.* Arielle mused to herself as she nodded her head in greeting.

William was confused by her reaction to his presence and wondered if the sight of him had some ill effect on her. The shake of her head and lack of speech mimicked her behavior in his coach the night before causing him to draw a concerned look across his face.

"Perhaps I have come at an inopportune time. Forgive me for my presumptions," William stated most sincerely, holding his felt hat close to his heart.

Arielle felt the urge to speak but could not quite gather her words before William spoke again.

"I am in possession of one of your gloves found under the seat in my coach. Its mate however seems to have vanished. Hopefully, you know of its whereabouts so the pair will be intact again. You never know when the occasion may arise to don your gloves and race into a storm." William teased a bit, trying to add a fraction of levity to the tension he felt in the room as he withdrew Arielle's glove from the pocket of his long woolen overcoat and presented it to her.

His gesture proved what she had been thinking. Business it was. The return of an article lost and nothing more. His teasing tone struck a raw nerve, taunting her weary spirit, causing her to bristle. She must thank him and send him on his way at once. However, he was a visitor to her home and she would remain gracious no matter how tempted she was to reprimand him.

"Mr. Clay, your thoughtfulness is once again my gain. Meeting your lovely aunt last eve was a pleasure I shall not soon forget. I apologize for taking you out of your way last eve and now, on this occasion of returning my glove. I had quite forgotten about them and assumed they were in the satchel I carried home from Chestnut Heights. I am sure I shall find the mate I seek there. I best let you be on your way before my foibles have consumed any more of your time." Arielle maintained a pleasant smile that barely put a dent in the dimple gracing her right cheek. As she spoke, she moved ever so slightly toward the front entry suggesting to William that he was being subtly motioned to take leave.

Just as he was about to respond, Elsbeth entered the hallway and approached the handsome duo. Arielle, with the ease of charm she had been taught so well, turned to her to make introductions.

"Mum, I would like to have you meet Mr. William Clay. Mr. Clay, this is my mum, Lady Hargrove."

Elsbeth raised her right eyebrow and smiled a quizzical smile as she acknowledged their guest while concurrent with her reaction, William bowed in formal greeting. Elsbeth was taken back by his stunning stature and finely tailored outer garments. He was truly a fine specimen whom she would welcome at anytime across her threshold. If his Aunt Emma was any indication of his breeding, Elsbeth felt confirmed in her thoughts that he would be an ideal catch for a genteel young woman such as her Arielle.

"Mr. Clay, I am pleased to make your acquaintance and it seems that I owe a debt to you for the assistance you lent my daughter after her injury last eve."

William masked the puzzled look that threatened to overtake him, not understanding the reference to injury conjured by Lady Hargrove. He felt it best to listen rather than turn asunder the dialogue that must have been earlier exchanged between mother and daughter.

"I am merely pleased to see that Miss Hargrove is, um, well-healed and none the worse for it," William generalized, glancing from Elsbeth to Arielle.

Arielle held her composure, thankful that William was perceptive enough to respond as he did, yet agitated that in his effort to remain neutral, assumed she was 'well-healed' and 'none the worse for it.' Her emotional wounds still held a sting as potent as tincture on freshly cut flesh.

"Mr. Clay, we are just about to be seated for our evening meal and would be most pleased if you would join us." Elsbeth offered with a strong desire to have more time to become acquainted with Mr. William Clay.

"Thank you, Lady Hargrove. Your invitation is very kind. I am otherwise engaged this evening and actually must be on my way lest I be delayed for my appointment. Perhaps some other time."

Arielle had heard such polite expressions before and knew the likes of William Clay would stay very clear of the Hargrove manse and its residents. She knew he would be glad to be rid of any remembrance of the stormy night and the addled young woman that was nothing more than an inconvenience. *Why else would he so quickly return the glove and come calling with another pressing appointment on his heels? Yes,* Arielle thought to herself. *This will be the last audience with William Clay.*

Chapter Six

Washington, District of Columbia

I an waited patiently in the dining room to be joined by the ladies of the manse. He had thus far remained very conservative with his liquid refreshment having consumed only one glass of scotch since returning from the Capitol. He apparently was not at the ready to splash another bit of the potent liquid into the void occupying the glass in his hand. He stood as Elsbeth and Arielle entered, wanting to do what was proper, fairly aware he had done anything but that the night before.

Arielle took her usual place one seat away from her mother while her parents flanked each side of the substantial mahogany table. Although at opposing sides, Ian and Elsbeth's positions held a place of balance that provided a much-needed anchor for the evening meal. As Arielle became engrossed in the radiance of the room, she allowed the dance of the candlelight in its gentle breeze-driven waltz to lull her nerves as a calming grace centered over her like a mother's reassuring embrace. For a moment, the faceted crystal drops suspended from the room's large chandelier transfixed her. Their brilliance seemed to form infinite prisms to her soul.

With a wave of her hand, Elsbeth signaled for the dinner service to commence. Her temperate style, quite in opposition to
Ian's manner, made her a favorite among the household staff.
Though generally well-intended, Ian's style held a gruffness that
spurred action by the staff but left a floodgate of animosity in its
wake. His presence kept the staff stiff and at the ready like well-
drilled soldiers whose only misfortune would be to provoke the
ire of their leader, Sir Ian Hargrove. Ian quite enjoyed the moniker of Sir bestowed upon him. His work in England and Wales
had made him a leader in industry, particularly the coal industry.
His motto was, 'See your opportunities and take them.' His business acumen was seen from a spectator's position as stalwart, and
his philanthropic pursuits placed him high on the scale of achiev-
ers who kept the needs of their countrymen in focus with country
first. He rarely opposed establishment and the laws that governed
his business operations for he was generally at the forefront of
shaping the laws. Ian relished the recognition and honor the
knighting tradition lent him and quite preferred being referred
to as Sir, even by his wife.

Elsbeth sensed a quiet in Ian this eve that veiled him in
an uncharacteristic softness. His tender demeanor was typically held in safe reserve for public occasions that warranted
a less brisk approach where he knew full well that the pressing
of palms, in a seemingly sincere handshake, might lead to the
acquisition of a supportive business associate or a loyal lobby-
ist. Elsbeth witnessed Ian's tender side on the limited occasions
when an intimate exchange occurred between the two of them.
She wondered what triggered the reflective stance he assumed
as he randomly moved the roasted beef and vegetables about his
dinner plate with the tines of his sterling fork, periodically pausing to retrieve a bite.

Just as Elsbeth drew enough strength of purpose to break the
quiet, Ian cleared his throat, directing his gaze first to Elsbeth
then to Arielle. Again clearing his throat with greater fervor than
before, he placed his white damask napkin in a rumpled mound

beside his plate and slid his chair a short glide away from the table.

"I must apologize," came the three words from Ian's mouth -- words that Arielle hoped to hear from her father with explanation but, she cringed to think that he would use this setting with her mother present to repent his errant ways.

"I must apologize for not being very sound company. Elsbeth, as you were kept late last eve with your charity work, I was unable to render a sufficient amount of sleep which I am afraid has taxed me greatly."

Arielle was ready to fume, yet, rather than fully open the damper on the fire that raged within her, she settled back and waited for her mother's response. How like her father to place the burden of his actions on her mother.

"Why, am I to feel so flattered, Sir Ian, for want of my company you sacrificed a good night's sleep?" Elsbeth chaffed attempting to relieve the discord.

"Elsbeth."

"Now, now. Arielle has seen a difficult night as well and it seems most fortuitous for us to enjoy our good fortune and count our many blessings," Elsbeth concluded as she smiled, delicately glancing back and forth to her husband and daughter.

Ian was at once stunned to imagine that Arielle would have spoken to her mother about last night's events, at least the parts he could recall from the drunken daze that had overtaken his good senses. *If Arielle had revealed details, how could Elsbeth maintain the calm resolve she exhibited?*

Arielle watched her father's face, observing his pallor. As much as she relished the effect her mother's words had on him, she felt compelled to redirect his concern and rescue him from himself.

"Father, Mum is correct, as usual, in suggesting that we over-look, for the present, the predicament to which we found our-selves last night. You, as you note, having been shorted a night's rest, and I having encountered a demon or two during the storm."

"Yes, Sir Ian. Arielle is wise beyond her years, exhorting the wisdom of a sage."

"You will allow me then, ladies, to retire to my study. I have some paperwork requiring my attention before dawn and, Lady Hargrove, before you take leave to your needlework, I find it most desirable and necessary for you to join me in my study."

"Certainly I will," Elsbeth responded, delighted whenever Ian wished to share her company. Maybe he would also share his thoughts and quell the ambiguity that piqued her curiosity.

The three exercised the paces necessary to spur them to the conclusion of their meal. Arielle made the first move to exit. Excusing herself from her parents company, she decided that in light of her father's request to meet with her mother in the study, she would remove herself to the rear of the house and enjoy the plants and tapestries in the conservatory.

Arielle and her mother spent a good deal of time nurturing miniature gardens they cultivated in Wardian cases. The lovely, glass-enclosed, terrarium-like housings brought tasteful touches of nature into their home. On occasion, when calling on a house-bound sick friend, Elsbeth would deliver a Wardian case to place at the friend's bedside for a cheerful reminder that the healing wonders of nature could be had for nothing more than the effort of a glance.

Arielle looked about the conservatory, taking in the scene and thinking how nice it was to be surrounded indoors by growing things, particularly when March in Washington's out-of-doors carried a chilly wind with little foliage to warm the eye or provide contrast against the brick, concrete and marble structures that so monogrammed the capital city. She panned the art about the space. Some pieces were unattributed leaving them with no signature or marking to denote the artist or maker. Her eyes caught on a landscape painting by J. F. Kensett hanging on the wall near the piano. It was a favorite of hers for its ability to draw her in, its brushstrokes were as swept with tranquility as the scene itself.

She contemplated sitting at the piano. She was fairly accomplished with the instrument, a beautiful, square Steinway grand piano with a brilliant rosewood case. It had been purchased for her tenth birthday. Her fingers were at once comfortable with the ivory keys and after only limited lessons, she became very adept at memorizing classical and contemporary pieces. She often gave impromptu recitals when her parents entertained but tonight she would forego the instrument that gave her much pleasure. Tonight she felt hard-pressed to find a song to justify the events of late and subdue her dismay, for her father's unusual behavior was seared in her memory.

She moved away from the piano, touching it lightly with her fingertips to find comfort in literature. The Hargrove manse was never lacking in reading matter whether it be Ian's study, the parlor, or conservatory. The conservatory's single windowless wall was fully stacked with hand-rubbed mahogany bookcases. Arielle gave a cursory search of the shelves, her eyes lighting on a volume to which she extended partiality. As an avid student of the work of Shakespeare, she selected a favorite passage from *A Midsummer Night's Dream*. The passage was marked with a pressed flower, a pansy. The delicate, yet hearty botanical's petals had remained well intact and were showing little signs of decomposition since she last gingerly opened the pages to reflect upon the words within.

Act I, Scene I's exchange between Lysander and Hermia fell across her lips as she read aloud. Lysander, "How now, my love! Why is your cheek so pale? How chance the roses there do fade so fast?" Hermia, "Belike for want of rain, which I could well beteem them from the tempest of my eyes." Lysander, "Ay me! For aught that I could ever read, Could ever hear by tale or history, The course of true love never did run smooth; But, either it was different in blood..." Shakespeare's copious prose, in the calming surrounds of the conservatory, were the gentle strokes she needed to feel at peace and absorb herself in the lives and times of others.

The walls of glass in the intimate room projected the space into the landscape beyond the panes, drawing Arielle's eyes to the garden still damp from last eve's rain. She was comfortable and at ease, having separated herself to the far side of the manse in the sanctuary of the conservatory. The room would keep her a healthy distance from the turmoil that was sure to come from her parent's repartee in the study.

I an walked around the dining table to Elsbeth's chair and stood directly behind her placing his hands tenderly on her shoulders.

"My mind is heavy with thought Elsbeth, and as dearly as I would like to spare you, there is a matter I must discuss with you. Before I lose my verve to speak openly, I suggest we move along to the study. It will provide the private venue necessary for our conversation.

"Sir Ian, you are frightening me. Is someone ill? Is your position in jeopardy? What has happened?"

"Come, Elsbeth. I shall explain what I know."

The walk from the dining room to the study felt like one of the longest journeys of Elsbeth's life. She could not fathom what could have occurred to garner such an effect on her husband. He was at once visibly distraught and in thought. Stepping back, Ian allowed Elsbeth to precede him into the room and, once both were inside, he turned, pulling the large doors together just shy of having their brass findings latch in place. He motioned for Elsbeth to take a seat in one of the large, deeply tufted, leather wing chairs that served as comfortable companions just opposite his desk. Elsbeth declined, finding herself wont to stand to hear the news he appeared ever fast to relaying.

"Come, Elsbeth. I beg you, take a seat," Ian pleadingly cajoled as he completed the last paces that placed him at his desk's edge.

"No, Sir Ian. I must decline your suggestion, for you fill me with so much trepidation that I feel the need to stand erect, on my own authority, prepared to hear what you seem so compelled to relay."

"I am afraid Elsbeth, that which we have feared most has come home to roost like a wayward carrier pigeon and our options have been quite narrowed."

"That which we have feared most? Has someone been taken irrevocably ill? Is it Arielle? Oh please, let your news spill forth lest I conjure a world of worry as I await your pronouncement," Elsbeth begged as her face became twisted with agonizing curiosity.

"I hold before you correspondence, the authenticity of which is confirmed by the details contained within."

"Correspondence from whom?"

"One, Olivia Smithfield, spinster sister of Dr. Edmond Smithfield of Nantymoel, Wales. Her letter states she has knowledge of Arielle's birth that could be known only by one entrusted into the confidence of Dr. Smithfield himself."

Elsbeth's complexion became ashen as she gripped the wing of the leather chair next to her and, grappling for support, moved to the front of the chair and fell into the welcoming well of the seat. *Why.* She thought to herself. *Why, after all these years, would Olivia Smithfield contact them? What information could she possibly have at her disposal and why would it benefit anyone for her to come forth now?*'

Elsbeth swallowed hard as though doing so would clean away the news that left such a distasteful residue on her palate.

"What news does she have? What might her brother have told her? How unscrupulous was the man to discuss Arielle's birth with another?"

"Scruples and acting in proper haste are of no consequence now for the deed has been done and we must decide how to handle this Smithfield woman."

"We might do best to dismiss her correspondence," Elsbeth encouraged, thinking that ignoring the receipt of Olivia Smithfield's letter would eradicate the truth of its text.

"Elsbeth, the woman is determined to discuss this matter with us and will not be held back. She expresses the burden of her knowledge and the need to set the truth free before she is deep in her grave. She notes that her poor health has prompted her to make this very difficult decision and, only after careful consideration for all involved, did she take pen in hand to draft this letter."

This was all far too much to fathom, far too much to believe, far too much to accept, yet Elsbeth knew the much feared time had come as she looked up at her husband with tear swept eyes.

"We should have been more enlightened than to think that our avoidance of the truth would make it any less real. You appear very earnest in your conviction that this woman cannot be put off but there must be some way to delay her, to send her a message that Arielle has been told. Therefore, there is no necessity for further contact with us. That should allay her desire to have an audience with us."

"Believe me, my dear Elsbeth, when I say that I have wrestled all day with any number of schemes to avert this situation. I have come to the end of the longest rope I could throw myself with nothing more than frayed nerves. At the very least, we must allow her to journey here and, upon her arrival, we will focus all our energies on keeping Arielle from her presence. If the woman is compelled to meet with us, avoidance will not be an option but we can spare Arielle any details we wish to withhold."

"I just cannot understand the significance of Arielle's birth to this woman. Why is this of any matter to her?"

"The content of her letter further states that there are facts not already known to us which she must discuss."

"Not known to us? Dr. Smithfield was very swift the day of Arielle's birth and, as he placed her in my arms he made little eye contact. Do you think he knew something he failed to share with us?"

"By the very nature of his work, the man had to go with much haste, leaving little time for formalities."

"Oh, Sir Ian. This is all too much to bear. Our dear, sweet Arielle. If the truth be known to her will she understand? Will she forgive us? Will she accept the reality that she is not a child of my womb?" Elsbeth whimpered, as she relived the heartache of her barren years and the joy that consumed her when little Arielle was placed in her arms that very first day a score of years ago.

Ian stood close to Elsbeth and rubbed her cheek, wiping away a trickling teardrop that released itself upon her face, thinking to himself how ironic it was that something like adoption, which held so much hope and joy, could hold so much anger and despair. They would work out the details of their next encounter with Olivia Smithfield tomorrow when their minds were fresh. For now, adoption and secrecy were the ever present shadows casting themselves among Elsbeth, Ian, and Fiona as she slipped away from the doors of the study, once again carrying alongside the burden of her eavesdropping.

Chapter Seven

Ian and Elsbeth's fitful night's sleep could only be matched by Fiona's. *What to do? What to do?* The recurring chant paraded about the night dreams of the three. Fiona jumped out of bed with a start realizing she had overstayed her waking time by an hour and would be hard pressed to properly ready herself for her duties that included seeing to Arielle's toilette. She bantered about the room like a moth stricken by flame, finally composing herself enough to leave her bedchamber adjacent to the kitchen and ascend the back staircase that took her to Arielle's room. *Arielle was adopted.* The phrase struck Fiona's nerves like so many needles running skittishly across her skin. She wondered how the news would affect her mistress if the truth were presented to her. *Oh*, Fiona thought. *It is not for me to even contemplate.*

Had she minded her own business, she would never have been privy to Sir Ian and Lady Hargrove's private conversation. It was enough she had become aware of scuffling sounds in the foyer two eves past only to see the master of the house listing off balance in the shadows as Miss Arielle swiftly fled through the main portal letting the door go closed behind her. The

Hargrove's would handle this their own way and it was none of her concern. *But, what if they never told Miss Arielle? The letter sounded urgent and, was it not Miss Arielle's right to know? Some action has to be taken.*

Fiona fiddled with her apron and adjusted her cap before placing her knuckles against the six-paneled door to Arielle's room, giving a light rap before turning the faceted crystal knob to enter. Arielle had already lifted the shades, allowing the morning sun to filter its way through the ecru panels of Belgian lace that hung next to the windowpanes. Fiona thought Arielle looked radiant and well rested. It was obvious her mistress had not shared her night of unrest.

"Mornin', Miss Arielle. Unless me eyes deceive me, ye look like the night was good ta ya despite of all what's been goin' on."

"Going on? Of what do you speak, Fiona," Arielle queried as she gathered her sterling brush and comb set. She handed it over to Fiona as she selected the appointments that would grace her hair for the day.

"Oh, I don't mean nothin' by that Miss Arielle, jest the rainy weather an' all sorta puts a body on edge."

"Maybe you just need a good book to take to bed with you. There is nothing like a story well told to take your mind to distant heights and introduce you to characters you would never meet otherwise. Reading is a delightful way to escape the bonds of the moment and can be quite liberating."

"Aye, it sounds like an idea I might adopt as me own. I mean, 'ere's definitely more to be read every day in this house, of 'at I'm sure," Fiona blurted as she rigorously brushed Arielle's hair, her hands shaking as she continued twisting sections together and holding them up in place with two large mother-of-pearl barrettes.

"Fiona, you seem as nervous as a titmouse held captive by a cat. Get hold of yourself or I shall have nary a hair left on my head."

"Sorry it is that I am, Miss Arielle," Fiona apologized as she studied the looking glass that captured Arielle's image and wondered who sired this magnificent creature.

"Here, Fiona. Help me into my dress."

Arielle had selected a simple but lovely lavender gown with a small lace insert across the bodice and pouffy leg 'o mutton sleeves. Three rows of purple velvet trim enhanced the full circumference of the gown's bottom edge. Its fitted waist formed the perfect silhouette for Arielle's shapely figure.

"Will ye be needin' the cape that goes with yer gown, Miss Arielle?"

"No, it can remain in the armoire for I have no business that calls me out today."

"Very well. I'll tend to yer nightclothes and the beddin' whilst ye 'ave your mornin' meal. Go on 'bout your day cuz there's no use frettin' over the surprises a new day brings yer way." Fiona caught herself speaking aloud the words her mother used to recite to her whenever tension overtook their modest Irish cottage.

"Fretting? Fiona is there something you would like to tell me?"

"Oh, no. Miss Arielle, I just got caught up thinkin' 'bout family and was gettin' a little homesick for my mum. Them words of 'ers just come back to me is all."

Arielle shook her head and rolled her eyes ever so slightly in an effort to pass off the drivel emitted from Fiona's lips. Even though her chatter was of some merit, the girl many times chose such odd venues to deliver her thoughts that the listener was forced to muddle through to make any sense of her dialogue.

As Arielle exited her bedroom, Fiona began fluffing the bed linens, giving them a vigorous airing while she thought better of tangling herself in any involvement with the origins of Arielle's beginnings. She would hold her tongue for now, for it was not her place to bear news of which she knew little fact, and she dare not hazard a conjecture about the repercussions she would suffer for putting her ears and nose in the business of others.

Ian collected the files he needed for his committee meetings and rooted through a pile of papers atop his desk to locate those most pertinent to the proposals he wished to pursue once he met the rigors of his office. He placed his files and several letters in his supple leather attaché. His eyes fell upon the envelope addressed expressly to him from Olivia Smithfield. For fear of leaving its contents in open view, he placed it in the pocket of his overcoat, picked up his valise and, entering the foyer where he donned his very dapper derby, he stepped out the front door. Prior to taking the necessary steps that would place him in his waiting carriage, Ian reached into the pocket of his frock coat to retrieve his gloves. He was not aware of the document that slipped from the security of its cloth surround to the very public concrete below. He was off in his carriage in an instant.

⌐⁓

"Driver, stop!" Alexandra's abrupt command came as her carriage sallied up to 1322 Vermont Avenue, Northwest. *So*, she mused. *This is where that willowy wisp of a nit calls home. I might have known it would be one of the fussier addresses in the city. The little snip has obviously been spoiled and sheltered from the more colorful, exciting sides of life. Her family should be caught quite off guard by the revelation that her personal effects are being found about Washington in the private cab of a man who is worldly wise and experienced well beyond the weak flirtations of an English lass parading as a street urchin!*

Alexandra stepped down from her carriage and looked up at the stately brownstone. She drew in a deep breath, gathered her skirts, and made her way up the brick steps to the front entry. As she raised her hand to bid a knock on the door, she became aware of a parchment envelope beneath her right boot. Alexandra read from the beautifully scripted face of the envelope noting that it was addressed to Sir Ian Hargrove. She bent down and lifted the envelope from its resting place. Upon further inspection, she saw that it bore an English postmark and its flap had been unsealed leaving the contents victim to the curiosity of its finder. Alexandra removed her glove and, as deftly as sap runs from a tree, slipped the letter from its sheath. She opened it wide and read all the paper had to offer with an eyebrow raised and the genuine sweep of delicious satisfaction crossing her face.

Well, my, my, my. Good fortune has certainly befallen me today. This news should bring the little strumpet, Miss Hargrove, down a few notches. William will never want a thing to do with her once he knows the truth about her! Alexandra's thoughts brought an enormous grin of victory as she placed the letter back in the envelope and, holding it in her left hand, knocked upon the door.

Within moments, Fiona answered the knock and, pulling the door back full-wide, greeted the flaxen-haired visitor.

"I have come calling to see Mrs. Hargrove," Alexandra announced presenting her card into Fiona's palm.

Fiona dipped into a brief curtsy and after reading the face of the card responded in kind.

"Oh, sorry I am Miss, but Lady Hargrove is not about. I'll be more 'en happy to leave your card fer 'er though. She's real good she is 'bout checkin' on 'er callers fer the day."

Disappointment fell across Alexandra's face but appeared to go unnoticed by Fiona who flicked the card with her fingers. Alexandra had more impetus than ever to want to share her items in hand, yet, with the mistress of the manse inaccessible, she would have to be delayed in her presentation of the glove Arielle left behind in William's coach. *And, of the letter, what do I do? If I take it to William, I will have to explain how it came into my possession. If I leave it with this 'Bridget' there would be no way of knowing if its contents were ever made known to Arielle.* Alexandra contemplated the fact that the impact of the letter she held in her hand far out levied the glove she had come to return, even with every reflection of impropriety she wanted to attach to it. *No, I need to pass the letter along, but keep it on its premises.*

"Fiona?" Arielle called out to the girl not having heard the knock on the door. She stopped, frozen like a statue upon focusing on Alexandra Whitaker. Alexandra headed the list of all the abominable sorts that could ever set foot in her foyer. She wondered what on God's green earth brought her and how she was able to locate her place of residence. Arielle knew she would certainly not invite her in for she had had enough turmoil in her life of late and could not imagine any good coming from an encounter with her.

"Oh, my, my, Miss Hargrove. I do apologize for my early call, but I thought you might miss your glove. I wanted to get it to you before too much time elapsed. With the fluctuating weather and all, one never knows when another storm might come upon us -- some things can be so...unexpected."

Arielle did not trust a word emitted from the pouty lips of Miss Whitaker. Her syrupy-sweet delivery was laced with an essence of castor oil and it was not going down easily. She had seen Alexandra's talons fully displayed and would not be taken as her prey. Fiona handed over Alexandra's card. Arielle placed it in the silver compote on the hallstand.

Alexandra moved forward and presented the glove to Arielle. It was indeed a match for the one William delivered the previous day. Arielle accepted it from her and, as she started to speak, was cut short by Alexandra's second presentation.

"Additionally, Miss Hargrove, this envelope is intended for you as well."

Arielle took the envelope from Alexandra's hand and looked it over.

"This is addressed to my father. Why do you say it is intended for me, and how is it in your possession?"

"Why, it came to me quite unexpectedly, by chance you might say. I noticed that it was from England and it would seem any letter from your birthplace sent to your home address would be information intended for and of interest to everyone in the Hargrove manse," Alexandra relayed, quite pleased with the explanation she conjured.

Fiona was horrified. Only one letter from England stood out in her mind and if that letter be one and the same with the letter that Miss Whitaker handed over to Miss Arielle, she felt she must do everything within her abilities to remove it from her possession.

"I can take that fer ye Miss Arielle, sos ye won't be worryin' with it 'n all," Fiona offered as she stretched her hand outright to receive the envelope.

Something in Alexandra's presentation and Fiona's restless demeanor signaled discord for Arielle, however, she held her reserve and took great restraint looking directly into Alexandra's eyes as she levied words of caution toward her.

"Be aware, Miss Whitaker, that I am not in the practice of reading material that is posted to another -- a practice you might do well to follow. You will however, be credited for the goodwill you manifest by returning both the envelope and the glove to their rightful parties. The sincerity of your actions continues, I see, from the night 'ere we first met," Arielle responded, her words laced with a trace of acidity as she held her ground with her nemesis, Alexandra.

"I sincerely feel you should let curiosity take its course, as I know I would, and read the little epistle found within. There is nothing like a tender revelation to stir the soul, or shock the senses as the case may be." Alexandra's face beamed with pleasure as she continued her very pointed conversation, keeping her piercing eyes equally aimed at Arielle and the posted letter Arielle held in her hand.

"Miss Whitaker, your time in my presence has ended. I have had quite enough of your display of poor judgment and poor manners. Be on your way before I have you formally escorted from this residence. This home is fully staffed and I will have no difficulty gaining assistance at a moment's notice." Arielle's words came slow and direct as she tested every measure of her patience. She would not accommodate another moment of Alexandra's insufferable being.

"Very well, there is no need to threaten me. My visit is complete, in fact, more so than I had anticipated. It is quite queer how circumstances have worked to my advantage and, I am afraid, not to yours. Ah, well, you may never know since you appear content to remain ignorant of the contents of that envelope!" Alexandra blasted her parting words in a final attempt to challenge Arielle to read the piece of mail addressed solely to Sir Ian Hargrove. As she turned to depart, she tossed two calling cards on the carpet. "These came in tandem with the letter, if you care to know."

Arielle could not close the door to the manse quickly enough on the retreating skirt edge of Miss Whitaker. *Blast her.* Arielle thought as she latched the door, drew a deep breath, and leaned her back against the heavy slab of paneled wood as though the additional weight of her body would assure that no further intrusion would come from the golden gargoyle. *What could be so exceedingly fascinating about the contents of this simple looking letter that elevated Alexandra to such a lofty state? Was she bluffing or had she truly read its contents? Was she reading Fiona's behavior correctly, or was she simply succumbing to the recent odd mix of circumstances letting her nerves get the best of her?*

Fiona had remained quietly at her side, a soundless stone at the ready to safeguard her mistress. As Arielle turned toward her father's study, Fiona broke her silence, once again requesting that Miss Arielle hand the envelope over to her so she would not have to worry with it. Fiona picked up the calling cards, placed them in the palm of her right hand and curled her fingers over them hoping Arielle missed her actions.

"Fiona, thank you, however, I am perfectly capable of returning this piece of correspondence to my father's desk. I am sure he will realize it has gone missing since Miss Whitaker, if her claim is true, says she found it just outside the door. He must have dropped it on his way to the office. It must hold little importance since he has handled it so carefreely." Arielle assured Fiona, then put her hand forward. "The cards, Fiona. I'll have those as well."

"Yer right, Miss Arielle. Sure I am, there is nothin' te interest you in that letter, it's jest a note te yer father is all and nothin' fer ye te concern yerself with," Fiona spoke, handing over the cards, failing to realize the suspicion that mounted in Arielle despite the fact her words were spoken to divert Arielle's interest in the letter's contents.

"You seem to be exceedingly sure about this letter. What awareness do you have that I have not? Is there something you need to tell me, Fiona?"

"Oh, me goodness, I think not. My mum always lectured me 'bout the difference between need and want. I might want somethin' awful bad, but then there might not be the need, ye know, the requirement of havin' it or tellin' it, as the case may be. I think ye need to jest let the letter be."

Arielle dismissed Fiona. She held the cards and letter in her left hand as she stroked the face of the envelope with the fingers of her right hand, following the lovely flow of the indigo script. The very tips of her flesh were nearly tickled by the finely raised grain of the stock as she gently passed over the address again and again, looping up and down in a writing rhythm, as though the recurrent exercise would bring her calm and confirmation. She ceased the fondling of the stock and stared at it long and hard, taking it in her right hand and flapping it against her left hand in indecision. *Confirmation. Confirmation. I cannot believe I have let this blasted woman unravel me so that I would dare consider reading mail not intended for myself. But, Fiona is acting quite odd herself. Perhaps it is in my best interest to read the contents. Perhaps something is wrong with Father, he has been so bizarre and this letter will explain it all. Mum has been quieter than the norm, so possibly she too is worried about Father, or could it be herself? The letter has been here, and no one has mentioned it. However, of course, I am not privy to the contents of all the packages and letters that arrive, why would I be? No, this is not meant for me. I will think no more of it.*

Arielle's petticoats made a slight swishing sound under her lavender gown as she turned to enter her father's study. With gusto of motion, she hurled the envelope toward the top of his desk, hoping to cast away any thoughts of it. The envelope missed its target, bounced against the edge of the desk and ejected its contents that drifted to the floor like pieces of fine down plucked from a well-endowed webbed fowl. Arielle immediately regretted her action as she moved forward to retrieve the escaped calling cards and tri-fold of paper.

The bottom third of the creamy white stock became raised as it landed on the lush Bristol carpet to reveal the signature of an Olivia Smithfield. Arielle's eyes moved several lines above and she read, "You, Lady Hargrove, and your daughter deserve to know the truth of that day." She looked at the cards in her left hand and there, nearly rising to meet her eyes, was the name, Olivia Smithfield, underscored with London, England. Arielle closed the letter, keeping the remainder of the composition hidden from herself. *The truth of that day? What does this mean? Who is Olivia Smithfield? Her name has never been mentioned in our home. What can she know that my parents do not? And, yet, she says I deserve to know the truth of that day as well. Why has Father not said anything? Or Mum too? Is this the reason for the odd tone of this household? The letter mentions me, so Alexandra was right. How can Alexandra know more about me than I know myself? I cannot, in good conscience, read my father's mail, but, how can I in good conscience not? I will face this moral dilemma at another hour. At present, I must seize the opportunity to gain understanding about all that has transpired of late. My options are very limited. Fiona, despite her immature ramblings, will not reveal what she knows. Obviously, Mum and Father are keeping quiet and, as for Alexandra Whitaker, she is hardly to be believed. It would bring her great pleasure to have me seeking her counsel for my own torment. No, my options are narrowed to one. I have no better choice than to read for myself that which has fallen before me.* Thus, with trepidation of spirit and a guiding force of one, Arielle re-opened the tri-fold and began reading every single word of Olivia Smithfield's letter from its beginning to its revealing end:

March 1897

Dear Sir Ian Hargrove,

It is with sincerity and burden of heart that I present myself to you with this letter. Though we have not yet made one another's acquaintance, the inevitability brought by our common bond compels me to request a meeting with you. My poor health places me in an unequivocal position. I must share with you some facts not already known to you regarding your daughter's birth. As you will remember, my brother, the late Dr. Edmond Smithfield, was instrumental at her birth and delivered her to you. On many occasions, I served as mid-wife, assisting my brother with his enormous workload. One such occasion involved the birth of your daughter. I am not proud of what transpired that very day, but the outcome has benefited us both. Please believe me when I say I wish I could remain silent, but the knowledge I have may not go with me to my grave. You, Lady Hargrove, and your daughter deserve to know the truth of that day. I know there is much at stake, but the merits of this information far outweigh any detriment we may all suffer. Soon, I will book voyage to America so I may, at long last, correct the wrongs that my brother and I put in place. Until then, I remain indebted to you for the care with which you honor my request.

Sincerely,
Olivia Smithfield

Silence. Deathly silence filled her ears and, as abruptly, there came a void. Everything and nothing collided at once meeting eye-to-eye. Tears flowed, and no matter how fervently Arielle strained to find a clear field of vision, her focus remained askew, her thoughts scattered into nerve shattering pieces. *I should never have dared read this letter. How can this be? What does it all mean? Father had used the word 'inevitable' the night I had to flee his rage, and here it is again within the text of the Smithfield letter. What does she mean by 'was instrumental in her birth and delivered her to you?' Why does she say 'to you' and not 'for you?' Perhaps she erred in her penmanship.*

Arielle shook her head and wiped the tears from her face so her droplets of despair would refrain from falling onto the letter, potentially smearing its ink and warping the parchment. She needed to return the letter to its envelope as unscathed as possible. There was no need for her parents to know she had any knowledge of the letter. *But, when, oh terrible sorrow, when were they going to come forth with the 'inevitable?' When? I have no alternative but to transpose the contents of this letter for my own keeping in case the need should arise for my own protection to present its contents.* With a shaken spirit and hand, Arielle selected a piece of parchment from the upper desk drawer and put pen to paper to copy, word for word, the missive from Olivia Smithfield.

With the letter neatly returned to its envelope, though unaccompanied by the calling cards, Arielle rested it on the blotter of her father's desk, then slipped her copy into the bodice of her gown and stepped into the foyer, closing the study door behind her. As she began her ascent of the staircase, Fiona caught a glimpse of her. She knew from Arielle's tear-stained face and reddened whites of her eyes that she had to have read the very same letter waved about earlier by Miss Whitaker and overheard the eve before as the topic of discussion with her master and mistress.

'Twill be a bit rough goin' 'round here, 'twill indeed," thought Fiona as she fiddle-faddled around in the parlor having the good sense to let Miss Arielle be to herself.

Closing her bedroom door behind her, Arielle collapsed to her bed, rolled to her side, and sobbed dreadfully deep sobs as though she would heave her insides out. Her wails became absorbed into her mattress. She rolled to her back, her sobs and breathing becoming more shallow. Feeling some relief from her display, yet still, quite agonized, she rallied enough to calm the sobs and force a plan of action. Her greatest calm of late had come from Emma Willard. She must return to Chestnut Heights, if for nothing more than to revisit that calm, and return the dress so graciously lent by the grand dame of Washington society. Arielle felt comforted in Emma's presence and relished a repeat of that sensation. She sensed she needed a neutral party and would find such balance in Emma Willard. *Yes,* she pondered. *At tomorrow's sunrise, I will ready myself to place a call to Mrs. Willard. She might be just the one to make sense of it all, for I truly cannot.*

Turning onto her side with her head nestled on her pillow, she fell into discordant slumber. Thoughts danced about her mind, uninvited, and unwelcomed. Dreams forming a wicked web spun of words, people, and fragments of paper, presented themselves all about her in a chaotic chorus inharmoniously shouting, 'inevitable,' 'truth of the day,' and 'delivered to you.' Arielle tossed and turned in the torment of it all, thrashing her arms to shoo away the inexorable demons. She was confronted by walls that untowardly blocked her passage, prompting her to turn and attempt a previously unsought path. Her limbs rooted through the murky madness, aimlessly striking out at her illusory adversaries, never making contact as she grappled for an exit to flee. Clouds, thick and dark as smoke, ran full speed toward her making her gasp for air as the masses of cumulus nimbus formations bombarded her.

Arielle was engulfed in a frenzied search to rescue herself from the voices growing louder and harsher with each step she attempted. Just as she felt she could take no more, her legs gave way. She stumbled, falling full face to the softest ground where her plight was cushioned by aromatic mounds of rose petals brilliantly hued in pinks and reds. There were no stems or thorns to be found, nothing to pierce the serene beauty of the moment. She gathered in an armful of the lush carpet of petals, tossing them in the air, letting them cascade her full length as she anointed herself with their rich fragrance. What had been fearsome, ominous clouds were no more. Having given way to splayed rays of sun extending from sky to earth, the rays were like rigid fingers of icicles whose glistening crystals shed caressing moisture to all below. Arielle continued to look skyward as though seeking some meaning for it all from a source bearing far greater power than herself. Her eyes winced just the slightest bit as they sought protection from the radiating gleam of sunshine emanating from the brilliant, crystalline beams. Nearly blinded by the persistent light source, she very snuggly closed her eyes, finally shutting out all the confusion and pain. She was alone and mercifully, sleep unobstructed by dreams had come.

⌒

" Fiona, I will be needing my cape after all." Arielle issued her request as she made final adjustments to the full-length vision she captured of herself in the carved cheval that stood in the far corner of her dressing area.

"Is it an appointment 'at calls ye out this afternoon, Miss Arielle?" Fiona inquired, hoping not to be reprimanded for her failure to mind her own affairs.

"I have business to which I must attend and ask that you tell my mum, if she precedes my return, that I will join her at the dinner hour, if not before. Actually, it is more a visit to a friend. There is no need for concern."

"Will ye be needin' my help with that satchel wots sittin' at yer door, or is it jest somethin' ye'll be wantin' me te stow fer ya?" Fiona asked, every inch of her body consumed with curiosity.

"You may take it to the front door for me, I will manage it after that."

"It has a very fond resemblance to the satchel ye was carryin' when ye stepped from 'at fine carriage the other morn, or maybe it's jest my imagination is all." Fiona continued along the same path of inquiry, hoping to satisfy her need to know as she placed the lavender velvet cape about Arielle's shoulders.

'Why, Fiona, you are as transparent as a pane squeaked clean by a thorough rub. Enough of your dillydallying around the subject of this satchel. Of course it is the one that I had in my possession the other morning when you observed my arrival home. I am returning it and its contents to its owner. Now, that will have to fully satisfy you for the time being for I do not wish to delay my departure. Please see that the carriage has been prepared. You will find me waiting in the parlor. You may summon me when it has been pulled 'round in front."

Fiona retrieved the floral tapestry satchel and, following her mistress' orders, carried it downstairs placing it next to the large palm near the front portal. She stroked the top of the bag, moving her thumb up and down the fabric in a swishing motion, enjoying the feel of the heavy, colorful cloth, wishing all the while she could ride along with her mistress as innocuously as the satchel and be swept into the magnificent home owned by the one Miss Arielle would visit today -- the one whose carriage she had admired, the wealthy Mrs. Willard.

Chapter Eight

Late March 1897
Washington, District of Columbia

Arielle's preliminary arrival at Chestnut Heights had been met in darkness with such rain swept haste it had not afforded her the opportunity to appreciate the magnificence of the mansion and its extensive grounds. As her carriage entered, broad iron gates spread forth like welcoming appendages. Her conveyance continued on its way along the circular drive. She drew in a breath of suspended awe at the sight of the stately Italianate manse built of brick and sandstone and ornamented with one-story classical columns. It was fronted on the entry level by a loggia with multiple marble arches that lent an air of motion across the full width of the dwelling's facade. Centered on the second level were double, multi-paned doors that opened onto an ample balcony elegantly trimmed in a bowed iron balustrade. Space above the upper windows was adorned with an embossed fruit and swag ornamentation that softened the very regimented architecture of the grand house. Large gas lanterns framed each side of the main portal where below them enormous jardinières filled with dwarf junipers stood sentry on either side of the door.

The evergreens in the large urns provided year-round color and life to the otherwise florally deprived porch.

Arielle was sure that as soon as the spring season arrived, Simon Peabody would have numerous arrangements displayed from the cutting gardens he monitored so carefully in his gardening log. *That Mr. Peabody, what a unique little oddity he is*, thought Arielle as a smile crossed her face at the image she stirred of him. *I wonder if he will be about the premises today? And, oh, what is the name of Mrs. Willard's houseman? It began with a T. Theodore. No, that is not correct. No, not Thaddeus either. Oh, I am usually so good with names. His name has to come to me before I approach the door. Thomas. Yes, that is his name. Thomas.*

With full confidence that she could now properly acknowledge Mrs. Willard's houseman, Arielle exited the carriage. She reminded the driver to wait for her to complete her visit for her return home. He handed over the tapestry satchel that acted as a vessel of transport for the items she would direct toward her acquaintance at 2460 16th Street Northwest. Emma Willard would not be surprised by the return of her dress, but the other item neatly tucked among its folds would most certainly peak the curiosity of anyone who beheld it.

With a sure grip on the cloth bag, Arielle raised the edges of her cape and dress to clear the way for her boots to find sure footing on the staircase leading her onto the loggia. As she entered the vestibule and faced the massive six-paneled door, she looked up and hoped that once it opened, she would find within the comfort and support she so needed.

Her firm grasp and movement of the brass knocker brought Thomas to the door within seconds. He smiled a broad greeting, his eyes acknowledging that he had seen this pleasant visitor before.

"Thomas, I believe."

"Yas, mam."

"I am Arielle Hargrove and I have come to pay a call on Mrs. Willard. I hope I am calling at a convenient time."

"Oh, yas, Miz Hargrove. Please come on in. I'll g'won in get Miz Willard. She'll be pleased ta see ya. Youse can g'wain the parlor and waits jest a lil' while for her ta join ya."

Thomas motioned for Arielle to enter the large room to his left. She remembered it well from her first visit to Chestnut Heights that chilly, rainy eve when only a few kernels of the day's fire remained to warm the ballroom-sized space. The room was even more compelling at second sight, the colors in the carpets and upholstery were much more vibrant in day's light, especially when viewed by a mind less muddled by an evening of confusing events. Arielle's eyes wandered about as she took inventory of all the special touches placed by its owner.

Her boots settled into the plush pile of the large area carpet. Oversized botanicals of lush leaves in deep greens appeared as though suspended on the tips of the carpet's wool loops. The room's walls were bathed in vibrant crimson. Rather than overpower and engulf her, the rich red plaster cloaked her in welcoming warmth. It was just the balm she needed.

The fireplace was free of the embers and ash that had met her virgin visit to the manse. A velvet lambrequin edged in silky fringe embellished the rich woodwork of the mantel. It was embroidered its full width with a trail of white tipped ivy and provided a soft landscape for several objects d'art placed along its surface including a grouping of porcelain animal figurines, small bronzes and assorted trinkets. The mantel appeared to be offering a smile as tall vases anchoring each end lifted its corners in a welcoming grin.

A Pembroke-style table next to a settee held a daguerreotype of a young man and young woman. Arielle gave particular focus to the picture. If she were not mistaken, the young woman was William Clay's aunt. She supposed the man to be his uncle. The pair were dressed in fine suiting. *A special occasion,* she thought. *Perhaps a wedding.* Next to the frame laid an album thick with pages that appeared to be slightly worn from fingertips fondling the edges as its contents were viewed page-by-page.

Arielle glanced away, her eyes catching on the uppermost embellishments of the columns partitioning the room's salons. The golden acanthus leaves on their capitals were lush. Draperies with deeply swooping swags and jabots were gracefully hung at the large sash windows. She found the parlor's expanse to be quite the contrary to gaudy or extravagant. The attention to detail exuded precision and care. She was sure the hand the late Mr. Willard placed in the creation of this magnificent home forever comforted his widow.

Very few minutes passed before Emma made her appearance. Her hair was in her signature chignon, as smoothly upswept and twisted into place as the first time Arielle saw her. She was a fine figure of a woman and exhibited a spirited, yet graceful pace as she entered the room exuberantly scooping Arielle's hands into hers, making her feel instantly welcome.

"My dear, I am so glad you have returned. I have sensed we have unfinished business to attend. Your departure the other morn after your meal left me feeling unsettled, for I felt I should have done something more to assist you. Oh, but now you are here and we can chat like old friends. I have prayed that all is well with you. I hope that is so. To what do I owe the pleasure of your visit to Chestnut Heights?" Emma concluded her robust welcome, as she nestled on the settee next to Arielle and glanced at the tapestry bag near her feet.

"Thank you, Mrs. Willard."

"Call me Emma, dear. It makes me feel young and makes the wrinkles fall away. Otherwise, I shall be inclined to turn and look for Horace's dear departed mother to enter the room. No, there need be no 'Mrs. Willard' between you and me."

"You are so kind, um, Emma, to have me call you so. The fact is, since our first meeting, you have bestowed nothing but hospitable generosity toward me and I am most genuinely grateful."

"My nephew, William, is an excellent judge of character. He would not consider you among his friends nor bring you to me if he did not hold you in high esteem." Emma's eyes sparkled as she spoke of William and gazed at Arielle.

Arielle's mind was suddenly bombarded by a vision of Alexandra. She wondered how Emma could be so jaded by her nephew's charisma to think he could so keenly judge character when Alexandra, to whom he appeared so faithful, was so abhorrent. *No,* Arielle mused, *Emma's dear William is 'a few stripes short of a Windsor tie' if he thinks Alexandra merits a caption of 'fine character.' Of course she would be blind to her nephew. She is a woman closely bonded to family and the entire concept of family, as she explained when she described her relationship with the residents of her home. Her handsome nephew has her head so turned her vision is askew. I must put Alexandra and her misguided nephew out of my thoughts and be thankful Emma has come into my life.*

"You have been so gracious to allow me to wear your gown. My mum has always instructed me with an axiom repeated on many occasions by my grandmum, 'Never a lender nor a borrower be.' Shakespeare I believe. I have always felt the phrase lacked the humanity inherent in doing for others, however, it seemed most prudent to return that which I borrowed to sweeten the lending that has come from you."

"It is amazing how burdened we can become with semantics and the will to do what is right. You may consider the dress given, not lent by me. There, that absolves us both from your grandmum's interpretations."

"More like her admonitions. But that is not kind of me to say. She has departed this earth and I must not speak ill of her. My mum always told me she treated me with cool aloofness because she had come up hard, having to work at an early age to help support her mum and siblings since her father died young from consumption. But, enough of that."

"I will have Thomas take the satchel upstairs," Emma stated as she reached for a small etched crystal bell perched next to the settee. It rested on a round vitrine filled with a collection of bejeweled enameled boxes with intricately precise detail. Their beauty caught Arielle's eyes as she returned to the matter of the satchel.

"Please, if I may ask you to delay calling Thomas for a moment," Arielle requested as she reached to stop Emma's hand before the bell sounded.

"Of course, Arielle dear. There is actually no hurry to have it removed from the room. I just supposed we were finished with it and it could easily be dismissed."

"Mrs., um, I mean, Emma. You have made me feel so welcome and comfortable and, as I have stated, I am very grateful, so, what I have to say next I hope will in no way be viewed as over-burdensome or taking advantage of your many kindnesses to me. You know, when I first came to your home, something troubling had happened in my life. I suspect I may have some answer to the events of that eve and would like to take you into my confidence. There is no other to whom I feel I may openly talk. My family is not an option at this time. If you think my request too bold, I shall fully understand."

"Arielle, you remind me of the daughter I always dreamed of having and, had I been so fortunate to bear a child, I would feel most successful as a parent if she came to me for guidance and counsel during troubled times as well as pleasant. You do intrigue me and can be assured anything of which we speak shall remain only with us. I shall do all within my measure to assist and comfort you. You are naturally not at full ease for the unfamiliar is always that way," Emma's words came slow and soothing as she patted Arielle's hands studying the lovely, worried eyes of the dark-haired beauty before her.

Arielle felt fully enveloped by Emma's warmth. Had she harbored any doubts about coming to her home, they had drifted away with Emma's sincerity. Still, she was hesitant to unfasten the satchel, but she knew that revealing the contents of the letter that consumed her thoughts was possibly the only way to exorcize them from her body and soul. There would be no better time than now to open the satchel and release those curious words into Emma's universe, to hear her reaction, gain her insight, and be soothed by *her* words.

Words. How they could build or destroy, hurt or heal, encourage or dissuade. Arielle knew she was in need of some healing words to build her confidence and gain encouragement to pursue the answers necessary to find a resolution. She turned and unfastened the woven bag, reaching in to lift the sleeve of the dress that wrapped itself like a protective arm around the folded piece of parchment. She handed it over to Emma who held it, waiting for instructions from the one who kept it safely in her care.

"Before you open and read from the paper I have given you, I must explain how it came into my being and hope you think no less of me when I have finished. The original letter was sent to my father. I handwrote the copy you have before you. I felt it important enough to transcribe for my use so my father would not find his letter had gone missing. A visitor to our home claims to have found the opened letter on our front porch and encouraged, actually taunted, me to read it. I am somewhat taken with guilt for having read my father's mail, but it seems I was meant to have done so, for it essentially fell open at my feet. At any rate, although I am remorseful, the deed is done and there is no undoing it. Please, Emma, read the letter and you will see why I am wrought with confusion."

Observing a well of tears rise in Arielle's eyes, Emma gently touched her knee, then slowly opened the letter penned to Sir Ian Hargrove by Olivia Smithfield. She gave little expression as she read the text, only once lifting her eyebrows in unison and taking a full breath at the conclusion of her reading. She looked up to witness the anxious expression on Arielle's face waiting to receive her opinion.

"Arielle, I am pleased that you have chosen me to read this letter. You are right to want to know more and it would be most difficult to keep the knowledge of the contents of the letter to yourself. Its ambiguity warrants clarification."

Footfalls in short, exacting strides, could be heard advancing from the rear of the house and continuing down the long hallway toward the parlor. Emma halted her speech as she waited for the recognizable gait to meet its destination. As sure as Monday follows Sunday, Simon Peabody rounded the doorway framing the parlor and stopped cold in his tracks as though stunned by the presence of the two. His gaze, which did not have far to fall considering his stature, fell to Arielle whom he recalled from her previous visit.

"Oh, my, my, my, my, my, Miss Emma. I do apologize most profusely for coming upon you and your guest so. The garden is displaying so many signs of the cusp of spring, I was inclined, and inspired for that matter, to call upon you to join me for a safari of sorts through the structured and unstructured wilds of your landscape. But, proceed as you must. The garden and its delights await my planned adventure for two at your convenience."

Simon ended his invitation with an attempt to bow but, in the enthusiasm of his delivery, he had risen to the tips of his toes and the effort of the bow nearly cast him forward, so he quickly shifted back to his heels to find a proper balance.

"Oh, my, my, my. Ladies, you must excuse my awkwardness. And, it is Miss Hargrove, if my mind registers correctly. Yes, I would know those eyes anywhere." Simon squinted his eyes until they formed narrow slits as he studied Arielle's orbs through the confines of his wire-rimmed spectacles.

"Now, now, Simon. You will be thought quite the flirt if you continue to admire Miss Hargrove's features as you do. We do not want our guest to feel uncomfortable, now do we?"

"Oh, my, my, my. I apologize most profusely once again. By no means do I mean any harm or disrespect. I find great fascination with the scattered flecks of gold that radiate in her eyes. Yes, quite rare and quite -- fascinating!"

"Simon, you seem equally fascinated with the progress of the gardens. I am sure Miss Hargrove would enjoy participating in your 'safari' as you so exotically term it. Let us all take on the sights to behold with our own eyes whether they be flecked or unflecked!"

Emma looked to Arielle for her approval. She knew the girl would benefit from a walk and there could be no better time than now when the gardens offered so much promise of beauty to come. She knew Simon would relish a fresh pupil to hear his discourse on horticulture and such an outing would rescue them all from the awkward moment at present. She hoped Arielle would not think she was dismissing the subject of the letter and decided she should clarify her suggestion.

"We all have busy days with our own agendas. Sometimes the impromptu is the necessary ingredient for relaxation before we return to the rigors of our schedules. Arielle, if it is agreeable with you, we can take an abbreviated tour of the gardens with Simon and still find ample time to continue our discussion. I have a name to share with you when we return to the parlor, and, as Simon knows, my day is not complete without a visit to my garden. We need not look too far to see that all that occurs in life is replicated in the garden."

"And, oh my, for Miss Emma, you are the epitome of what I shall next say. Those who show a love of nature are truly indeed graced with a refinement beyond all others. Culture grows in the gardens, yes it does indeed!" Simon passionately exclaimed.

As their guest nodded in agreement, Emma rose to her feet, followed in suit by Arielle. Simon, whose pleasure showed from the tips of the wispy strands of his silver hair all the way to the springy steps of his little feet, began his short, exacting strides, retracing his previous steps as he led the two to the rear of the mansion for a look at his labors.

Arielle, at first disappointed at the interruption to her conversation with Emma, found Emma's segue to be the proper tonic of relief from the tension that had grown inside her. She was secure in her intuition that Emma would not abandon her cause. Her mention of a name she said she had to share with her upon their return to the parlor left her waning with curious confusion. She knew Emma only meant to give her reassurance that all hope was not lost and there were actions to be taken.

"How are you Mr. Peabody?" Arielle politely inquired.

"Oh, wonderfully well, Miss Hargrove. Yes, wonderfully well!"

Simon opened the French doors leading to the rear yard. The wide, double doors formed a frame for the picturesque scene beyond. A quick burst of wind thrust itself against the mullioned panes catching Simon off guard and flinging him upon the patio like a fly flicked from a loaf of bread. The door flew back upon its jam nearly smacking Emma flat against her face as she quickly back-stepped to dodge the oncoming assault of the hinged architectural appendage. Not to be thwarted, or have his pride diminished, Simon scrambled to his feet, adjusted his garments, corrected his eyeglasses that had gone askew, and reached for the door handle to assist the ladies in their exit.

"Well, Simon, you are so kind to test the whims of the weather for us. I do hope you are none the worse for wear." Emma expressed her concern with a mischievous gleam in her eyes, finding some humor in Simon's unplanned flight to the stone patio. Her cursory evaluation of his condition gave her cause to continue on the path the trio had set forth, finding no further concern warranted regarding his well-being.

Arielle observed the immediate area adjacent to the rear doorway of the house. It was partially covered in flat fieldstones that were visually drawn together by narrow masses of moss that formed lush green crossroads. Shade from the heady architecture of neighboring chestnut trees and shadows cast from the walls of the dwelling preempted sunlight from drying the stones. The moist environment had encouraged a rich patina to form across them lending Old World character to the landscape of the city residence. The lattice of espaliers blanketed with pyracantha flanked the French doors and were positioned against the brick and sandstone masonry walls. The thorny evergreen was still heady with red-orange berries.

"Come, ladies. Let us follow the path to the parterre. The boxwoods are fragrant and many of the perennials have begun their emergence. By May, the parterre should be ripe with foliage and spring blossoms!"

Enthusiastically, Simon stepped from the fieldstones onto an ivory-gray path consisting of thousands of oyster shells. The randomness of their size and irregularity of their shapes created an informal, yet suitable surface to protect one's footwear from the earth's mud and dust. The shells, slightly shifting to and fro with each footstep as the threesome traversed the path, created sounds similar to shards of glass rubbing one against the other as the trio made their way over the discarded remnants of homes once inhabited by mollusks.

"The oyster shells are a wonderful addition. I enjoy the texture they add to the space and the definition they impose on the walk. However did you gain such an abundance of them?" Arielle queried as she took pleasure in the sound emanated underfoot from the shell pieces.

"Bridwell's Oyster Bar at 615 7th Southwest, a favorite stop for a pint of Heurich. It is a local brew, a touch heavy on the rye, but a nice, heady lager none the same. At any rate, yes, at any rate, the boys in the kitchen over there save shells for me and, every once in a while, haul a wagon with a bed full of them. So, I have been able to pack quite a firm base for the walk. They provide substantial stability for the movement exercised across their surface," Simon boasted, proud of his acquisition and the friendship his patronage at Bridwell's had produced.

"It seems the shells act as a beacon engaging nature's creatures as well, for my very presence upon them makes me feel like a conductor for a choir of chittering birds and squirrels. They veritably sing out as I make my promenade," Emma said as she smiled and waved her hand like a maestro with a wand toward the trees and hedges that formed the risers for her winged and bushy-tailed madrigals.

To one standing still, the path clad with oyster shells seemed to dissipate into the verdant landscape as it continued on its way, curving between dense walls of evergreens. The three came to

the end of the shells where a black iron gate, very Gothic in ornamentation with open panels shaped like cathedral windows,
greeted them denoting something special to be exposed beyond.
The gate's panels were crowned at their peaks with a lancet finial
and were surrounded top and sides by a privet hedge, a thick,
arched surround of neatly manicured yews. Several fieldstones
placed under the gate's threshold separated the oyster shell walk
from the pebble lane that began on the opposite side of the gate.
The lane led the way to Simon's pride and joy -- his elaborate
parterre.

Arielle was quite impressed with the appointments Simon had
designed for the magnificent formal garden he had laid out for
Emma's Chestnut Heights. The symmetry of the multiple beds,
like sextants from a central hub, filled the large expanse with
pathways and numerous pieces of architectural garden embellishments. Large urns waiting for plantings, statuary, a sundial and
gazing ball added delicious dimension for the eye. Low hedges of
crisply clipped boxwoods anchored the parterre's beds that were
enhanced with specimen trees and artistically trimmed topiaries.

Just as Simon had noted, borders were beginning to show the
rebirth of a wide variety of perennials. Periwinkle with its waxy
green leaves was ready to leave its low lying winter status and rise
up to form its thick blanket of green around a square pond with
stone coping. There was no sign of the vinca minor's flowers, but
Arielle knew their lavender-blue blossoms would soon appear. She
could only imagine the breadth of the colorful beauty to come
when all the blessings of the garden were reaped upon summer's
arrival.

At the far end of the parterre, sat an ornate iron bench heavily
cast with filigree. It was nestled among beds of pansies exhibiting
a vivid display, the amethyst faces of each five-petal blossom full
wide with black and yellow markings, giving each distinguishing
characteristics. One section of the bed of pansies was distinctive
with white pansies that were exultant with their infusion of deep
purple.

"I see, I see. You admire the *pensee* as our French friends would say, or Viola cornuta where the lovely blossoms find their root," Simon beamed as he walked closer to the colorful beds to review their progress.

"Arielle, Simon selected these flowers especially for this area of the garden because he knows my fondness for them and their royal purple color. It soothes me to have their velvety faces meet mine whenever I come for a quiet moment of reflection -- they invoke thought."

"They certainly thrive in this location -- obviously well chosen by you, Mr. Peabody."

"Yes, you see, you see, Miss Hargrove, the pansy is very stable and gives quite a show at a nominal cost to one's pocketbook, if I may say so, with its lengthy blooming calendar. Why, Miss Emma and her guests may enjoy these bloomers into September with little care and maintenance. They are fairly protected from direct sun, finding sanctuary in the northwest portion of the property. Yes, you see, they are most appropriate here."

"You can benefit many fold from picking pansies for bouquets as they are thus encouraged to produce yet more. It is always love-ly to have a bundle to pass along to a friend who will know you are thinking of them. You probably noticed a vase filled with them in my dining-nook when you had tea the other morn. I feel renewed when fresh flowers are in my midst."

"Mr. Peabody, the landscape is more lovely than I could ever have envisioned. I see your Dusty Miller is coming back strong. What are the sprigs of green I see near the borders of the beds over there?"

"Oh, those my dear, those are some of my favorites for the del-icate little flowers they produce. Iberis sempervines or Candytuft is to the right. It will eventually sport small white blooms with a light sweet scent. Next to the Candytuft is Calliopsis drummondii or Coreopsis. Its yellow, daisy-like flowers should give a constant show throughout the summer. They are particularly effective edg-ing plants."

"What a great talent you have. The quadrants you have designed make each section of the garden a refreshing room unto itself. You have created a giardino segreto! It is truly a gift to have such golden hands!" Arielle extended her praise to the man whose abilities she held in high regard. His eccentricities served him well in garden design. "There is nothing prosaic about your work!"

"Prosaic, ahh, prosaic. Thank you. Yes, thank you."

Emma laughed, "Indeed, there is nothing dull or commonplace about Simon."

"I should say," replied Arielle.

"Ah, I presumed, yes, I presumed you were a woman of culture Miss Hargrove, the first moment we were introduced. Your knowledge and interest confirm my conclusions. I am certain, yes, I am certain I am within my bounds to say that you must return to Chestnut Heights before the drama of the gardens reach their denouement."

"I should enjoy that greatly, for already I feel a great temptation to linger here," Arielle responded without the slightest sense of hurry coming over her.

"You can see the Almighty's influence more at this time of year than any other. It is as though nature's bounty preaches a sermon about immortality. Immortality, yes indeed." Simon appeared to glow with pride as he surveyed the emerging signs of spring.

"And, Lord knows the gardens are a full-time focus for Simon. He is meticulous and has quite a penchant for all things botanical. He says he finds little more depressing than a garden whose inhabitants have remained well past their prime. You will nary find a browned leaf or spent blossom loitering under Simon's watchful eyes. Yes, Simon, you are outstanding. This preview of things to come has been a most informative pleasure. Now, before Miss Hargrove and I begin to 'wither on the vine,' I suggest we save for another day the next garden stop on your 'safari' and take tea together in the parlor. Simon, I would invite you to join us, but for now, we have some private matters to which we must attend. I know you will understand. Perhaps we can dine together this evening," Emma kindly suggested, knowing Simon was accustomed to being excluded from her personal visits with friends.

"Yes, Miss Emma, yes. I look forward to that very much, yes, very much I do."

"Very well."

"Mr. Peabody, this has been most enlightening and reviving. There seems nothing better than a breath of fresh air to cleanse the soul. Thank you." Arielle finished her words to Simon with a small curtsy then turned to trail Emma through the gardens back into the equally lovely manse.

The two found their seating in the parlor, selecting the identical positions they had taken at the onset of their visit. Emma leaned forward to gain closer proximity to Arielle as one does with a close confidant, and took her hands to hers. She smiled at the beautiful young woman, thinking about the delicate nature of the situation at hand and hoped her advice would aid her well. They had not known each other long, but from their short encounters, Emma's fondness for the girl grew.

"Your welfare is of paramount concern to me and I fear you will not feel of sound mind until the questions that have so unsettled you find some reply. There is a woman on F Street that you must see. She has established quite a notable reputation for the skills and perceptions she applies with great dispatch to matters of uncertainty such as yours. She was instrumental in solving the case of a threatening letter-writing campaign that was nearly the undoing of one of the Congressmen. The threats were so severe that he was on the precipice of vacating his seat when Miss Pennybacker, after heated surveillance, nabbed the perpetrator just as he slipped another carefully composed note under the Congressman's door. Yes, you and Miss Morgan Pennybacker must have an audience with one another. Though she and I have never met, she knows of me, as do I of her. You will find, my dear, that the longer you abide in Washington, the more intimate the city becomes with bedfellows who are not so much strange as they are competitive, and at times, contemptible. The political arena can be a rough and stuffy place. But, oh, here I go, rambling on. Give me a moment. I will write a letter of introduction for you to present to Miss Pennybacker and you will be prepared to proceed on your way."

Emma squeezed and patted Arielle's hands, then slipped away to her desk where she selected a lively piece of ivory stationery bordered with a pattern of petite rosebuds. She had consciously avoided the black-bordered stock that so frequented her correspondence since Horace's death. Arielle observed the tidy stack of stark stationery that lay on the drop-front of the desk. She recalled having seen a similar style of paper used when her uncle passed on. Her aunt had explained at the time that the stationery was representational of her bereavement, its wide black border would increasingly grow narrower as her period of mourning reached its close.

Arielle felt a sense of renewed expectations. Her time in the garden had given her a lift. The changes she witnessed in the plantings from their winter to spring status bore relevance to her current state. Change was as inevitable in the garden as in life. It signaled that something would be altered or different but, the truth remained that change, in and of itself, could be for the better, not necessarily for the worse.

She knew she must not think otherwise or she would go mad in the process of raising questions and doubt. She must adapt to the world that was changing around her or be neutered like a seedling blown from its earthly mooring never to find itself viable again. She felt sure there were answers to her questions available for the finding and, thanks to Emma's recommendation, Miss Morgan Pennybacker would be her guide to map the proper course.

How was it that one evening's events could ricochet one's life about until it fell into so many discordant fragments? Arielle was full with thought as she waited for Emma to complete the letter of introduction.

Emma's effortlessness of grace was something pure to behold. It came to her as second nature, an innate charisma. Arielle had met many well-to-do sorts, but none held a candle to the woman who sat before her. Emma Willard was a rare gem indeed and Arielle was glad to count her high on the roster of her friends.

"Here, my dear. Take this note along on your visit to Miss Pennybacker. I understand she can be imperious, so do not find yourself put off by her manner. In the long run, her style will serve you well," Emma said as she handed the note over to Arielle. "I have left the flap of the envelope unsealed so you may read what I have written prior to presenting it to Miss Pennybacker."

Arielle's youth refreshed Emma and her plight ignited Emma's innate willingness to minister to others, to make a difference, to offer hope. She liked this young woman and wanted to do all in her power to aid her. Arielle appreciated Emma's openness and all of her efforts to soothe her.

"I cannot thank you enough. I am met with some trepidation, for this is all so new to me, however, your kindness and assurances strengthen my resolve to follow this through. Thank you so very much, Mrs., I mean Emma, thank you very much. My life is so much richer for having you as a friend."

Arielle smiled as she took the note close to her with both hands, then, releasing one hand, gathered the folds of her dress to lift its front edge from the floor as she walked out the main doorway of Chestnut Heights.

"Take good care my dear," Emma advised. "I have an abiding faith in you."

Arielle was unaware of the roving pair of eyes peering from behind a lush holly on the front corner of the mansion as she made her way to her waiting carriage. Simon Peabody found himself to be just in time for her departure as he rounded the front of the grounds to catch a parting glimpse of Miss Emma's young guest. Pursing his lips together, he moved his mouth from side-to-side and pulled the fingers of his right hand through the sparse strands of hair remaining on his nearly naked head. He rolled his eyes about their sockets, then shook his head as gusty winds swept about the exterior of the manse. Large leaves from mature, waxy evergreens were cast about Simon's face like a battalion of barbs enlisting their forces against him. He stepped back, vigorously swatting the advancing branches from his face in self-defense like one who suddenly came upon a fully inhabited and very angry hive.

Securely inside her carriage, Arielle was oblivious to the extemporaneous jig Simon performed just yards from her. As her carriage pulled away and rounded the far end of the lane, Simon's ears rang with the clip-clapping rhythm of the horses' hooves on the heavily pebbled drive, their shoes kicking stone back upon stone in choreographed movement. He rubbed his facial skin to ease the sensation of the painful pricks still piercing through his pores from the hostile holly.

"Blasted shrubbery!" Simon exclaimed in a wind-muffled bellow as he squinted to see the last of the vessel of transport carrying Miss Hargrove away.

"Fascinating. I say, fascinating. Yes, she is most fascinating. Hope she returns. Yes, hope she returns," Simon breezily muttered, feeling less than sated, desiring to know more about the business of the fair lass whose arrivals and departures lent an enchanted fixation with which even his beloved subject of horticulture could not compete.

Chapter Nine

Washington, District of Columbia

Morgan Pennybacker, oddly enough, was named not for the famed J.P. as she would most prefer to believe, but for the breed of horse her father raised on the family farm in Virginia where she was sired a score and ten years ago. An earnest, hardworking native of the Leesburg countryside, the disciplined Jackson Pennybacker trained his daughter with the same thorough dispensation he afforded his horses. He taught her to be obedient to and consistent with signals, to be honest and to be straight-forward. The senior Pennybacker always gave his daughter clear messages so she, like his horses, could reach her full potential.

Like a strong, well-mannered horse, Morgan benefited from her father's good training. His Morgan's were versatile, they were as well suited for driving as they were for riding, and they were attractive with good confirmation. He gave them good care and good treatment, gaining a great deal of inspiration from the challenges he incurred while achieving his objectives with his livery.

The dedication placed toward his horses was no more than he drove in Morgan's direction, instilling in his daughter cordial hospitality, a passion for adventure, and enough horse sense for her clever mind and sturdy shoulders to maneuver the most challenging situations. Morgan's fondness for the handsome, gentle creatures and her father's sage teachings gave her insight into the behavior of man and beast. She felt a fond kinship for the regal creatures and a great liking for their rich, chestnut brown coats.

Her horse sense was put to work on a daily basis as she dealt with the public in the small needlework shop she established eight years earlier in the District of Columbia. An outgrowth of fireside evenings spent with her mother, Pennybacker's Stitchery offered excellent instruction, fine threads, yarns, linens and canvases. The shop kept Morgan grounded the way the farm centered her father. He would on occasion remind her that the free spirit for which they both were known was an attribute to be handled with respect. Unharnessed, it was no better than an eye out of focus, a ship off course, or a train without benefit of a track.

Morgan's needlework required focus and precision. She always took great care as she guided the needle up through the Aida cloth and brought it down again piercing the fibers of the cloth with utmost control. As she worked, she heeded the words espoused by her mother whenever she was tempted to exercise haste, 'Speed without accuracy is of little value.'

Her store generated steady revenue. Its contents kept her interest. However, restlessness challenged her reason for being and sent her in search of diversions from the little world of orderly spools, laces, pins and needles all neatly confined at Pennybacker's Stitchery.

Arielle stood before the entry to 247 F Street focusing on the golden numerals imprinted on the clear transom over the door. A hunter green sign was suspended perpendicularly from the storefront by a wrought iron bracket formed in a meandering wisteria vine motif. It confirmed that she had indeed come to the correct address. 'Pennybacker's Stitchery -- fine needlework, finishings & findings' read the scripted black letters. *Ah, findings.* Arielle thought to herself. *How coincidental it is that the vocabulary for a craft fits the vocabulary for a trade or, had this all been well-thought-out by a very thorough Miss Pennybacker?*

One week had passed since her encouraging visit with Emma Willard and, though she had gathered verve enough to arrive at the stitchery shop, she was not wholly confident about her decision. She drew in a deep breath, determined to see her decision through. She would at least meet on this one occasion with Miss Pennybacker. She felt no harm could come from presenting the little details she knew and, after all, Miss Pennybacker, as her professional confidant and guide, would advise her as to what logical steps should be taken.

The reflection from the street on the door's window obscured her view of the interior of the shop, but the handcrafted 'OPEN' sign stitched in petit point welcomed her. Placing her thumb on the worn brass latch, she pressed down, pulled the door toward her and stepped inside. The interior held no mystery. There were cabinets displaying samples of work, bolts of fabric, rolls of canvas, bins filled with luscious yarns, racks of colorful threads, patterns, stitchery books and cards with needles.

Pennybacker's was, for the needlework enthusiast, as delectable as a candy shop's offerings to one with an inexorable sweet tooth. Shelves, pigeonholed compartments and bins burgeoning with fastenings, findings, threads and cloth ranged from simple to ornate. On a small counter near the front of the store was a gleaming National cash register, a spike holding pierced receipts and a stack of white paper bags to transport customer purchases. The shop held a stillness about it. Arielle observed there were no other patrons milling about or, for that matter, was there any human form to greet her.

Suddenly, the mantle of stillness fell away with the flutter and flourish of feathers against a wire cage.

"Whoa, boy. Whoa boy. Step up son," came the mixed lyrical message emitted from behind the curved beak of a parakeet gaily outfitted in its bright plumage of buttercup yellow and lime green.

Arielle, with her frayed nerve endings feeling every bit of their unravelled status, jumped and twitched a bit. Upon spying the source of the commotion, she cast a smile toward the feathered warbler and moved closer to observe its beauty. The bird began hastily jumping from perch to cage floor and back, gaining a momentary foothold on the sides of its wired fortress. He began repeating his nervous flight about the cage all the while stirring up bits of seed that became airborne and scattered to the linoleum floor. Arielle stepped back attempting to still the bird's agitation.

'Whoa, boy! Whoa boy!" the bird squawked catching Arielle somewhat amused as it danced its impatient two-step about the cage.

The squeak of a door caught Arielle's attention. She turned her head to one side toward the source of the high-pitched sound. A wisp of a young woman with braided strawberry blond locks fastened into a tidy bun at her nape, stepped through the doorway and, squinting to focus through the narrow lenses of her wire-rimmed glasses, offered a half-issued smile toward the shop's visitor.

"Now, now, Peepers. Remain calm. Remain calm. May I be of assistance?" The somewhat nasal inquiry came from the young woman whose arms were abundantly filled with fabric and patterns that threatened to spill forth with any further movement.

"Perhaps, I may return the offer," came Arielle's reply as she reached forward to catch a portion of the unbalanced load and followed the young woman to the nearby counter top where they both freed themselves of the teetering merchandise.

"Thank you. I have the propensity for impulsive behavior on occasion, which tends to make me think I am more prepared than I in reality am -- or, so professes Miss Pennybacker. She's trying to break me of it, but she says it would seem I am kin to a mule. Oh, I am so remiss. There I go, speaking first, thinking later. Do you need help with your needlework?"

"Oh, I see. You are not Morgan Pennybacker," stated Arielle, finding herself caught somewhere between a place of amusement at the young woman's behavior and uncomfortable with the private revelations of one prone to impulsively broadcast random thoughts.

"Oh, my, no," came the firm and still nasal response. "I am Agnes, her assistant. Agnes Fielding."

"Remain calm. Remain calm," retorted Peepers.

Her *assistant*. Arielle was taken back a bit by Agnes' statement, wondering if this efficient, yet somewhat bungling young woman was solely an assistant to the wares and customers of Pennybacker Stitchery, or could it possibly be that she assisted the reputedly effective Miss Pennybacker with her investigations? Arielle began to question herself and her decision to come to 247 F Street. She began to question her reliance on Emma's recommendation. She had not known her very long, but her intuition persuaded her to continue to garner hope from her advice.

Arielle could gather no immediate reasons for the feelings that welled inside, but she knew deep in her being that she must pursue the paths that had taken her to Miss Pennybacker's door. Turning back and leaving forever latched some critical portions of her history would render her unsated and unsettled -- sensations she was less than willing to take on as lifetime companions. *I must not be so critical of the young woman named Agnes. I must allow her more than the potential errors of a first impression to formulate an appropriate opinion.*

"Miss Pennybacker, is she on the premises today?" Arielle queried as her eyes studied the young woman, searching her face for confirmation that her decision to remain was sound.

"Oh my, yes. Unless Miss Pennybacker is involved in a case that takes her away from the shop, ah, I mean unless she is otherwise engaged, she is either visiting her father or working in her office. She spends little time upstairs in her apartment -- I think it holds little interest for her. But, I guess that is enough from me. Would you like to speak with her?"

"Yes, that would be much appreciated."

"Give me just a moment. I will let her know that you are here. Oh, forgive me. Whom may I tell her is calling?"

"My apology is in order. I should have introduced myself. Please tell her that Arielle Hargrove is here to see her."

"And, will she know the nature of your visit?"

Arielle felt the young woman inquired not so much to be intrusive as she was intent on being thorough in her presentation to Miss Pennybacker.

"I have a matter which needs her expertise. It will be best for me to explore any details directly with Miss Pennybacker, if you will be so kind to announce me."

Agnes was used to the second-class status that enveloped her when new clients appeared on the scene. She knew Morgan's reputation drew people to the shop and Morgan was the person indeed whom they wanted to see. Agnes' supporting role was not diminished by such treatment. She was confident with the position she had been given and knew that even though Morgan held the business reins, her role, which she performed well as Morgan's right-hand girl, kept her in an enviable and secure position.

Their working relationship began quite simply when a 'Help Wanted' sign drew Agnes' attention as she strolled through the shopping district. Agnes had no family attachments to refrain her from traveling on Morgan's whim. She appeared capable enough to keep the shop organized and to advise customers, and she got along exceedingly well with Morgan's beloved parakeet, Peepers. Hiring her was of little risk as far as Morgan was concerned.

"Miss Pennybacker asks that you come into her office. Here, I will lead the way," Agnes motioned through the open doorway for Arielle to follow.

The two proceeded through a narrow hallway that held very little brightness except for shallow shafts of light emitted from a doorway that appeared to be reserved for storage and another room whose door was open almost fully wide. Agnes approached the door and paused just inside.

"Miss Pennybacker, I present Miss Hargrove."

Agnes signaled Arielle to come forward. Arielle thought her legs might fight the reflexive impulses from her brain that ordered them to move, but their hesitation was brief. She drew a deep, cleansing breath of courage bolstered by Peeper's exclamation of "remain calm" and moved forward to make her acquaintance with the renowned Miss Pennybacker.

The office was not what Arielle had envisioned for the owner of a needlework shop. Far removed from any fluff or frills, the office appeared very tailored, very tidy, very Eastlake in influence affixed with simple appointments. Barrister bookcases with leaded, stained glass panels in an Arts & Crafts inspired design lined the walls. The honey-yellow stained oak cases were abundant with books. The room was nearly void of bric-a-brac. A lamp with a very angular stained glass shade illuminated the desk's top where a blotter, two inkwells, a notebook, several volumes of files, and stacked leather bound ledgers with gilded lettering adorned the organized surface. A utilitarian umbrella stand beside the doorway gained Arielle's curiosity when she caught sight of a black leather horse whip mixed among an assortment of black umbrellas, some with carved wooden handles and some that appeared to have handles made of ivory or bone.

Natural light filtered through hinged wood shutters mounted against a moderate window just behind the desk. All about the walls were simply framed renderings of horses. All had expressive faces and were drawn with one medium in sepia tones. *Morgans,* Arielle thought, *a noble breed. Perhaps a precursor of Miss Pennybacker's reputation.* The room took on the atmosphere of a stable's well-fitted tack room, so much so, that Arielle's nostrils imagined they were filled with the heady scent of freshly cleaned leather. The room was a mise en scène of equine pursuits.

Her eyes moved quickly about the room as she continued her cursory inventory of its contents before settling her visual attention upon the one whom she most needed to focus. There she sat, the one person who could possibly, objectively disentangle the bonds of lies and truths regarding her heritage. Once again, Arielle's reflexes threatened to derail her. As she began opening her mouth, she feared the air passing over her windpipe would not allow an intelligible sound to produce itself. But, with much conviction, and a well-placed silent prayer, she rallied, even mustering the ability to trim her face with a pleasant smile of cordiality. Her words came smoothly with the precision that one finds when having rehearsed, if only moderately, the manner in which a conversation might unfold.

"Miss Pennybacker, thank you for seeing me without benefit of anticipation. I have a letter of introduction for you from Mrs. Emma Willard who speaks very highly in your regard. Her confidence that our meeting will find a satisfactory result has prompted me to visit you today. I hope I am not in error, having failed to make an appointment."

Morgan reached forward to accept the envelope Arielle presented. She lifted its flap and removed the letter. Her perusal of the correspondence was thoughtful, yet brief, and holding it slightly askance, she glanced up at Arielle. With a sincere depth of focus emitted from her dark brown eyes, Morgan looked squarely into Arielle's face as she verbalized her thoughts.

"In point of fact, Miss Hargrove, you needed but to mention Mrs. Willard's name to engage my attention. She has earned the respect of many and I readily count myself one among them. Her letter references a search upon which you wish to embark, and she feels you would benefit from my involvement. I am, of course, more than happy to oblige, but I will undoubtedly need some pertinent information to set my course. Please make yourself comfortable," Morgan stated, motioning to Arielle to take a seat in the chair opposite her desk.

Arielle made the necessary few steps and sat in the slatted-back chair. Its leather cushions and wide, Adirondack-style arms were in sharp contrast to the more ornate furnishings that filled the Hargrove home. The details of the room's furnishings momentarily enveloped and consumed her. She noted their difference from all that was known to her yet, in tandem with those thoughts, she felt a strange alliance with the office of Morgan Pennybacker. She had a sensation, a feeling of comfort that transcended immediate reason, yet gave her the impetus she required to surge forward with her quest.

Morgan handed the letter over to Agnes who took a quick glance at its contents before refolding and slipping it back into the confines of the envelope. She held it securely, rubbing her fingers across the surface, appreciating the fine stock of the stationery that imported Miss Hargrove's request.

Agnes knew the Willard name and the respect the woman had earned for her philanthropy and unselfish generosities that she quietly bestowed. She never flaunted her affluence, as was the pattern set by many of her equally wealthy peers. *Yes,* Agnes thought. *With such endorsement, Miss Hargrove's case will be delicious to pursue, and certainly a pleasant, stimulating diversion from the daily routines of the stitchery shop.*

"Bear with me as I make some notations to focus our field," Morgan stated, selecting a pen from the ink well as she slid a blank piece of paper onto the blotter that protected her desktop.

Arielle felt the recurring reticence wash over her, but, emboldened by Emma's counsel, she immediately dismissed its hold by centering her focus on the mission at hand. She had within her the gift of Emma's words.

"I am embarrassed to speak about a matter so private, yet, I clearly must find answers to my questions, all the while requesting the utmost discretion."

"You will fully benefit from the very essence of my propriety and that of Agnes as well. Confidentiality is no stranger to us, rest assured, Miss Hargrove. It comes with the territory and I have built my reputation upon it," Morgan stated with conviction readying her hand to write.

"Bear with me as I make some inquiries. Besides Mrs. Willard's referral, what precisely has led you here?"

"Recently, I was made aware of a letter sent to my father from a woman in England, London I believe, stating that she had information regarding my birth that was not known to my parents. She stated that she must meet with them -- that she was ill and would need to see them soon."

"I have a simple question, but nonetheless important. What is it about this letter that makes you curious to know more?"

"Events of late, in my home, have been askew. My father's behavior has been unnecessarily erratic and my mum has appeared drawn and worried. The letter has been kept from me and quite accidentally came into my hands. Upon reading it, I began to question its contents and the intent of its author. At the very least, I need to know more about her and the doctor she mentions."

"The letter was penned by a woman in England. You are sure of that?"

"The envelope bears the postmark of Great Britain."

"Was her name at all familiar to you?"

"No. I can say I have no recollection of anyone by that name."

"And tell me, by what name did she identify herself in the letter?"

"Olivia Smithfield was the name signed. Here is her calling card. Additionally, she made reference to her brother, a Doctor Edmond Smithfield. I want to know more about Olivia Smithfield so I may put to rest all the demons that her letter has stirred since its arrival. I have written down a copy of the letter for you," Arielle finished, retrieving the copy of the letter from her handbag, feeling quite relieved to have finally aired her knowledge regarding the Smithfield letter.

"Coincidence serves us well today, Miss Hargrove, for I have planned an April buying trip to England to select merchandise for my shop. The challenge for a business owner such as myself is to keep steps ahead of the latest whimsy by offering something fresh and new that promotes an interest in needlecrafts. In fact, Agnes and I set sail at the end of the month. If you choose to engage my services, I can begin to pursue this matter immediately upon my arrival in London," Morgan stated as she continued to make strikes with her pen upon the papers before her.

Arielle wondered what further notations she could be making and actually found the motion of her penmanship curious as her strikes became strokes that appeared to take on a series of forms. Morgan was at once aware of Arielle's gaze and promptly stopped the work of the pen in her hand. She looked at Arielle as though awaiting her response.

"Oh, yes. Why, of course. You give me very good news. This is more than I had expected. I am most pleased that you will pursue my case and with such dispatch. Yes, most definitely, please consider yourself hired."

"Miss Hargrove, I must remind you that although we will employ every measure within our means, in point of fact, there are instances, however rare, when all avenues have been exhausted leaving no viable path for us to embark. We will have reached a dead end, an impasse, and as frustrating as that is from our perspective, it can be devastating to our clients."

"I have every confidence in your abilities and, with God's good guidance, we shall all be well served. There is the matter of your fee."

"If it is agreeable, one half is requested upon securing our services with the balance due upon conclusion. Agnes will draw up the paperwork."

"You say you sail next week? I will be, of course, anxious to hear word regarding even the smallest detail you deem relevant to my concern. How shall we remain in contact?"

"I am prepared to suggest that you accompany us. Your parents may feel refreshed not to have you underfoot while they sort through Miss Smithfield's request. In point of fact, your desire to visit your homeland, one would think, will seem a reasonable sojourn and will not place you under undo scrutiny by your family. I should say, from your accent, I have made the assumption that England is your native soil."

"You are correct that my accent is of British origin, and I have family in England, however, before arriving in America, I lived for several years in Wales."

"Very well. Let me share our travel itinerary. Agnes and I board the train to New York on Wednesday, April thirtieth at ten o'clock in the morning with a brief stay in the city before setting sail to England. Work out the details and meet us at the Baltimore & Ohio station at New Jersey and C streets, Northwest. If, for some reason, you are delayed, or elect not to book the journey, we will wire information to you via Mrs. Willard to avoid alerting your parents."

"If I may ask, what will be your first course of action?"

"Quite logically, it makes the most sense for us to start at the source. We will locate Olivia Smithfield and see what we can glean from her. Hopefully, she will be amenable to responding to our questions. But, not to worry if the process fails to go that simply, for we never approach a case with only one plan in force and yours will receive the care and depth of expertise for which we are notorious."

Morgan finished her somewhat self-righteous dialogue and drew in a deep breath that not only raised her shoulders to attention, but also seemed to lift her like a hot-air balloon from her chair. She walked around the side of her desk to face Arielle as Agnes presented her with the paperwork she had directed her to draft. Morgan quickly perused the document and handed it over to Arielle.

"In fairness to all, my fee is non-negotiable nor refundable. I feel compelled to disclose that fact, although I find distasteful and uncomfortable the business end of my investigative work. Agnes is a real help in that regard."

"Business is business. I fully understand. I shall arrange very earnestly to join you Wednesday the thirtieth for the journey to England. Until then..." Arielle's words trailed off as she handed forth an envelope with cash she had withdrawn to pay for Morgan's services, seeing the sum's use not as a frivolous expenditure but an investment in her future. She glanced at the papers on Morgan's desk. With precision of pen she had skillfully drawn a paddock full of horses. Her work was the gestalt of the equine style she obviously so revered. Muscular, Morgan horses with expressive faces and gracefully curved necks adorned the paper stock. They were kin to the livery displayed on the walls surrounding her.

Morgan stood as Arielle prepared to exit the office. She placed her hand in the pocket of her waistcoat. Her fingers came upon several coins that she jingled back and forth, seemingly oblivious to the noise they emitted. Her behavior seemed more habitual than purposeful as though the coins were a simple substitute for tender carrots she could have at the ready to offer to her equine friends. Some might view her fidgeting as a nervous tick, but Arielle quite doubted there was anything that would unsettle Miss Pennybacker. She seemed as strong and determined as the breed she displayed on her walls.

Agnes, having given Arielle a receipt, escorted her back through the corridor to the doorway that opened into the stitchery shop.

"If I might say so, Miss Hargrove, you are wise to choose Miss Pennybacker. She is widely known for seeking a successful resolution with great dispatch. You can feel confident you are in good hands."

"Ain't that the truth? Ain't that the truth?" Peepers repeated as he resumed his nervous strut about his cage while Arielle made her way to the front door.

"Uh, oh! Uh, oh!" Peepers repeated moving his clawed feet back and forth in a stuttered prance across his perch. "Remain calm. Remain calm."

"Pretty girl. Pretty girl," came his repetitious refrain bringing a smile to Arielle's face as she lifted the latch to the front door and crossed the threshold to the sidewalk beyond. Turning toward home, she was unaware of the form that stopped dead in its tracks at the sight of her, its shadow cast across the pavement by the midday sun.

Alexandra was halted by the happenstance of encountering Arielle Hargrove once again pounding the city streets. *Washington could certainly use a few more avenues to broaden the distance between myself and the sight of her!* Alexandra muttered to herself and stood stone-cold as Arielle made her way across the street to a cable car and disappeared from view.

Alexandra glanced at the sign above the door of the storefront Arielle had exited. *Hmm,* she mused to herself as she broke her frozen spell and, putting her legs in motion, made her way to the entry. Pressing on the latch, Alexandra opened the door and stepped inside. *A stitchery shop and she left without the slightest parcel.* Alexandra reasoned. *Surely, she could find something to peak her interest. At the very least, the twit might be in need of a skein of yarn or a bundle of floss to busy her idle self, yet, she left empty-handed. Who works in this place?* Alexandra's thoughts bounced around in her head like so many table tennis balls running amuck in need of a well-aimed paddle. *I must make some inquiries. I will not be satisfied unless I do!* Alexandra, feeling very much alone with her thoughts, was snapped to attention as the railings of the parakeet known as Peepers broke the brief moment of quiet and resumed his telling refrain.

"Uh, oh. Uh, oh. Uh, oh," Peepers chanted as he acknowledged the presence of the flaxen-haired visitor whose shadow now cast itself over the goods and services of Pennybacker Stitchery.

Chapter Ten

William Clay was a man of letters as much as he was a man of means. He was born into a world of business and high finance that provided a very comfortable cushion upon which he might have rested his wealthy derrière. Instead, he elected to take the self-imposed action of completing what he felt was his true self by expanding his university studies. A man of conviction, he was not prone to whim as were some of his peers who, like himself, had been reared in the comfort of a feathered nest.

He discarded the trappings that would have classified him as a bon vivant and thoroughly thought-out his courses of action, balancing social requirements and pleasure with astute business associations. His law degree from Georgetown University denoted a sense of accomplishment and integrity for which he was keenly proud. His engaging good looks, charismatic ways and financial status, were visibly enough to see him through the finest social circles, but, he was never one for an easy ride. He opted to work hard, expanding his holdings while dabbling in a healthy dose of philanthropy, which he felt kept him grounded by causes bigger than himself.

William was just returning from one such meeting near the Executive Mansion. Pennsylvania Avenue remained gaily adorned with red, white, and blue buntings -- visible remnants of McKinley's inaugural festivities. Deciding to stroll the shop windows before returning home, he turned from Pennsylvania Avenue onto 14th Street, crossed over E Street and walked until he came to F Street and turned right. He admired the footware in the window at Edmonston & Company. The store's sign as 'agents for celebrated makers' boasted of men's, ladies and children's shoes and slippers in all grades and styles including Laird, Schober & Co. from Philadelphia, Pennsylvania, and Stacy, Adams & Co. from Brockton, Massachusetts.

William continued on his way, pausing to glance into the window of his custom tailor. The man was renowned for exquisitely cut suits, fitted to a turn, enabling just the right amount of shirt cuff to become exposed at the wrist, and the proper break to appear in the leg of the trousers. A warm wave of acknowledgment came from within the shop as the expert tailor himself quickly identified the prominent passerby, and, issuing forth a welcoming gesture, encouraged him to enter. Feeling every conviction of pursuing his walk, but at the same passing not wanting to offend his talented associate by ignoring his greeting, William reversed his steps and paused in the open doorway where the scent of freshly cut cloths and iron-heated woolens permeated the shop's space.

"Gooda day, Mr. Clay, gooda day! So nice-a to see you," came the energetic welcome from Antonio Genovese who, benefiting from his Italian grandfather's expertise as a first-class tailor, carried on the fine family tradition in his F Street shop.

His parents arrived in the United States from Sicily a score of years earlier placing him in need of a livelihood. The streets of Washington, abounding with men who made their living in suits and held demanding positions that virtually forced them to exhibit an impeccable valet, gave Genovese Gentleman Tailor the perfect venue for success. Indeed, Genovese's reputation had caught the attention of the Executive Mansion where several presidents commissioned Antonio to design classic, conservative suits. Besides the finishing details that included a hand-embroidered label denoting his business name, Antonio's signature touch was an initial to personalize the suit with the purchaser's single monogram embroidered on the inside chest pocket. It was a subtle, elegant inclusion. Like an artist's signature on a finished canvas, Antonio's last threads of embroidery gave him the satisfaction of another completed masterpiece.

"Mr. Genovese, good day to you too, sir. It appears from the activity I see in your shop that business has not slowed since the inauguration. With the new administration will come a fresh stream of customers who will want the expertise of the Genovese hand! I surely hope your appointment book will not fill so quickly that I am left waiting in line for you to, pardon the pun, suit my needs!" William chortled, laying a sincere compliment on the merchant whom he enjoyed for his friendship as much as his textile skills.

"Mr. Clay, you knowa therea will alwaysa be an extra page-a in the booka for you, gooda sir!" Antonio exclaimed very animatedly. He moved his hands in the air with his right hand drawing his fingers together to his lips in a kiss that he threw toward the ceiling like a 'thank you' to powers above for blessing him with William Clay.

Having bid one another adieu, William continued along F Street, crossing over 13th. The F Street area, now almost completely transformed into commercial storefronts, had been predominately residential just decades earlier. William enjoyed the mix that still existed. The lot of shopkeepers who maintained residences above their business establishments had become fewer and fewer as the price of rent escalated encouraging retailers to share commercial space by renting the square footage above to other retailers. The businesses provided a variety of goods and services and many had maintained their good names through more than one generation. C. Schneider Hardware, Evans Dental Parlor, J. Louis Florist, S.A. Reeves Grocer, and Hoover & Snyder

Shoes Shop were among the merchants whose windows William purveyed as he strolled the 1200 block of F Street.

A stop at his favorite tobacco stand supplied him with a mild cigar that he snipped and lit to savor for the remainder of his walk. The cigar had a particularly good draw and he held his head back ever so slightly as he drew in another breath, momentarily holding the smoke, then dipping his chin down a bit as he exhaled. *It does not get much better than this.* William mused to himself as he walked along the sidewalk enjoying his cigar, nodding at passersby, taking note of the crisp, refreshing spring air.

His promenade came to a decided halt as his body came up hard against the slender frame of a woman in a hasty retreat. Her prodigious pace caused the wind to nearly be knocked completely from her as their bodies collided, sending the woman to the pavement. She gasped, drawing in a full breath of air as she attempted to right herself and maintain her dignity with her exposed petticoat. She held a fixed focus on her handbag and a small piece of paper that had flown from her grasp.

"Good Lord, what a bungling fool you are tromping the streets with abandon without a care for the ladies of this city! Why, where were you raised, sir, in a barn?" Alexandra exclaimed, fussing with her skirt, scooting her feet under herself and raising herself to stand full face with the one who so caught her ire.

The smoke that swirled about William's face began to dissipate as he held his cigar down to his side and waited for Alexandra to recognize the perpetrator of her accidental assault. He would have reached to assist her, but with all of her scrambling to regain a vertical state, he was sure any effort on his part would only serve to annoy her and place him on the receiving end of an impromptu flogging.

Alexandra picked up her handbag and shook the long skirt of her gown, shimmying all the layers underneath into place. As she completed her ritual, she began to look up beyond the veil of smoke and into the face of the one who pound her to the pavement. Her eyes fluttered in surprise as she realized her error in pronouncing the one before her a 'bungling fool.'

"Uh, oh, William. My goodness. How careless of me..."

"Oh, but the error is mine not to have noticed a 'lady', as you put it so sweetly, my dear Alexandra."

"But, you know, of course William, that I would never call you a fool."

"And I would never call you a...well, touché, my dear. Let us call this one a draw. You seem to have dropped this piece of paper as you 'took flight.'"

"A piece of paper? Whatever do you mean?"

"This was emitted from your fingertips as you took your fall."

"How can that be? Why, I have never seen it before. It must have flown out of the stitchery shop on the heels of another customer as I peered at the window display."

"Well, in that case, I will take it and dispose of it properly."

"Uh, oh, ah, no. I can certainly dispose of it here," Alexandra fervently reached forward taking the paper from William's hand. She opened her handbag to deposit it inside.

"You seem to have more than a fleeting interest in that scrap, Alexandra. Here, let me see it."

"William, do you not have better things to do than harass the ladies of Washington. Now, come along. My stomach is gnawing at the sides. Be a dear and take me to the Vienna Dining Room at 9th and F for my midday meal," Alexandra purred as she slipped her arm through William's and snuggled herself beside him while she kept a firm hold on the handbag that served as a trusty receptacle for the purloined piece of parchment she envisioned would well serve her scheming purposes.

William was not disposed to wrestle with a wildcat. Alexandra's prowess for manipulation was no stranger to him nor was her suspicious behavior. Rather than challenge her intentions this day, he deemed it best to continue their promenade as peacefully as possible, even though a well-placed gibe in Alexandra's direction was a pleasure William was seldom able to forfeit.

"Alexandra, you do intrigue me."

"Oh, William. I am delighted to hear you tell me so," Alexandra perked nearly raising herself on the tips of her toes as her grin spread clearly across her face.

"I am intrigued, my dear Alexandra, by your sudden interest in needlework. As I recall, you damned every bit of stitchery as, 'the crafty creations of the lonely-hearted, singles, spinsters and dowagers alike.' Are you perhaps sending a signal that for you all prospects are past and the vision of partnership with good cloth and good thread make for the perfect match and good life for you?"

"William you are such a tease. Of course I have no time for or interest in needlework. I am far too focused on others to find any benefit from such menial pastimes."

"Then why the stop at Pennybacker's? A curious retreat for one who is so contrary to the work of the hand."

"You simply are not listening to me, William. As I have said, my interest in others takes me places I might otherwise never tread. Simply because handiwork bores me to no avail, does not mean that I do not find curious its attraction to others. I was on a fact finding mission and nothing more, believe me."

"Oh, I *believe* you were on a mission. Of what I am *not* so certain is how your mission will benefit others," William concluded, making his point, knowing full well that his repartee with Alexandra was going to do little more than continue in circles.

A midday meal at the Vienna was a decent suggestion on the part of Alexandra even if she was attempting to divert his attention from the discussion of needlework and the spark that fired her curious interest in Pennybacker's. The Vienna was known for very tasty, generous fare, and William had worked up an appetite fit for the portions served there. He was also not ashamed to have Alexandra on his arm. She could always be counted on to turn many heads, particularly when the shiny blond strands of her flaxen hair glistened in the noon sun. She carried herself with an assured gait, her head and shoulders held high, and although she took short, feminine steps, her feet showed great intent of purpose as they moved her on her way. Her skin was fair with a stray freckle sprinkled here and there, mostly in the vicinity of her nose. A small brown mole just below her left eye on the cusp of her cheekbone further distinguished her face. It was a subtle mark that at careless glance appeared to be a spot of soil, but upon more discerning observation, was a mark of beauty, one petite detail in combination with her posture, hair, skin and eyes that projected a beautiful image flawed only by an intense personality.

Alexandra's green eyes, as clear as marbles, held in their center a piercing, foxlike quality ready to infiltrate anyone new to her den. Her ability to ensnare her prey with her watchful stance was typically focused on the female sector by which she felt most threatened. Men, however, were not exempt from the power of her penetrating green orbs. Her eyes had been duly known to render men enchantingly captivated or burn them to the core as she easily cast them away. William had come to tolerate Alexandra's talent for acridity lest he negate the promise he made and upset the Whitaker family, more specifically the late Andrew Whitaker, patriarch, founder of a large textile company, and dear friend and benefactor of the late William Clay, Sr.

William's father drew him into his confidence shortly before his passing to make him fully aware of the financial assistance his longtime friend, Andrew Whitaker, had provided when the very rapid growth of his business interests placed him in the unenviable position of being overextended to the point of bankruptcy. Andrew lent the necessary financial resources that allowed the Clay Companies to thrive while purchasing real estate that William's father was able to renovate and turn over for sale at profits great enough to continue his company's expansion and fully pay back all monies owed to Andrew.

Though all of the debt had been paid in full, William Senior's gratitude for Andrew's generosity never faltered. Bill, as friends informally referred to him, maintained that, even in his absence, his son must honor the indebtedness he felt was owed his friend. So, William was more than obliged to keep pleasant company with Alexandra as a courtesy to her father and a pledge to his father's memory. William knew full well how he had benefited from the kindnesses and business savvy of Alexandra's father. He lived what some might define as an extravagant life but, with all of its abundance, William concentrated very seriously on his private practice. He had established a very highly regarded reputation with his clients who placed the utmost confidence in him as their railroad and corporation lawyer.

William and Alexandra stepped off the curb to crossover to the Vienna, dodging manure that lay upon the pavement emitted from passing horses. The residue did little to mar the beauty of the day. The cooler spring air and gentle breeze eliminated the potency of such noxious aromas that would be strongly sensed in the heat and humidity of July and August.

Watching one's step was a necessary maneuver William had fine-tuned for reasons beyond the streets beneath his soles. Success and access in Washington dictated enormous finesse on one's feet for anyone desiring to frequent the most advantageous social and political circles of the city. He, through a healthy combination of God-given talent, intelligence, charisma and monetary clout, had positioned himself among the leaders of the city and was proud of his influential status that found his name high on many a matron's list of eligible men they would be pleased to have sire their grandchildren.

As the handsome pair halted and waited for a trolley to pass, William was distracted by a passenger whose fair skin and raven coiffure so resembled one he had come to know in only a fleeting way. The pleasant memory of moments with her lingered like a well-chosen word. The trolley was filled to near capacity, but her presence within its space could not be missed. *Yes, it is indeed Arielle.* The very Miss Hargrove who had dismissed his call on her residence as that of a mere messenger sent to return a wayward belonging. Her mother had given him a more enlivened reception than her offspring. *Why am I so spellbound by her, so drawn to know more?* He could not be certain but he sensed their eyes met. It seemed that for one brief moment, as he stood waiting and she sat moving slowly by, her gaze fell upon him and a glimmer of recognition passed across her face. Whether that was what he saw he could not be sure, but he was sure that was what he wanted to see. *A beauty, a true, rare beauty is what she is.* William pondered to himself, hoping the words going around in his head were not uttered audibly for Alexandra's vexation. But, vexed she was as soon as she became aware that William's attention had been diverted. As the trolley neared the corner and began its turn, Alexandra caught sight of the form that held William's interest. *Retched fate is testing my spirit to its very limits.* Alexandra silently fumed, wondering how much more she could stand to suffer from the existence of Miss Hargrove whose timing was proving to be disastrous in her efforts to gain William's sole attention and affection.

Alexandra placed a tender squeeze upon his arm and looked up, casting an adoring gaze toward his deep blue eyes. Her motion triggered him to pat her arm pleasantly, as one might touch the body of a faithful hound, signaling her that they could continue their walk, the path was now clear.

As the two entered the vestibule of the Vienna and were greeted by the maître 'd, Alexandra released William's arm to precede him to their table. The dining room was buzzing with the conversations of patrons who abundantly filled the restaurant reputed for its deliciously varied menu and high-profile clientele. Alexandra normally enjoyed glancing about the room, taking delight in the eyes that looked her way, espying her from tip to toe, but she had lost her appetite for such empty advances and was presently only remotely interested in dining at all. If she could gain no sustenance from William, food would nary satisfy her soul.

William held her chair as she settled into the seat then took his place across from her. She laid her handbag in her lap and placed a white linen napkin over top.

"You continue to guard your secrets well I see," William gibed as his eyes followed her hands to her lap where they lay securely clasped across the large linen square.

"Have no fear, Alexandra," William continued, "You are among a friendly audience for the time being."

"For the time being?" Alexandra questioned wondering what William was implying.

"My guess is that most of the present patrons have never made your acquaintance so they have not had the opportunity to find you otherwise than a faithful ally."

"Is that not a bit harsh, William? I have always been faithful where you are concerned and will continue to be so no matter what the cost." Alexandra spoke through her teeth. She was using every muscle in her face to keep them from becoming clenched.

"The cost to yourself, my dear, or at the expense of others?" William retorted, deliberately avoiding her attempt to pair the two of them.

"Really, William. I cannot fathom what has so provoked your ire that you take such exception with my behavior and express such a tone with me. I have been the recipient of a very trying morning and only seek your good company to right the day. Do forgive me, but you are the one who perceives that what I hold in my lap is a secret. You have far more important concerns upon which to focus than a silly scrap of paper in a lady's handbag with the random pen scratches of an idle hand that found its way into my path today. Please assure me that I am not destined to be a victim of both pavement and parchment by your very hands today!"

"I do find curious that you claim no awareness of the 'scrap of paper' as you call it, however, now you mention awareness of markings made by 'an idle hand.'"

"I think we should cast aside all conversation about this and treat it as the rubbish it is," Alexandra finished, firmly stating her opinion while maintaining a grip on her calm.

Though his implications and uncharacteristic disposition were bearing down hard on her nerves, William was too important to her to create a scene or speak angry words that, once spoken, could never be retracted.

Quite used to getting her way regardless of the toll taken on those in her wake, Alexandra wanted desperately to find a forecast for smooth sailing to carry her through the remainder of the afternoon with William. *I must put an end to this awkward banter, she thought to herself. His work. I will ask him about his practice, yes, that will do.*

William was tossing about his own thoughts. He realized that he was being boldly direct with Alexandra and possibly unfair in his suspicions about her intent and the paper she nestled in her lap. *But, did I not hear her blurt out something about 'pen scratches?'* As he best recalled, the piece was folded into fourths and she had not opened it in his presence. Nonetheless, it was ridiculous for him to badger her any further. It was his duty to extend every kindness to her despite the fact that on many occasions he felt like reprimanding her for behavior he found less than genteel.

In unison they began to speak, bringing smiles to both, breaking the tension that had begun to escalate. Graciously, William signaled Alexandra to proceed.

"I was just going to inquire about the new location for your office in the May Building and wondering if you feel well settled with the other law offices that surround yours," Alexandra smiled, leaning forward in a natural show of interest as she awaited William's response.

"The space is quite adequate and convenient. I was fairly familiar with the neighboring lawyers so we have a comfortable rapport with one another and, because most of them are occupied with court cases which do not involve my clients, we are able to avoid the animosity and competition of showmanship that becomes a necessary act of forte in the courtroom."

Alexandra was very pleased with William's response. He seemed always at ease when he spoke about law. She had chosen the perfect topic to set their conversation on an amiable course and was grateful for that.

"In fact, my work soon takes me far from the courtroom. One very significant client who is headquartered in New York has set an appointment for one week from today for me to review a new contract that will increase his holdings double-fold. The merger he pursues is quite large and not without some risk, so my services are needed to review all the documents before the deal is signed and sealed."

"Your client is in very competent hands and one would hope he would see to it that you are extremely well compensated."

Alexandra could see from William's expression that she had tread on sod that he likened to crabgrass. Compensation and topics related to that ilk were of distant concern to him. His good fortune, with enormous wealth at its base, did not defray him from being skillfully prepared for opportunities that came his way. No, William was no bon vivant, and did not want to be thought as such. He wholeheartedly preferred to be portrayed as an average man. Those who proclaimed that he enjoyed a continuous run of good luck were unaware of his hard work and the masterful way he managed business affairs as adeptly as he managed people. He had a style that made success appear easy. His quick thinking and charisma found many a deal deemed tenuous, sealed, and, found heretofore lackluster acquaintances forever pledged as friends.

William vowed never to have himself serve the money at his disposal. Instead, he felt the money must serve him and those in need about him. It was that very philosophy that led him from the dry warmth of his coach to the heavily rain soaked pavement days before when a lone, jet-black coifed female form made its way through the damp darkness of night only halting in flight at the outreach of his welcoming arms. There it was again, that vision of the beautiful sodden stranger, a vision that had become a recurring memory that he could not shake from the deepest recesses of his mind. *Why is she so much with me?* William reflected, looking for answers with much conviction, not wanting to dismiss the images of Arielle Hargrove from his mind.

Alexandra wondered where she had lost William, for he had become unmercifully quiet and distant. Determined to gain his attention once again, she prepared and delivered her next inquiry.

"So, travel takes you away from Washington and me again? Shame on you. You know how bored and aimlessly detached I feel when you have left me alone in this city, William. I trust your business will be concluded swiftly so I will hardly have the opportunity to miss you," Alexandra purred like a cat well rubbed, waiting to make its next demand on its master.

"You flatter me, Alexandra, yet, I have to wonder how anyone, including yourself, could become bored with all the sights and activity that abound here. Come, let's make a call on my Aunt Emma. Maybe she can inspire you to involve yourself in the missions and work to which she devotes herself at St. John's. She finds her efforts most rewarding and she has never been heard to express boredom. A visit to Aunt Emma might be just the cure for your aimless blues," William concluded with a big, questioning grin, knowing Alexandra would balk at charity work.

"William, you know full well how busy my days are. Why, I hardly have time to do all that I need to do for myself much less worry about the concerns of others. A call on your Aunt Emma will be pleasant enough. I am however sure, there is no need to raise her hopes that I will join the ranks of her missionary devotees," Alexandra finished firmly, though, within the same breath, she traded exclamations that she suffered from sincere boredom for proclamations that her days were full.

"Oh, Alexandra. As I recall your father exclaiming on many an occasion, 'I would call you sweetheart, but the word gets stuck in my throat.'"

Alexandra threw off William's recitation of her father's words, dismissing them as she had whenever her father uttered them. Her father's ounce-of-vinegar-laced speech had always torn at her nerves, for though she felt doted upon by him financially, their personalities from time-to-time came into caustic conflict.

No, she had no need to join the work of Emma Willard, for a far greater mission loomed on her horizon and its pursuit would require her full focus, as far as her green-with-envy orbs could take her. She would precipitate the undoing of Miss Arielle Hargrove with every ounce of her being. She held close her little handbag. *The paper inside will be enough to undo sweet, little Miss Hargrove. It is confirmation of her meeting at Pennybacker's. Here is her very name, written on a piece of parchment enhanced with the etching of a horse head. I'll wave this in front of the little miss and make her answer to her motives for being in the stitchery shop. She will have to answer to me.* As William and Alexandra exited the restaurant, Alexandra smiled with confidence. She had a plan and she knew it would take her far.

Chapter Eleven

The visit to Pennybacker's had provided all that Arielle could hope for at this juncture in her search. Morgan had been receptive regarding her need to gain clarity from the text of Olivia Smithfield's letter. Arielle felt disburdened in her presence despite Morgan's formal manner. Co-mingled with her distracting penchant for doodling, Morgan's conduct projected a calculated reserve that served to hold her clients at a distance. Arielle was willing to indulge Morgan her peculiarities. She deemed her formality akin to steadfast sincerity, and her horse doodles seemed a portent of her active mind and attention to detail. All were worthy traits that would serve Arielle's best interests when implemented by one with the fine reputation that thoroughly preceded Miss Pennybacker.

Arielle removed her hat formed of a lush purple velvet, deep in color, very much like a mature eggplant. It was styled with an upsweep to one side that held a full plume dyed to match. As she placed the hat on the ornate brass stand atop her dresser, she paused to think how quickly summer would be upon the city and her wardrobe would convert to fabrics and accessories less burdensome in the heat and humidity that were as certain as death and taxes to come to Washington.

There were other more pressing burdens Arielle would just as soon see packed away. *Oh, how heavy is my heart.* The words spilled across the fullness of her lips as she brushed the tips of her fingers across the delicate plume of her hat hoping to extract comfort from the wistful caress. She pondered how quickly one's life could take a turn. To be one day full of bliss and at the next hour caught up in confusion. Her scattered thoughts found their point of focus on the letter, a simple piece of parchment that, by nature of the written word conveyed upon its surface, became a messenger of uncertainty, of curiosity, of grief. Olivia Smithfield's declarations, lacking specificity, conjured a wealth of scenarios that left Arielle feeling overly burdened and fatigued.

She moved to the récamier upholstered in moss green damask. It was positioned on a pleasing angle near her unlit fireplace. Gathering a woolen throw that was draped across the lengthy lounger, she pulled it up across her shoulder and settled back, placing her head upon an inviting, cut velvet pillow edged in thick, tri-color cording. She needed to be nurtured and would create her own forum for it.

Surrounded in her room by objects of beauty that brought her pleasure, and cuddled on her couch with a wrap that enveloped her with warmth, she gained a sense of security that found her eyelids unable to resist slumber as she acquiesced and prepared to drift off to sleep. Sounds about her were rendered increasingly faint, as the tick of her clock became a far away pendulum of peace relaxing her mind and body. Soon the dark chasm of slumber took her on an unplotted black and white journey. A large, bold doorway opened carrying in its path a thrust of bright light surrounded with a mist of rolling gray clouds. Out of the mist appeared a small, rather formally dressed man who extended his arm forward with an outreached white-gloved hand. At the very tips of his fingers, incased in beaming white cloth, was a piece of aged parchment rolled and tied with a shiny satin ribbon that securely held a single immature rose. He moved forward in short, precise steps, all the while extending his arm, presenting the diploma-like document with a faint, foggy whisper, "Here, here."

Arielle reached out with every essence of her being, stretching and reaching, and leaning and searching through the mist and the clouds and the light. The more she stretched and reached and leaned the more endless became her search as the clouds cascaded back into the mist and the bright light became a hushed glow fading into vacuous darkness. She whirled about in confusion and frustration, grappling with the vaporous air, her arms slicing through the blanket of gloom and pitch-blackness that enveloped her. Voices danced about calling her name over and over until she could take no more of the inharmonious chorus and threw her hands tightly over her ears muffling the relentless sounds that persistently pounded her brain. A gasp brought her reeling to an upright state. Her hands moved rapidly to her chest as fantasy ran full force into reality. Before her stood an impeccably dressed figure, albeit clothed in an apron, with an outstretched hand.

"Miss Arielle. I said, would ye be takin' yer tea in yer room or should I be settin' it up in the parlor fer ye?"

"Fiona, you have scared the wits from me! How can I possibly think of holding a cup and saucer stable when you have left me trembling like a feeble octogenarian? Remove yourself from my presence and give me time to collect myself."

"I beg yer pardon. I heard ye speakin' and callin' out so I came into yer room. I ken see now ye was frettin' with a dream or some nightmarish vision wots got ye out 'o sorts and not actin' like yerself. It's sorry I am fer comin' 'tween ye and some demon wots got hold of ye. Ye think ye'd be thankin' me, but I knows when my services aren't needed so ye can jest call me when the mood passes, I mean, when ye see fits," Fiona's words ran on in her own bumbling, inimitable way. She bowed and ducked, twisting the corners of her apron all the way to the door that she quietly closed behind her as she entered the quiet of the hallway beyond.

Arielle felt tears free-flowing down her cheeks. *It seems the pain of leaving the dream has taken its toll on me. Nightmares and demons. Why, the girl's imagination is running rampant or, could it be that she knows me better than I know myself? I am most assuredly in no position to remain objective. I am confused, weary, drained. I have been less than fair with Fiona. She is merely performing the rote duties of her day and here I am awaking from an unsettled tomb of questions and doubt, casting aspersions at a simple soul whose very existence in our house is measured by her diligent care of my person and possessions. I must call the girl back and correct any misunderstandings.*

Arielle brought the conversation with herself to a halt, swinging her legs over the side of the récamier, readying herself to stand and check her décolletage in the large oval cheval in the far corner of the room. One, lone corkscrewed tendril of raven hair fallen from its place just behind her right ear was the only remnant of disorder visible in the aftermath of her dream. Arielle gently searched her hairline with her fingers, locating a loose hairpin that she deftly used to secure the non-conforming coil. Feeling less unsettled, she proceeded to her doorway and took in a hefty full breath as she opened the door, releasing herself to the world she attempted to escape.

Voices could be heard emanating from the foyer. Arielle could clearly segregate Fiona's Irish brogue from the other female voice. *Oh, must I be tormented the livelong day? Is there no relief from this creature?* Arielle fumed to herself as the voice of Alexandra Whitaker floated like hot air through the cavity of the foyer walls wafting its way to the hallway above where it landed soundly on Arielle's ears and nerves. Proceed forward or retreat? Arielle knew her choices and the latter was certain to be a more pleasant alternative than engaging in a face-to-face audience with Alexandra. *What could possibly be gained from any communication with her? Yet, here she is again, showing the verve to appear at my threshold, testing the limits of my threshold of patience and congeniality.*

Proceed I must, the words came terse and low as Arielle began her descent of the staircase in slow, ladylike, yet, deft as a panther fashion. Making her turn on the landing, she saw the lower edge of Alexandra's wool cape, identifiable with its border of loop and floral designed soutache braid she had observed from the trolley only hours earlier as it passed along 9th street.

"Ah, there you are. This simpleton does not seem to understand the importance of my seeing you. She has been standing, twisting about, insisting that you were unavailable to visitors when, here you are, as fresh and ready as ever to be in the public view," Alexandra finished as she caught the warning look flashed her way by Arielle.

"I advise you to be cautious as to whom you call a 'simpleton' and never utter that expression again toward Fiona. Words, particularly those cast in haste, have a way of inflicting irreparable damage. Indeed, the exercise of caution is something you should take in a daily dose. Perhaps the apothecary needs to double your dosage. Since you are intent upon seeing me, let us get along with the purpose of your visit. Can it be that you have 'found' another of my gloves?" Arielle felt slightly playful as she dangled the idea before Alexandra that her pair of gloves still missed a mate.

"I cannot be concerned with your irresponsible attention to your wardrobe, my dear. For all I know, leaving articles of clothing behind is a ploy you employ to require men to call on you. An outer garment this time, an undergarment next, there is no wonder a steady suitor is nowhere in the midst and surely none as fine as Mr. William Clay," Alexandra continued her degradation of Arielle's character as Fiona quietly stood on languishing in the fact that her mistress had come to her defense.

Alexandra had hit a raw nerve. Arielle never intended to leave her gloves behind, yet, just as Alexandra described, her carelessness had brought William Clay straight to her door.

"Fiona, I want to speak with you but, as for now, it would be best for you to see if you can be of any assistance to Cook. I will show Miss Whitaker out."

Fiona complied with her mistress's request with some reservation, sensing a growing animosity between the two women and wondering if it was safe, and even wise, to leave the two to their own devices.

"Show me out! A bit premature, I think! I will not leave until I have had a word with you," Alexandra nearly shrieked as a stern expression overtook her face.

"A word? You, Miss Whitaker, have overstayed your words! Definitely one too many!" Arielle retorted, her calm reserve maintaining its hold for outward appearances though she felt her nerves might defy her at anytime.

"Well, if you care not for my words, let me show you what I have on paper!" Alexandra exclaimed as she reached into her petite handbag and withdrew a small scrap of paper. Presenting it with a determined thrust of her wrist and retracting it just as rapidly, Alexandra awaited Arielle's response with an expression of satisfaction much like a cat having fully consumed a tasty, unassuming canary.

"So, you see, I know you had a meeting with the illustrious Miss Pennybacker, no doubt to elicit her services and see what light she might shed on your less than glowing background."

"You know nothing of the sort and I find it quite disturbing that now, on more than one occasion, you have looked me up for the express purpose of deviling me."

"I am merely trying to be of service to you and this is the thanks I get. The truth may be difficult to bear, please do excuse my choice of words, but you need not be so hostile toward me -- though your shabby beginnings would promote the coarse, ingrained reactions that you exhibit here!"

"Once again, you mention my beginnings. You know nothing and are simply bullying me. My best advice to you is to leave this very instant and be quite certain that your sniveling, conniving, insolent, poor excuse for a lady self never darkens my threshold again!" Arielle railed as she attempted to regain her composure by slowing to a halt the trembles running through her limbs that threatened to bring her asunder. She motioned to the doorway, finally taking Alexandra by the shoulders and turning her toward the large mahogany door. She gave her a gentle, yet firm push that catapulted her out of the house.

"You have not heard the last from me," Alexandra's voice trailed off as she found her footing outside on the landing, determining that her point had been made and she best be on her way.

Her day was indeed complete. She had found just enough evidence of Arielle's path of inquiry to cast the ominous shadow of fear over her. *Yes. Now the good Miss Hargrove will be left fretting over what she thinks I know. Pity the girl set her sights on William. A fool she is to think he would have any interest in her in the first place and most definitely not now. Yes. This should take care of the little snip.* Alexandra concluded her silent proclamation, turning her head to look back at the portal to the Hargrove manse, raising her eyebrows in a farewell gesture. *Good riddance to the crow-haired pest.* Alexandra's venom spewed. She recoiled with the sudden burst of cold air that swept over her as March placed its windy touches on the best and worst of the city.

⟨⁓⟩

Arielle shivered, closing the door on her unwelcome visitor, shutting out the gloom that spun about the foyer. The chill in the air was as much a result of Alexandra's visit as it was the wisdom of Mother Nature to shoo away the woman's wicked ways.

Why am I so undone by that woman? She extracts the very good from me. But, I cannot dwell on that now. There are details to be put in place for me to proceed with my trip. Mum and Father will understand my desire to return home to visit, but, I must secure their approval before involving Fiona in packing my garments.

Determined that dinner would be the best time to test their moods, Arielle returned to her room to collect and freshen herself for the next ordeal of her day. *Oh, how I look forward to a suitable end to all of this and to be done with the shadow of Alexandra. A spell of gloom has been cast over me since our first meeting, and her erstwhile presence, seemingly at my every turn, is taking a supreme toll on my well-being. I must put her out of my mind and not allow her to distract me from my focus.* Arielle shook her head ever so slightly as she reached the crest of the staircase attempting to silence the voices within that fought with her conscious self. *And, what about William Clay? Oh, the words that flowed from Alexandra's venomous mouth, as caustic as they were to hear, must be true. Mr. Clay made his appearance at my home for the single intent of returning my lost article of clothing and nothing more. Yes, he probably called on me out of curiosity and a banal desire to find just how far he could make a go with me, the woman of little virtue, whom he found loose on the dark, damp city streets.*

Arielle felt her reserve weakening as she entered her bedroom and made her way to the small, carved-back chair at her dressing table where her unfinished floral needlework lay. She fondled the piece to locate her starting point then glanced up catching her image in the mirror. Her discontent was magnified. She was pale and drawn and did not fight the desire to blame every crease in her brow and shadow beneath her eyes on Alexandra's willful, unremitting ways. As much as she would like to believe she had endured the final performance by the woman, common sense, and the recent history of her acts, assured Alexandra's script was far from complete.

Fleeting pain suddenly startled Arielle. She winced, drawing her finger back in a jolt from the slender implement of distress. She had been in a trance-like state working the needle and yarns in and out of the cloth when the plunge of the needle snapped her back from her daze. Squeezing her finger with great firmness of pressure, she forced a rounded droplet of blood to hold itself suspended on the edge of her index finger. The mere happenstance of her careless action held more significance than the prick her finger endured.

For Arielle, it was a reminder of the pain and confusion of spirit she suffered not knowing the extent of her heritage. As she placed her injured finger to her lips, sucking away the warm red fluid from her skin, she put pressure on the small, self-inflicted puncture wound with the edge of her teeth. Pulling her finger away from her mouth, she swallowed, allowing the metallic and brine-like taste of the crimson fluid to glide over her taste buds and waft down the receptive cockles of her throat. Blood. Her blood. Her bloodline. She would not, could not rest until she pursued, with all fullness of intent, the answers to the myriad of questions that so burdened her soul.

The formality at the dinner table was stifling. Ian and Elsbeth's minds were as much caught up in the circumstances of late as Arielle's, yet she knew she must penetrate the stagnate air of confusion and concern to move forward with her plan.

"Father, Mum. I am so pleased we can be together this eve to discuss something I am most earnest to pursue. I have felt at odds with myself for a day or so and can only attribute the sensations to homesickness and a desire to be surrounded by that which is most familiar, my roots, so to speak. As fascinating as it has been to become established here in Washington, I feel an uncompromising desire to part the embrace of this fair city and return to visit England and Wales, if even for an abbreviated stay. Please grant me this single wish to which I have given extreme thought and care."

Ian and Elsbeth fixed their eyes upon their only child's face, closely observing every subtle wrinkle of her beautiful brow as she conveyed her request to journey away from them. Ian's first inclination was to respond with a firm 'nay', standing soundly on a resolve to keep Arielle protected and close at hand. However, it came to him that with her away, he and Elsbeth could invite Olivia Smithfield to visit and, in Arielle's absence, relieve the woman of the burden she proclaimed to bear. *Yes, such an arrangement would be most agreeable for all*, thought Ian. *There is no time to hesitate, for correspondence to Miss Smithfield must be made forthwith.*

"Arielle, your mother and I too have felt the longing for home and the benefits provided by visits with dear friends. We had however hoped that you would find Washington to your liking, enough to consider it a place worthy of permanent residence. My appointment is very likely to be extended, and your mother and I have discussed the possibility that we may remain here for years to come. Nesbitt is quite capable of managing the colliery, thus freeing me to widen my concentration on matters involving my commission here. But, enough of that. You have asked for our guidance and prudence and you shall have both." Ian cleared his throat and, casting a darting glance toward Elsbeth, continued his response.

"Your mother and I are in wholehearted agreement that you should begin your journey soon, before the week is out, if you wish."

If Elsbeth had not been chewing a portion of bread that kept her jaw engaged in the process of shifting the tasty leavened piece from tooth to tongue and back again, she would no doubt have issued a stifled shriek of disbelief upon Ian's endorsement that Arielle take leave of them. A shaft of terror ran the full length of her body. Every extremity felt an unwieldy surge of angst while Ian's words shot clearly through her as precisely as the blade of an arrow focused squarely on its target by a skilled marksman.

Elsbeth rallied her strength, deciding to wait for an explanation from Ian. His many successes had not been wrought from lack of forethought. She maintained every confidence that her husband traveled a secure path that would not place their relationship with their daughter at a crossroad. Her terror was apparently evident as she raised her eyes and observed the concerned expressions washed over each of their faces. Both appeared ready to take leave of their seats to catch her ashen body if it began its fall from the confines of the dining room chair. However, she swallowed the remaining wad of bread and, with a deep draw of breath, stiffened her shoulders and drew herself up in a show of confidence as she emitted several carefully chosen words.

"You do know how very much your father and I love you, Arielle. We have, from your very beginning, wanted nothing less for you than the best the great gift of life has to offer. It is important that you keep my words close to your heart, rendering them as inseparable as the petals comprising a freshly bloomed rose," Elsbeth's words, full of emotion, began to crack as her voice defied her intent to remain strong.

Oh, how rapidly the years have passed. Far faster than one in youth can ever foresee. One has but to blink and old age is there with less vitality of skin and less vigor of spirit. The young woman before me was once cradled in my arms. She was a tiny babe with simple needs for survival. Needs freely and lovingly bestowed upon her by her father and myself. Oh, the agony I suffer now. Yet, I would travel no different course today than that of previous days. We have created a home, a family, and a history of which to be proud. Neither shame nor doubt shall tarry at our doorstep. I must sweep away all fear, grinding every particle of it into dust as easily eliminated as it is created. Oh, God, please ease my pain of this moment and guide me with your infinite wisdom. Elsbeth's thoughts swirled around in her head ending in a brief, silent prayer for sapient counsel from the Almighty.

Her eyelashes, moist from the onset of tears held back in a stoic effort not to appear undone by Arielle's request, received a gentle dabbing from the delicate, lace-edged handkerchief clutched in her hand. Lest her daughter be wrought with suspicion about her emotional response to the prospect of a trip abroad, Elsbeth, feeling a divine renewal of fortitude, breathed a cleansing breath of air and drew her lips together in a pleasant smile.

"Forgive me, my dearest Arielle," Elsbeth continued with her smile intact and a sparkle developing in the outermost recesses of her eyes. "It seems that although I am in agreement with your father that travel is certainly acceptable, I was not prepared for everything to happen so quickly. I simply need time to adjust. My little girl, our little girl, is a young woman and, though growth is naturally a process of life, I am afraid it sometimes hits me hard when thoughts of losing you cross my mind."

"Oh, mother. I will never be lost from you. Our bond cannot be severed by a trip to England, for my stay will not be overlong.

You and father can enjoy time together without me underfoot knowing I am safe and secure under the watchful eye of Auntie Leta. No one could have a more caring watchdog than Father's dear sister and, Father, I can make a call on the colliery. You know how keen my interest is regarding the coal business." Arielle paused as she saw the mixed look of pride and unacceptability cross over her father's face.

Ian stared at the girl, his girl, this beauty so like him in so many ways yet fortunate enough to have been spared his difficult disposition. She projected a sophisticated deportment carefully nurtured since birth by her mother. She was a prize. Early on, before she was a half score of years, she rode with him to the colliery after her studies, intently observing all the activities there. She listened to her father question the foreman about production, watched him absorbingly as he made notations in the daily books, and heedfully winced as workers, whose pace was not up to Hargrove standards, were verbally thrashed, then sent back deep into the mines to inhale the dusty soot that clung like a second skin to their clothes and faces.

Their work formed a queer dichotomy. It brought ease and comfort to families whose fuel the colliery supplied, while in the same measure, the work remained physically draining for the pit brow employees who worked long, strenuous hours. The workers had little choice. Most were limited in their options for a trade by nature of their breeding, having grown-up as children of pit brow workers themselves. It was their life's lot and a way of life that met their basic needs, keeping food on the table, and the cover of shelter over their loved ones.

"Now, now, Arielle. I know you have a strong business head but, I must advise against your being too heady with pronouncements in that vein beyond these walls. Your mother has worked very diligently to school you as a gentle young lady with pursuits befitting your gender. The next thing I know, you'll be wishing my retirement, taking my very shoes and stepping within to trod a path most unsuitable for a genteel young woman. Before your mother has lost patience with us both, I suggest we return to the matter of your holiday and see to it that Leta is notified you will soon be in her company. When last she wrote, I was concerned that living alone proved too severe a drain on her sanity. She complained of bouts with nervousness and sleeplessness, and a general malaise that limited her activities beyond her home. I have not been quite sure what to think of it all since Leta always seemed to have come to terms with her unmarried status."

"Sir Ian, my goodness. You must know your own sister, and women for that matter, much better than you imply. Leta, having spent years as a spinster, is of less relevance than her advancing years and the proclivity toward dyspepsia. Your dear sister is suffering the demons of the advanced feminine state and nothing more. She is a feisty one and will not succumb to life's passages without a fight. A visit from Arielle is just the tonic she needs to remove her mind from herself and savor the spirit of youth."

"Then, Mum, I have your blessing?" Arielle questioned, pleased to hear the change in her mother's attitude toward her departure.

"Yes, as long as you do not delay your return. I will indeed miss your company and worry over your absence. Even though I know you will be in comfortable and secure company with Auntie Leta, you will be innermost in my thoughts."

A well of tears began to form along Elsbeth's lower eyelids as she contemplated bidding even a temporary adieu to her daughter. Goodbyes had never been her forte and seeing Arielle off would not find her free of sadness. No, when the time came, a trip to the rail station would not be part of Elsbeth's itinerary. She would say her goodbyes from the familiarity of her hearth, and just as steadfastly be found at the threshold with lamps of welcome brightly lit for Arielle's anticipated return home.

Chapter Twelve

Horace's death and Emma's sincere regard for her requisite year of mourning had cast an unfamiliar shroud of gloom over Chestnut Heights, holding at bay the warmth and merriment that traditionally exuded from the walls of the stately mansion. During the darkest period of Emma's depression and adjustments to Horace's passing, she explained to William that her days of grand entertaining had seen their end.

"I have been diminished to one half of myself and feel the good has been taken from me. Nothing will ever be quite the same. I was two and now I am one. Social invitations have already been made awkward, for couples find it much more balanced to include a pair rather than a single widow such as myself. My life as I have known it has been altered without my choosing and I must adapt, I know that. It will take a great deal of time for me to heal, for Horace's death is a severe blow. He was my greatest fan and I shall miss him exorbitantly. But, go forward I must or be lost to a future too dreary to conceive. In time, I am sure I will come once again to delight in the simple pleasures of entertaining a guest or two at a time, but the bells at Chestnut Heights have sounded the final knell for grand galas and expansive dinner parties."

"Aunt Emma, as I listen to your words, I can barely believe this is the great voice of reason and encouragement upon which I have come to admire and so consistently rely. You have always been my best counsel, and in appreciation of your services rendered on my behalf, I am duty-bound to insist that you give yourself time, and certain adjustments will follow. Let Chestnut Heights be your salvation from despair. You know how much your happiness here meant to Uncle Horace. He, more than anyone, would want you to maintain normalcy, never allowing the walls of this grand home to become quiet and dreary. It may not seem so now, but your best days are ahead of you."

"Your Uncle Horace will always remain with me, though I feel so alone without him physically here."

"My dearest aunt, you have me and my heart always, as well as a multitude of others who hold you in the highest regard."

"I am but an old woman whose best years have passed."

"Quite the contrary, my dear aunt. You, most of all, know every age has its own grace."

"You have been a true gentleman since the day…"

"Since the day, Aunt Emma?"

"Yes, my dear William, since the day you were born."

William's words comforted Emma. His handsome face and kind expression reached out to her good senses. He had always been her favorite nephew, their bond resembling that of the most secure mother and son. Horace was also quite fond of William. Emma knew the intense admiration they held for one another. Horace had taken the lad under his self-educated wing, teaching him early on about the importance of real estate holdings, diversifying and developing a field of interest that would form a solid foundation upon which he could fall if all other speculations erred on the side of disappointment or failure. Horace's business acumen was one of sound judgments fueled by keen insights. William heeded his advice and, through several successful real estate transactions, became interested in corporations and contracts spawning his concentration on a legal career.

Horace was proud of William's personal success, crediting the young man for his relentless drive that never faltered. Emma knew William too was suffering with Horace's loss, and his anguish was compounded by her desolation.

William's loving kindness enveloped her. His words held sincere credibility and emoted all that was good, giving her pause to reconsider the tenor of her remaining years at Chestnut Heights. From this day forward she determined that the healing process would find her making steps, no matter how minute, to return to her title of 'Grand Hostess', letting Chestnut Heights breathe without the burden of a heavy heart.

She knew that Horace's being would remain ever present and immensely felt by her. In the way the ground, newly turned by Simon's shovels and spades, held its moorings, in the way the freshly trimmed blades of grass regained their stature, and in the way the house itself stood in regal respect for the lord and master who gave it its first breath of life when it was no more than a series of architect's strokes and calculations waiting to take on a life's form, Horace's imprint was permanent. Even the random creak of a floor board seemed to represent a word from Horace, a reminder that though seemingly still, there was movement among the beams and joists that connected the house to itself and to the couple who made it their home.

These were sensations that would not be removed by death, for they held a heartbeat of their own, unstoppable by limitations brought forth by Father Time or the wieldings of God. Horace's spirit would forever abound. That knowledge provided Emma with comfort beyond the caring words and acts of kindness generated in great force by the many friends and business associates who filled the parlor the day she laid her dear Horace to rest. Gone he was, but with her remained years of affection and devotion that would sustain her as she made her way through painful grief to find something that would bring balance back to her life.

William knew his aunt was doing the best she could, and he would not fault her for that. He was relieved after several months when word came to him that she was once again fervently engaging in tea parties and other small-scale social gatherings with her lady friends. The level of chatter at those events, so enjoyed by the fairer sex, inevitably escalated to a pitch happily side-stepped by his gender. His male associates much preferred the smoky walls of the library where hearty guffaws, cigars and a bar well stocked with brandy could be enjoyed. Yes, indeed, the passage of time had prompted Emma to resurrect her Ladies Tea Guild.

⁓

A group of well-coifed and elegantly outfitted ladies descended the steps of Chestnut Heights as William approached with Alexandra practically welded to his arm. The ladies enjoyed their double-take glances cast William's way as they took advantage of gathering as much sight as they could of Emma's tall, dark, handsome-as-a-rogue nephew. William recognized many of the women as dear friends of his aunt's whom she welcomed for sewing circles, book club gatherings and afternoon teas. He nodded in recognition, much to their delight evidenced by the smiles that crossed their faces and the chatter that ensued as they continued their departure along the sidewalk. Alexandra beamed, fully assured in her own egotistical way that the ladies were caught up by her beauty and envied her companionship with William.

"Look at the old biddies, William. Why they are so taken by your choice of a partner that they have taken second looks. I must say, I do admire their taste."

"My, Alexandra, I was unaware of your clairvoyant skills until this very moment. So, you have taken to reading minds, have you?"

"I have not taken to reading minds or anything else, you know that. It is perfectly clear that the old gals were admiring me and wishing themselves in my place. Anyone with even the simplest mind could see that."

"What I see, my dear Alexandra, is that *you* appear to have the ability to see that which is not within full view."

"Oh, William, honestly, you do love to torture me! You know I am much more pleasant when you agree with me. Is it so difficult to accept the fact that others envy me, especially when I am in your company? Can you not plainly see that?"

"See? Do you suggest the beauty that basks before me does not blind me? Yes, I know what I see, Alexandra. Now, let's move along and see how Aunt Emma has faired from her afternoon of tea and toddies."

"More like tea and biddies, if you ask me."

"No one is asking at the moment. It would serve you well to pretend your tongue is engaged in search of a tea leaf that has fastened itself to the roof of your mouth. Its retrieval should keep your tongue free from wagging for a time."

"Why do you choose to annoy me so? You tease me to the core. If you continue, I will shrivel up and die like a spent rose. I should turn right around and find company that appreciates my candor. I would think that you, of all people, William, would find my free spirit refreshing when so many of the young women today are wont to drone on and on about their domestic accomplishments with the highlight of their day being how many stitches they have tatted on a sampler. It is enough to make one shriek with boredom! If you ever find me wallowing in such pursuits, please promise you will take a gun to the temple below my lovely golden locks and end it all lest I suffer an inconceivable existence."

"Alexandra, you have missed your calling. Such high drama should be played out on the stage. We must knock on Aunt Emma's door now before the curtain rises on your next scene."

"William!"

"Now, save it for the New National, my dear girl."

Alexandra felt like fuming, but wisely held her tongue. She was savvy enough to know when William had had his fill of her antics. Although it took a considerable amount of energy on her part to stifle her thoughts that were waiting to billow forth, she did so in hopes that he would take more time with her.

Thomas quickly responded to the rap on the door and after a broad-grinned greeting, led the two visitors to the parlor to await Emma's entrance. He shook his head ever so slightly from side-to-side as he stepped from view, thinking what a special man Mr. William was to be able to tolerate Miss Whitaker. *Beauty or not,* Thomas thought to himself, *that woman would worry the horns off a Billy goat.*

Alexandra was an infrequent, but familiar visitor to the Willard's and Thomas, who had in the past overheard several interchanges between the two, marveled at William's calm resistance to her antagonizing ways. *Yes, that Mr. William is a saint, he is indeed,* Thomas pondered with another shake of his head as he walked toward the kitchen to announce the latest guests to Chestnuts Heights.

Emma was praising her staff for the magnificent display they prepared for her lady friends. She was fond of her staff, many of whom had been with her since the inception of Chestnut Heights and therefore knew her style and standards well. Emma took nothing for granted and, though she paid her household staff reasonable wages, she never slighted them the recognition they deserved for a job well done. She had just concluded her remarks when Thomas approached. She responded with gleeful enthusiasm at the news that William had stopped by to pay a call. She quickly exited the kitchen to join her nephew in the parlor as Thomas followed close on her heels to complete the remainder of the announcement he intended to deliver.

"Miz Willard, wait up jez a minute, Miz Willard! I jest needs te tell ya that Mr. William has that light haired lady friend with him and I jest want ya te be prepared, that's all."

"Now, Thomas, it is unlike you to make commentary regarding my guests."

"Oh, I knows that, Miz Willard. I don't mean nothin' by it, it's jest I know how special Mr. William is te ya and I specially hates te see anyone put a spell on your good day is all."

"Thomas, you are very kind to protect me so, however, if it is Miss Whitaker of whom you speak, I have no doubt that my dear nephew will keep a mindful watch over her. You needn't worry about me when William is present."

"Yez, Miz Willard. You knows best, as always."

William rose to his feet and walked to greet his aunt the moment he heard her footsteps rounding the parlor doorway. Alexandra remained seated, only moderately tolerating William's obvious attachment to Emma. She was pleased to rest upon the settee of the 'queen of Washington society' for it gave her another tale to spin when she gathered with her equally competitive cluster of female companions to share the latest brag. But, the loving attention William paid to Emma required a performance of acceptance that left Alexandra feeling drained. She felt no need to fuss with her attire or her coiffure prior to having an audience with his aunt, for she felt cocksure her appearance was impeccable --for how could anyone conceive of her otherwise?

William lovingly grasped Emma's hand, bowing momentarily, then placing his lips against the top of her hand where the skin was indiscriminately dotted with light brown spots of varying sizes. The random blemishes of age were sprinkled over what had been smooth as ivory skin and, though it had surrendered to less elasticity and the transparency that comes with passing years, the tenderness exchanged upon its surface was not altered by time. Emma drew a breath of satisfaction as she formed a simple curtsy in response to William's greeting. She turned toward Alexandra, noting the young woman's tolerating stare. Always the gracious hostess, Emma welcomed her female guest.

"Alexandra, I am so pleased that you have chosen to visit this afternoon. Why, it is so very refreshing to be in the company of young people when one has spent several hours with her peers. Oh, you know I think the world of the ladies who share tea with me, but there is much to be said for the lift one gets when surrounded by the younger generation. Yes, it does my spirit good to see you both. What brings you here today?"

"Aunt Emma, Alexandra was curious about the work you perform through St. John's at the settlement houses and I thought, what better way to satisfy her inquisitiveness than to come straight to the source? I knew you would be able to shed light on any of her inquiries."

"First, Mrs. Willard, may I beg a cup of tea?"

"Why, of course dear," Emma complied with Alexandra's request pouring a fresh, hot cup from the Herend teapot still warmed by a satin cozy.

"How interesting and surprising I must say, Alexandra, if you do not mind my being so forward. However, I cannot remember, in even the recent past, any concern for the less fortunate being expressed by you. That is not to say that one's interests cannot change. By any means, you now have my curiosity peaked."

"Mrs. Willard, William is correct about my interest as far as your work is concerned. I am, as always, dedicated to avoiding the plight of others," Alexandra said as she lifted the tea cup, took a hearty sip and swirled it about the inside of her mouth much like a rat savoring its food.

William and Emma both snickered as Alexandra attempted to rectify her statement. She undoubtedly realized how her innermost thoughts had audibly surfaced and now needed to find a way past her less than altruistic comments to end the humor Emma and William enjoyed at her expense.

"You see, Mrs. Willard, if I may clarify, I am happy to know more details about the work you do even though I have no intention of participating myself. Why, William can tell you how filled my days are. There is truly no time to dwell on others, and, I might add, William, that you are a cad for laughing at me and making me feel uncomfortable in your aunt's presence when I have come here with nothing but good intentions."

"Quite the contrary, my dear girl. I am happy to show you how to begin your days with the interests of others at the forefront, while still allowing ample time to focus due attention on your own concerns. The satisfaction gained from adding a ray of light to the lives of those less fortunate than ourselves is immeasurable by words. Their need is no less great and many times can only be grasped by the heart. Until you know their world and make it your own, you can have no hope or plan for assisting them. I can only tell you the warm feeling that wells in your heart when you look into the eyes of someone whose day you have improved. Such gratitude bears neither timekeeper nor price. You are welcome to join me on one of my visits to Purdy Court. It will be a time you will never forget. To truly benefit the less advantaged, we must see, we must know. The goal is a better life for everyone. Our involvement is the only answer, and it provides our opportunity to serve, to eradicate injustice. Join me."

"You see, Aunt Emma, that is exactly what Alexandra fears most about your volunteer work, that it will cling to her memory and remain a vision she will not soon forget. Is that not correct?"

William finished his jab at Alexandra, which found her most disconcerted. She was not blissful. A series of caustic oratories felt ready to fly from her lips but, as her better senses took hold, she decided to hold further comment toward William until they found themselves in a solitary state. She thought over her options for retort and decided it best to try to divert the conversation to other topics.

"Mrs. Willard, you know, despite William's teasing, I have the greatest respect for you and your endeavors on behalf of others. In fact, that brings me to another project about which you are the benchmark for others. William informs me, and as I behold from the tea you hosted today, you are entertaining again. Chestnut Heights has not given pleasure to the masses for some time now and it would behoove you to throw a grand party especially in this inaugural year."

"For what occasion or reason would I find justification for that which, as you say, 'behooves' me?"

"If for no other reason or occasion than sheer fun and the celebration of the life ahead of you."

"Whoa, Alexandra, can it be that you have a philosophical side? I am in awe!" William leaned forward for Alexandra's response as he threw his latest barb her direction. The vagaries of her behavior kept him simultaneously challenged and confused. She could be as charming as a Nightingale and as venomous as a viper.

"Yes, my dear tell us more," Emma asked with curiosity, eager to hear where Alexandra was headed with the idea of a large-scale event at her home.

She actually was not sure her heart would ever be healed thoroughly enough to host a grand party without Horace at her side. He had such a way of making all their guests feel exceptional even when poking fun, and without him she was unsteady in her verve. She felt she needed more time before she would be equal to the task of hosting a gala affair.

Emma turned her head from the two as she lifted her gaze to a far corner of the room and recalled the time when the enormously popular actress, Ellen Terry, made a cameo appearance at the conclusion of one of their dinner parties. She had come directly from the theatre, having drawn the final curtain call on her lead in Macbeth. Although no longer in costume, her face was still fully laden with ample doses of cosmetics that provided a dramatic effect, especially to her eyes heavily outlined in charcoal black, all quite suitable and necessary for the stage, but expressly dramatic when viewed in a drawing room.

Her fair face was icing smooth with rosy hued rouge highlighting her cheekbones and a ruby red glaze covering her pouty lips. Her thick, knee length hair, for which she was notorious, hung unleashed over her royal blue velvet cape. Her entrance made quite a show with remaining guests vying for a moment to stand near her or catch her eye.

Miss Terry was accommodating to a point and then felt the urge to make a dramatic sweep of her cape to clear the space before her for passage. In so doing, she reached behind her back and gathered her cascading hair over her forearm as one would a treasured cloak. As she proceeded forward, Horace, who with the other gentlemen had consumed his fair share of brandy that eve, stopped her in her tracks as her gesture caught his attention and he pronounced, "We thought you would tarry a bit longer Miss Hairy!" to which the men outwardly laughed as the ladies forced every bit of restraint to keep their quivering cheeks and lips from forming into full blown smiles.

No one was certain what Miss Terry's response would be. She continued forward, turning her head to the right over her shoulder and, catching Horace's sheepish grin, a mystical spell overcame her as she transformed herself into Lady Macbeth. With great conviction and boldness of diction she exclaimed, "Think of this good peers, but as a thing of custom; 'tis no other. Only it spoils the pleasure of the time."

Horace gave Macbeth's retort in his best imitation of the tragic character, "What man dare, I dare. Approach thou like the rugged Russian bear, the armed rhinoceros, or the Hyrcan tiger; take any shape but that, and my firm nerves shall never tremble. Or be alive again, and dare me to the desert with thy sword; if trembling I inhabit then, protest me the baby of a girl. Hence, horrible shadow! Unreal mockery, hence! Why, so; being gone, I am a man again. Pray you, sit still."

"You have displaced the mirth, broke the good meeting, with most admired disorder," Miss Terry continued.

"Can such things be, and overcome us like a summer's cloud, without our special wonder? You make me strange even to the disposition that I owe, when now I think you can behold such sights, and keep the natural ruby of your cheeks, when mine is blanch'd with fear," Horace retorted.

At this moment one of their guests interjected, "Horace, do you truly think you can keep up this dialogue with Lady Macbeth at such a late hour?"

Miss Terry continued, "I pray you, speak not; he grows worse and worse; question enrages him. At once, good night. Stand not upon the order of your going, but go at once."

Then, another guest exclaimed, "Miss Terry, you and Horace are divine! We beg you for an encore!"

As the group of friends moved along with the two thespians thoroughly engaged in their Elizabethan exchange, a round of applause gave pause to Horace's recitation of lines as Ellen Terry smiled and raised her arm that was free of tresses in the air. She swirled her hand in a subtle motion as it climbed into the air like a pocket of smoke rising to dissipate. She delivered her closing lines on her impromptu performance at Chestnut Heights.

"A kind good night to all!" Her words floated into the night air as she exited the manse with drama equal to that of her striking arrival.

The following day, Emma sent her apologies for what she termed 'Horace's playful twist of vocabulary under the influence of spirits.' Soon after, she received a very cordial response from Miss Terry saying that the evening was *'nothing in which to split hairs'* and, whenever her schedule permitted, she would be pleased to visit, *'at least the lady of the manse.'*

Horace kept life at Chestnut Heights from becoming mundane. Emma only hoped she could continue to add the spark that gave memorable flare to gatherings there. Horace affected her like no other. He always made her feel grand, like a queen. The minute she entered a room, he would smile and say, 'You look so beautiful!' It seemed he never tired of passing compliments her way and she adored him for it.

"Are you quite alright, Aunt Emma? We seem to have lost you for a moment." William's tone sounded his concern that possibly his aunt had taken ill.

"Oh, my, excuse my temporary absence. I was just having the most wonderful memory of a night when the unexpected happened at one of our parties and your dear Uncle Horace put his years of delving into the works of Shakespeare to use in a spirited delivery with Miss Ellen Terry. His performance was one I hoped Miss Terry would find forgettable, or at the very most remember as a moment of good humor among friends. Oh, it was a stimulating exchange and quite memorable for our guests. The visit by Miss Terry even made its way to the society pages of the Star and the Post which found Horace disappointed only, as he teased, that his performance deserved some acclaim and mention on the theatre pages. It was indeed a grand time. Oh, there was never small talk with him. He always began with a story."

"Yes, he was good company," remembered William.

"That brings us back to my idea, Mrs. Willard. Why, my idea encompasses your interest in the theatre and make-believe. It will make for an evening of intrigue and great drama," Alexandra encouraged, sitting forward on the edge of the settee as she went to work selling her idea to Emma.

"Intrigue has already entered the arena, for I clearly do not know what you are suggesting, my dear. Please spell it out before those of us in the dark go mad with curiosity," Emma urged, looking at William for confirmation that he too was as clueless as she.

"Why, a Masquerade Ball, of course. It has all the very best components for success. Guests may come in costumes as simple or elaborate as they wish with the requisite wearing of a mask. The mask is a must. Oh, it will be such great fun to guess who's who and watch how the evening unfolds. I have found that people are apt to be considerably more bold and at ease when their identity is protected by the guise of a mask."

"Is there any chance that one who already is bold by nature will become more docile when her visage is covered by false decor?" William playfully asked, waiting with eyes ready to wince at Alexandra's retort once she absorbed the direction of his question.

"You treat me like a red-headed stepchild, William! I am trying to encourage your aunt to extend invitations to a themed gala that not only is perfect for a woman with her talent for hosting grand affairs but also will be the talk of Washington society for months to come. The Masquerade will be an excellent means for guests to reveal or keep secret their identities, thus providing great mystery to the night. Please say you will seriously consider this idea, Mrs. Willard."

"I can say that I am amazed at my reaction to your suggestion for I am not feeling totally opposed to an event of such proportion. Actually, it could be quite fun and something refreshingly different for this season of my life. It will also aid in taking everyone's mind off the city heat. Now, it would be premature for me to decide one way or the other until I have taken some time to organize the party on paper and examine some issues that relate to my widowhood. I do appreciate your idea. It has been a long time since I felt enthusiasm about being surrounded by large numbers of people, and I am feeling good about our conversation." Emma sorted through her thoughts as she spoke reflectively finding the preceding moments some of the most pleasant she had ever spent with Alexandra.

Alexandra smiled. Her plan had worked. An evening with William in formal attire was just the venue she needed to exercise her charm and be held close by her handsome escort. It would take some weeks for Mrs. Willard to formulate plans for her Ball and extend invitations. William would be engaged with assisting his aunt which would give her the freedom she needed to take a little excursion to a London flat. Alexandra cut her eyes from side-to-side. A Cheshire grin overtook her face as she merrily voiced her pleasure to herself. *Yes, things are coming together quite nicely indeed.*

Chapter Thirteen

Late April 1897
Washington, District of Columbia

Thoughts of travel took hold of Arielle. She was easily unsettled by change and needed time to adjust her thinking before she found a level of comfort with the idea of leaving all that was known to her for the less familiar. She felt a sudden surge of nerves as adrenaline rushed the full courses of her veins. She closed her eyes rather than succumb to the toppling sensation that sent waves of anxiety across her skull and through her limbs. *Risk. I am taking a risk, putting myself out for all to examine, shedding my privacy, exposing my being.* Arielle shuddered and sighed a deep down heavy sigh of resolution. *I must cancel these thoughts.* She spoke aloud, momentarily tormented by her inability to feel free of her inhibitions, her self-imposed guard, her first and most protective reaction to decline all change and say, "No."

She glanced out her bedroom window as a subtle breeze became more invigorated, catching in its wake the branches of a mighty red sunset maple. The breeze sent thousands of seedlings from their tenuous holds. They spiraled through the air like battalions of whirligigs and spun ever so delicately to the ground, littering the fieldstone patio and grass beyond. She watched their rotating flight. The clutter generated by the annual spring shedding event was made bearable with the knowledge that the tree's emerging leaves would offer a lush umbrella of shade kindly welcomed on a heady summer's day. For a moment, Arielle's mind reflected on the fall season when leaves from the same specimen would fall to the earth making sounds like crisp raindrops. Imagining the sound of cleansing rain provided her momentary solace.

God grant me serenity from myself, she proclaimed as the words flowed over her tongue and through her lips in an effort to garner emotional assistance from a power above. *I must think of this as a trip to visit my dear Auntie Leta, my home. All is familiar to me there. I will be safe. Nothing Miss Pennybacker uncovers will be so alarming. It will all be in my best interest and I must go forth. I must face the fear that leaves me so divided. Enough of my backward thinking, for it serves no purpose but to paralyze my every action.*

Arielle opened the large doors of the ornately carved armoire housing her wardrobe. Flame finials crowned both corners and the top center of the over-sized piece. It had belonged to her father's mother and memories of her childhood came rushing forward. She fondly remembered the many occasions when her grandmum took her to her room and opened the massive doors to expose her beautiful array of dresses, cloaks, hats and shoes purchased from the trunks of the finest coutures. She let her make selections from her finery, a dress for a ball, special slippers for her feet, and a stunning jeweled comb for her hair. Her grandmum would sing wistful tunes as Arielle danced about the room in a fanciful waltz, making graceful efforts not to lose her footing in the too large shoes and gowns. She touched the fabric of one of her dresses, stroking the folds of its full skirt, remembering how she lifted the weighty volumes of cloth in her grandmum's gowns. She would twirl and raise the lush fabrics about her like an accomplished matador presenting his cape. *Ah, these are the thoughts of childhood and carefree days. What I would give for such piece of mind.*

She looked in the mirror at the gold briolette earrings adorning her earlobes. The facets on the pear-shaped amber quartz stones dangled and danced in the room's light. They had been her grandmum's and were a treasured heirloom she hoped to pass to her daughter some day.

She continued to fondle the crimson taffeta, its moiré pattern casting reflective highlights about the space as it captured the sunlight emanating from a nearby window. A single teardrop fell onto the cloth and melded with the water stained effect of the fabric's weave. Her reaction to her thoughts of childhood caught her off-guard. Her emotion came from deep inside, yet felt at the very edge of her skin. She swiped her cheek with her right hand, rubbing into the fine pores of her porcelain skin the moisture and loving thoughts the tear provoked to savor, not wipe away, the memories and their last days together.

Grandmum Hargrove was a treasure. She prided herself on her dedication to the Bible and all it stood for, professing her purity and abstinence from the vices of society, having never smoked or chewed tobacco, nor sipped anything stronger than fully steeped orange pekoe tea muddied only by a spot or two of cream.

Arielle had always been enchanted by her cup and saucer collection, well represented with lovely floral patterns by Royal Dalton, Spode and Coalport. She and Grandmum would go to the china cupboard, discuss the patterns, then select a set to carry to the tea table where the hot beverage was enjoyed with warm, currant speckled scones and luscious Chantilly cream for spreading.

She recalled that her grandmum's passing had been expected however, that knowledge served as small solace for Arielle as the family gathered waiting for her final day. She had been quite lucid nearly to the end until the emphysema that plagued her took her parting breath as she patted the shiny raven locks on Arielle's head with short, soft touches until her fingers stilled. She had had a warm, wonderful laugh that made Arielle giggle and feel happy inside. Now, she lay silent. She did not stir, there was no beat of life. Arielle took her grandmum's cold hand in hers, squeezing it a double squeeze, hoping to resurrect a pulse, to trigger action from her heart, but there came no response. She remembered her mother touched her shoulders to guide her away while her father kissed his mother's cheek, and then lowered her lids, placing her in dignified repose.

Arielle missed her laugh, the tea parties, and the love that came so freely. An unexpected second tear fell upon the watermarked taffeta. It was as though her grandmum had joined her for the moment so each could shed a tear, then be done with the sadness. A smile crossed her face as she recalled her grandmum's playful nature and her ability to turn a sad event into an opportunity for growth. *It is time to grow!* Arielle expressed with gusto as she waltzed about the room spurred by a heavenly presence, placing garments from the armoire on her bed for packing. From the distant recesses of the four corners of the room, the essence of her grandmum's tunes playfully filled the air and Arielle's spirit captured every loving beat.

Clothing, enough for several weeks should be quite sufficient for my stay. Auntie Leta will enjoy a shopping outing so I will be able to happily embellish anything lacking from my packing. Arielle mused, as she laid out the pieces of her wardrobe in organized fashion with each slipper and boot assigned to its proper gown. She would leave to Fiona the task of properly placing each outfit and accessory in her luggage for safe travel across the ocean. For now, her bed came calling. A good night's rest was in order if Mother Nature would allow.

Beyond her bedchamber's walls, the wind wailed. Every shingle billowed in the wind's wake, as their hinges and latches held their moorings, refusing to succumb to the potent tug-of-war initiated by the forceful currents of air. Foliage and branches swayed forward and back, again and again until Arielle, entranced by the sounds of their motion, could listen no more. She closed her eyes tight, pulled the covers up over her face and tried to imagine that all was calm until the next burst of wind broke the stillness. She received only temporary dispensation from the mournful whistle circling about the exterior of the manse and felt encompassed in a capsule she had no recourse but to endure. A whirlwind of thoughts cast themselves about her mind like fragments of spit soil until she finally drifted into sleep.

A tap came to her door the next morning. "Come in," she summoned, expecting Fiona's little freckled face to appear. Instead, the portal held the form of her mother. Arielle thought their conversation had ended with her mother's quiet acquiescence regarding her departure. But, it seemed for Elsbeth, final words had not yet come, for she needed to be in Arielle's presence, to be close enough to see, to be close enough to feel.

Elsbeth's mind reeled with feelings, with emotions that ran deep. She knew she had cleared a path for Arielle to partake of a journey unknown to them all, with an outcome just as precarious and the thoughts made her quiver. She shook off the edges of the feelings threatening to disarm her. She wanted these last moments with Arielle before her departure to have substance, to render an inseparable bond between them that could not be brought asunder by any person, place or thing.

"Mum, I had hoped to see you before I left this morning."

"The train, I believe you said it is scheduled to depart the railway station at ten o'clock a.m.?"

"Yes, Mum, you remember correctly. I can see the worry in your face but, Mum, please remember I am a young woman quite capable of being on my own and fighting my own battles. You have raised me well and, after all, you know I can nary go far astray under the scrutiny of Auntie Leta."

"Yes, my darling, I know. It is just that I want to feel as though my arm of protection can span the great waters and reach out to you from any distance. It is hard to let you go, though I know I must."

"It will be no time at all before I return. We both have that with which to look forward! I had thought Fiona would have come around to pack my things away. There is no wonder what is causing her delay."

"In Fiona's defense, I asked that she refrain from entering your room until I had come and gone. I just needed to be with you without Fiona, your father, or anyone else. I just needed time between the two of us."

"Really, Mum. You need not fret over my absence. I will return and it will be as though I never left."

"Arielle, how I hope your words are true."

"You suggest I would be false with you, Mum?"

"Oh, my dear, no. Any doubts are my own," Elsbeth explained, realizing she was treading on tenuous ground and must watch her next verbal step lest she send red flags of questions and distress Arielle's way.

"I mean, my dear Arielle, that I do not ever want to see you altered in a bad way by any circumstance you might encounter. I want only the best for you, always."

"I understand that more than anyone. You have always lent your fondest attentions in my direction. I do not take for granted an ounce of the love and care you have extended my way superseding your own needs."

"I fear you credit me beyond what I deserve. However, I am very moved by your words and will hold them close to my heart hoping we never lose our bond."

"That which is cast in love can never be lost," Arielle expressed with a smile as she leaned forward, throwing her arms about her mother as the two embraced one another with a sustained hold.

"I love you, Arielle. You give me great joy. Joy. It is such a petite word holding abundant repercussions."

"I love you, Mum," Arielle spoke soft and lovingly as each savored the sweet scent of the other until the two broke their embrace setting in motion the final stages of Arielle's preparation to leave.

It was only moments after Elsbeth left Arielle's room before Fiona's fidgety self lighted in her doorway.

"Miss Arielle, I hope ye won't be blamin' me fer not bein' 'ere earlier to help ya but, Lady Hargrove gave me strict orders not to enter yer room 'til she said so, so 'ere I am now."

"Fiona, I understand. Your work has been made simple, for I have laid all my clothing out. You need do no more than put everything carefully in my bags and trunk and place them downstairs within the hour. I must leave by quarter past nine. That should provide me ample time to meet my train to New York."

"Yes, miss," Fiona dipped, then quickly stood fully erect, admiring the exquisite display of clothing waiting to be packed away, soon to be worn about the streets of England and Wales.

Having made all of her selections and completed her morning toilette, Arielle was now watching time. She was trying to escape its presence with other thoughts but kept being brought around to how painfully slow the hour was passing by the measured pace of the ticks and tocks from the clock on her mantle. Time, the ever-present harbinger of moments found well spent or wasted, was keeping a ponderously slow watch over her now.

Her thoughts were twisted. Mixed wishes for time's expedience came to the foreground while in the same thoughts, she yearned for an enormity of time that would find her outliving the span set by her ancestors. Why should she wish her life away by aching for time to pass quickly? In less than an hour she would be at the rail station to meet Miss Pennybacker. It was time to order that her carriage to be prepared for the drive to the station. If all went according to previous arrangements, she would soon be seated in the car of the train that would take her, she hoped, to the answers to questions that seemed to multiply.

Arielle disliked the area nearby the station. Though it was a mere three blocks north of the Capitol building, dirt seemed to find a comfortable existence in every nook and at every curb. The patrons were an urban montage of shabby, crusty street sorts in need of a good scrubbing sitting among the fashionable, upper crust. Fine, well-appointed ladies and derby clad gents, many with the daily news tucked as wedged bastions of intellect under their arms, waited for cabbies, the men pacing the sidewalk to keep warm in the late April chill. Arielle gazed skyward at the very tip of the station's Italianate clock tower, its spire regally pointing to the heavens. Rising beyond the peak of the spire and centered over the main portico that provided access to the station's ticket windows was a barren flagpole. The threat of inclement weather it seemed, kept Old Glory from being raised this day. Arielle took note of the absence of the national symbol of freedom and missed its presence as she watched everyone go about his or her business without missing a beat.

She stepped back as her carriage pulled away, having let a porter tag her baggage for New York with transfer instructions for the White Star's SS Britannic to England. She put her belongings with her ticket on a handcart to await the arrival of her train. Her journey would begin its first stages in moments from now. It would be only a matter of time before Miss Pennybacker shed some light on her situation, she was confident of that. She felt less than confident about what her reaction to it all would be.

Reading matter. I should have brought my latest Journal with me. What a silly twit I am to have forgotten. Oh, it might be just as well, for Miss Pennybacker and I will be able to have a chat during our ride to New York. What am I thinking? She may not speak a word my direction the entire trip. Arielle bounced contradictions back and forth, then, glancing again at the clock tower and seeing the time for her train to arrive fast approaching, she determined herself to cross the street to the newsstand to purchase reading material for what she imagined might prove to be a very droll, sedentary passage.

She quickly stepped from the curb, looking both ways but, in her haste, she misjudged the speed of an approaching four-in-hand. The driver was relentlessly attempting to slow the grand looking beasts, but to no avail. His knuckles pulled white against the reins as he shouted "Whoa, boy, whoa, boy!" in a frantic plea to slow the horses. His horror was compounded when the young woman stepped directly in his path and was trampled to the ground by the hefty force of the horses. Gasps could be heard over the screech of the carriage's brake that the driver applied with all his might, but no amount of strength could alter the ravages suddenly thrust upon Arielle's body as she lay limp and lifeless on the cold, hard macadam. Women stood stoically still, their hands clasped to their mouths trying to stop the shrieks of terror that instinctively rushed from their lungs. Several men dashed to Arielle's side, one removing his frock coat, gently placing it under her head in an effort to soften the blow that had consumed her entire body. She showed no motion, for she had entered another place where the sights and sounds of the day were instantly obliterated.

"Oh, my God, she's dead," sobbed one woman who turned away seeking support from her companion.

"Get help, get help!" shouted several others, one pointing to a flat bed wagon to be used as a method of transport.

From the crowd of spectators stepped a plump, elderly man with thick, wavy, white hair and a mustache to match. He pulled his pocket watch from his vest pocket and, after noting the time, reclosed it and let it hang loose by its fob. *The coroner will want to know the time of death, poor girl.*

"Move away, it's ol' Doc Lovering. Give the man some room!" ordered a young lad as he observed the doctor's presence.

Those gathered parted, creating an almost ceremonial guard for Doctor Lovering to pass through. He shook his head as he approached the petite frame lying ever still. He knelt beside her, taking great caution not to move any part of her body abruptly. He opened her eyelids only to find a distant stare and then rested two fingers of his right hand on the side of her neck. As faint as a whisper sucked away by a wistful breeze came the faraway rhythm of a pulse.

"She remains barely with us," Doctor Lovering announced, very matter-of-factly with an empathetic measure of relief showing in his eyes.

"Let us get some help here. You men bring that flat bed on over. There is a board in it that we can rest her on. When I say 'move', the four of us will carefully lift her, and I mean *carefully* lift her onto the board and into the wagon for transport to the hospital. This young woman needs immediate medical attention!" Doctor Lovering systematically barked his orders to the crude gathering hoping the young woman's pulse would still be found upon arrival at Providence.

Morgan and Agnes stopped at the curb observing the small crowd and sudden movement of a flat bed wagon toward the spot where a group of four men stood waiting.

"I wonder what the fuss is all about? Looks like something has happened, Morgan. An accident or something," Agnes said, lifting her chin to get a better view.

"Well 'something' certainly covers the gamut of all that is possible! Of course, *something* has happened, but it all looks well under control. We have a job to do and a train to catch so we had best be on our way. Come along before Peepers blows away in the breeze," Morgan exclaimed, grabbing Agnes by her cloak to get her aimed toward the terminal.

Peepers cocked his head, moving it from side-to-side as though befuddled he had to endure yet another voyage with the mismatched duo he relied upon for his comfort and care. Morgan insisted there was no one to whom they could entrust Peepers' well-being so, much to his chagrin, he remained an unwillingly companion, accompanying Morgan and Agnes on all of their excursions.

The men, under the doctor's careful supervision, gathered Arielle's limp frame from the pavement ever so cautiously. They placed her on a half-inch thick length of plywood sheeting that would be her gurney for what those present feared would be the final ride of her life. Doctor Lovering's roundish form was projected into the wagon with much assistance from the men who had lifted Arielle. He sat beside her, watching intently for any change in her condition, but none came.

"Was anyone with this young woman?" Doctor Lovering queried the group receiving no response.

"Move along then, without a jolt, if you will," the doctor shouted his order to the wagon's driver.

"Get to Second and D Streets Southeast with measured haste man, for we have no time to lose!"

The words no sooner exited Doctor Lovering's mouth than the wagon was in motion, its large, multi-spoked wheels rolling past the railway station, urgently on its way to Providence Hospital.

A very smartly appointed landau made its way in line to the curb at the terminal's entrance. The coach had waited for several cabbies to pull away that had lingered to gawk at the accident. The driver secured his team, then opened the high glossed door for his charge to exit. Most of the bystanders had already taken notice of the fine looking, Vanderbilt green turnout. It was a standout on any occasion and particularly now as it stood among the predominantly black cabs and broughams frequenting the station. As the passenger presented himself in the doorway, several women took particular notice of the exceedingly handsome man in a finely tailored, coal black coat. He was tall in stature with deeply dark brown hair, its volume enhanced by the slightest wave. His eyes soaked in the moderate sunlight that seemed to add an extra glimmer to the deep blue of his expressive orbs. He heard one woman gasp, then giggle to her lady friend as she acknowledged her embarrassment upon realizing that the striking gentleman had looked her way when he heard the outward sounds of her admiration.

William smiled, as he was wont to do, to ease her momentary social discomfort, not identifying in his own humble way that his

eye contact with the maiden sent flutters of excitement and anticipation throughout her limbs. He turned and continued up the
ramp of the station's entrance, his promenade muted by the blend
of scattered voices coming together to form an indistinguishable
hum. He was able to decipher dribbles and drabs of conversation
as he proceeded on his course, none of which seemed of any pertinence. As he rounded the concourse just inside the terminal,
he cited the ticket window indicating his train's departure time.
Standing behind a small-framed woman holding a cage with a
rather anxious parakeet, he joined the line of passengers to confirm his travel.

"Uh, oh, uh, oh," came Peepers' dancing response as he sashayed on the roost within his wired confinement.

William, not to be put-off by a bird, and more than ready for
his business trip to get underway, looked past the hapless-looking
creature.

"Morgan, I still find it a shame, and more than a trite un-
settling, to begin our holiday with a commotion of questionable
status occurring nearly before our very eyes and ignore its occurrence as though it were an invisible act. It seems quite against
your nature to dismiss an event in such fashion and, you know,
I speak this with all due respect to your superior judgment and
experience."

"Agnes, in point of fact, it is best for us to make every energy
of our focus that which benefits our client and cast our time and
talents toward a successful conclusion on her behalf. You must
remember to stay the course. We need not divide our interest."

"But, I am certain Miss Har," Agnes' words were halted in
mid-stream by Morgan's arched eyebrow raised in tandem with
a stern look.

"Agnes, I will not remind you again to be ever present of the
fact that the anonymity of our client, particularly when we are
about in a public place, is paramount to maintaining the professional status I have achieved. I will not have you forgetting yourself
at the onset of our journey, placing in jeopardy the good name of

our client. For now, keep your eyes on Peepers and keep him calm before the floor of the station is paved with his plumage."

Agnes held her tongue. She knew she was no wit to Morgan's intimidating style and realized she had become caught up in the excitement outside the station. *I must remember to maintain my focus as Morgan says.* Agnes repeated the words over in her head as she spied the handsome gentleman in line behind her. *Oh, my God, he is a gorgeous creature.* Agnes nearly swooned, causing a slight shift in Peepers' position in the cage.

"Uh, oh. Whoa, boy," Peepers chirped, emitting a grin from the handsome man behind him.

Agnes looked William straight in the eyes, then glanced away, embarrassed by her obvious show of admiration.

"That is quite a bird you have there. I once had a parakeet, but he never spoke a word," William broke the uncomfortable moment for Agnes with his repartee.

"Not a word?" Agnes questioned.

"No, not *a* word, *dozens* of words, it would seem. He was a relentless pluck, very spirited, forever brandishing a phrase. I am afraid though that the looseness of his tongue was his undoing, for after shrieking "Fire! Fire! Fire!" to a new housekeeper, she thought it prudent to release One Way, as we called him, and true to his name, he never returned." William smiled and a playful grin overtook his face as he shared his bit of fiction with the susceptible stranger before him.

Agnes surveyed his face and within the moment perceived that the gorgeous man was having a little poke at her. Agnes smiled, sending a tiny laugh William's way. He laughed in return and all was equal as Morgan, Agnes and William resumed their status in line, moving forward to confirm their tickets and secure their seats for their ride by rail to New York.

"I say, Morgan. There has been no sign of Miss, I dare say, your client. Shall I look about the station for her?"

"No, Agnes. In the economy of time and efficiency, we need not waste a moment searching for someone who clearly is not going to show. We have had no confirmation from her these past few days, therefore, I would surmise she has laid full confidence in us and will await our telegram."

Agnes turned her head away from Morgan to roll her eyes. Staring straight back at her were Peepers' steady pupils.

"Remain calm, remain calm," came his refrain.

"Oh, shush, you silly bird."

"I see Peepers has found you out."

Agnes blushed at Morgan's words. She was rarely able to disguise her feelings from her and Peepers lent little assistance in her favor.

William observed their interchange only to find the eyes of Peepers upon him.

"Pretty boy, pretty boy," Peepers exclaimed as he paced along his trapeze-like perch.

Agnes looked up and smiled at William thinking her business trip could take on a touch of pleasure if he became her handsome traveling companion.

"No. No one seems to have any information regarding this young woman," Doctor Lovering informed the admitting nurse as Arielle's limp form was removed from the makeshift plywood stretcher to a more suitable hospital bed.

"There was a small purse beside her, its contents remained fairly intact despite the force of her fall. There was no time to examine it earlier, but we could certainly have a look now. The poor girl's family should be notified at once," Doctor Lovering said as he handed the purse made of intricately tatted navy lace to the nurse who carefully spread its drawstring opening to reveal all within.

"Ah, doctor. Here we go. She has her calling card with her. Her name is Olivia Smithfield."

"And her residence?" the doctor queried.

"None listed, sir. Just her name is all."

"Well, we best get Miss Smithfield to an examining room. She has suffered a severe trauma. We must do all we humanly can. Try to locate her family, if you will. I would urge them to come as quickly as possible. The presence of loved ones at a time like this is sometimes the deciding factor as to whether one survives or succumbs to the events at hand."

The nurse moved quickly, her white uniform fashioning no contrast to the ghostly white aura that had overtaken Arielle's complexion. Her condition was dire. No movement or prompt by the doctor or hospital staff elicited any cognitive response. She had entered a realm well beyond their walls, untouchable by their reach but, they hoped, penetrable by their voices of encouragement and inquiry.

"Miss Smithfield, if you hear me, please squeeze my hand," Doctor Lovering spoke loudly, yet with an earnest gentleness as he held the hand of the young woman who lay so peacefully before him. He hoped to feel even the faintest reaction to the tender clutch he maintained on her lifeless palm.

No movement came. Her pulse had strengthened every so slightly, yet not enough to proclaim her out of harm's way.

"We can only hope the 'morrow will find her back with us. Until then, if no family is found, it will be necessary to run a notice in the newspaper. There must be someone who will miss such a fine young woman." Doctor Lovering patted her hand as he signaled the nurse to wheel her away to a semi-private space for safekeeping where she would be near watchful eyes for the remainder of the day and the long evening that lay ahead.

The good doctor watched as the narrow mobile bed made its way down the sanitized corridor then turned into a doorway of the room that would secure the young woman for the night. Providence had seen its fair share of 'Jane Does' but this one was a standout among them. Her fine features and attire separated her from the likes of the street dwellers he treated whose alcohol abuse and lack of proper hygiene made them ready candidates for hospitalization.

"Well, I must turn my attention to others in need," Doctor Lovering rationalized as he took note of the hour on his time-piece and replaced it securely in his vest pocket. It was well past time to head toward home and have a well-balanced meal while awaiting the callers in need of medical care certain to cast their shadows on his doorstep before bedtime.

⌒

Morgan, Agnes and Peepers settled into their seats. From a bird's eye point of view, all was right with the world. Morgan, and particularly Agnes, always found leaving their home base the most difficult portion of their journeys. Packing, secur-ing the storefront, and making the final closure of the door, were rigors of the travel process. They had all been successfully com-pleted. Now their trip could officially begin.

"Why must it be so difficult to leave?" Agnes mused aloud.

"The why is ever present, Agnes. One is leaving the known for the not so known. There is the requisite uneasiness associated with that. There is a sense of lacking control that arises when it is the unknown one faces. However, and, in point of fact, that un-easiness can provide the zeal to know more, the adrenaline that has us spring from our haunches to satisfy the curiosity to see all that the wide, wide world has to offer."

Agnes wondered on many occasions if Morgan was as confi-dent as her words and tone conveyed. She viewed herself as more timid, however, if she dared suggest the word timid, Morgan would remind her that the word 'reticent' was entirely more complimen-tary. So, in Agnes' own, reticent way, she listened to Morgan's ex-planation regarding why it was so difficult to leave home and sat quietly back in her seat waiting for the motion of the train and its jostling reverberations on the track to lull her into compliance with the standards set by her employer.

The train's whistle blew an abbreviated warning sufficient enough to lend heed as it exited the station. William rested his head back. He peered out the window to the platform beyond where a solitary flaxen-haired woman stood. Her resemblance to Alexandra was uncanny. He took a second parting look. No, it was not she though the woman prompted him to question Alexandra's whereabouts. Prior to leaving for the train station, his secretary informed him that Alexandra visited his office when he was out and left the message that she would be away for several days. She left no details regarding her destination or intended return. Whenever she slipped away without his knowledge, concern for her well-being weighed on his mind. His word was his bond and he had given her father his word that he would keep watch over her. He knew Alexandra's strong-will would forever challenge his patience. His friendship with her father and the generosity Andrew Whitaker bestowed on him kept William tied to her. She would have to breach his trust, or cause humiliation beyond repair before he would revoke his guardianship over her.

Each sway and sashay of the train created a lullaby that overtook Agnes' desire to remain awake. She acquiesced as her body became ensconced in sweet harmony with her vessel of transport's motion along the tracks.

Morgan slipped a notebook and pen from her valise. She began to fine-tune her agenda, but the left to right lurch of the train along the segmented rails of the track jolted her back and forth. The walls and windows of the car rattled in response to each vibration. Morgan's pen took flight along the surface of her pad of parchment leaving unintelligible script. *Hmmm,* she thought to herself. *Pristine penmanship will have to wait until journey's end.*

Chapter Fourteen

Early May 1897
London, England

The streets of London were turf well trod by Morgan. English wares were exceedingly popular among her clientele and were priced affordably, allowing a fair profit to be had in Washington. Her visits to the bustling city of fog, drizzle and bland victuals were far more frequent than she could ever have imagined as a young girl in Leesburg, Virginia high astride the back of a hearty thoroughbred.

London was as significantly prosperous and prominent as it was poor and pitiful, a social dichotomy of rich and poor amassed together in servitude to one another's needs. Fine ladies and gents strode the thoroughfare, some on foot, others with benefit of highly glossed carriages pulled by the finest horses, equipped with deluxe fittings. At the same time, simple beggars, costermongers and street urchins brushed alongside them sharing the same ground and air, yet without access to, or the ability to achieve, the fancy trappings of the velvet gloved gentry in their midst.

As Morgan disembarked the ship, she corrected the lapel on her frock coat, its pointed tip having caught against the inside

edge of the long navy woolen outer garment that covered her tailored dress to its full ankle length. An ever-present sense of order
was pursuant to Morgan's prodigious attention to detail and as-
pirations for perfection. Her standards knew only a master of the
highest caliber and she rode no one harder than she rode herself.

Agnes knew full well that to assist Morgan Pennybacker she
was to be alert at all times, listen intently, and maintain precision lest Morgan lose her patience and dismiss Agnes from 'the
very room in which we stand' as she had been wont to exclaim on
more that one memorable occasion.

Even Peepers' intuitive powers found him chanting 'Uh, oh,
uh, oh!' as he promenaded in a flurried two-stepped pace about
his cage.

With no greater than a few long strides between them, Agnes
shadowed Morgan, her right hand clutching the metal handle
atop Peepers' cage while her left hand remained propped below
to stabilize the journey for the colorful, winged cargo teetering
within the confines of his small, portable aviary.

Morgan seemed in a particular hurry to acquire transport
away from the Docks that consumed inshore acres bordering the
Thames south of London Bridge. At the Pool, cargo ships clustered, awaiting orders to unload their manifests of colliery coal,
metal, lumber and other products of the vast industry from the
north. Cabbies lined the length of the dusty board walkways waiting to take on their next fare while their horses, many of them old
nags, halted to feed and rest before taking their hooves again to
the pavement generously laden with excrement from the likes of
their kind.

Agnes, with exception to the concentrated stronghold she
maintained on Peepers' cage, was thoroughly absorbed by the
view she garnered of the Docks as she continued her promenade
down the ship's gangway entranced by Morgan's rapid gait. The
serene, clear water of the tidal river made the Thames a pleasant
contrast to the pungent air and noise that surrounded the hurly-
burly of activity before them.

Cartwheels and horseshoes clamored against the pulverized stone remnants comprising the streets. Stone dust wafted into the air and coated everything within its midst. Agnes coughed to clear her throat of an airborne cluster she sucked in as she opened her mouth wide to warn Morgan to beware of a load of beams that were about to make contact with her back as a careless laborer, who had just passed by with an extended load of boards on his shoulder, stopped and turned to greet the driver of a passing livery. Morgan, ever quick to react, sharply stepped aside, artfully dodging the potential onslaught of lengthy lumber aimed for her stately head.

"Watch yourself young man!" Morgan admonished, regaining her composure as she continued to pursue her quest to exit the Docks as rapidly and safely as possible.

"Aye, it's sorry I am mum. It's a good 'ead ye 'ave on 'em shoulders an' I ken see why ye'd be wantin' ta keep it that way!" The young man shouted, admiring Morgan's handsome accoutrements.

"Mind your load and your manners, young man," Morgan replied, keeping her pace unaltered, nary missing a step, despite the careless gesture by the young laborer to throw her off course.

Agnes shook her head in reprimand at the young fellow whose wide grin exposed a hollow gap on the upper level of his mouth where a tooth had gone missing. He winked at her, attempting to bow with his awkward load, as his words spilled forth in a thick cockney accent.

"'Oodn't ya know. I 'ave upset the likes of yer friend 'ere as well. She's still quite a comely lass though, even with the scowl she's presentin' me with, or maybe after bein' at sea fer so long, it's jest 'er smile's gone an' capsized!"

With his final words, the lad threw his head back belting out a raucous laugh as he turned, catching the eye of his buddy and gained additional pleasure to find his mate laughing along as well.

Morgan's nostrils flared in aggravation and immediately filled with the noxious odor of freshly emitted horse manure. City dwelling had made her less tolerant of its aroma that was greatly enhanced by the recurring sweep of breezes and the hefty concentration of the droppings along the Docks. She cast her head away from the impudent lad and continued her fast gait to a waiting cabbie, knowing she was more than ready to be free of the unsavory surrounds before her.

T he interior of the hansom cab was a welcome retreat. The small black carriage efficiently held Morgan and Agnes but, lacking space for Peepers' cage, the wired assemblage came to rest upon Agnes' lap for the duration of the ride into the city proper. The negligibly padded leather seats and walls of the very basic turn-out lent the only relief in the intimate space as the cabbie ordered his nag onward, sending his occupants lurching forward then back against the well-worn leather interior. Morgan closed her eyes to gain some escape from the rigors of travel.

The passage from New York to London had given her much-needed time to reflect on her assignment. Daily promenades on deck lent a refreshing air to her focus on relaxation all the while serving to maintain her clear head for the investigative work that would take paramount importance over the selection of threads and linens for the shop. She was determined to get to the bottom of the mystery that surrounded the cryptic letter from Olivia Smithfield. Such revelation would be the least she could do to serve her client well.

Though anxious to review her written agenda for the call she intended to make to Olivia Smithfield before noon on the 'morrow, she knew such review would have to wait until she was free of motion and well refreshed for the night in the plush surroundings of her hotel room. She had read the letter over and over and kept it folded and secure in a pocket in her outer garment for easy access. The desire to read the letter once again overtook her concern for the effects the motion of the cab might have on her intestines. Her shipboard journey had provided sway enough as the ship rocked in lengthy swells brought on by worsening weather on the seas. She had withstood that motion and would persevere to ignore any onset of queasiness. A refreshing, though languorous waft of air drifted through the cab's windows giving her renewed fortitude. She withdrew the document and proceeded to read it through again.

March 1897

Dear Sir Ian Hargrove,

It is with sincerity and burden of heart that I present myself to you with this letter. Though we have not yet made one another's acquaintance, the inevitability brought by our common bond compels me to request a meeting with you. My poor health places me in an unequivocal position. I must share with you some facts not already known to you regarding your daughter's birth. As you will remember, my brother, the late Dr. Edmond Smithfield, was instrumental at her birth and delivered her to you. On many occasions, I served as his midwife, assisting my brother with his enormous workload. One such occasion involved the birth of your daughter. I am not proud of what transpired that very day, but the outcome has benefited us both. Please believe me when I say I wish I could remain silent, but the knowledge I have may not go with me to my grave. You, Lady Hargrove, and your daughter deserve to know the truth of that day. I know there is much at stake, but the merits of this information far outweigh any detriment we may all suffer. Soon, I will book voyage to America so I may, at long last, correct the wrongs that my brother and I put in place. Until then, I remain indebted to you for the care with which you honor my request.

Sincerely,
Olivia Smithfield

The woman had clear intent on making public, at least to the Hargroves, information that had been held silent for a score of years. The information itself and the woman's motives were a curiosity that intrigued Morgan, kindling her desire to meet with Miss Smithfield in as timely a fashion as possible upon arrival in London. She hoped Smithfield's poor health would not jeopardize the gleaning of information necessary to answer the questions surrounding Miss Hargrove's case.

The wrongs, the wrongs. Morgan repeated Olivia's words. *What could they be? And, will tomorrow's dawn bring the answers?* Only time would tell.

Chapter Fifteen

E lsbeth spent an interminable week going about her usual tasks in rote form with few quiet moments of repose. She was consumed with thoughts of Arielle. She hoped Arielle's stay with Leta would prove much more settling than the thoughts of impending disaster looming ever present in her mind, threatening to suck stability from her moorings. Her feelings for Arielle were deep down, deeper than any words could properly relay. At the very moment she determined herself to begin anew, feeling refreshed with hope that all was well with her daughter, Ian burst through the front portal wielding a newspaper, summoning her to join him immediately in his study for what he proclaimed was 'most shocking news!'

She gathered her thread-loaded needle with the cotton lace work she had been creating since the hour past and scuttled forth to join her husband. Why she had not elected to set her work aside, leaving it in the parlor to be rejoined at her future leisure, she was not certain. Perhaps the mere transport of the work in her hands added security, something she could stroke and lay permanence to as Ian shared the news he waved before her in a gyrated fashion, his chaotic motion mimicking a victim of palsy. His muscles suddenly lacked structure and substance as his limbs, overtaken by emotion, shook.

Oh my God. Elsbeth silently expressed. *How many times of late have I found myself in this position, seated in Ian's study, awaiting some life altering news delivered as deliberately as the honed blade of a guillotine? Why must life be so difficult? Perhaps, without the difficulties and pain, I would not appreciate the joy and happiness that so often graces my life's experiences. Oh, how I pray for a measure of peace to grace the days before me.* Elsbeth sighed a deep down sigh as she took her seat in the leather chair near Ian's desk, its large wings enveloping her in a protective stance, its nailhead trim forming a bastion about her soul.

She sucked in a hearty breath, her chest heaving as it took on its full force of oxygen and then, with a smooth, almost effortless and benign exhale, she let go of the cleansing air as she waited stoically to hear her husband's news.

"Sir Ian, you have brought me once again to my wits end. Forgive me for saying so, but, I am feeling sincerely strained. There is little more I can tolerate. Please tell me there is n'er more to fear."

Ian studied his wife. The worry lines that crossed her brow gained more prominence this night as though they anticipated taking permanent residence on her face.

"The woman has been under our very noses and there is no telling what tales she has spread about our personal lives. She knows nothing about the travails of Washington life and how the most minute of details can flare briskly into an unstoppable fire of rumor and innuendo!" Ian's voice escalated as he slapped the rolled newspaper against his palm, then threw it with precise aim into Elsbeth's lap catching her quite stunned.

Elsbeth remained seated, though there was little about her countenance that remained still. Her heart beat fast and she could almost hear her bones rattling as she searched her nerves for composure. Ian spun about his desk holding his forehead in brief contemplation, shaking his head and muttering several phrases before his eyes took hold of Elsbeth, her stunned stance maintaining a hold over her.

"Shake it off, woman. Shake it off. We have no time to waste. From henceforth we must take action to stop head-on this woman's agenda." Ian watched Elsbeth as he barked his command while pacing the floor in a traditional path chosen many times before evidenced by the compact variation in the pile of the otherwise lush carpet gracing the hardwood floor of his study.

"Elsbeth, have you heard a word I have said? Speak out woman and let me know you have heard what I have said!" Ian's agitation intensified as he awaited his wife's response.

"Sir Ian," Elsbeth's words came slow and low. "I am shaken by your demeanor and the fact that I find myself sitting with the daily news on my lap which has been thrust at me like a discarded bone. I have absolutely not the slightest idea of whom you speak and, with Arielle abroad, with no word since her departure, you must forgive me if I am less than receptive to playing a guessing game. Please, do not insult my intelligence. You must be forthright. Tell me in short form what so engages your ire this eve."

Ian studied his wife's face. He knew she was a sensible woman and generally took great patience with the tasks at hand. Her comments gave him fodder for thought and he realized he knew of whom he spoke because he had read the Public Notices in the day's Star and she had not. His senses were overtaken by one particular notice and, finding himself so afflicted by it, he realized he commenced railing before Elsbeth was cognizant of the source of his rage. He composed himself and, sitting on the edge of his desk, reached for the newspaper resting atop her lace work.

She watched him, engrossed by the slow motion manner he employed to remove the newspaper and gingerly leaf among its pages to find the notice that had brought his pleasure of reading the daily news to an abrupt halt. She was pleased that her husband sensed her alarm and ceased his gregarious display. He was not always so wont to end a session of outrage, letting his emotions simmer until morn, with grudges held intact for days beyond. But, this night was different and for that Elsbeth was grateful.

Ian opened the newspaper to the classified advertisements where the heading Public Notices presented itself in bold, black letters. He read aloud as Elsbeth followed the written words with her unbelieving eyes:

PUBLIC NOTICES

URGENT
Seeking responsible party or parties.
Any person or persons who may be family or friend
of one Olivia Smithfield is/are requested to contact
Providence Hospital at your earliest dispatch to lay
claim and care for her immediate well-being.

Words were slow to form on Elsbeth's lips. She gave a second reading to the notice, her eyes blurred with disbelief.

"Olivia Smithfield, here in Washington without having called on us at first arrival. How can this be? Her letter clearly indicated that she wanted to meet with us. Why would she come and not let us know? There can be no one else here whom she would contact. But, Providence Hospital? What is the meaning of that? Why would she be there? Her letter did make reference to her ill health. Perhaps she was so stricken upon arrival that she had to seek medical care immediately, yet, even at that, she could have sent word to us that she was hospitalized. Why does none of this make sense?"

"Elsbeth, this Public Notice would never have been posted unless this woman was in dire condition, unable to function on her own behalf. It appears she was able to give her name and nothing more, which, now that I have time to reflect, stands to our advantage. Perhaps she has not had the strength to spread what she claims to know of us since we have not directly been informed by the hospital."

"What will we do, Sir Ian? Whether she has spoken of us or not, the fact remains that if we respond to this notice, we will be associated with this woman in a public way."

"We must assume she has said nothing of us since we have not been summoned. We must go to the hospital and ward off any tales she may be intent on spinning."

"To the hospital? How can we go to the hospital without arousing suspicion that we have some prior association with her?"

"We will say we are friends of a Smithfield family and upon reading the notice in the newspaper, were compelled to find out if this woman was of one and the same family."

"That may seem all and well, but how will we explain our knowledge of her once we are before her with medical staff possibly surrounding us at her bedside?"

"Elsbeth, there are times, and I dare say this is one of them, when we cannot foresee all potential outcomes and must act on our best instincts as we await the final toll, hoping we have proceeded to our best advantage."

Elsbeth's mind became mixed with images of Ian and herself standing before Olivia Smithfield, her body in a stark white shroud, encircled by a field of doctors and nurses uniformly clad in bleached-white garments. The caregivers were standing guard over her person with accusing eyes cast at the two of them as though they were being held up for judgment, that they owed some explanation for their presence in her room. She imagined Olivia Smithfield's face, her fixed eyes staring like dark, icy lumps of discarded coal. Elsbeth shook her head, trying through such agitation to rid herself of the thoughts and images that bounded about her mind. *Why can things not be simpler?* She questioned herself as she continued to prepare, through a mental dress rehearsal, for the visit she knew her husband would have them make to Providence. *Providence, the benevolent guidance of God or nature. How ironic.* Elsbeth mused silently.

She wondered how she would garner even one ounce of sleep with such mighty burdens of thought holding countenance over her.

How she wished they could dash off to the hospital now and save themselves the hours of doubt and denial that lay ahead in anticipation of their face-to-face encounter with Miss Smithfield. *What could she know and why did she feel so exceptionally compelled to discuss with us something that happened a score of years before? She should let the sleeping past remain dormant. Her visit will do nothing but harm to our family.* Elsbeth sensed the dread deep down as though it seeped into her marrow, causing her to recoil as her bones and muscles nearly atrophied in response to impending doom. *Shake it off. I must shake these sensations off.* Elsbeth counseled herself, looking at her husband who had made his way to the bar fully refreshed with claret, brandy and scotch.

"May I pour a nightcap for you Lady Hargrove? A sip or two of scotch may help settle the turmoil that wretches our souls this eve."

Ian set two glasses forward as he steadied himself with one arm on the mahogany bar, the other on the crystal decanter generously supplied with the deep amber potion.

"Oh, Sir Ian. Why is it that you think filling one's veins with intoxicants is the solution to the events that meet us this day?"

"My darling, Elsbeth. The events remain the events. There can be nary little change in them, however, you and I, on the other hand, may alter how these events effect us at this very moment by taking advantage of the liquid refreshment that lays quite openly before us."

"With all due respect, Ian, we must keep our faculties about us. We will be best with heads that are clear thinking and unaltered."

"If you, my dear, feel your head is clear and unaltered as we speak, then by all means forego a friendly drink with me."

"I am merely stating that it seems unwarranted to indulge excessively."

"One drink is hardly in excess though, I cannot promise what might be consumed pending the outcome of this woman's bantering," Ian pronounced while he poured an over-ample serving of scotch that sloshed over the rim of the knobby crystal glass and onto his fingertips.

He lifted the glass in a high salute. The sticky liquid that slipped off the rim and down the sides of the glass was ignored by him as he took a hardy second sip before extending a glass of claret to his wife.

"Here my dear. No harm can come from one glass.

"The glass is not my concern. It is that within the glass that concerns me."

"Well, I can suggest nothing more to you except that you drink what is in your hand to steady your nerves. This seems no time for temperance. Consider it a nightcap of sorts so you may go off to slumber, ready on the 'morrow to face the devil knows what!"

Elsbeth took the glass from Ian partly in compliance and part-ly to quell the butterflies that danced about her abdomen. She was never as inclined as was her husband to succumb to drink as a means to salvation. In fact, she had witnessed several occa-sions when Ian needed to be rescued from the very potion that he thought would provide escape from the excesses of the day.

In a slow siphon, she took a cautious draw of liquid from her glass. The warm, red wine passed through her lips with ease and over her tongue, its heady bouquet coating her taste buds as it made its way down her throat, warming her torso and coursing through her veins.

Ian was correct. He knew her all too well. She needed some-thing to file away the edginess that chiseled its way all about her. She heaved a hardy sigh and set her glass on the desk's rich brown leather inset bordered with an embossed gilded edge.

"Finish the wine, Elsbeth. Gulp it down sending the demons with it!"

"I fear we may be creating our own demons, Sir Ian, or at the very least enhancing the authority they have over us. They may not be sent away but come at us full force. We must not weaken our stance by allowing this jewel of a liquid to consume us and render us incapable of facing the harshest news."

Elsbeth nearly sang out her plea as her voice ascended a scale, then her lips came in unison with the edge of the stemware. She took another sip, this one more lingering than the previous and looked at Ian who was fully replenishing his glass with another round of scotch.

"My dear, in my years at the colliery there have been, as you are aware, conflicts not easily resolved where emotions run high and much is at risk. My success has been built upon a foundation of perseverance reinforced by long-term plans that must be in place so day-to-day efforts support those long-term goals. We are in the midst of a conflict, at a critical crossroad, and how we aim our course will determine the outcome at the end of our journey."

"Of what course do you speak?"

"Why, the course we have been invited to set out upon by Olivia Smithfield. It remains uncharted at best, thus we must proceed with due caution while working from our long-term plan."

"Sir Ian, how can we develop a long-term plan where Miss Smithfield is concerned when we have no more than a hazy clarity regarding why she desires an audience with us?"

"Elsbeth, Elsbeth, Elsbeth. I am a very successful businessman and I pride myself on that fact. I will not attempt any bandaged-style solutions to this situation. We must devise a plan in order to proceed. I have to know, and must have a long-term plan. Tell me Elsbeth, what do you see as the long-term plan?"

"Long-term plan, long-term plan. You are making my mind spin. You are not conducting a council meeting, we are talking about our daughter's well-being. This is a matter of humanity, not a matter of your being satisfied as a businessman that there is a long-term plan you may present at a meeting to remain in your company's annals for fiscal review!"

"I am going to have to end this conversation right here, right now, if we do not devise a plan." Ian's words became more adamant and equally more slurred.

"This is no time for the burdensome weight of stubbornness to raise its ugly head. We gain nothing by such conversation and, I dare say, Arielle becomes the victim of our squabbling. May we detain such thoughts of master plans until we meet with Miss

Smithfield and review her dialogue with us? We should have more insight on the 'morrow. You have oft, on more than one occasion, said anything done in haste has unintended consequences. Please, Ian?" Elsbeth stroked her husband's shoulder as she had her say, then laid her head against the same spot, closing her eyes, praying for an amenable response.

Quite contrary to the norm, Ian made no immediate reaction. He seemed to enjoy taking in the moment as Elsbeth's warmth and calm soothed the anger and uncertainty stirred in him by reading the Public Notice. He cocked his head down, his nose resting atop her neatly coifed strands of hair, their graying-brown mix sweetly scented by the rose water wash she rinsed daily through her thick tresses. The scent was as recognizable as the backward slanting script of her signature. *Moments such as these are too few,* Ian reflected.

The mutual thought merged in space as the two held their pose with nothing more than their breaths and heartbeats competing with the lovely silence. Ian placed his glass on his desk and put both of his arms about his wife's waist. He drew her closer against him, feeling calmed and comforted by her nearness. He rubbed her back, stroking back and forth at first, then his touches took on a circular motion. Elsbeth responded to his loving touch by placing a tighter grip on his waist, then, lifting her head from his shoulder, she looked past the graying growth atop his upper lip and gazed directly into his eyes. Shifting her eyes side-to-side in their sockets, she searched her husband's eyes that earlier, having been consumed with such rage now seemed content. She placed her left hand on his chest, moving upwardly along the buttons that fastened his waistcoat then settled on the knot in his silk tie. Wiggling the knot in a slow, fondling fashion, her adept fingers loosened the hold it had on his neck, allowing his shirt collar to fall free from his skin. Elsbeth kept a grip on his tie as she used it for leverage in concert with the tips of her toes to lift herself up to his face.

He removed one hand from her waist raising it to stroke the full length of the side of her face. His fingers came to rest on the bottom of her chin as he tilted her face up toward him. He studied her classic looks, the bone structure of her well-defined face, bright eyes with ample lengthy lashes, delicately arched brows, a regal nose, and full lips. Elsbeth stared as Ian took roving inventory of her face and she of his. He could be so gruff yet, she saw none of that now. This was the Ian she stood by through the most tumultuous times and the most dear. He provided for her and sought her well-being though sometimes at the price of her nerves. She had learned to adjust to his ways, not changing her basic principles, just not bringing them to the forefront on some occasions.

Once again, Ian stroked her face, then ran his fingers across her lips. Elsbeth moved her lips and opened them just barely enough to let the tip of her tongue slip out to glide over their surface, tasting the essence of his fingers and lightly moistening her lips with her warm saliva. He watched the smooth glide of her tongue and gazed upon the resulting gloss glistening as it beckoned him. At once, his lips came down on hers as sure fitting as the proper poles of a magnet. Her lips welcomed his as the contact and pressure of their pulsating lips engaged them in pacifying euphoria. His moist kisses moved about her face and down her neck, sending tantalizing ripples throughout her torso causing a familiar warmth to form in the recesses of her loins. Ian drew her even tighter against him, his manly bulge coming up against her in full arousal. Elsbeth felt swept away, her mind free of any litter the outside world cared to spew. She answered Ian's call with hungry kisses and groping hands as the two shed each layer of their garments. Feigning no fear of discovery by household staff, the two cast aside the scourges of the day and made, sweet, passionate love on the study floor among the rumpled and strewn classified pages of The Washington Star.

Elsbeth's glances Ian's direction over her morning tea were a reserved blend of succulence and shyness. It had been some time since they had partaken of the carnal pleasures shared by husband and wife. She felt the titillating sensations of her younger days, last night's caresses and resulting climax having called forth scenes from their early married years. Elsbeth waited for Ian to look up and catch the lingering glow emanating from her face but, he was intently back to business, using his pen to make hastily etched notations on a large white notepad. He cleared his throat several times and occasionally scratched through a portion of his writing, shaking his head just prior to the strikeouts he dealt to the written words with his pen.

"Ian."

"Not just yet, Elsbeth, I must keep my concentration."

"But."

"Not just yet, I said. Be patient woman," his words spilled out falling sharp against Elsbeth's ears.

She knew better than to attempt any additional interruption to the fervor he demonstrated with the pen and paper. Obviously, his passion for her was short-lived. Elsbeth took in her thoughts and replayed them in her mind. Her merry mood shifted, causing a heavy curtain to fall over her good spirits. Had she a mirror before her, she would have instantly seen the alteration in her expression from one of pleasure to one of dissatisfaction. *Oh, he can be so abominable. He tries my last nerve!* The anger stirring throughout her body at his dismissal of their conversation brought her to thoughts of dramatically pushing her chair away from the table, standing abruptly, pouncing her boot firmly against the carpet, and exiting the room in a huff. She knew such behavior on her part would gain her nothing. Ian would simply hold an interminable grudge against her and never share the details of the draft he crafted. She needed to know how he intended to proceed, how *they* would proceed, in the pursuit of answers to Miss Smithfield's letter and surprising arrival in Washington.

She tossed about her options, deciding to take another sip of tea, hoping the mild stimulant would warm her soul and soothe her nerves.

"Ah, huh, we have a plan," Ian announced as he put the final touch on the paper that held his attention.

"Elsbeth, have you heard, me? We now have a plan. Are you going to respond?"

"Oh, I see. Your all-consuming companionship with your notepad has ceased and you now desire companionship with me. Perhaps I am too focused on my morning victuals to find any curiosity with the work that has so involved you at our dining table this morn."

"Elsbeth, cast your sensitivities aside. I must review this plan with you before we head to Providence."

She knew her emotions were getting the best of her. Of course, she was curious about 'the plan' but, she was also hoping that the pleasures of last eve would have had some staying power and softening effect on Ian. Why was he a man of such clear vision where business was concerned, yet so out of focus in relation to her feelings? She knew she would never have the answer to that question, so she might as well listen and show interest in his plan.

She put her teacup down in the security of its saucer and, clasping her hands together, she rested them on the linen covered tabletop and lent her full attention to her husband.

"Please, sire, let me hear 'the plan.'"

Ian, satisfied to finally have her attention, ignored the edgy tone in his wife's voice as he lifted the notepad and shifted his eyeglasses to read aloud his strategy.

"We, upon arrival at Providence, will show the Public Notice to the head nurse and," Ian's sentence was cut off by Elsbeth.

"The Public Notice may be somewhat in disrepair having been consumed by somewhat more than reading last eve," Elsbeth interjected, her playfulness returning, hoping to glean a warm, visual stroke from her husband.

Ian looked up from the notepad and over the rim of his glasses. He caught the playful expression on his wife's face that drew a half smile. Elsbeth softly smiled in return and allowed Ian to continue his reading of 'the plan.'

"As I was saying. Once we have presented the Public Notice, we will say we are responding because we know a Smithfield family and want to err on the side of caution, that we would feel remiss if we ignored this public plea for assistance."

"And you think our sensitivities toward this 'public plea' as you call it, will assure us an entrance to Miss Smithfield's hospital room?" Elsbeth queried, still feeling quite insecure, not knowing what her future held.

"Elsbeth, we have gone 'round about this before. Assurances are the product of the Devil. I have no crystal ball to guide me. This is a risk we must take and, I dare say, one we can afford to lose. We know nothing of Miss Smithfield. For all we know, she wants to share information with us that shall never reach our Arielle's ears. And, with Arielle away, we can determine her intent, act on it quickly, send her on her way, and be none the worse for it."

"Ian, I wish I shared your optimism. Forgive my reticence. This subject captures my mind and disables my tongue. I too, want nothing more than to bring an end to the turmoil this woman has spun yet, I am severely uncertain about my ability to confront her. Such is the task of far stronger souls than myself."

"And that my dear, is the reason I shall be fully at your side during our approach and subsequent visit to Miss Smithfield. Fear makes a feeble guide and you must shield yourself from it. With a strong resolve at your core, you can summon the strength from within to carry you successfully through this challenging time. Come, my dear. Get your wrap and we will be off to set our plan in motion," Ian concluded, reaching his hand out to signal her it was time to go.

Elsbeth stood upon Ian's signal and with a degree of reluctance, walked to the foyer where she donned her coat, hat and gloves, familiar trappings providing comfort for the unfamiliar to come.

E lsbeth approached the concrete steps with trepidation, feeling moderately weak in her knees as she moved her legs forward to take the first riser up to Providence's entrance. Her boots balked at the coarse texture of the upper landing. She shuffled her feet and fought the urge to bolt back to their carriage and be quickly on her way to the security of her home. Ian took her arm, softly forcing her forward with every determination to see the job through. He pushed on the hefty dual doors with thick glass inserts, opening the portal full-wide for their entry. Both were taken back by the heady smell of ammonia wafting about the halls, masking the essence of infection and bodily fluids. The aromas lingered despite vigorous efforts by two maintenance personnel busily scrubbing the sheets of white linoleum that ran through the halls and rooms.

Ian cleared his throat, motioning to Elsbeth to move in the direction of the front desk. As they approached, a rather dour woman looked up from her desktop, then glanced down again making no further eye contact until Ian spoke.

"Excuse me, madam. We have come as the result of a notification and..."

Before Ian's sentence had been completed, the graying woman in full nurses' regalia made two severe marks with her pen across the short stack of papers resting before her and gave a glance toward a notebook laying on the top right corner of her desk.

"You'll need to sign yourselves in," the white-haired maven flatly ordered with no more warmth in her voice than the center of a once hot biscuit forgotten in a cold lunch pail.

Elsbeth tugged at Ian's coat sleeve with as little motion as possible to avoid alerting the nurse to her action. She had hoped they would not have to give their names. Remaining anonymous was of extreme importance.

"Madam, if I may explain..."

Again, Ian's sentence was cut to the quick as the stout woman repeated what were becoming droning words.

"You will need to sign yourselves in."

"Yes, madam. We will do so, just as you say, as soon as you give us cause to do so," Ian's words came quickly with just enough confusion mixed among them to summon a reaction from the plump old bird.

She narrowed her eyes in a questioning squint as she readied herself to challenge the willing opponent before her. Her lips moved to one side as her facial muscles pulled them back in a smirk, and, moderately nodding her head, she looked Ian straight in the eyes.

"Your 'cause to do so', as you put it, falls into the category of hospital policy and, as an officer of that policy, I must insist that you comply!"

"We will be graciously ready to comply if you are willing, as an officer of policy, to hear our plight, for without your voice in our matter we may well need to be on our way."

"How might my voice serve you?"

Ian hoped his perseverance would garner him a dialogue with the human balustrade blocking his advance to Miss Smithfield's room. He was determined to engage her in sufficient conversation to distract her from the visitor's log and thus keep his name from public view.

"Your voice, madam, is obviously one of authority and prudent judgment of character. Had you not such qualities, you never would have been placed in a position of such high regard. It is to our great benefit that our paths cross this day so we may both reflect on how crucial we are to each other's plight."

The hefty matron cleared her throat and, in dubious fashion, studied the face and demeanor of the one before her who seemed to possess an endless reserve of words. For her, the night had been long and she was in spare humor to delay a moment longer with this one so intent on avoiding her first rule of signing-in.

"My only plight this morn comes from the distress I suffer at your tongue, which, at its flapping, detains you from doing that which you must."

"We much prefer to see to Olivia's well-being than dally about with the formality of signing-in. Please tell us how she is. What is her condition? What progress is she making? We are so concerned for her we must see to her best interests. Please keep us not a moment longer from her bedside, we implore you."

Elsbeth watched the matron bristle as Ian's last words commanded her to action. She found herself rubbing the smooth, satin finish of her gloves, seeking the most ready source for something to calm her nerves and distract her from the outburst she could see brewing in the nurse's being. The matron placed her large, puffy hands on the desk top for support to raise herself out of her chair. Her face had reddened, she was prepared for battle, and Ian was her enemy. Elsbeth kept her eyes on Ian who took a healthy step back as the nurse, now at her full height, leaned forward and spoke in a very commanding tone.

"You, sir, may not speak another word in this hospital. This is a place of care and healing and you will NOT compromise the policies or mission of this institution. You insist you are here for the well-being of one Olivia Smithfield, yet you refuse to follow hospital policy and in so doing put others at risk."

The nurse turned her attention to Elsbeth, keeping her body firmly planted toward Ian, lest he make any further verbal advance her way.

"Madam, you have had little say in this matter. I can tell you that Doctor Lovering has insisted that, in the patient's best interest, only members of Miss Smithfield's family may enter her room. If you have proof of such relation, please present it at this time or I will have to insist that you both be on your way."

"I can only say that my husband and I received a letter from Miss Smithfield asking us to meet with her. We were in that process when we read the Public Notice that placed her here. We will only be a moment with her. If you will please allow us to see her," Elsbeth's words trailed off in a kind, pleading manner as she awaited a verdict from the head nurse.

"You appreciate, I am sure, the fact that I must follow the rules, and you have yet to show proof that you are related to the patient. At this time, I must ask you to remove yourselves from the hospital unless you are in need of care yourselves."

Elsbeth was surprised that Ian remained mute. She knew however, that he did not want to make more of a scene than he already had, or possibly be recognized by another visitor to the place. It had been their good fortune that no one had shared the space since their arrival except the distant workers cleaning the floors. Elsbeth was feeling the need of care and thinking that another moment with this woman might find her cascading to the floor like a withered flower. *Oh, how I hope Ian will say his 'good day' and move on.* She looked his way, still diligently rubbing her gloves, their smooth satin finish taking the brunt of her worry.

Ian looked at Elsbeth and again at the nurse. He thought about the point of his mission and the current failure of his plan. He would need to leave this place now. His usual manipulation of people and events was falling against a formidable rival. Other than the impossible notion of racing through the hospital's halls to locate Miss Smithfield's room, he truly had no alternative but to vacate the place and return at another time -- a time when this head nurse was not on duty. He turned to Elsbeth, took her arm and moved toward the hospital's exit doors.

"Good day, madam. My wife and I came in good will and will leave in the same verve. Please tell Miss Smithfield that the couple she hoped to share some news with was here asking about her. She knows where to find us." Ian spoke his final words to the nurse confident this would not be his final visit to the halls of Providence hospital.

Chapter Sixteen

May 1897
London, England

Olivia Smithfield was a slight woman and, for her, time and infirmity had not been kind. Her illness had taken its toll and dramatically underscored her fragile state. Her white hair, dusted with patches of silvery gray, echoed her parchment white skin. Her body was surrounded in a rippling sea of cloud-white sheets that granted her an ethereal air. Arthritis had distorted her joints and made them appear as fleshy twigs.

The bony fingers of her right hand clutched the rolled edges of her over sheet's top cuff in a seeming death grip. She was a ghastly sight, one that would ward off visitors if any came to call, but visitors were non-existent. She had spent a lifetime maintaining a close-knit circle comprised of her immediate family. Now, only one remained. She hoped, at all costs, to avoid any inquiry from the realm outside her walls, but her troubled conscience and time's impatience were altering the rules of her safe haven.

She breathed in disinterested breaths. They appeared to softly rock her body as oxygen drew its way up her throat into the back of her mouth, causing her chin to tremor. As air moved up through her nostrils, then naturally moved out, she was put to peace until the next breath came to stroke her body, causing the whole laborious process to repeat itself yet again.

Her mind strayed to thoughts of the course upon which she elected to sail her self-directed ship. The end of her journey was fast approaching with the revelation that, at best, she had operated her life with a misguided map whose representations not only charted a poor plan for herself, but for others as well. If she indeed was captain of a fool's ship, so be it. There would be no turning back. The past could not be undone, however, with her last breaths, she hoped to right her ship and stave off the waves of disaster threatening to turn it and her final words asunder.

She heard the tingle of a bell, its sound muffled amid the sleep-like trance dulling her senses. The sound came again, equally as muted, like a clapper going against its metal confinement but never making a strike of any notable force. There was a shuffling sound against the darkly stained and scuffed floorboards and the dull thud of footsteps descending stairs. Beatrice, her caregiver, had responded to the uncommon intrusion into her dull den of quiescence.

Olivia could hear voices, muffled to be sure, their distance from her and the effects of her weakened state made the utterances anything but clear. She could discern the sex of the voices. The visiting voice was that of a woman. Olivia tried to rouse herself, to force her eyes open to make sense of the sounds that seemed so beyond her reach. Everything was drifting away. She felt as though her weary body held no more significance than a withered leaf cast off by nature's cycle. She rolled her head from side-to-side trying to gain the strength to attempt to open her eyes again, but her efforts failed.

Beatrice was taking some time at the door. It appeared she was engaging in a verbal exchange. Olivia could hear her distinctive, husky voice. When she would go silent, another unknown female voice could be heard. Olivia heard the door close. There were the sounds again. Footsteps were coming together, mounting the staircase and approaching the doorway of the room she feared would be the place of her last breath.

The footsteps were much closer now, coming through the small entryway to her room. Footsteps, numerous footsteps, she was sure of it. She had been mistaken, for there were more footfalls than those attributed to one woman and Beatrice. There was a third pair of feet coming along the hallway heading in her direction. As the final pair of footsteps became louder with their approach to her room, she attempted to lift her head from her pillow.

"Miss Smithfield, mum. You 'ave two visitors, ladies they are. I 'ave told 'em, mum that yer in no condition for visitors, but they 'ave come ta see ye none the same. I'll stay with ye, mum. If the company's too much fer ye, ye just squeeze me 'and and I'll escort them from yer room. This first one 'ere's told me 'er name is Pennybacker and 'er friend is Fielding. They say it's important that they speak with ye, mum, or I wouldn't of let 'em call on ye."

Olivia lifted her chin as Beatrice spoke. It was as though the orchestrated movement of her chin signaled her comprehension of Beatrice's words. She took several breaths and, though shallow, they formed a force within her body causing her chest to heave upward. Beatrice took her hand in hers and, feeling no squeeze, looked at Miss Pennybacker to proceed.

"Good morning, Miss Smithfield. We regret coming to call under such circumstances. My assistant, Miss Fielding, and I have been retained in response to a letter sent from your residence to America. The document recently drafted by you came to our attention. It is with the utmost care that we deliver this notification and ourselves to you. We beseech you, on behalf of our client, to exercise extreme prudence in this matter. If you will allow me, I will read the contents of a letter received by a Sir Ian Hargrove, closed with a salutation by one of the same name as yourself, Olivia Smithfield.

Morgan shifted the crisp parchment among her able digits, unfolding the page to its full length, making every word legible for her reading.

"Uh, hum." Morgan cleared her throat, ready to go about the task at hand even though the woman before her appeared unable to sustain a friendly social call, much less endure a matter of business.

Morgan read through every word of Olivia's letter, pausing ever so briefly at the line reading, 'one such occasion involved the birth of your daughter.' Morgan observed Olivia's face. Her eyes were wide shut, her eyebrows raised, her eyeballs rolled about underneath their lids as though they were searching to speak. Her lips, parched from exhaustive mouth breathing and days in bed, nearly cracked as she spread them to speak. Her tongue, lapping at the dry roof of her mouth, had difficulty projecting itself forward to communicate as it laid nestled in a lump toward the back of her throat. Slowly, with every degree of purpose, her tongue came upon the inside edge of her lower teeth. She took a heavy chested breath, arching her back in an attempt to raise her shoulders from the bed and with great effort she spoke.

"Ari..." her body slumped back against the sheets that had become her second skin. She slowly wiggled her head side-to-side, searching again, her eyeballs rolling back and forth under the thin, wrinkled skin of her upper lids.

"She is clearly trying to tell us of Miss Har..." Agnes stated, breaking the momentary silence only to catch a stern eye from Morgan who snipped her last word in half.

"Agnes, remember your duties here which include, first and foremost, the anonymity of our client. We additionally, in point of fact, do not want to put words in her mouth."

"Oh, my. I stand corrected. I was just..."

Morgan stopped Agnes in mid-sentence with a raised eyebrow and solid stare that conveyed, without a doubt, her desire for Agnes to be seen and not heard. Peepers broke his silence by strutting about his cage with wild abandon. His fitful prance was startling in its spontaneity. All of a sudden, in a winged flurry, he created a miniature dust storm comprised of feathers and feed that consumed his closely confined arena nearly obliterating him from view. Morgan, who was not easily distracted, was finding Peepers' behavior bordering on annoying. She cut her eyes to Agnes. Agnes took Morgan's stare as much as a reprimand for herself as their winged companion.

"Our time here is limited and we must make the most of it. Just keep your hand busy at note taking. And, Peepers, you will be advised to settle yourself. Now, Miss Smithfield, I must continue by asking what you know of the birth of Sir Ian Hargrove's child."

"Excuse, me mum, but can't ye be thinkin' that me dear Miss Smithfield is not in the best way for ye to be talkin' to 'er now?" Beatrice questioned with a worried look across her wrinkle-laden forehead.

"Miss, uh, Beatrice, it is, I must urge you to allow me to continue. My attempts here are pragmatic, that is, I must get to the truth, and the only person who can validate that truth for me lays before us now. Bear with me. It is most practical for me to continue my questioning. Miss Smithfield has started this thing in motion and obviously wants to see some result before her condition further deteriorates. We must move forward so her wishes will be assuaged."

Morgan again cast an eye at Agnes who dutifully continued taking notes. Agnes was always duly impressed with Morgan's ability to make her actions appear as though they were as much to the benefit of the person before her as to herself. By suggesting that she needed to satisfy the wishes of Miss Smithfield, she was providing comfort and trust that theirs was a common goal.

Agnes looked down at Olivia's frail form thinking how she pitied the poor soul for waiting to tell her hidden story until the hands of the reaper were all but on her shoulders guiding her away for eternity. *Why had she not put this information in writing? Delaying like this, until her final hours, puts at risk the chance that her story might never be told. Perhaps the information was too bold to be told in any form. Perhaps the writing of it was too painful or she feared any written document would fall upon the wrong eyes. Perhaps, she felt the only way for the information to be heard was from her own lips in her own time and now, as she prepared to be called away, God had set a timetable for the telling. Whatever her reasoning,* Agnes thought, *I still pity her and will opt not to query Morgan with any of my thoughts.* As she observed Miss Smithfield's shallow breaths, she felt decidedly less sure that this woman would ever find the strength to share her tale.

"That said, we must give Miss Smithfield a moment to collect her energy so she may respond with useful answers to the questions that must be asked," Morgan continued, showing some compassion for the woman's condition.

Morgan was not well pleased that Olivia Smithfield was so weak. She anticipated from the letter that she would be well minded enough to let her story flow with the added impetus that her poor health was chasing away her optimum days.

The rapid advance of her condition was an unanticipated finding for Morgan, leaving her a bit short of temper. She had hoped to have more ready news for Miss Hargrove that would not only find Morgan best pleased, but would also boost her reputation for speed and accuracy. She knew however, that good things take time and, unless this 'key witness' for her case expired, she felt sure she would obtain her desired results to the satisfaction of all involved. *I must exercise care and patience so this woman, so key to the events of a score and two years ago, will not step through death's door before releasing herself from the guilt of days gone before.*

Morgan paced a bit, her feet performing a three-step pattern, first right then left then right again, with a pivot onto the left and a momentary pause steadying herself, transferring her weight to reverse direction leading right again. The process was repeated four times as Morgan's motions removed her from Miss Smithfield's bedside, then brought her back again, all the while periodically jingling a handful of coins in her frockcoat.

Standing was beginning to take its toll on Agnes. She discreetly shifted her weight from one leg to the other not wanting to draw unwarranted attention from Morgan or ruffle the feathers of Peepers. Morgan turned so her body was directly aimed at Olivia's bedside.

"Would ye like ta 'ave a seat mum? I mean, ye's welcome to a seat even though I'm thinkin' it's best fer ye to let Miss Smithfield 'ave some peace. She's really quite weak an' it won't be doin' 'er no good to use what strength she's got remainin' tryin' to talk with ye," Beatrice spoke with raspy sincerity as Morgan contemplated her next actions.

Of course the woman was weak. However, she was the one who raised the banner of suspicion about Miss Hargrove's birth and only she could provide closure for her client. Her task might be deemed distasteful, but it was her task to complete, distasteful or not.

"Miss Smithfield. Please remain with us a few moments more. We have come because you summoned us through your letter. Our visit is of your doing. Now, it is imperative upon you to explain, or clarify, the nature of the events to which you have referred. You have tapped our curiosity. We want to know what it is you wish for us to know."

All eyes were on Olivia as her breaths became increasingly labored and her eyelids fluttered until they were fully closed. Her lips fell open and her mouth breathing became heavy. Her lips came together and her tongue made a brief survey over her lower lip. Her lips came fully together again, then opened to reveal a sound reminiscent of an earlier uttering, "Ari..."

Morgan, Agnes, Beatrice, and even Peepers leaned in full attention to capture Olivia's vocalizations only to be thwarted by her mouth breathing, renewed in full earnest. Her breaths seemed to come from deep inside a cavernous space that took full charge of her. Morgan attempted another question determined to make precious every conscious minute she had with Miss Smithfield, but there was no chance of bringing Olivia back from the well into which she descended that found her flailing for strength and fighting for her life.

Chapter Seventeen

London, England

*H*umph. *So, this is where the snitch lives,* thought Alexandra as she gazed upon the stately brownstone that housed the flat of Miss Olivia Smithfield.

"A rather comely place for a snitch." She repeated the epithet aloud, smiling as she found pleasure in its repeating.

She eyed the lengthy staircase as she prepared to lift her skirt's hem off the pavement to make her ascent to the landing level and ring the manual bell to gain entry. An uncommon hesitation overtook her, causing her to draw back her foot.

Review. Review. The words teeter-tottered against the walls of her skull as she attempted to bring into balance the dialogue she intended to conduct with Miss Smithfield.

I have come this far and heaven knows I, of all people, deserve to learn the truth about dear, sweet, limp as a dishrag, dull, old, Arielle Hargrove. Oh, how the very slip of her name across my tongue casts a bitter taste. How William can find any delight from her is of grave mystery to me. But, all that attraction will end soon enough. Miss Smithfield is the needed key. She, and she alone, will unleash the door behind which festers years of secrecy. Another grin crept across Alexandra's face like a cat well placated by a lap of warm milk. She nearly let out a purr as she aimed her eyes upward and began her ascent.

Upon each footfall, her enthusiasm for her mission winded her more than the quantity of stairs themselves. She caught her breath, steadied herself and reached toward the large, round, brass knocker.

Tarnished, like dear, dear Arielle's reputation, oh, a pity. She cast a sarcastic grin at the knocker whose surface was indeed in need of a good rubbing.

As she lifted its ring away from its base and began to click it down upon itself, the door moved inward ever so slightly. Alexandra was surprised and drew her hand back, waiting momentarily for someone on the other side to proceed with its full opening. One hinge creaked as though asserting a feeble warning to proceed with caution. Alexandra decided she dared not say a word until she discovered who or what was on the opposite side of the door. With the toe of her booted foot she inched the door back, bit by bit, until it was open full wide for her to review what lay beyond. Dense darkness permeated the space. Her opening of the door provided the only intrusion of daylight into what could be designated a tomb of darkness. The pitch black that enveloped her as her eyes squinted to adjust from natural to subdued light did not undo Alexandra. In fact, the severely silent void made her eerily curious about her next encounter.

As her eyes established a comfortable union with the space, she could discern that heavy draperies covered all the windows keeping any remnant of light from the first floor rooms. A narrow strip of light emanated from the second floor, throwing a beam like a scepter down the staircase. Its tip zeroed in on Alexandra's boots, granting a magical cast to the high gloss of their ebony leather. She looked down at her glistening boots then followed the beam's path as it directed her to come along. Lifting the skirt of her gown, she made her way up the steeply pitched flight like an assured alley cat placing its paws firmly with pads full down. In a proud prance of cocksure intent, she paused only briefly for the sounds of any life form.

"Could the old girl be dead?" Alexandra quickly questioned, and as rapidly dismissed the thought.

Though there was a delicate air of mustiness she attributed to the quaint furnishings and closeted state of the flat, there was no wretched smell of decay. No, she was certain there was no body rotting away, not that the sordid sight of deteriorating human flesh would turn her intestines. She was tougher than that. Her only regret would be having missed the opportunity to meet with Olivia Smithfield, befriend her, and learn firsthand the nature of the great secret she held.

Alexandra continued her ray drawn path to the doorway where the beam found its origin. As she peered inside, she observed that one panel of the drapery on a far window had been pulled to the side. It hung in a haphazard fashion against a decorative bracket that exposed a narrow flash of natural light. The light shown upon a wall of framed watercolor paintings of roses in shades of deep and pastel pinks. What the room lacked in light was indeed most generous in furnishings with a lady's vanity, large dresser, chest, and several over-stuffed chairs, their down cushions in need of a good plumping. Brocades and English chintzes played off one another in texture and variety. Fabric prints, some large, some small in scale, complemented one another in a warm, hand-me-down style, like it had taken years to accumulate the pieces to achieve the perfect mix.

Alexandra's eyes continued their compass about the room until they came upon the bed. There was an ivory matelassé coverlet neatly folded and stacked across the bed's foot. Her eyes swept along the upper surface of the dense cotton blankets overlaying the bed sheets where she could barely make out any form until, at the uppermost portion of the bed, she was taken back by the sudden representation of a head. The blankets, appearing nearly flat upon the bed, held no indication that a body laid among them.

"My, my," Alexandra mused, "She is indeed in a very bad way. There is barely any body remaining for her flesh to cling."

She observed the coarse gray hair surrounding the cap of Olivia's skull. It was lackluster and resembled the dull pallor of her equally chalk-like skin. At immediate glance it was impossible to discern that any life remained with the form. If indeed she had expired, it had happened with immediacy and absolutely just prior to her arrival.

Alexandra inched her way closer to the bed, her eyes taking direct aim on Olivia's abdomen to note whether there was any movement up and down from her lungs to her diaphragm. Seeing no visible exercise in that region, her eyes advanced to Olivia's face where her eyelids lay fully lapsed across her eyes. Not even the flicker of a reflex showed itself. Suddenly, Olivia's mouth fell open in a ghastly gape with her tongue's tip protruding to the inner edge of her lower lip. It remained resting there as she took a heavy-hearted breath. A slowly drawn snore reverberated through the back of her throat as she was drawn deep into the chasms of sleep. She repeated the process of deeply drawn breaths accompanied with more guttural sounds from her open mouth.

"Be…a…" Her darkly distant sounds attempted to form a voice that she willed anyone within range to interpret.

"Be…a..," the sound came again, lacking the identical force of the first.

Alexandra observed Olivia's struggles to speak with new respect for the woman.

The snitch is really having a difficult time. She is so frail, and, yet trying with all her might to get someone's attention. Alexandra bounced her thoughts around her head, still firmly focused on Olivia's every motion. *Perhaps I should answer her call, but I have no inkling to whom she is referring.* At that moment, Olivia's eyes shot open like some pain of realization had taken over her reflexes. She looked at the figure before her, squinting, then forcing wide her eyes, trying to bring into full focus the image at her bedside.

"Ari…" her voice trailed away and her eyes willingly joined the departure.

A shallow puff of air grazed the surface of her tongue and flowed across her lower lip into the limbo of space.

Ari. Ari. She thinks I am Miss Hargrove. How sweet is that? Alexandra's entire being was met with an adrenaline rush as she reiterated Olivia's repetitive sounds. *Ari, Ari, Ari,* Alexandra repeated under her breath in a nasty snarl with the muscles of her upper lip raised to one side, her head gyrating in resentful acknowledgment. *Why am I constantly subjecting myself to such humiliation? Why have I not learned to avoid these entanglements at all costs? This woman, these people, Arielle Hargrove, the whole lot of them, are of no importance to me, yet their countenance consumes my days!* Alexandra railed and looked prepared to pitch a fit as the names and faces of the entire clan of souls consuming her every waking thought passed through her mind's eye.

I will be damned if they can think they will have the best of me! No! I shall prevail! Alexandra's body shouted, her voice in subdued silence as she leaned closer to Olivia's bedside.

"Well, good morning. There you are. I had hoped you would be well fit to receive me. So, you think I am Miss Hargrove. What do you know of her? Tell me now. Let me hear from your lips what there is to tell of Miss Hargrove. Speak woman, before you have no strength left to fill your lungs with air. I have little time and no patience for your weakness. What secrets do you harbor about Miss Hargrove?"

Alexandra was supremely disappointed to find Olivia Smithfield in such a state of demise. She sincerely thought her visit would produce just enough fodder to be the undoing of Arielle. *No,* she thought, *this is not going well at all. How am I to inform William, to turn his head from the low-life he seems so smitten with if this woman remains tight-lipped? I must forge a new plan. Or, better yet, yes, perhaps it is to my best advantage to agree with her!*

"I *am* Miss Hargrove, your precious Arielle." *Oh yes, she is a fine looking girl, if you care for that look!* Alexandra's eyes nearly popped from her head as she stared at Olivia's face and felt a bad taste come into her mouth as she imagined having to savor being Arielle Hargrove.

Olivia's eyes garnered the fortitude to open sufficiently to view the face before her. She felt woozy, as though the simplest motion might send her world catapulting beyond control. She stared and stared and searched the eyes of the one whose face hovered before her like an ominous cloud ready to dump an unwelcome forecast across her face. *Who is this one so intent on joining my bedside? Who is this one joining in the ritual of my inevitable death? Who is this one who holds no resemblance to anyone I hold dear? Who is this one?*

Alexandra held her vigilant stance waiting for Olivia to become more aware so she could question her about the letter. But, Olivia retreated into a far distant fog, her eyes barely catching the light of day as her lids slid in heavy cloak over her pupils blocking any vision, good or evil, from her sight.

She held the very last image to come before her eyes as clearly as if she had been healthy and strong and fully alert. She knew what she saw before her and she knew it was neither her caregiver nor the one in whose birth she had participated. *No,* she thought. *This is not Beatrice, nor is it my dear Ari...Oh, I can stand no more.* Her thoughts drifted to the far recesses of her mind and, as she slipped further and further into sleep, her visitor, hearing sounds from the stairwell, slipped further and further into the recesses of the room.

⌒

B eatrice came along quickly. She had not wanted to leave her charge for long, but necessities called her out for the briefest period of time. When she left, Olivia was deep in sleep. She expected to find her just the same. She realized how the weight of her morning caregiving had rested in her bones as she lifted her legs, step upon step, up the staircase to the Smithfield flat. Her legs felt heavier with each tread. The balls of her feet rested only momentarily upon the surface of the steps leading to her daily wage. She had grown fond of Miss Smithfield and felt more akin to her than not, knowing she was nearly all but alone. How sad it must be to come to this moment in time when the healthy shell of a person is thwarted by the failure of the body's inner workings.

She reached the landing just outside Olivia's door and peered in to see if she was just as she had left her. She lay passive, a low rise in her chest verified for Beatrice that she was still one with this world. She put her parcel down and carefully rustled through its interior until she came upon a small tube of salve. Pearson's Lip Balm was her destination. Olivia's lips were so dry. It seemed that with every sip of water her lips became even less hydrated. Beatrice hoped Pearson's would do the trick. Untwisting the cap, she squeezed a healthy dab of the clear, gooey gel onto her index finger and ever so lightly spread it across the folds of her charge's lips. Olivia barely stirred during the process, only moving slightly to root her lips toward the source of the motion bringing comfort to her mouth.

Beatrice turned away, removing a handkerchief from her sleeve's cuff to wipe the goo from her finger. As she did, she heard a low rumbling sound and turned back to Olivia to ascertain how hungry she might be. Her appetite had been non-existent and her gastric sound had become subdued to the point of oblivion. It was not unusual to hear such darting gurgling sounds from her, so Beatrice interpreted them as reminiscent of signs of life and forti-tude. *Thank the Lord, my prayers are bein' answered,* Beatrice thought to herself as the sounds came again with renewed strength. It was as though they emanated from a place beyond Olivia's immediate realm, as though thrown with a ventriloquist's skill to the far cor-ner of the room. Beatrice listened intently and watched for any sign of restlessness from Olivia. She remained sedately ensconced in a dream-like trance. The sounds came again, as distant as their predecessors. Beatrice turned and searched the room with her eyes, her pupils straining to see in the half-dark space lit only by an isolated beam of daylight. Again, the sounds. Gastrointestinal eruptions that could not be controlled by shear force of will.

Alexandra sucked in her abdomen until it was nearly concave yet she could not thwart the sounds popping 'round and 'round within the walls of her stomach. She held her hands across her mid-section hoping to subdue to silence the inner workings of her body, but they were guided by an uncontrollable power with a life all their own. She had tucked herself into a far corner of Olivia's bedroom near a dormer window where the ceiling line angled down forcing her to duck her head and lower herself to fit the awkward space. She was partially hidden by a tall, narrow lingerie chest whose height left only enough space between its top surface and the ceiling for a few small picture frames to adorn it. She watched as Beatrice looked about, squinting toward the source of the disturbance breaking the deathly quiet of the room.

The natural beam of light shifted across the room's expanse as the earth's axis sent the sun on a luminous mission of revelation. Alexandra's image was brought into full view. She tried to draw herself back however, she had no further place to go. Beatrice gasped as the form of the flaxen-haired woman came before her. She was stunned to find someone lurking in the room and was having difficulty forming words. Once formed, she was less than certain she could project the words beyond her lips. A shudder sent itself through her core, then to the far edges of her extremities. She wanted to cry out, to gasp loudly with an assertive show of will but, as the strength to do so boiled within her, she stopped the feverish rush at its simmering point to keep from disturbing the one whose care came under her guard. In a tone as hushed as one could deliver having been scared witless, Beatrice kept her eyes on the face of the flaxen-haired intruder, held her body tightly composed to itself, and began to speak.

"What business have you here?" Beatrice's words came forward in a directly crisp, protective style.

Alexandra felt prepared for the inquiry knowing she might be found out at some point. She began to step forward. Beatrice held her arm away from her body with her hand up, palm forward, in a halting signal causing Alexandra to delay her advance in mid-step. She rested against the lingerie chest for support as she readied herself to respond.

"Stay where you are missy, and answer the question that's been posed you." Beatrice maintained her firm, hushed tone, looking away briefly to monitor Olivia's response. Seeing that she remained in a deep sleep, Beatrice returned her attention to their intruder.

Alexandra was not best pleased to be talked to in such a tone however, since she was truly cornered, she had little option but to give some explanation for her unwanted presence.

"Speak up, will you. But, mind you, I'll not be 'avin' you upset Miss Smithfield."

Ah, so this sickly soul is the snitch herself. I was right. Alexandra's thoughts scurried around in her brain like a loose ball of mercury as she prepared to spew her toxic response to Beatrice's inquiries.

"I suggest you speak to me in a proper tone, as I am due." Alexandra cocked her head in a flare of intimidation as she placed her feet firmly side-by-side and, having stepped beyond the angled eve, drew her body up to full stature.

"Ye, a perfect stranger, trespass and want the likes o' me to talk civilly to the likes o' ye? Why, what would be the sense in that? Ye are the one who needs to be offering up an explanation and, mind ye, it had better be now." Beatrice was having no part of the bold tone being cast her way.

"How daft can you be? I have come here to see my mother."

"Yer mother, is it?"

"Yes, my dear mum. We have been parted for a lifetime and only recently has she made me aware of our relationship. I, of course, had to come. Her letter to me was so sad and full of devotion. She told me she was ill but, oh my, I was under no impression that her health was indeed so grave. Oh, my, this is just devastating to behold." Alexandra tried to make her eyes well with tears to add validity to her fiction but, none came, so she winced and looked down, taking one hand over her eyebrows to cover both of her eyes in false dismay, shaking her head in disbelief.

"Yer mum."

"Yes, my mum."

"Next thing ye know ye'll be tellin' me yer, Miss Ari..."
Beatrice's words were cut to the nub by Alexandra's quick retort.

"I am Miss Ari..." Alexandra's words caught in her throat as
Beatrice stood and glared her straight in the face."

"Have you any siblings?"

"Why do you ask?"

"Just askin?"

"In all fairness to my mother, that is, my mum, I am unable to
respond."

"In all fairness, you need to take your leave at once and not return until you have some proof to your story beyond your words."
Beatrice pointed to the doorway leading to the hallway.

"Very well. But, when my mo...um, mum regains consciousness, she will be most displeased that you have treated me with
such discordance and sent me on my way. Heed my words, you
will not be in her good graces." Alexandra walked to the doorway, nodding at Beatrice with her eyebrow raised in a threatening
arch to indicate she had not heard the last from her.

Alexandra turned into the hallway carefully clutching a wad
of her skirt lest she drop the small rectangular frame held captive
among the striped folds of French taffeta. She waited until she
fully descended the stairs and came into the natural light, well out
of Beatrice's view, before she exposed her ill-gotten acquisition.
The sun's glare obliterated the image under the piece of glass
protecting the three by five inch sepia daguerreotype. Alexandra
gave the frame a slight tilt bringing into complete view the subject
in the frame. There before her was the childhood version of the
one she so detested. There before her was, although a wee child,
the one who now drew the attention of her William. There before
her was the one whom she would see ruined if it took her last
breath. There before her was confirmation that Olivia Smithfield
was indeed Arielle's mother. *Yet,* she thought, *whom had she known
to get a photograph of the girl, and why would they have kept his or her
quiet about her? Could it be the likes of Beatrice?* Alexandra queried,
her thoughts turning to the woman who formed a wall of armor

in protective encampment about Olivia. *Of course. She knew I was Arielle. She began to say it and I cut her short. How perfect is this! I must return on the morrow and hope Miss Smithfield is alone. If her caretaker suspected my identity, then I shall have no difficulty convincing the dying twit, Miss Smithfield, that I am her long, lost, sweetie, sweet Arielle. Oh my, things are going much better than I had ever planned!* Alexandra put a skip in her step as she sauntered away with thoughts of tomorrow while the truth of yesterday rested firmly in her clutch.

Chapter Eighteen

S hallow breaths glided along the torso of her weary body. Her mind grasped for the familiar amidst a fog-strewn reservoir of thought that held her persistently captive. The assault to Arielle's brain, suffered weeks before, was not relinquishing its hold on her. During waking moments, her head moved about, her chin lifted up and then drifted left to right, seemingly searching for a proper path, a way out of the quagmire, a beacon home. With her back to the doorway, she faced a wall that bore a window no larger than one offered to a jailed prisoner. She lay on her side, swaddled in crisp white sheets that just skimmed her chin.

Earlier, a nurse on her morning rounds directed a surname at her that would have normally escaped her attention, but of late, the name was foremost in her vocabulary. *Smithfield.* A name that was foreign, yet familiar, distant, yet ever present in her muddled mind.

Smithfield, a quite common name, yet it resonated with Arielle. "Smithfield. Miss Smithfield." *Yes. The nurse seems to be calling to someone.*

"Miss Smithfield?"

It was an appellation about which she felt less than comfortable, but she could barely remember why.

"Miss Smithfield?"

"Yes?" The response came with simple affirmation yet, so faintly through Arielle's lips, it went unheard.

As the word departed from her mouth, simultaneously her head began rocking ever so slightly in search of the source of the one calling out to verify her identity. *Who is this one calling to label me, to call me from my tunnel of darkness?* She felt herself spiraling deeper and deeper into a fog.

"Smithfield? Miss Smithfield?" The voice was different. It sounded like a man. She heard the words in rapid-fire repetition, pelting her consciousness like tiny pinpricks that made her wince against their assault. Was there no escape from this name, this woman, this unknown person who kept reoccurring in her life?

"Yes?" Arielle's breathy response searched for something familiar, "Yes?" and sadly again, she went unheard.

Voices. Voices. What are they saying? It is all so garbled, so unclear. Who are they? Are they speaking to me? Where are they? Where am I? Mum? Mum, is it you? Here I am. See. Come, Mum, come. I need you. Father? No, not Father. But, who? It is a man. A kind man. Oh, I know this man. Help me. Here I am. See. I have to go. Help me. No. Oh, no. Where is he going? Oh, his voice is faint. Was he here? Is he gone? Oh, his voice has gone. I am alone. Where did they go? Come back. Please, come back. Help me.

Just as he turned to leave the room, Arielle's head made a half turn toward the doorway of the room as sleep came calling, beckoning her to seek answers in elusive slumber. Her body felt too weak to allay the din of muffled voices echoing about her. She momentarily succumbed to slumber and was drawn away from the world she was trying so desperately to seek. *This must be a temporary cocoon,* she mused as her body became restless and began to stir.

The rustling of sheets and creaks from the springs of the iron bed stopped William in mid-stride. He hesitated, wondering if he imagined the sounds. He hoped his visit would provoke some response from Miss Smithfield. He shook his head, indicating the doubt he cast over what he thought he heard. Doctor Lovering had made arrangements with the hospital's administrator for William Clay to visit his patient. He had queried William to petition the courts to be Miss Smithfield's Guardian ad Litem since she was incapable of representing herself. His guardianship as her court appointed special advocate would safeguard her interests.

The rustling and creaking became repeated. William did an about-face and was totally stunned by the sight his eyes witnessed. Raven hair, twisted about in matted ropes, framed a porcelain white face -- a face whose beautiful image he carried in his mind's eye. He would never forget her radiance, nor would he want to. Here, in this godforsaken state, lusterless, alone and detached from all that was familiar, her beauty and grace called to him. A lump caught in his throat and he swallowed hard to clear it. His hand went against his chest to catch his heart that began to race as though beating time for two. He took in several breaths, drawing on his reserve of calm, hoping some could be found. His briefcase fell from his clutch, its thud to the polished linoleum floor receiving only a moderate jerk response from him for his concentration was cued directly to the fragile form before him.

He took steps, cautious steps, to her bedside. His proximity to her confirmed not only her identity, but also his distress with that confirmation. Deep concern overtook his face. He wanted to speak, but was rendered momentarily mute. His eyes studied her face and searched every detail of her bone structure, muscle and flesh, for a sign that all would be well, that her fog would lift, that the Miss Hargrove he had begun to know and wished to know so well would rejoin their dance on earth.

Her eyes were tightly closed, fringed by lush India ink lashes. Her skin held no color beyond a tinge of pink on her right cheek, an imprint forced upon it from the pressure of her face having rested upon the pillow. He wanted to touch her, to reassure her, to comfort her. He did not know if he dared do so, yet, he questioned if he dared not.

Propriety aside, his heart spoke and he rested the able fingers of his right hand on her brow. He let them rest there, lingering, allowing the warmth of his fingertips to fuse like a healing pulse into the distant recesses of her mind. She shuddered and her eyes moved under her lids as though she wanted to respond. He stroked her forehead, softly, gently, tracing back and forth, back and forth with the pads of his fingers as though reading her thoughts in a loving Braille. She shuddered again, this time with a sigh. William removed his hand from her forehead and rested the tips of his fingers against her right cheek. He put his thumb and forefinger on either side of her earlobe, exerting a soft squeeze. Her temperature felt normal and he felt a modicum of relief for that. He brought his hands to rest upon the bedrail, its cold, rigid, harshness was in strong contrast to the soft warmth and beauty of the dear patient he observed.

William wanted to speak to her, to say her name, but wrestled with the ramifications of doing so. His actions, had they any effect at all, might startle or embarrass her, responses he would never want to impose or evoke. Yet, his time alone with her was limited. Soon, the nurses would make rounds and, once he revealed her identity, her family would surround her, he would have no place there. But, inform everyone he must. Miss Smithfield, bed 1A, was nonexistent. All, on their best authority, were trying to reach someone who had never been there. Here lay someone very real to him and growing dearer.

A myriad of scenes flipped through his mind as he recalled their first meeting on a cold and dreary evening when her pallor resembled the one he now witnessed. He recalled the sensation that overtook him as he swept her off the pavement raging with precipitation and held her wet, delicate body against his. He had not anticipated the emotion that came over him as their cheeks brushed one against the other, flesh to flesh. Then, there was the visit, the visit to her home to return a lost belonging. He felt that had not gone well. Her response to him was less than he had hoped. He felt that perhaps he had not presented himself, or the purpose of his visit, well. When he spotted her on the streetcar, he was sure impressions had gone awry with Alexandra on his arm. Miss Hargrove, of course, would have no idea that he was duty-bound to escort Alexandra and answer to her whims. It would take an act of Congress to release him from the responsibility and debt he felt he owed Alexandra's father in his father's name.

He shook his head in an attempt to negate and dismiss the complications that threatened his attraction to and admiration for Arielle. *Why must life become so complicated? When next I see Alexandra, I must explain our relationship.* William knew that would be no simple task. Alexandra was more stubborn than a rejected mule. She would not be put off easily. His soul was not for sale for it now solely belonged to Arielle. He hoped she would soon be aware and feel the same depth of commitment that captured his inner being.

His thoughts came back full circle to the matters at hand. *First, I will make a call on Doc Lovering and explain my find. It might be best if he delivers the news to the Hargroves. Next, I will tell Aunt Emma. What a blow this news will be.* He knew she was very fond of Arielle and would do anything in her power to help the young woman. All planning aside, Arielle's recovery was in the hands of God, and William prayed that God would shine his healing light and favor on her. William also knew he could not leave Providence Hospital without trying to communicate with her.

With his hands firmly grasping the bedrail, he leaned forward so his face paralleled hers. His deep blue eyes were transfixed on her. As the atmosphere of the room encircled them, the space became their space, the moment became their moment. Nothing else existed in this world of two. Two bodies, two minds, two hearts. Nothing could penetrate the focus he held on Arielle. As he stood and stared, he began to speak.

"Miss Hargrove?" William's voice was smooth and comforting. "Miss Hargrove?"

William tried not to show his disappointment when she failed to respond. He was typically not easily discouraged and this moment would be no exception.

"Miss Hargrove?"

Still, no response, no reaction, no flicker of recognition.

"Miss Hargrove? It is William Clay. I have come to help you."

Arielle lifted her chin ever so slightly, turning her head to the left as though reaching toward the sound. His voice was muffled, garbled, but she knew it was he. *That voice again. That voice, for Miss Smith...*Arielle's mind began to swoop away then come back.

"Miss Hargrove, William Clay here."

There it is, that voice again. Oh, so far away. Come back. Come back to me.

"Miss Hargrove?"

*There. That is it. Yes. Hello. Yes. Where are you? Stay with me. Come closer. Oh, I cannot hear you. Please stay...*Arielle's brain was letting her linger longer.

"Miss Hargrove, I," William stopped himself as he observed a change in Arielle's expression. He was certain her lips attempted to form a smile.

"Miss Hargrove, I," William's words again were cut short as the identical expression reoccurred on her face.

William felt so jubilant to see the change in her that without hesitation, he took her hand in his hands and held onto her in a warm clamp. Arielle's eyes rolled back and forth under her closed lids. William rubbed his right hand over the top of hers to encourage the smile to return to her face.

"Miss Hargrove, open your eyes. It is I, William Clay. Please open your eyes for me."

Arielle's indiscriminate searching under closed eyelids continued. William was determined not to tire of the routine he was putting into play to elicit the pleasant, smiling response from

Arielle. *She hears me. I know she hears me.* William was committed to persist and do all in his power to mitigate her suffering.

"Miss Hargrove, let me see your beautiful eyes."

Again, Arielle's expression was pleasant and then, ever so slowly, her eyes formed slits that began opening wider and wider as she welcomed in the light around her. Her eyes shifted side to side in a slow, drugged squint. Her lids opened and closed, opened and closed, as though it took every effort to lift them and keep them in motion. William's adrenaline began to flow and he could barely contain himself. He was so pleased to see her coming alive.

"Miss Hargrove?"

"Yes? What? Yes? Yes…" her voice was faint, her throat dry, she gave a weak cough on her last word.

It had taken every measure of strength for her to respond and, now, her body rebelled. Her lids rolled to a tight close, her lips rested, one against the other, and she fell into deep repose. *Chaos.* She felt inflicted with fragments of chaos that sucked all sense of normalcy from her. She needed to be replenished. Her body tossed side-to-side as her subconscious mind grasped for a vision that would bring her calm. A visit to the garden never failed to bring her back to her true self. The serenity of the garden would form a soothing balm smothering the privation seeking to overcome her. Hedges and trees formed a green mantle that wrapped her in secluded comfort. She was in her own paradise. Blankets of rare and exotic orchids and ewes dominated the understory resulting in a colorful and densely textured carpet. She felt the rhythm of the plantings, flowers and shrubs alike, co-existing as nature's harmonic blend and their graceful adagio lulled and lured her to a renewed calm. Was it her dream that soothed her? She tried hard to decipher the images and sensations occurring as she slept.

William took the fragile hand he still held in his care and lifted it from the bed sheets. Bending sufficiently to make contact with her delicate flesh, he placed his lips upon the sweet nectar of her skin, not to draw sustenance, but to brand an eternity of healing strength he prayed would nurture and sustain her for the hours and days of recovery ahead. He took a breath, but only after taking one for her.

Chapter Nineteen

Alexandra questioned how she allowed herself to become caught up in the 'good deed expedition' that was Emma's pet project. Certainly it was not of her choosing, nor would it ever be. *Father told me compromise in life was a necessity. Oh, why must I always be plagued with making compromises!*

Agreeing to accompany Emma on her mission of mercy to First Street was a weak moment on her part indeed. William was so insistent about her going and, she did need to pull his mind away from questioning her antics. He was growing too close to her plan to ruin Arielle, seeming to keep a keen eye and ear on every move and word. *Slums, slums, slums, and more slums!* A stone's throw from the Capitol, the sights and smells nauseated Alexandra. She would as soon hold her head over a retched garbage pail and inhale the germs and vermin within. Purdy's Court, just thirty-five yards from the Peace Monument, was a human trash receptacle in her eyes. *Peace. How could that word be used to name a monument surrounding the likes of this? Could peace be so swarthy and disgusting? Absolutely disgusting! How could anyone live like this?*

To Alexandra the men and women inhabiting Purdy's Court, many Italian immigrants, were like large rats living among decaying walls and decaying windows smeared with feces on their decaying world. *Putrid. The entire place is putrid. There is not the remotest corner free of the smell of poverty. Imagine. The auspices of the Woman's Home Missionary Society oversee this place. What a name for a group of white gloved, garden club, society doyennes of domesticity. These women are from the finest homes in Washington, the political elite. Why would they elect to taint themselves with the likes of these...vermin? Oh, a hasty retreat seems the only viable option. William will forgive me. Heaven knows he always does. He might be disappointed, but, what of it, he will get past it, he will have no other option.*

Alexandra watched Emma as she entered the hovel that housed the Brown family. There was no Mister Brown, for he had vacated the family several years prior when wanderlust came calling on him. He left the misses home with four mouths to feed. The four mouths had grown to six. It seems the misses was intent on spending her lonely nights in the company of any man who could pleasure her. Her needs were simple enough. A friendly smoke with the strike of a match to ignite very limited conversation was usually all that was needed before a secluded place could be found for Mae Brown and any male suitor to roll about in a horizontal position. After a brief period of time spent rubbing their bodies one upon the other like a bar of Fels-Naptha against a stubborn stain, their union resulted in an extended period of heavy breathing and a loud moan from Mrs. Brown as the innermost core of her female sensitivities succumbed to the stiff male organ that found its way inside her. The up and down, in and out, lubricated motion, cast titillating sensations throughout her body, arching her back, extending her nipples, reddening her chest, and causing her to imagine realms far beyond the dingy walls she inhabited. She closed her eyes and let every beautiful, ecstatic moment descend upon her. Her crotch pulsated, aching for more, but having shot his wad, her suitor, well sated until their next turn in the sack, withdrew his member and rolled off on his merry way. Shortly, as the calendar clocked by, she was no longer 'on the rag' and her tummy blossomed with new life inside. So it went for many of her lot. The burden of boredom, the crisis of confidence, and the pity of poverty doomed her to an inevitable cycle that Emma and her fellow doyennes hoped to reverse. *Reverse?* Alexandra mused. *How could she reverse something so dramatically askew and inbred? These people were impregnable to any efforts at reversal. For them, this is their way of life.* As far as Alexandra was concerned, the denizens of the alleys had made their beds and could lie in them.

Ugh. Alexandra grumbled to herself as she lifted her skirt's hem properly high enough to prevent the crusty scum of daily existence from touching its edge. She sashayed with careful aplomb lest the fabric of her bouffant ensemble brush against any manner of the unsightly environmental carnage before her. *Ugh.* Alexandra felt like shrieking as a four-legged creature, a rat, skittered across the alley, its tail sweeping behind, making a pen's width clearing on the ground's surface, ironically offering the only fresh path Alexandra had witnessed since her arrival. She drew her body back its full length, stretching a few more inches taller as her spine extended in a show of resolute force. Though she felt like retreating, she was determined to stay the course just to show William and his dear aunt that she could and would.

Emma greeted Mae with a pleasant smile and a gentle touch of her hands. *Oomph!* Alexandra thought, while her outer self maintained a pleasant expression. She forced herself to look glad to be there. *Touch that woman, I should say NOT!* Alexandra's mind screamed with clenched teeth. It was bad enough she was surrounded by the impurities of these despicable people. She was most assuredly NOT going to allow any of their vileness to make contact with her pure skin. *Oh, get me out of here.* Her words raged in her head as she watched Emma move to take a seat offered by Mae's outstretched hand. Mae extended the identical offer to Alexandra.

"Thank you, but I will remain standing. It seems I have been sitting most of the day. It will do me good to stand for a while," Alexandra explained with a sweet as sugar smile, not because she feared Mrs. Brown would take insult from her decline, but because she was determined to have a secure excuse not to sit on the pilled, stained and worn-to-near-thread-bare chair that Mrs. Brown ultimately took a seat upon.

Alexandra discreetly pulled her tussie-mussie to her nose as Emma and Mae spoke, attempting to thwart the noxious airborne odors from traveling through her nostrils into the depths of her sinus passages. *There is no telling what disease with which we will become afflicted just keeping the same unwholesome space with these people. William owes me a great debt for stepping into this pitiful pit of wasted humanity!*

Emma had a leather satchel filled to the top with staples that were everyday pantry items for her but were luxuries for the Browns. Thomas had carried the bag in from the carriage, its heft more than Emma dared lift. Sacks of sugar, flour, oats and potatoes comprised much of the weighty cargo. A crock of butter, blocks of cheese and jugs of milk rounded out the load. Emma had Cook bake two dozen cookies that she brought along, always sure to enter with something to sweeten the home.

"My, Miz Willard, you are so kind. I can't tell you how much your kindness means to me and my family," Mae shared while her sad, tired eyes came alive in a dance as they moved in happy rhythm from Emma's face to the bountiful provisions and back again.

"My dear, I know they will be put to good use. You have new mouths to feed so I am certain you will not squander these resources, or, should I add, I trust you will not."

"Oh, no Miz Willard. You can be sure of that."

Alexandra had watched and listened to all she could bear. The smells were overcoming her level of tolerance. Smells. As far as she was concerned, she smelled a rat. A big, fat, pregnant rat who needed to have her womanhood cut out instead of receiving another hand-out lest she bring anymore scum-sucking, dirty little rug rats into the world to drain the good from society. Alexandra blew air through her closed mouth making her lips reverberate like those of an exhaling horse. Both Emma and Mae looked up as her sudden show of exasperation drew their attention.

"Oh, pardon me. A flea, I mean, a fly, buzzed across my face. I was attempting to frighten it away. I am afraid I am causing a ruckus. Please excuse me a moment. I am just going to step outside."

"Stay near, my dear. You do not want to wander far." Emma cast a warning her way as subtly as possible, not wanting to offend Mrs. Brown.

Alexandra stepped from the dank, dusty confines of the Brown's ramshackle dwelling onto the narrow sidewalk that put her immediately at the curb. She looked left and right, but could not locate Thomas or the carriage that would assure her retreat from what she guaranteed would be her first and last visit to Purdy's Court.

The day's heat and humidity had squandered itself all over the city with no sign of relent even though dusk was setting in. The evening pall, a mix of haze and the hour, drew emphasis to the virtual absence of anything green. *Of course,* thought Alexandra. *Other than a rich pile of fertile manure, and the fertile Mae Brown, there is no reason for any life form to exist on this ground. These people cannot tend to their own needs, how could they ever nurture the smallest sprout?*

She continued her search for the carriage, walking along the narrow sidewalk spotted with spit, debris and decay. She turned into an alleyway hoping to find the tethered horse and carriage. Several mangy dogs paraded by, nonplused by the fetid conditions, seeming to bask proudly as they pursued their next acquisitions. As she made her way into the alley's depths, she became aware of the sound of footfalls keeping pace with her own. *Thank God, Thomas has found me,* she surmised as she stopped and turned only to find a burly man, three times her size, right upon her skirt tail. She froze, waiting for him to pass by but he remained fixed.

She took a step to move beyond him but he blocked her body forming a sweaty, human wall of fear. Again, she lifted her foot to shift away, anything to maneuver herself into a position to flee. A lustful smile came over his burnished lips revealing a grin short of several teeth -- those remaining were tarnished like deeply tea-stained linen. They were alone.

The alley was deadly quiet and, for once, so was Alexandra. She was stunned by his presence and chilled by his manner. His short, thick fingers reached out and grabbed her toward him, the stubble on his face rubbing like coarse sandpaper against her fair skin. She bristled and winced at the unpleasant sensation as she freed her arms to flail at him. Quickly, he caught her arms up, pulling her more tightly against his hard torso, sucking the breath from her lungs, rendering her speechless. With one arm, he kept her locked in a firm grip. She was trapped without air. He brought his other arm down along her throat, watching her face all the while, seeming to gain pleasure from her displeasure. His callused hand maintained its unbroken journey along her collarbone down to her breasts. He paused, taking his time, fondling her breast, attempting to move away the fabric on her bodice to reveal her flesh. He rubbed over and over her nipple until she thought it would be raw from the rigorous stroking of the corset against her skin. A hardness came between them shocking Alexandra into retained silence as she felt a heat come over her in a crimson wave of panic, not passion. Her body began to go limp as his hands left her chest and the two of them collapsed to the cobblestones. Resting to her side, he brought his hand under her skirt's layers, rubbing his fingers against her pantaloons, digging their stubby tips into the soft cushion between her legs. As he reached toward her waist to tear away the linen obstructing his next show of force, Alexandra, having been given back the use of her throat by the collapse to the ground, let out a shrill, ear-piercing scream. Her wailing siren startled her attacker who thought he had muted his prey. He removed his hand from her most private parts, lifting it to cover her mouth. She turned her head and rolled her body to the side, letting another equally chilling scream sound her warning and signal for help. Despite her ample resources, they could not keep her from harm's way.

Upon the initial scream, Mae Brown and Emma halted their conversation, sitting at attention with ears cocked to interpret what they had heard. The second scream brought them to their feet. Simultaneously, they exited to the street looking for the source of the plea. Several neighbors exited their spaces and joined them in the search. Emma saw her carriage stopped at the opening to an alley, the tethering straps dragging on the macadam, only the carriage's brake and the horse's good will keeping both in place. What had been a search party of several grew into a crowd with Emma and Mae leading the swarm of gawkers toward the alley. The pack moved along the sidewalk in massed rows, in shoulder-to-shoulder unison, driven by their common objective, then down into the belly of the alley. There they saw a tall, thin, negro man hovering over a small, blond woman who was flipping about on the pavement in the fashion of a prize flounder who had every intention of escaping the filleting knife's edge.

The crowd became incensed, the adrenaline of several men converging into robust action as they rushed forward to save the victim from her attacker. Emma gasped and shouted to bring them to a halt, but she went unheard. The men were nearly upon the man they viewed with hatred. They would not allow a man of his kind to touch the woman who lay helplessly in the alleyway under his domineering stature. Again, Emma called out in earnest, her voice a faraway drone in the din created by the rush of angry men. At once, the group pulled the negro up, grabbing his legs and arms in stock-like strongholds, subduing any immediate use of his limbs. Emma's legs felt like preserves without sufficient pectin. She ambled forward, pushing away at shoulders with desperate politeness, making her way to a spot where she would be heard. As the first blow came from a fixed fist catching Thomas in the pit of his abdomen, rendering him unable to protect himself,

Emma's form made it to the forefront of the anxious crowd and her words came with unrelenting authority.

"Unhand that man this instant!"

Her voice rang out in a desperate peel to rescue Thomas. Another fist, ready to lay claim to Thomas' rib cage, was thwarted in mid air by her words.

"Unhand him, I say!"

The men turned toward the source of the request, wanting to know more before relinquishing the hold held on the man they saw attacking the young woman.

"I say, unhand him. This is my man servant, my employee, this is Thomas."

"Mam, he may be who you say he is, but he was attacking this lady. You heard her screams just the same as us," came the claims from a brawny young buck who kept a firm grip on Thomas.

"I tell you, he had nothing to do with her screams. He is my trusted employee and I insist that you release him at once."

The men eyed each other, not one able to think or act solely, as though the group had formed a brotherhood whose bond could not be broken.

"Alexandra, speak up! Tell them to let Thomas go!" Emma's words were firm with a hefty dose of exasperation lacing her lips.

Alexandra remained still, her eyes closed with arms folded across her chest in corpse repose.

"Alexandra!" Emma shouted, using all of her lungpower to rouse Alexandra to her senses.

There was still no response. Emma moved forward, stepping beyond the border formed of men, women and children who stood in anxious silence waiting to see what would next occur. Emma cast a stern eye toward the men who held back Thomas, then bent down next to Alexandra looking toward Thomas with a reassuring eye.

"Alexandra, answer me! Answer me at once!" Emma sent her verbal order, placing her hands on Alexandra's to unclasp them.

"Oh, let me be! Can you not see how humiliated I am?" Alexandra whined as she shooed away Emma's attentions.

Appreciating Alexandra's state of dishonor, but needing to defend Thomas' honor, Emma continued her plea to the obstinate girl.

"Alexandra, there will be time for you to tell me what happened, but, for the moment, you must tell these men that Thomas was here to help you or harm may come to him."

"Thomas, Thomas, Thomas. Can you think only of him? Is anyone concerned with my welfare? Here I am, practically ruined, battered, bruised and in need of a thorough scrubbing to remove the adulterations to which I have been subjected!"

"Mercy me, Alexandra. You will have my sincere attention as soon as Thomas has been released."

"Oh, yes, release him, let him go!"

Alexandra's words seemed genuinely sarcastic prompting the men to keep their hold on Thomas. Emma decided she must use another tactic with Alexandra to elicit the response the men needed to hear to let Thomas go.

"Alexandra, did someone attack you?"

"My Lord, yes! Of course! Are you a ninny? Why else would I lay prostrate like this on this filthy pavement?"

"Alexandra, was Thomas the one who attacked you?"

"He was chasing the man who attacked me, of course! Are you all so lame that you cannot see the obvious?"

On her words, the men released Thomas from their clutches. He stood, shaken, yet relieved to be free of their bondage. Emma disregarded Alexandra's poor manners, knowing the girl had a short fuse and that her mouth was prone to house a sharp tongue, particularly if she felt threatened by any person, place or thing. It seemed therefore, there was nary an occasion when caustic words would not find the opportunity to fly from her lips.

"You see you have taken actions based on assumption alone. We must all take heed and remember that much responsibility lies in the eye of the beholder. Come dear. Let me help you to the carriage," Emma comforted as she assisted Alexandra into a sitting position.

As Emma got Alexandra up to her feet, she turned to the group who had been Thomas' captors.

"You have heard, there is someone in your community who has committed a crime against this dear young woman and it behooves us all to find him so he may not repeat his offensive behavior. I must ask you all, did anyone see the man and recognize him?"

"We were here alone. I am the one who saw him and I dare say it will be a cold day in h..." Alexandra's words were snipped by Emma.

"My dear, I know you will give us a complete description. However, since I assume you do not know the man, nor had you seen him before, you cannot provide his name or place of residence. Perhaps someone here saw him and recognized him."

"Miz Willard."

"Yes, Thomas."

"Is it okays if I's speak Mam?"

"Most certainly, what is it?"

"When I heard Miz Whitaker screamin' I 'ad just pulled yer carriage up ta the alley. I seen a man down on de groun' wrestlin' with Miz Whitaker soz I's jumped off de carriage and run fast as I could. De man, he seen me comin' an' he jumped up an' ran all de way ta de end of de alley. I can't tell you much about 'im 'cept he was 'bout six feet tall an' kinda heavy. He run wid a limp, kinda draggin' 'is left leg an' he was wearin' dark brown pants an' a brown shirt wid a rip on de left sleeve at de elbow."

"Thomas, thank you for that and for your efforts to protect Miss Whitaker. We can all be thankful to Thomas for saving us from a situation that could have been much worse."

"Much worse! My word, I have been mauled and..."

"Alexandra, this has been very trying. Let me get you to Providence. You need to be seen by a doctor. Mae, I will see you another day. And, gentlemen please apprise me as soon as you have specific information about this man. He must be dealt with by the authorities."

Assisted by Thomas, Emma and Alexandra boarded the carriage. Alexandra paused before she took her last step into the coach. She turned and looked back down the dingy alleyway nestled under the spreading shadows formed by the umbrella of the Capitol dome. At that moment, she mentally declared she was done, over, finished with humanitarianism. In a single visit, she had given all to charity she would ever give.

Chapter Twenty

D octor Lovering's cart passed through the hazy city streets toward his destination. As a prelude to the heat and humidity to come, a gauzy gray screen had formed that filtered the landscape. It was as though an artist's implement brushed the air to soften and mute the crisp edges of the trees, the buildings, and all else within its spectrum.

He reviewed the address William Clay had given him and looked at the numbers on the large brownstone before him. *This be it*, he announced as he readied himself to leave his cart. He approached the steps of the manse with enthusiastic caution. Sudden news, whether good or bad, could propagate an alarming effect on any listener. He took the final step to the door and, using the knocker, announced his presence.

"Good morning, sir." Fiona dipped in a half curtsy as she drew back the door.

The doctor stepped beyond the vestibule into the front hallway and offered his card to the freckled-faced girl with the Irish brogue. He knew many of Washington's elite, having examined more of them than they would ever care be revealed, but he

232

was not familiar with Sir Ian Hargrove or the rest of his family. William had offered the doctor a summary of specifics regarding the family's head and their tenure in Washington from Wales. William felt it would be best, and more appropriate than coming from him, for the physician to present the news about Arielle to her parents. He surmised they might view him as 'the perfect stranger,' someone new on their scene and not yet a member of their society of trust.

Fiona examined the card and examined the man before her -- a cursory check she performed more out of curiosity than security.

"I'll summon the misses. Wait here, if ye don't mind." Fiona pointed to the parlor as she dipped and bobbed, affirming her request as she started off to find Lady Hargrove.

"Wait up. May I inquire, is Sir Ian Hargrove in as well?"

"Aye, aye, if yer sure ye want me to be callin' 'im," Fiona looked at the doctor with a one-eyed squint, raised eyebrow and cocked head.

"And for what cause would I not be sure?" Doctor Lovering returned the same one-eyed squint, raised eyebrow and cocked head reaction to the housekeeper.

Fiona was taken aback. She was used to her comments being dismissed, her thoughts passed over. The doctor's facial expression intimidated her more than she felt it mocked her. She found herself cowering into a deeper curtsy and quickly spun off to find the lord and lady of the manse.

Within moments, Ian and Elsbeth entered the parlor, having approached from opposing areas of the dwelling. The doctor raised himself from the settee, a minimal task considering his short stature. Elsbeth kept to Ian's shadow as he made his way to extend his hand to their visitor.

"Doctor Lovering, I understand." Ian's greeting was firm in voice and handshake.

"I am Sir Ian Hargrove and this is my wife, Lady Hargrove." Ian's firm grip lost its potency and, as he withdrew his hand, his face bore a complexity of emotion.

"Sir, Lady Hargrove, I am the bearer of news. Forgo your worried looks, for it is not bad tidings I set before you but news of hope. For you, it is a day to rejoice in the lost being found."

"Lost? Found? Of whom or what do you speak? Do not speak in riddles my good man, state your purpose," Ian's words came with strong resolve.

"Your daughter, Arielle. I have news of her whereabouts, news of her recovery."

"Arielle? Her whereabouts? Are you mad? Our daughter is under the guardianship of my sister in London. She is on holiday. Collect yourself, sir, lest you find yourself on a fool's errand."

Doctor Lovering was less than humored by Ian's tone. He felt his body become slightly rigid as it tensed-up to do battle, albeit verbally, with the pompous slouch before him.

"The only fool of which I am aware is the one who will not see because his mind's eye is closed, limiting his vision, and, you sir are that fool."

"Why, you have the audacity to enter our home and speak in such a fashion? Tell me, sir, why I should not escort you to the door this very moment?"

"Because, if you do sir, you will be depriving yourself of information and an opportunity."

"Opportunity? What opportunity and what information?"

"The opportunity to know the truth about your daughter."

The doctor's words were so direct, and coalesced with the news of late, that Elsbeth felt faint and sank into a nearby chair, its upholstery cushioning her assent. A sensation of heat overtook her, creeping from her torso up her neck to her chin's edge. A steamy heat and suffocating closeness overcame her. She tugged at the ruffled collar of her blouse attempting to release its encroaching closeness. The double layer of ruffles threatened to choke her. She pulled at the rippling edges of silk to allow any extract of air to seep against her skin and refresh her to normalcy.

Doctor Lovering was instantly at Elsbeth's side. He took her hand, placing his fingers on her wrist to check her elevated pulse.

He was never without the mobile hospital that allowed him to erect a limited triage whenever a crisis of medical distress occurred. His black bag held a score of quick alchemies to treat any minor affliction whether it be of physical or psychological origin. He anticipated an alarmed response from the Hargroves but had not expected Arielle's father to be so arrogant or her mother to be so overwhelmed.

"Please, man, state your purpose. You can see the toll your presence extracts on my wife."

The doctor could also see the tension building in Ian, but was in no way obliged to tell him.

"Your daughter, sir," Doctor Lovering glared at Ian then turned to his wife. "And, if you will allow me, Lady Hargrove, was the victim of a very serious accident. She was rundown by a team of horses several weeks ago." The doctor's words were halted by Elsbeth's gasp.

Ian and the good doctor came upon Elsbeth, one on each side, forming protective pilasters as she swayed in an erratic swoon to the doctor's devastating words. Dizzying vertigo stirred queasiness in her stomach causing her to gulp back what she was afraid would be an uncontrollable need to vomit. Her world became black as total darkness spread across her mind. Her eyes closed tight to stop the motion that so unsettled her.

"Elsbeth," Ian called out to keep her with them.

"Lady Hargrove, bear with me for the news is not grim. Your daughter's condition has seen some improvement."

"Some improvement?" Ian questioned the weak and variable adjective selected by the doctor.

"Your daughter is beginning to exit the trauma she suffered. There was an apparent deep assault on her brain. It has taken some time to heal. As the swelling subsides, she is given to moments of lucidity." Ian interrupted the doctor's explanation.

"My God, man. Why were we not consulted before now? Why in God's name has it taken so long for any word to come to us?"

"If you will let me continue, I will explain what little I know. Miss Hargrove was struck and rendered unconscious. She had no personal belongs to speak of other than a small purse that held only one piece of identification. It was a calling card and on it the name, Olivia Smithfield. The going assumption was that she was she. Her condition offered no option to question her directly. Had we had such access to 'the source' we would most likely not find ourselves in the predicament of today. However, what is is and we must accept that and move on."

The doctor took a much-needed pause to gather his thoughts for the remainder of his delivery while Ian and Elsbeth shared a wide-eyed look of surprise that Arielle had one of Olivia's calling cards in her possession.

"Miss Hargrove's, your daughter's, identity only recently became known when a lawyer friend of mine agreed to visit whom we thought was Miss Smithfield. He came solely to represent her interests due to her weakened state and the fact that no immediate family had come forward to see to Miss Smithfield's well-being."

"A solicitor? A solicitor aided in Arielle's detection?" Elsbeth's words came in a pant as she attempted to regain her composure, opening her eyes full blown as though ready to welcome in all that would be cast through their lenses.

"Yes, Lady Hargrove."

"And this solicitor, this man, how did he know our Arielle?"

"Lady Hargrove, he told me the two of them met under rather stormy circumstances, quite literally in fact, and he introduced her to his aunt," the doctor's words were cut to the quick by Elsbeth's rapid-fire question.

"His aunt? Arielle then met his aunt? When? Who is this man? Name him now."

"William Clay, Esquire, nephew of Emma Willard, widow of the late Horace Willard. He is from fine stock, as any turn of the society pages would tell you, and was extremely dismayed at the revelation that whom we thought was one Olivia Smithfield was none other than your daughter. He came to me quite shaken with the news."

"Hmmm." Elsbeth felt a mysterious release of tension filter through her body. Clay, William Clay. What pleasure the mere mention of his name brought. A relieved smile began to form its upward curve on her lips, until she was brought back full circle to the question of Arielle's actual condition and prognosis.

"Our daughter, how is she now? We must see her." Elsbeth's voice choked as her words caught in her throat and she envisioned her dear Arielle, battered, bruised, lost, alone and forever damaged by her accident.

"She is in quite better stead than was the case some weeks before."

"That tells us little. Please, be more candid in your description," Ian snapped with Elsbeth's lips on his heels ready with the same retort.

Doctor Lovering was not warming to the two before him. He understood their anxieties, yet was feeling less than accommodating, particularly toward Ian whose demeanor fit that of a rakish pit bull. He had, over the years, questioned the practice of medicine and his pursuit to aid and improve the lives of others. His was not an exacting science, but his successes far outweighed any losses. For him that was reward enough. For now, he would put at bay the tension stirred by the two and continue on his course as advocate for Miss Hargrove.

"Your daughter, sir, has moments of lucidity, but those moments are few indeed. She is in a semi-conscious sleep for the majority of her day. She has however called out twice, and on both occasions references were made to you both. We can only pray her progress will continue on a steady course and," he added with a sharp look at the two, "a healthy environment to which she can return after her dismissal from the hospital."

The doctor dealt his words as a reprimand, for the behavior of the two did very little to warm the cockles of his heart. He looked skyward, searching for counsel and grace, fixing his eyes on the coffered ceiling and finding calm in the repetition of the box pattern created by the dark-stained beams. *God I pray,* the doctor began his silent dialogue with his Creator, *that goodness bestows itself on the whole lot of them.*

"We best be on our way," Doctor Lovering urged.

"May I offer passage in our coach?" Elsbeth graciously offered.

"I shall decline your kind offer and proceed to Providence in my cart. I will await your arrival at the hospital and assist with your entry to your daughter's room. The duty nurse can be a force to maneuver. It will be best for me to make introductions to clear your way."

Ian knew exactly about whom he spoke. She would be quite surprised to see him return under the escort of the good doctor.

"Yes. I will be quite pleased to see that duty nurse again," Ian revealed aloud, realizing his slip of tongue.

"Again?" Doctor Lovering queried.

"Again, as we return to visit Arielle as she finds daily progression."

"I see," the doctor replied with a question mark forming as he studied the less than honest expression on Ian's face.

"By the way, this card in your daughter's possession, this Olivia Smithfield. Who is she?"

"That, sir, is a curiosity that will have to wait," Ian said with frigid formality. "We must see to Arielle and we must see to her now.

Chapter Twenty-One

Washington, District of Columbia

Sequestered to rooms for healing, the ill and injured were architects for the serene atmosphere consuming the hallways of Providence as Emma entered with Alexandra, the two having been released to its sterile floors by Thomas. Emma sent him on to William's home with a note requesting her nephew's presence at Providence at his most immediate opportunity. Lest he become alarmed that she had taken ill, Emma prefaced her note with a notation about Alexandra and, 'an unfortunate event of which you should be made aware.'

Alexandra was examined by a doctor who, much to her chagrin, found her, 'none the worse for wear' and suggested a warm bath with Epson salts and a lengthy rest in bed to soothe her bruised body and ego. She curtly excused herself from the doctor's presence and began swirling her skirt about in a tornado-like funnel. As she stormed toward the examining room door, she ran smack-dab into the firm, broad chest of William Clay. Though surprised, the recognition of the one whose torso she gazed upon spread sweetly over her like warm fudge on a stirring spoon. She was more than willing to devour every rich morsel his handsome physique offered until her thoughts took a nasty turn.

Her body bristled as she stepped back, recalling what brought her to the hospital and on whom she placed the ultimate blame. She used her hands to push away from him as though she were casting off an unwanted toy boat by giving it a hearty push down river. But this boat did not buoy or sway, it remained steadfast, eyes stern and focused on its course. Alexandra twisted her body about, then stomped her feet in frustrated defiance at William's demeanor. She expected a warmer reception and knew she deserved it after all she had endured.

"How can you be so mean and hurtful? Oh, look at you looking at me that way! Nobody understands me and I try so hard! Can you not see that I have suffered this day? Can you not see that I..."

William, merely by his gaze, snuffed out her words, forcing them to trail off as he observed Alexandra was unchanged, her vehement nature continued to spew forth. She took her hands, balling them into fists that took aim for his chest. Before her first advance allowed them to pummel upon him, he took both of her fisted hands into his in a vise-like enclosure and, maintaining his firm, yet gentle grip, he looked directly into her raging eyes and spoke with resolute reserve.

"Calm yourself, Alexandra. I know you are very trying." William cleared his throat at the subconscious misstatement.

"That is to say, assuredly, the experiences in Purdy's Court have been most trying. I understand you have been quite shaken but are, by doctor's estimates, physically unharmed and, for that we shall all be thankful. Let's put this behind us. If you wish, my aunt has offered her home to you where she and her staff may look over you. It might bring some comfort to be alongside friends and rest amongst Aunt Emma's tender loving care."

Alexandra felt ready to explode! *No one is taking into account how I feel, how I have been treated, how I have suffered, how I want things to go! Oh, how I want to scream!* She jerked her hands away from

William's clasp with such force, just as he released his grip, that her fists came back hard against her bosom causing her to cough and almost lose her balance.

The series of motions only increased her ire as her sense of control plummeted. It was all about control with Alexandra, and the loss of it sent her into a tornadic tailspin. William appeared to be directly in the course of her rage. She was losing patience, what little she ever had, and she was determined to have him to herself. Aunt Emma might be her key to turn the lock on his heart. Thus far, that key failed to have him beat a path to her door. He was always the gentleman and generally kind to her, but that was far too little. She sensed he felt an urgency of obligation that blocked any wisp of passion from revealing itself. *Oh, how I adore him, his wonderful good looks, and all of his wonderful money.*

Her father had left her well set, but it was William she wanted. He was the best and the ultimate prize she would conquer and have as her own. Yet, she was her own worst enemy for, in her haste to draw him near, her actions repelled him further away.

William looked at her and recalled her father's last words to him before his death. Alexandra was Andrew Whitaker's sole offspring and, though he knew she was far too spoiled to make herself amenable to others, she was the light of his life. On more than one occasion he teased that she was certain to make some man quite miserable someday.

Alexandra was in her teens when her mother died leaving her father to totally dote upon her. She persisted with her arrogant behavior knowing her father would never disclaim her and actually, quite the contrary, he seemed to revel in making excuses for her.

There was the time, shortly after her mother's death, that Alexandra stormed into the middle of a lavish affair her father held for executives of his company, its subsidiaries, and their wives. The gaily-clad guests were engaged in lively conversations over goblets of the senior Whitaker's finest port. Alexandra drew the room to a hush with a startling scream. The guests turned to face the source of the disruption, taking into full view Miss Alexandra Whitaker, encased head to toe in muck-like mud. Her father made his way through the throng of guests to the room's median where his daughter took center court, trembling and spewing mud-soaked epithets. He was quickly at her side, leaning in to quietly inquire about how she came to be in such a state. It seemed she had taken a late evening ride when a sudden storm ensued and her mount slipped, tossing her onto the water soaked terrain. She exhibited a few fitful twists and jerks away from her father's calming hand and ultimately honored his request to leave the room and refresh herself.

After her exit, he looked about the room, smiled at his guests and said, "It seems my darling Alexandra has fallen victim to some mudslinging, of the literal and not verbal stature, and from her horse no less. I trust we would have noticed a pungent aroma in the room had she fallen in stable remnants. But, enough of that, the night is young and we have much to celebrate!"

He signaled the orchestra to resume play and the wait staff to refresh drinks. It was as though Alexandra's storm had rapidly passed into the night leaving no damage against the atmosphere of the evening.

Unfortunately, for Alexandra, her father's doting and placing her at the center of his universe, had rendered her vulnerable to her whims, enabling her to demand attention, both good and bad. Days before he breathed his last breath, he asked to see William alone. Knowing he had forever secured his daughter's financial welfare with his own monies, he laid the burden of Alexandra's happiness upon William.

Now, Providence was her stage. Little did she realize her anger would not soon abate, as she became aware of voices several doors away. A large charge nurse was holding back a man and woman, her arm outstretched, insisting they wait. A small, roundish man came upon the three and at that precise moment, Alexandra heard the name that brought her to her knees.

"Nurse Hildegard, these are the patient's parents. I will vouch for them. You have my word, they are who they say they are and it is in the best interest of our patient, Miss Hargrove, that they see her, and she them." Doctor Lovering motioned to William and Emma.

"Sir Ian and Lady Hargrove, I introduce to you Mr. Clay and Mrs. Willard. Without Mr. Clay, it may have been some time before we realized the true identity of your daughter."

Ian and Elsbeth, still visibly shaken by the events of late, nodded in recognition of the doctor's introduction.

"We thank you, sir," were Ian's simple words as he turned and guided Elsbeth in the path taken by Doctor Lovering.

Alexandra's legs went weak. Her knee joints failed to hold their steady lock and she collapsed to the floor, landing in a kneeling position as though she was prepared to beg or pray. Her sudden cascade to the floor went unnoticed by the group gathered near Miss Hargrove's room. William pretended to ignore the commotion beyond the doorway to her room, though he kept a vigilant eye on Arielle's kinfolk, wanting to join them, to go to her, to take her in his arms and reassure her that she would soon be well so they could begin a life together.

Suddenly, his leg jerked as if the ground tremored with a large serpent attempting to draw him into the earth's chasms. He shook his head to awake from the fantasy he conjured only to again feel the jerking motion. He looked down to find Alexandra clutched to his leg tighter than a kitten to its mother's tit. She was not one to let her feelings be ignored. The expression in her eyes was sincerely pathetic, in fact bordering on mad. He thought most certainly she was about to lose her mind, if it had not already taken its leave.

He knew full well that Arielle would remain confined to Providence for some days ahead. Doctor Lovering assured him he would keep him abreast of her progress. Upon his arrival this day, William had passed her room giving only a glance to her delicate form in the bed. He dared not enter with Alexandra afoot. It was best to focus on her needs and find her situation stabilized. He had no idea Arielle's name would be announced in the corridors for Alexandra to take heed.

As William bent low to cradle Alexandra and bring her up from the floor, Emma approached with both eyelids and brows lifted high as she searched William's face for answers to the questions swirling about her mind.

"William, is it true? Is dear, sweet, Miss Hargrove a patient here? My word, did you know? What has happened? Is she terribly ill? Oh my, why was I not informed?" Emma, as was her nature, was calmly disappointed.

"Aunt Emma."

"Oh, forgive me for not allowing you to answer one question at a time, I am just so gravely concerned."

"Aunt Emma, you see..." William's words were circumvented as Alexandra reared with an aroused roar.

"Remember me? Remember why we are here? Remember what I have suffered? How can either of you find any importance with any topic other than me? Me, me, me! Look at me! I need your full attention!"

Any activity or motion in Providence's corridors came to a steady halt as Alexandra's railings garnered everyone's attention. Sir Ian and Lady Hargrove were not privy to Alexandra's outburst for they had entered their daughter's room having been given permission by Nurse Hildegard who yielded to the doctor's authority. Alexandra's extreme emotion brought forth the methodical and determined footfalls of the nurse who rapidly made her way to the three from whence the commotion came. She was not well pleased.

"This is a house of rest and healing! Must I remind you of yourselves?" The head nurse's words were executed with utmost authority and sincere intimidation.

"We are, of course..." William's words, meant to appease, were stopped short as Doctor Lovering sidled up to the nurse to speak on behalf of the three, two of whom he knew well, and one whom he felt assured he would learn more about, like it or not.

"Let the four of us step over here where we can sit in privacy," Doctor Lovering said as he ushered the three away from Nurse Hildegard and into a small room adjacent to the nurses' station.

Emma guided Alexandra along, then came up beside William, and with reserved resolve looked him in the eyes and spoke.

"William, my dear, William. You must explain to me about Miss Hargrove. Did you know she was here, in the hospital? When last I spoke with her, she was leaving for England. Why, I had no idea she had not sailed. Did you know, William? Did you know?"

William cut his eyes to Doctor Lovering who nodded approval for William to answer his aunt as forthrightly as their oaths allowed. Had the doctor not come to him asking him to represent an indigent patient, William would never have been cognizant of Arielle's accident. He knew she was in the best of care under the doctor's watchful and disciplined eyes. He equally knew he had been retained in a strict confidence that did not permit him to share his knowledge of her whereabouts with anyone, not even his beloved aunt. The doctor knew, had it not been for William, his patient might still lay without proper identity, a lonely cast-off, orphaned by society with no kin to lay claim to her well-being or care.

Alexandra listened intently as well. Every hair on her body bristled as her nerve endings reacted to the news that William knew more than he had previously shared. *Ooh! Arielle Hargrove is like a wart that continues to fester and grow with no hope of removal. She continues to arrive at every turn! No wonder she had not interfered with my visits to Olivia, she was not even out of the country! Ooh!* Alexandra's thoughts whirled about her head in rapid abandon as she fought with the memories of having carefully planned her visits to Miss Smithfield's hoping not to be confronted by Arielle.

Had I known the pesky little wench was disabled, my energies would not have been so divided. Ooh! Even bedridden, she controls my actions and wastes my precious time! I must get William and myself out of this place that houses this annoying imbecile before he is sucked into her spell. How could he find any fascination with such an insipid piece of humanity?

Oh, what could he be thinking? He must learn the truth about her, and the sooner the better. I must find a way to make him see the truth. My word, what is the truth? Oh, I am so confused. Stop, Alexandra. Stop. Stop and think. Alexandra you know what you need to do. Thinking of herself in the third person always seemed to clear her mind. *First, you must get away, out of this place. You must distance William from her. Take him away with you. Have him focus on you, forget her. Then, you will be able to set him straight regarding her beginnings so he will never, ever want a present or future with the likes of her.*

"Alexandra? Alexandra?"

She heard William's voice, though it seemed muffled, as if she were hearing through wax clogged ears. Her name reverberated back then forward, like the sweep of an unlatched screen door banging away from, then back against its frame. Her senses awakened with each strike of his vocal chords.

"Alexandra, do you hear me?"

She drifted from her self-imposed stupor and looked at him straight away. She watched his lips move, forming the sound of her name. She wanted to purse her lips against his. Instead, she began to swoon, lulling to his strength and good looks. William reached forward and gathered her in his arms that enveloped her like the able wings of an eagle. She softened in his embrace, nearly cooing as she looked into his eyes for affection and found pedestrian concern.

Doctor Lovering was the next to speak as he observed the drama unfolding among the unwilling cast of characters.

"William, Mrs. Willard," Doctor Lovering began with a decided mock bow. "Miss Whitaker will do well to accept your invitation. I have consulted with the physician who examined her. Her bumps and bruises are best treated at home. With a good night's rest and friendly companionship, she should be well on her way to recovery from today's events. Rest assured, I will call on your home tomorrow to confirm her good health. Now, you will excuse me, I must make my rounds. Good afternoon to you all."

"Good afternoon to you all." Alexandra mocked the doctor's words with a sneer. "Here I am, suffering. Suffering I tell you, and all anyone seems to care about is that wimpy snippet Miss Hargrove."

William ignored her slight to Arielle not wanting to be caught up in Alexandra's maelstrom. "Alexandra, I know this has been a particularly onerous experience for you. You have felt firsthand the dangers of life under such abject conditions. My understanding is that Aunt Emma warned you to remain close at hand, yet you ignored her sound guidance. Though I do not fault you for what happened, for you are the victim in this, you have learned a hard lesson. You will be well served to divorce yourself from some of your stubbornness and heed your best interests."

"Oh, William. Take me. I mean, take me home to my own bed. I have much to ponder and my servants can tend to my needs. A good night's rest in my own home will be just the tonic I need to plan my days ahead."

"You sound as though you have a mission in mind," Emma surmised as she watched a glow come about Alexandra's face and a gleam settle in her eyes.

Alexandra drew her lips up forming a little grin. "Oh no. A mission? Me? After all I have been through today? No, I am merely trying to think of a way to better the lives of indigents and lobby for the poor disenfranchised that is all. There are those in our midst who need to learn a lesson or two and, who better than me, to throw the book at them? I mean, educate them."

"I fear the trauma of the day has taken its toll. Come, let me get you home."

A wave of optimism came over Alexandra as she rotated her body to face William. She felt positive the tide would soon turn, and she would do everything possible to assure the resulting waves rippled in her favor.

Emma watched Alexandra's eyes nearly devour her nephew. *The poor soul thinks she has a chance with him,* pondered Emma. *But then again, if Alexandra did not think so highly of herself, who would?*

Chapter Twenty-Two

D ays were moving too quickly past. The business of selecting and buying fresh inventory for Pennybacker's consumed
Morgan, though her immediate interest was today centered on
the affairs of Olivia Smithfield. Of paramount importance was
what she hoped would be a defining visit to London's magistrate
to review court documents pertaining to births a score of years
prior. Records, if accurate as perceived, would undeniably prove
that Miss Smithfield, albeit unmarried, was Arielle's birth mother, as suspected, thus putting to rest, at least for the purposes of
the case at hand, the matter alluded to in correspondence from
Olivia to the Hargroves.

All the while, Miss Hargrove's absence in London was curious
and of concern, but Morgan was determined to move forward
without her. Contact with her Aunt Leta lent no news. The woman
was flustered and distraught there had been no correspondence
from her niece. She said she anxiously awaited the daily post for
any word regarding a change in her niece's plans. The uncertainty of Arielle's whereabouts, melded with the uncertainty of her

beginnings, kept Morgan on task and drew her like a magnet to learn more and sort through her findings.

Agnes walked along behind Morgan, keeping the cadence of her methodical pace, much like a cart at the rear of a horse with no alternative but to follow. She held a tight clutch on Peepers' cage periodically transferring it from one hand to the other as the circulation in her fingers was made to feel expired. She wiggled her fingers to rejuvenate the flow of blood to her extremities, drawing Peepers' attention with the flutter of her digits.

The courthouse was a stately building formed of large, dark, irregular stones patched together with wide seams of mortar. Its steep steps formed an equally daunting invitation to the main entry. Morgan paused only momentarily to establish her whereabouts, then made her unabashed way up the steps into the large vestibule that formed a holding cell before allowing complete admittance into the house of judicial assembly. Agnes and Peepers were more reticent in their approach. Peepers, remaining at the mercy of Agnes' whim, attempted to stabilize himself on the floor of his cage. He looked up at the mass of stone before him and exclaimed, "Whoa boy, whoa boy!" Agnes lifted his cage and gave him a look.

"Come along, Agnes," Morgan called down to her from the entryway. "We've no time to dilly-dally."

Agnes picked up her step and, in turn, Peepers perfected his two-legged stabilizing act on the base of his 'maison de plume' to keep himself from capsizing. There was no way for him to abandon ship for he was a captive, living at the mercy of his caretakers.

"Morgan," Agnes called to the one who outdistanced her by length of stride alone.

"Morgan, I say, Miss Pennybacker?" Agnes was prone to revert to a formal address when calls to the familiar fell on deaf ears.

"Morgan, I say hold up a moment, will you?"

"Agnes, what is it?"

"Morgan, it is just that with Peepers and all, I am inclined to need compensation, understanding if you will, for my failure to keep constant pace. Go ahead if you must, for I am feeling slightly short of wind. I will keep my eyes posted on your every turn and be ahead shortly."

Although Morgan preferred that their threesome move along in unison, she understood the burden born by Agnes and declined any negative retort.

"Very well. But, do come along quickly. An extra pair of ears remain an asset in matters worth repeating."

Morgan proceeded down the long hallway lined by doors until she read the gold rubbed letters on a set of frosted glass double doors where the hallway came to an abrupt end. She paused as she read, 'RECORDS.' Here were the doors that protected the area housing the facts she needed to know. As she studied the doors, she hoped the facts were more transparent than the opaque glass before her. A simple turn of the brass knob and easy push forward was all the effort required for her to step over the threshold and into the space that sheltered details of so many pasts and presents. *What a monumental responsibility the walls and people residing over this space endured to protect the census of generations,* she mused.

Morgan approached the counter. A tiny woman, her nose twitching like a church mouse, looked her in the eye. She would have looked her straight in the eye had she the stature, but such was not the case.

"May I help you?" Her generic greeting sounded mechanical, verifying the greeting had been delivered hundreds of thousands of times with no luster remaining for any new inquiries.

"Yes, you may. I have come to seek the records of my dear aunt. She lies gravely ill and has sent me to verify for herself and the family certain papers important to our lineage."

"What have you to show proof of your relationship?"

"Why, dear Aunt Olivia, barely able to speak on her own behalf I might add, gave me her calling card. Oh, my how she clutched it. She knew it held her best connection between your office and herself. As her representative, I am here to oversee the culling of facts regarding her birth and other pertinent data."

The woman looked Morgan up and down which consumed some moments for her lowly height preempted her ability to rapidly go from brow to toe on someone of Morgan's stature. She completed her evaluation by stepping on a wooden box that raised her to new heights, allowing her to see fully over the counter where she viewed Morgan nearly eyeball to eyeball.

Morgan placed Olivia's calling card on the counter's top. It lay still as though in quiet reverence to its owner. Morgan eyed the clerk, looking for a name plaque that would help her make a deeper connection with the woman. She knew that if you called someone by name, like calling in a horse from the field, you garnered more attention from them by invoking their given name.

There it was, a rectangular wood plaque with a name engraved across the brass plate, 'Rowena Nash, Clerk of the Court.' Morgan looked at the plaque, then at the clerk. She hesitated to assume the counter decoration applied to the woman on the riser before her, but she assumed so just the same. The clerk caught Morgan's wandering eye.

"Miss Nash, I appreciate your attention to my request. Due to my aunt's condition, I feel a sense of urgency to complete the tasks she set before me."

"I must tell you that under most circumstances a notarized letter is required from the party giving you authority to act on their behalf. I am dubious about allowing you to enter our files without such authority, however, you seem to be genuine in your manner and request. I am going to honor what you say are your aunt's wishes for I can see no harm coming to her, especially if she is in the condition you describe," Rowena Nash explained as she picked up Olivia's card from its place of rest with her slender, spindle-like fingers and examined it more closely.

A sudden commotion occurred on the other side of the door with the sound of metal clanging against the brass kickplate. There was a brief scrambling of feet, the door knob rotated, the door pushed open and in leaned Agnes as scattered in her mannerisms as Peepers' birdseed was in his cage.

"Pardon our fuss," Agnes exclaimed with a condensed huff and puff as she swung Peepers' cage fully into the room out of the sweep of the door she pushed to close.

"Whoa boy, whoa boy!" Peepers' call exited his beak in a higher than normal distressed pitch like a fine-feathered S.O.S.

"Now, now, Peepers. Be a good boy. We've a job to do today for Auntie Olivia," Morgan proctored as she cast a look to Agnes to collect herself.

"Olivia? Olivia? Whoa, boy. Who's Olivia?"

Rowena, at first somewhat taken off task by the display, looked at the threesome, stepped down from her perch and lifted the counter's hinged section to allow the entourage through.

"Now, and I mean now, Peepers, settle yourself. Relax." Morgan admonished.

"Relax. Relax. Peepers is a good boy," came his refrain.

"As I have stated, I am taking exception here. If for any reason you show cause for me to question my decision, you will have forced my hand. I will call you back and require that you vacate the premises. I must say, my curiosity compels me to ask, why do you carry a bird with you?"

"Actually, she does not carry the bird, I do," Agnes responded quite proudly, happy to take credit for her efforts.

"Agnes, oh, never mind. Miss Nash, the parakeet's name is Peepers. His reason for accompanying us is two-fold. He has never adjusted to being alone and is therefore prone to throwing uncontrollable fits in his cage. The process is quite disturbing to view. We fear for his safety. Secondly, and because of the facts I have just explained, Peepers has become part of our signature, our calling card. Wherever we goeth, he goeth, so to speak."

"Relax. Relax. Peepers is a good boy. Ain't that the truth?"

Morgan cut him a stern look, her eyeballs ready to emit fumes.

"I see." Rowena Nash skeptically reviewed the three, beginning to question the sanity of not only her decision but of the two women before her.

Miss Nash led them to a large room, very sterile in its lack of embellishments, with row after row of thick oak filing cabinets.

"Your aunt, Olivia, her last name?"

"Smithfield."

"Not to be rude, but how common is that? You will have to hope that in all of these records there is but one Olivia Smithfield born at the time of your aunt. Here, I will leave you with this cabinet. Everything is in order. Please leave the files as you have found them. If you have any questions, I will be where you first found me. Do not remove any documents for these are sacred public records." Rowena Nash turned, leaving the area in a quick pivot. She trusted that her charges would respect the sanctity of the place.

Morgan placed her hand on one of the long file drawers administering a hefty heave as she pulled the fully loaded weight of it forward. So many Smiths. The name filled the drawer as it did the next two opened by Morgan. She bent down, way low, to the bottom file of the cabinet's series. Rather than suffer a backache as she bent over the file, she plopped herself down on the cold linoleum floor and began sorting for the name Smithfield.

Just as Miss Nash stated, the files were in pristine order as Morgan flipped by the words that gave identity to so many. Albert, Bernice, Colin, Desiree, all Smithfields and all accounted for. Her fingers continued their search flicking by file after file until she reached the O's. Here lay a host of Smithfields whose paths may never have crossed but for these files. Oakley, Octavia, Odell, Ogden, Olga, and then, finally, Olivia. Morgan anticipated the file would be there, but the finding of it gave more merit to her mission. Now, all she needed was for the contents to verify what was thought to be true. She lifted the file from its place neatly nestled between Oliver and Orson. She stood and held the file close to her chest so none of its contents would spill forth. She walked to one of the long oak tables that remained free of clutter, their barrenness helping to assure that nothing would contaminate the historic records. Agnes and Peepers watched over Morgan's shoulders as she read through the file.

"Olivia Ralston Smithfield. Born March 4, 1833 to Katherine Jane Ralston and Jonathan Oliver Smithfield in Kentsgate Court, Manchestershire. Siblings: Edmond Randall Smithfield, born 1830."

Morgan was puzzled. She knew from Olivia's letter that she continued to use the name Smithfield, but she thought for certain that court records would show a marriage resulting in childbirth. Nowhere in the file was there mention of a marriage or birth. *Could it be that she had the child out of wedlock and thus maintained the Smithfield name or had her spouse expired early on and she reverted to her maiden name? As odd as that seemed, it was a possibility. Or, had she married another Smithfield and thus retained her surname? Why was it that this women elicited so many questions? Why was it that even her file, the record of her life, remained so vague? Why was there no marriage certificate, no evidence that she had ever birthed an offspring?*

Morgan returned to the filing cabinet and replaced the file protected on each side by Oliver and Orson. She began toward the front of the drawer moving from A to E where she honed in on the file labeled Edmond Randall Smithfield and began to read aloud: "Born March 18, 1830 in Kentsgate Court, Manchestershire to Katherine Ralston Smithfield and Jonathan Oliver Smithfield. Profession: Doctor, Nantymoel, Wales. Died: 1887 in London from indigestion after eating strawberries." *Cut to the quick by berries. How could something so fruitful lead to one's demise?* Morgan thought. She had heard it suggested that the gastric sensations brought on by some foods, berries included, simulated certain adverse conditions of the heart. Though the death was ultimately the result of a weak heart, the cause of death was attributed to the food most recently ingested. Thus, indigestion was the considered killer. *Poor man, a doctor at that, unable to diagnose his own ailment or to foresee the dark side of his future. Despite his training and experience he was incapable of predicting and protecting himself from a premature death.* Morgan pondered the inequities of one's profession and life.

"Morgan, of what interest is the brother? We were sent to discover what we might about Miss Smithfield."

"Agnes, do please recall the full contents of Miss Smithfield's letter received by Sir Ian Hargrove. In the text she reveals her brother's name and the fact that he attended Miss Hargrove's birth. Were he alive, his testimony to the facts of the day would be crucial to our investigation. We must seek out someone with more authority. We must again visit with Miss Smithfield. She is our best hope to glean details of that day. We must pray she has not passed through death's door or we will have to amend our plan."

"Morgan. I know you are of an abler mind than I, but, I draw your attention to the fact that, according to those records, Miss Smithfield was two score and four when Miss Hargrove was born."

"Yes, Agnes."

"Well, I am just saying, she was no spring chicken to be giving birth. It was a bit of a late start and quite strange if you ask me."

Peepers jumped to his swing, swaying back and forth in a concurring motion chirping, "Ain't that the truth? Ain't that the truth?"

Agnes smiled to have her words villified, even if by a bird, only to erase the smile from her face as quickly as it appeared with Morgan's admonishment.

"Do not be distracting me now. If these records are to be believed -- stranger things have happened, Agnes. We are reviewing the facts, the little that are known at this time, so we will be well-poised to move ahead efficiently."

Morgan removed her pen from her valise. She dipped it in the inkwell provided on a nearby table. She opened the leather-bound notebook she carried for dictation that served duly as a personal journal and sketchpad for her equine etchings. She jotted off notes about Edmond Smithfield, heavily underlying Nantymoel. She sensed Doctor Smithfield held more than a subtle connection to the Hargroves and she was hell bent to discover why.

Chapter Twenty-Three

Late June 1897
London, England

L ondon's haze from the previous eve's rain had given way to a spectrum of light bands passing over and between buildings, making the pavement dance. It proved to be a warm, but refreshing June morning, and Morgan was hopeful that 'rewarding' would be added to her list of the day's pleasures. Official papers in the office of records proved undeniably crucial in establishing the fact that no child had ever been born to Olivia Smithfield. *So, what is Smithfield's connection to Miss Hargrove's birth?* Morgan pondered. *I need clarification about the tenor of her letter, and the best source for such clarification will be Miss Smithfield herself.*

She hoped Miss Smithfield would be more forthcoming than she had been during their previous visit. The woman was indeed in frail health. Morgan could only hope she had regained some strength and that her delirium had passed. The questions she planned to pose needed to be fully understood and responded to with concrete answers to complete the puzzle whose pieces were still scattered at best.

Facts were not coming together easily, but easy offered no challenge to Morgan. Her thrill was in the hunt, the chase to the prey, with her trophy being the resolution of her case. One week had passed since the Pennybacker investigative threesome had seen Olivia Smithfield. Little did they know she had been in the company of an uninvited visitor who served only to confuse her fragile memory.

Morgan, Agnes and Peepers made their familiar pilgrimage to Olivia's brownstone. Even the sun's blessing could not remove the aura surrounding the structure. Each of its hand-hewed bricks appeared wrapped in vaporous gray like a portent of death, as though the building sensed Olivia's deterioration.

Gathering their breaths at the crest of the steep flight of stairs, Agnes used her free hand to bang the door's knocker. Within a shuffle of moments, Beatrice greeted them, looking less fresh than she had on the previous occasion. Caring for her charge was obviously an exhausting task. Morgan had seen this scene played out time and again. In cases of aging spouses, she had witnessed many a healthy spouse predeceasing their infirm husband or wife by the toll taken from the demands of infinite care.

"We hope we are not intruding, Beatrice. How is Miss Smithfield this day?"

"No change for the better I can tell ye. She's a strong one she is to have stayed with us this long. It's like she can't leave us yet. She knows somethin' we don't and won't go to 'er rest 'til it's 'ad its proper sayin'."

"May we step in? We will keep our visit to a minimum. There is a curiosity we need to make clear."

"I guess that can do no 'arm. She may not wake for ye, though."

Morgan and Agnes stepped near Olivia's bedside. Peepers' reaction was quite telling as he aimed his beak and beady eyes on her corpse-like form exclaiming, "Save my soul, save my soul. Whoa boy, Whoa boy! Save my soul, save my soul!"

"Hush, now," came Agnes' whispered reprimand.

"Save my…" Peepers' dissertation was cut short by a delicate shake to his cage causing his last word to sound like a hiccup.

"Has she awakened recently?"

"Only once in the last hour."

"May I sit next to her to see if she will rouse?" Morgan queried.

"Just fer a short while. My duty is to Miss Olivia and we both endured a very perplexing sight several days ago."

"Of what are you speaking?"

"Oh, nothin' really. I'd stepped out to tend to Miss Olivia's supplies. When I returned there was someone, a woman, in 'er chamber."

"Did she identify herself or state her intentions?"

"She was quite confusing I must say."

"Can you describe her?"

"Well, 'er 'air was flaxen like the sun."

"And her age?"

"I'm not the best judge of age on a good day, but I would say she was at least a score, with a few years added on for good measure."

"Did she offer any reason for her presence?"

Beatrice was feeling intimidated by Morgan. Her rapid-fire questions were leaving her feeling spent and sorry she had broached the topic.

"She kept insisting she was related to Miss Olivia."

"Related how?"

"Her words were that Miss Olivia was her mum which I knew could not be so."

"Please state how you know that not to be so." Beatrice was re-gretting any part of the conversation at hand. She needed to find a way to escape the topic.

"I'm not quite sure. Call it a hunch of sorts."

Beatrice felt heat come to her face as she attempted to dodge Morgan's interrogation. She could not allow herself to be lured to speak. She was a hired servant and would be true to her employer as asked.

"Miss Olivia will be tiring soon. It would seem that ye should be speakin' to 'er now lest she fall into slumber again."

"I understand and appreciate your candor." Morgan gave a curt smile. She would store in the recesses of her mind the information about the visitor. *If Beatrice did not recognize the woman, how would I know her?* Though she found Beatrice vexing, she could not allow anything to delay speaking to Olivia. She resolved to turn to the matter at hand.

"Miss Smithfield. Morgan Pennybacker here. You wrote a letter about Miss Arielle Hargrove and I have the need for more details from you."

Morgan realized she was sharing her client's name before Olivia and Beatrice but she could shield the name no more in Olivia's presence. It was paramount for Arielle's name to be spoken before time took its toll. Within the deep recesses of her mind, Olivia recalled the voice seeping slowly but surely to her senses. The tone was familiar. It had visited her before. She had responded to this voice before and would do so again. Morgan observed the movement of Olivia's eyes under her lids as her chin moved in a circular motion extending her neck as in search of the sound infiltrating her ears.

"Miss Smithfield. I need speak with you only briefly, if you will so oblige me. About Miss Hargrove, what do you want to say?"

Olivia's eyelids parted in a cautious squint, blocking the room's light from shocking her pupils. She parted her lips and stroked her tongue in and out over her bottom lip like a baby tasting its first pabulum.

"Ari…?" came her weak reply. "Ari…?"

"Miss Smithfield, we need to know more. How can we know more about Miss Hargrove?"

Olivia's eyes opened wider. She stared with distant intent at Morgan.

"How? Miss Smithfield? Tell us how?"

With her chest lifting up and down to billow sufficient air, Olivia's mouth prepared to form words.

"Maggie, girl. Maggie. Welsh girl. Maggie, Maggie Galligan. Nantymoel, Maggie."

"Maggie? Who is she, Miss Smithfield?"

With her last word came shallow breathing, closure of her eyes and a drift into dense sleep. Morgan was puzzled. She came to speak about Arielle Hargrove and heard nothing but three letters of her name. *Who is Maggie Galligan,* she pondered? *Welsh girl?*

"Beatrice, what do you know of the names you have heard before you today? Please, we bid you, tell us all you can."

Beatrice's eyes looked up and to the side, totaling taking their gaze away from the visitors. She knew she had taken an oath of sorts. She had been strictly instructed by her employer never to reveal any information about anyone who befriended her or resided with her. *Even in Miss Olivia's fragile state, I cannot and will not break that line of trust.* No, for now, she would reveal absolutely nothing and in respect to the name, Maggie Galligan, she could honestly say she knew nothing of her. Miss Hargrove was another story. She knew that name well. Miss Olivia had asked for her assistance to pen a letter to the Hargrove family. She acted with great mystery as she instructed Beatrice to write every word she methodically dictated to her. She had begun the writing of the letter herself, but found the task too difficult with her weary hands. Though the girl's penmanship was not the best, it would have to suffice. She shared no further details with Beatrice. With respect, Beatrice asked for none. *No. I will remain silent, as Miss Olivia has requested.* Beatrice's eyes redirected themselves to Morgan's stoic stare.

"It's sorry I am mum to not be able to tell ye more, but there's nothin' I can tell." Beatrice was pleased with the formation of her words. She had chosen them carefully and was proud no lie was contained within.

Morgan searched the girl's face. Beatrice's exhaustion peaked in her overall facial expression. Dark circles had formed under her eyes and she appeared in need of a good rest. *There can be no good to come of grilling the girl at this juncture.* Thoughts whirled in her head. *However, I am sure, though she may profess there is nothing she 'can' tell me, there is most assuredly something she 'will not' tell me. The shifting of her eyes and inability to make eye contact with me speaks volumes. If the results I desire do not come in due time, I shall have to revisit my questioning of her with greater force.*

"Very well, for now, Beatrice. We will be on our way. We bid you adieu and pray Miss Smithfield will continue to find comfort in your care. Be mindful of your own health as well."

Morgan, Agnes and Peepers took their leave with a new mission on their agenda. Olivia, immersed in sleep, had deepened the task of inquiry for Morgan. Who was Maggie, and why was Olivia so insistent about her? A visit to Wales appeared to be on Morgan's horizon and she would not deny that instinct. On the 'morrow, she would prepare to leave London posthaste and attempt to find all she could about a Welsh woman named, Maggie Galligan.

Chapter Twenty-Four

The spring and summer months could not pass too quickly for Arielle. She had spent so many weeks at Providence she felt as though the calendar had stopped counting off days and left her in an endless state of medical probing with numerous prompting attempts by the nurses to encourage her recovery. Her body's broken bones and bruises had sufficiently healed for her release. Most importantly, the bruises to her brain sustained in the carriage accident had left no ill effects on her memory or her ability to fully function as she had before. Weekly visits from Emma and daily visits from her parents lifted her spirits, but none of these well-wishers raised her enthusiasm and desire to be set free more than the occasional sighting of William Clay. He kept his visits brief, not wanting to overstay or overstep his presence.

The news that she would be released from the hospital to return home could not have come at a better time for, late one evening, in what revealed itself as a passage from a recurring dream, a man entered her hospital room and presented a paper rolled like a proclaiming document. She at first was apt to think she was deep in a dream sequence until she reached forward and took the document from his hand and felt it on her flesh. Carefully, she unrolled the piece to read its contents. It was a telegraph from Morgan informing her that her presence was needed in Wales. Arielle was quite surprised that Morgan was no longer in London and wondered what caused her to visit the village of Nantymoel where her father's colliery thrived nearby.

⌒

"Miss Emma. What have you heard of late about Miss Hargrove's condition?" Simon queried, the wrinkles on his little brow furrowed in concern.

"I am pleased to report she is much improved, Simon."

"Much improved, much improved, yes, that is good news indeed, much improved."

"Simon, am I mistaken, or have you taken a fancy to Miss Hargrove?"

"Why, Miss Emma, no, oh my no, oh, my no. The fact of time establishes I am well beyond her in years. That fact alone would put an end to any fool's heart such as mine thinking Miss Hargrove would ever take a fancy to someone the likes of me. Oh no, oh, my no. I simply wish for her recovery, oh yes, her rapid and full recovery," Simon's words bubbled from his mouth as his face turned a pale crimson matching the hue of his bow tie.

"Well, I believe your wish has already been answered for Miss Hargrove is to return home today. William stopped by yesterday afternoon to inform me of her restored good health. Perhaps she will be inclined to visit with us again one day soon."

"The thought of that alone brings me great pleasure, yes, great pleasure indeed."

The words were barely shy of Simon's mouth when the great knocker on the door to Chestnut Heights sounded prompting Thomas to proceed to the front portal. Emma and Simon moved forward to be in full view of the visitor as Thomas drew the door open to reveal Arielle.

"My word, do I dare believe what I see before my eyes? Dear Arielle, please come in. Oh, what a lovely surprise! My dear, you look...wonderful," Emma hesitated on her choice of words and hoped Arielle would not be put off by her delay.

The girl was pale and had lost a bit of weight, a loss more significantly notable on someone with her petite frame.

"Come, let's sit in the parlor. Cook will bring some tea and, how about some scones with Chantilly cream? Cook made some savory scones this morning and oh, my, they were so aromatic. Come." Emma gestured for Arielle to follow her. "Simon, why don't you join us too?"

"Good morning, Mr. Peabody," Arielle said with a brief wink his way. Her time sequestered in the hospital rendered her in a playful mood and who better to have a go with than her friend, Simon.

The crimson hue that had begun to dissipate reinstated itself across Simon's face. He was indeed smitten with Miss Hargrove though he was wise enough to know theirs would forever remain a friendship and nothing more. Simon looked from Arielle to Emma with a befuddled expression.

"My, my, Miss Hargrove. Oh, I must say it is a great pleasure to see you again. Oh, our prayers have been answered, yes indeed they have. Chestnut Heights has not been the same without your presence. And the gardens, you must visit all about the grounds before they lose their luster for I know you have always found the gardens enchanting." Simon's feet moved in a nervous dance step on his last words as his reticence in Arielle's presence revealed itself.

"It will be my great pleasure to view your lovely gardens but, with you as my escort, of course." Arielle smiled at Simon as he appeared to float off the carpet and grow inches taller with her suggestion.

"Very well, very well, yes, very well indeed. For now, I will take my leave so you and Miss Emma may take tea together and be at ease to converse unrestrained without a gentleman in your midst."

As Simon bowed and exited the room, Emma hastened Arielle to a two-seater settee in the corner of the grand parlor. The carved dos-à-dos covered in aubergine cotton velvet provided the perfect setting for the two to talk and exchange news. Emma was most anxious to learn of Miss Pennybacker's latest findings. She took Arielle's hand in hers.

"I am so delighted you are here. Tell me. How do you feel? Are you fully healed?"

"I am ready to respond to Miss Pennybacker's message. Thank you for having her recent telegraph delivered to me at the hospital. She is urging me to come to Wales. I feel that I have the strength to travel and will soon make arrangements to join her there." Arielle's eyes became moist with tears.

"Oh, why does it seem there is more to be done than can be done? My life's days, though fulfilled in so many ways, are at the ready to do more, though time does not avail me so, especially since the disruption of my pursuits with Miss Pennybacker by my hospital stay. I feel rested, yet so forlorn."

"Have no worries, my dear. It is the hallmark of a well-lived life that you don't feel you have enough time to do everything you want to do. Everything will come together for you in good time. I am certain of this."

Emma took Arielle's hands and patted them gently. Arielle felt immediately at ease and so fortunate to be alive and with her dear friend. Just as the two readied themselves to engage in lively conversation, the knocker on the front door resonated through the foyer. Thomas could be heard greeting a very familiar voice.

"Oh, my what a glorious day," Emma exclaimed as she rose to greet their handsome guest.

Arielle could not have been more pleased to see the unaccompanied William Clay step into the parlor. It was a blessing that he was devoid of Alexandra, for the good spirits she was feeling since exiting the hospital would surely be run asunder with her presence. As William looked her way, she felt a lovely tingling sensation emanate throughout her body. His being cast a spell on her and she was happy to linger in the spreading sensations his mere presence evoked. He smiled and gave a bow her direction as he kissed Emma on her cheek.

"Oh, William, isn't it just wonderful that Miss Hargrove is fit and back amongst us again!"

"It is indeed, Miss Hargrove. I trust your strength has returned and you feel no ill effects from your accident. Coming back to daily routines can be a daunting task after such a long hospital stay but, I must say, I have every confidence you will soon be ready to meet all challenges."

"Thank you, Mr. Clay. You are most kind. You have continually had faith in me when I do not. You and your aunt share a common trait of making one feel most welcome and secure. I am most grateful."

"William, Miss Hargrove, was just preparing to tell me about a trip she is planning. Oh, my goodness, I do not want to break a confidence, and William, I do not want to appear rude, but, Arielle, should we postpone our conversation?"

Arielle could not imagine a better and more welcoming audience to discuss Miss Pennybacker's findings. She knew so little herself that there was barely much to reveal. Alexandra had cast so many aspersions her way in William's presence, she wondered if she dared divulge the reason she had hired Morgan. *Perhaps Alexandra's premonitions will come to fruition. Perhaps I am all she says I am, nothing but a bastard child. Why would William Clay want to have any association with me?* Her thought processes were broken by William's voice.

"First, Miss Hargrove, I would like to request that you call me by my first name. It would seem we have spent many months addressing one another formally. My aunt has suggested that you might find the use of first names a comfortable form of communication. So, I therefore, wish to request your permission to refer to you as Arielle, if you deem this most fit, of course."

Arielle felt a flutter of ease and comfort float through her. She was so taken with this man, this William, she felt she could melt into a puddle on the floor from the heat of his thoughtful gaze.

"Why, Mr. Clay, if your Aunt Emma, takes no objection, I will gladly have you address me by my first name."

William smiled and gave a modified bow her direction. "Then, you will, in turn, call me William, I most sincerely hope."

"I will be most pleased to do so, William." Arielle thought she might swoon at their newfound familiarity.

"William, your aunt has been most kind to assist me with some personal information pertaining to my family heritage. The evening we met, an unusual occurrence in my home left me little alternative but to flee. Your appearance, though somewhat alarming for me, placed me at Chestnut Heights and for that I will always be most grateful. Meeting your aunt and having her warm friendship has made a curious time in my life more tolerable. I was reticent about speaking details of the occurrence during your visits at the hospital. If you will forgive me for casting aspersions her way, Miss Whitaker, on more than one occasion, had inferred that you would be less than pleased to know what has troubled me so."

"You may rest assured Arielle that Miss Whitaker has little influence on my interpretations nor is she my guide. I apologize for her inappropriate utterances and any harm she has cast your way," William smiled as he graciously spoke to allay her concerns.

Arielle felt at once confident any information she shared with him would be met with tender concern and the utmost compassion. She sensed a bond between them that she hoped was more than a mere reflection of the professionalism he was wont to exhibit as an attorney with his clients. She would put thoughts of Alexandra aside, as far aside as she could rally, for Alexandra was a force few could restrain.

With Emma at her side, Arielle proceeded to relay the events of the rainy March night, the letter posted to her father, her meeting with Morgan Pennybacker, and her plans to visit Olivia

Smithfield that were run awry when she stepped into the path of a carriage at the train station.

William listened intently with willing ears. He allowed Arielle's clearness of thought to flow without interruption, all the while gripped with battling emotions. He silently felt controllable rage as he questioned her father's behavior and the worry endured by Arielle as she tried to make sense of it all. It brought sensations of empathy and compassion to the surface of his skin.

Emma patted Arielle's hand as she set the final words to her story. "You have, my dear, been through such a traumatic series of events. I am glad you have chosen to share this information with William. He is a wonderful ally. I will return in a short while after I summon Cook for some fresh tea."

William looked to Arielle. He positioned himself in his aunt's abandoned seat on the dos-à-dos and stared into her eyes. They exchanged no words. The silence became not a void between them but a mutual bond, a quiet calm, lending their hearts time to render the growing lust filling their minds and loins. William's manner touched Arielle in an unexpected place, a place she hoped would be revisited time and again.

Chapter Twenty-Five

Lifted from its pallor since Horace's passing, Chestnut Heights found itself in the best of health this night as its welcoming walls breathed in and out with a robust blush of well-being. The house itself seemed to be fully at peace. Its stately columns and arched window ornamentation were beautifully infused into the Italianate style of the manse and ready to welcome Emma's guests. Her home looked beautiful inside and out. The gardens, bursting with color, made Chestnut Heights a Villa Ferrari, or translated, *House of Flowers.*

Emma was exceedingly pleased with Simon's imposed influence over all the plantings, including the parterre with its grid of clipped boxwoods planted in a rectilinear pattern. A nearby stone dependency acted as a trellis for a climbing rose bush. Through the allée, statuary mingled among leafy hostas and ferns lending a formality to the area. Emma quite often found herself drawn to the soulful retreat where a nearby butterfly bush attracted monarchs, tiger swallowtails, Baltimore Checkerspots, and masses of cottons that would barely light before going on their way. Simon

took particular pleasure in studying the variety of larger lepidop-
terans attracted to the shrub as they lingered to sip its sweet nectar. A carefully placed viewing bench lent the perfect perch to
take in nature's beauty.

Chestnut Heights was ready to pulse with energy. Emma
knew full well that hosting a grand party required the ultimate
in organization and an equally good mix of guests. Planning
the masquerade served a dual purpose. It took her away from
her grief and allowed her to fulfill the promise she made to
Alexandra after the incident at Purdy's Court. The girl indeed
needed something for focus beyond herself. Emma so hoped
the party would lift her spirits and assist William in appeasing
her, for Alexandra had been in a perpetually agitated state ever
since she learned of William's contact with Arielle Hargrove at
Providence Hospital.

Emma tended to the final details for her party. She assured every
lamp about the manse was lit with low flames emitting modest glows.
Daring shadows, prompted by the flames, cast themselves about the
manse's rooms giving the illusion of movement where none existed.
Glass curtains caught up by the night's breezes performed scarf-like
dances, lifting to and fro like a maestro's well-directed wand. Quietly
still, then suddenly vibrant with motion, the sheer draperies tiptoed
away from the lengthy panes of glass, loftily lifting their hems off
the floor in an airy, free-flowing style. Sashaying in a forward promenade they found themselves ultimately sucked back to the dark-
stained mullions, only momentarily returning to their places of rest
awaiting the next breeze. Exceptionally full palms, planted in large
urns, dipped their branches down and up as they waved in response
to the current of air circling the room.

Each room was enhanced with festive décor to delight her
guests. The first floor rooms were opulent and fragrant with
orchids and evergreens. Over-sized, eight-armed candelabras
placed on the floor, rising five feet in height, were fitted with a
colorful mix of chunky pillar candles, some red, some purple,
some green and some gold. Each lit wick maintained a brilliant

flame showcasing a gay, draft-swept rhythm at its pinnacle. The mahogany piano in the conservatory was draped with a favorite Czechoslovakian silk tapestry fringed in brilliant colors. In the grand parlor, arched pocket doors between the rooms added their own distinction and grace to the interior.

Hours earlier, Thomas had been absorbed with household duties and trips to the main threshold as large clangs from the manse's heavy doorknocker announced the arrival of boarders. Emma made it quite clear in her instructions to Thomas that she was not to be disturbed, and had suitably arranged a wardrobe for boarders who had not the proper attire for her masquerade. Rather than remain sequestered in their rooms while gaiety abounded below, Thomas had been instructed to offer every accoutrement necessary for new boarders to join the evening's entertainment. There would be three new guests this eve. Thomas had shown the two gentlemen and one woman to their rooms, sharing details of the festivities with each one. The men were quite enamored with the white wigs and fancy frock coats issued them whose tails and fine fabrics tied them to gentry.

The woman remained a curiosity for Thomas. She was at once familiar and yet somehow remotely removed. Her supplied costume consisted of a flaxen wig, scarlet frock, cut low at the neck, red satin slippers and a red sequined mask. Thomas thought it bold of Mrs. Willard to assume any female visitor would want to be outfitted so, yet, the hint of a smile crossed her face as she accepted the bundle from his hands. He wondered what this visitor must have been thinking. He would be surprised to know her thoughts were filled with delight. She let her imagination take her to heights entirely contrary to her normal being. She would rest, enjoy a refreshing toilette, dress and join the party below. With a costume she could truly escape from herself this evening. Yes, this was the perfect happenstance. It was her good fortune to have inquired at the train station about a proper boarding house. There were few in the city unaware of the fine reputation of Emma Willard.

Soon it would be time for the party to commence. Emma mentally reviewed her guest list. She knew with a new man at the helm in the President's House many of the men would be wont to opine about McKinley's chances of improving the state of the country. Some would hold their opinions to themselves while others would boldly share their allegiance to the current administration. Emma knew Washington inside and out. It was a city where loyalty meant a great deal. The smallest of favors could have far-reaching consequences. As for her, she always put principle above politics and that had served her well. She was quite pleased the dispiriting campaign season had concluded. *I just hope none of the conversation leads to a show of fisticuffs! The last thing Chestnut Heights needs is the threat of a duel!* Emma shook her head to cast off the worrisome thought.

⌒

The newly arrived boarder was the stranger among an established cast. She knew, therefore, she would either find herself duly ignored or the object of inquisition. Earlier, when she approached the first step that would lead her to the entry level of the Willard manse, she had paused in contemplation of the first steps she was executing to bring public that which had been kept private for what seemed an eternity. Timidity had overtaken her feet, causing each forward step to feel like an untoward effort to an untoward conclusion. It was as though her full life had been held captive by a sum of circumstances to which she could give little direction until now. Her feet persevered with methodical redundancy until she stood full face with the large mahogany door that would provide her entry into an uncharted territory of her life. She wondered if the completion of herself resided just beyond the finely crafted portal of Mrs. Emma Willard.

She had completed her unpacking. A chifferobe in her well-appointed room sufficiently held the gown she would wear for her special visit on the morn. A series of drawers provided ample space for the tools of her hobby she removed from her satchel. Textured paper, watercolor paints, a palette and brushes accompanied her wherever she traveled. She had long held an affinity for the flower of love with a fondness for roses in any color, but those in varying shades of red and pink were most prevalent in her work. With the palm of her hand, she grazed the surfaces of the completed paintings, taking in the beauty of the lush blossoms she captured in lasting bouquets. Her botanicals renewed her.

She glanced into the large oval mirror on the front of the chifferobe and was quite pleased with her attire for the evening. The sounds of movement throughout the large home and the melding of numerous voices let her know the party was well underway. It was time for her to make her way to the activity below. She picked up her mask and exited to the grand staircase.

She looked up. The rotunda above the first landing with its whimsically ethereal, frescoed ceiling featured plump images of cloud-enshrouded cherubs floating among billowy lengths of gossamer ribbon. The scene captured the guest's peaceful gaze. She was wont to savor the heavenly air the stylistic painting lent the space above. Lustres from a large chandelier spangled the space with a dazzling light display. Slowly, her red satin slippers made their way upon each stair tread, the wearer checking her mask, ensuring it had not gone askew. Peering through the mask's eyeholes while descending the unfamiliar staircase was a daunting task. She however continued on her steady course making final contact with the foyer's dense Bristol carpet.

Several heads turned her way as she cautiously entered. They turned back to their existing conversations just as rapidly. She was relieved. In due time, her path would come upon those for whom her course was set. For now, she must take this night to learn every morsel she could about the family she intended to see. Surely, someone knew Sir Ian Hargrove. Music filled the foyer to the upper rafters of the manse as a string quartet serenaded the crowd adding zest and bonhomie to the gathering.

Outside, a group of gentlemen commenced the lighting of cigars. They found the porch the most public part of the house. In the open air they greeted one another and all guests waiting to make entry. Spirits were high. The usual talk of politics ensued with one trying to assert his opinions over the other. Loud guffaws resonated into the foyer. The power of money and its influence in political races weighed down Emma's porch and formed a heady mix emblematic of Washington's political landscape. The identities of those on the porch, though costumed, could be easily revealed not only by their voices and portliness but also equally by their political determinations.

"Oh, Rainn," Wendell Reed exclaimed taking a hefty toke from his cigar. "We could not be more different politically but, bless us, we do share so much common ground. We have needed a candidate who would bring us together and I hope your man will do that. Time will tell if a day be before us to trumpet his progress."

"Wendell, your native status is revealing itself! Washington is so engrained in you, you appear to be taking a position on both sides!"

"No, you are quite wrong, Mortimer! I am not about to compromise my convictions with someone else's policies!"

"Bravo, gentlemen," Rainn grinned, "I raise my glass to salute you both for exploring the possibilities of this administration. We cannot become so entrenched in bureaucracy that we cannot be heard or maneuver enough elbows to make change."

"Well said, Rainn. I trumpet your words," Mortimer concurred as the group took hefty draws, the smoke from the tobacco filling their nostrils and the night's air.

"I can tell you, on nights like this I do miss Horace. There was never small talk with him. He always began with a story. Yes, gentlemen, he was good company," Wendell said as he exhaled and began to draw in another toke from his cigar picturing in his mind the magnificent soirees he had experienced at Chestnut Heights.

Suddenly, there was a tap on the shoulder of the one in the red dress. "My dear, you are exquisite! It is as though the gown had been commissioned for you!" Emma spewed, looking into the young woman's face and finding a familiar gaze from behind the mask. Emma squinted and cocked her head ever so slightly. No, it cannot be. Yet, there was something there.

"You must pardon me," Emma went on, "For a moment, I confused you with another. I do apologize and am afraid I appear to have lost all semblance of breeding. I am Emma Willard, and my dear, you are?"

The shoulders of the scarlet dress shifted in an effort to delay a response and then the wearer spoke. "Nothing would please me more than to tell you, but I should like to keep silent for awhile longer. It's not the done thing to reveal oneself so early on at a masquerade, now is it?"

Emma watched and listened closely. The British accent and dancing eyes were a perfect fit. Was it the flaxen wig that threw her off course? *No, what am I thinking. How silly of me. She cannot have come. William would have informed me.* Emma smiled and clasped her hands together in acceptance of her guest's privacy. For the time being, she would succumb to the element of mystery and intrigue her masquerade lent. Later there would be due time to ferret-out this beauty's identity. For now, she had a party to host and would not abandon her duties.

Wendell could take little more of the praise for McKinley. He was quite vexed by the gathering's full-throated endorsement of the country's new president.

"Do you not see how ill-fated his vision is for commerce? Why, without the freedom for corporations such as mine to lobby with our friends in government, we shall lose our competitive stature! Our ability to influence and sway public opinion is the only way we can ensure our growth!"

"Your Democratic roots are revealing themselves, Wendell. I think McKinley's regulations on corporate dynasties and tariff protection are the most substantive actions his administration has undertaken to date."

"Spoken like a roaring Republican, Mortimer, and I would like to toast you and your fine taste in presidents!" Rainn Howard cheered. He was never one to miss a controversy or a reason for libation. "And, Wendell, you can hardly put the blame on McKinley. Direct your ire at those in Congress. They are the ones drawing the legislation, overseeing and funding policy. They are the responsible parties so, may I suggest, you look at whom you put in there!"

"If we had not suffered Cleveland's tenacious efforts at tariff reform, we would have nothing to discuss gentleman. So, I say we raise our drink to Grover, for without him, the dear Major's deft eloquence and ability to keep prices at the workingman's level might never have been recognized!"

Mildred Moore heard the boisterous male voices coming from the porch. She knew some of the men had gone missing for a good while. Their rancor persevered as she set her feet firmly before Wendell Reed and placed one hand on her hip, leaving the other free to point her finger at the gathering.

"Tisk, tisk. What's this? Front porch politics? I know Washington is a very partisan town gentlemen but, tonight is the night to step aside all factions and put your energies into Emma's grand party! Before I am forced to endure another stinging rebuke from either side, I implore you to cease this discourse. Come, the ladies want their partners in to dance before the drink threatens to buckle your brains and your legs!"

"Oh, Millie. Let us have our fun. Torturing Mr. Reed is such great sport!"

"So, Mr. Howard, you are not opposed to revealing yourself as the bully? Why, you are treating me like a rented mule."

"Oh, what is Washington without some healthy finger-pointing and blame?" boasted Mortimer Eggers. "We must endure our arguments regarding the past for they portend the future!"

"Gentlemen, your opinions might drone on for hours, especially with Mr. Howard in the mix. I have oft' heard it said about

Rainn, 'He is a man who needs no introduction but could use a conclusion!' Come, there's a better party to be had inside. There's no need to resurrect failed policies from a previous administration! It is high time to set aside partisan differences and find a common ground for your efforts. You must be more forward thinking. We've just inaugurated the man. Give him a chance before striking the gavel!"

Mildred's fist came down sharply to her side in a ceremonial salute to justice as though it had been served by her very words. Washington skeptics made Mildred weary. She knew both parties had become so polarized it was difficult for negotiations to fetter out any reasonable compromise. She most assuredly was wont to quell the ardor of the group, get them inside and put a stop to conversation that would lead to frayed nerves and fractured friendships. She gestured again to lift them from their seats and, as they acquiesced, she herded them toward the main entry and into the throws of the masquerade where political rhetoric would dissipate into the gaiety of the evening.

"Oh, Millie. You know one can totally give up everything or one can fight for something. That is political sense," hailed Mortimer, his words trailing off as the determination of Mildred Moore spurred them forth.

"Come along gentlemen before you all try to reposition yourselves! It seems each side works with its own set of facts. You have dabbled in enough politics for one night!" Mildred Moore threw her head back with a laugh toward the entourage that was gaining pace with her.

A flurry of activity suddenly came through the foyer. Emma and the one in red looked to the gathering of stout men led by a rather round woman. The main hall and salons beyond were teaming with guests and gaiety. Emma had not lost her touch or title as a notable matron and doyenne of style. Her guest list had surpassed its circumscribed limits, for few ever declined an invitation to Chestnut Heights. The evening found the Willard manse thronged with society's elite.

"Take a deep breath. Can you smell it? Can you smell the rust of antiquity about us? Blood, birth, ancestry...we're surrounded by a coterie of high pedigree! This social assemblage makes for a most memorable evening! Come, Wendell, let's enjoy some good spirits to soothe our differences. Lead me to the punch bowl. A few swills will do us both good," Mortimer cheered as he looked among the crowd adorned with lavish costumes, wigs and masks.

Mildred leaned forward to give Emma a kiss on the cheek. She winked her eye, acknowledging her success in corralling the men back into the main party.

Much to Emma's delight, William appeared in the doorway. She knew him by his height and lush locks of brown hair. Clinging to his arm was Alexandra looking like a royal princess in her golden gown with a hefty bustle and cards of lace embellishing its high collar, sleeves and bodice. Notable sequins and pearls were sprinkled about the skirt of the gown adding weight and distinction to its design. Her golden slippers were a perfect match with adornments of polished pearls and knots of lace.

"I must say, Madam that you look radiant this evening," William said to Emma as he bent to kiss her gloved hand. At the same moment, the one in red caught Simon's eye.

"Miss Emma, Miss Emma. I must say, I must say, yes I must, that the young woman over there, over there in the red, bears a striking resemblance to Miss Hargrove. Have you seen it? Have you seen the resemblance? Is it possible they are one in the same? My, my, my. How wonderful that she and her good health returned in time for your affair! Yes, I believe she is Miss Hargrove indeed!"

Simon's exuberance with his rapid-fire speech pattern caught the attention of Alexandra. The mere mention of Arielle's name prickled the hairs on her neck. She turned and gave an angered look her direction. *How dare she postpone her trip abroad and ruin my evening with William! I won't have any part of this! She must be found out now!*

Alexandra looked directly into the eyes of the lady in red with a cold, squinted stare belying the heat building in her blood. She noted the dimples on her face and that angered Alexandra further. She had oft been told one had dimples because angels kissed their cheeks just before they were born. *Oh, the very idea anything as divine as angels had come in contact with this one! Absurd! She is the devil in disguise!* Alexandra moved in closer. Simon took note of Alexandra's proximity to the guest in red and at once determined he would intervene at a moment's notice. He would allow no one to harm Miss Hargrove. He would come to her rescue! Alexandra took another step forward making Emma's lovely guest exceedingly uncomfortable. She began to step back as Alexandra lunged forward with words and her arms.

"You are nothing more than a bastard child!"

Simon squeezed his petite form between the two as Alexandra's foot lifted from the floor to trip him.

"Out of my way you impish little man!"

Simon went down in a roll through the open French doors to the patio beyond. Alexandra, in her taunt, became embroiled in Simon's descent, and with her hold on the one she berated, the two joined him on the stone patio. Alexandra leapt up and, not to be quelled began to spew more of her venom.

"How can anyone be so lame as to tolerate the dribble from this little sprite? He does nothing more than proselytize about horticulture from dawn to dusk! And, YOU are nothing but a bastard masquerading in the appointments of a lady! This evening, even your attire captures your true persona! You should be ashamed to smear the low-class likes of yourself about this fine affair! You will never rise above your station!"

The red-attired guest tried rolling away from Alexandra and the nasty words she spate as Simon lifted himself up, which was a short task with his limited stature. Not to be throttled to the ground again by Alexandra, Simon grabbed at her ankles bringing her back to the ground which allowed time and space for the disheveled guest to stand. Others were beginning to gather with audible gasps as the sounds of Alexandra's vituperation carried throughout the lower corridors of the manse.

Alexandra continued to reel, "I so hate to cast aspersions on someone so perfect as yourself, Miss Hargrove, but, have you no manner of decency? Reveal your true self!"

William appeared around the corner looking in disgust and amazement at the scene before him. "Alexandra! What on earth?"

"William, you are always my voice of reason. Tell them about this trollop!"

"Your voice of reason? Quiet yourself. I see no good reason for your behavior! Perhaps *you* can explain yourself!"

"I desire only the best for you William and this, this creature, is not to be believed!"

A very angry Simon Peabody pulled Alexandra's mask from her face. He had stood all he could of the ruckus and verbal bashing escaping from the lips of the flaxen-haired bully. She would deride him no more. Alexandra was hotter than a lit match. She glared at Simon and began to lurch his direction when William, assisted by Rainn Howard and Wendell Reed, pulled her back and tried to contain the defiant twisting and turning emanating from her body. Simon was taken back. He thought he recognized her voice and should have known by her manner that she was indeed Alexandra Whitaker. A mask was an ineffective implement to disguise Alexandra's purposes or temperament. Any facades upon her flesh did not hide her true nature.

"Oh, you silly little sod!" Alexandra cast a harsh look at Simon. "Please, William. You know how I care for you. I have nothing but your best interests at heart. You must feel the same toward me," her words spewed forth in a painful plea.

William briefly brought his attention to Simon. "How are you doing, my man?"

"Quite well, under the circumstances Mr. Clay, thank you. It seems, yes, I say, it seems, Miss Whitaker always has a good word to share." Simon's sarcasm was evident in his facial expression as he brushed the lingering essence of the ground from his clothing feeling quite thankful to be out of harm's way.

"That said, Simon, Miss Whitaker owes you an apology." William turned to Alexandra. "You cannot make my heart and mind feel something they will not."

William cleared his throat realizing this was not the proper venue for a discourse about his relationship with Alexandra.

"Oh, William. How can you be so indulgent? Can you not see the humor in this? No disparagement was intended, for I speak only of what I see, and I clearly see a menacing little troll with whom I will not parse words and a woman who has no right to be in the company of the likes of us!"

"Alexandra, you seem to take great sport in the misery of others, created I might add, by your very hand. It may appear curious to you, but the guest you accost this eve is not whom you think. Do you ever wonder about the accuracy of your accusations?"

Alexandra was not well pleased. "I dare say! I need not waste my time on the frivolity of wonder when I for one know!"

"I fear Miss Hargrove is out of the country."

"Miss Hargrove is what?"

"Out of the country."

"Who then is this impostor? She should be ordered out immediately for causing me so much anguish!"

"Your anguish is of your own doing." William searched the face of the unknown visitor. He could see how Alexandra's confusion had come about. Looking into the visitor's eyes, flecks of gold danced about, tantalizing Alexandra while keeping Simon quite mesmerized. William knew the look, yet these eyes were missing the immediate attraction he had with a similar pair. He could not explain it, but the other pair drew him in with a longing for more.

"My darling, misguided girl. My grandmother, rest her soul, would oft say, 'The road to hell is paved with good intentions.' It seems your intentions are quite one-sided and not for the good of all. Have you forever forgotten your sense of grace? I must ask that you cease this spectacle once and for all and allow my guests to return to the gaiety of the evening while you regain your composure. Perhaps you need some moments to yourself." Emma kindly forged a wedge to halt Alexandra's collision course.

The one in red was for the moment dumbfounded by the scene. She was surrounded by people who before this 'eve had never existed in her life. *My choice of boarding houses was certainly ill-fated to incur the bad luck of being under the same roof with this nasty woman,* she mused. *However, this man, this William, seems to have not only a handsome head on his shoulders but a very level one.*

"Oh, no. I cannot be silenced! It is time for *her* to reveal her dirty little secret! This poor girl has a mother, or shall I say, 'mum', other than the one known to this assembly and her name is Olivia Smithfield! She knows she has lived a lie. Tell them, you bastard trollop. Tell them the truth so they will see that I am not the liar. The biggest liar of them all is standing before us!"

Alexandra's truculent manner made Emma gasp. She had heard the name Olivia Smithfield from Arielle. *How could Alexandra know it as well?* Emma was wrought with confusion, yet Alexandra's statement begged for more to be heard.

"Alexandra, cease this degrading repartee at once!" William admonished as he took Alexandra by the arm, holding her tight as she tried to wriggle away.

"I thank you, sir," came the soft voice of the one in red. "I do appreciate your upholding my honor in the presence of one so determined to bring me down. She has made an interesting claim, and may be quite surprised herself to find that I will not deny the identity of the one who raised me to be the lady that I am today."

"Lady! Humph! Oh, remove your sorry soul from my presence," Alexandra snorted, refusing to pull in her claws.

"On behalf of my aunt and myself, I extend our sincerest apologies for this uncomfortable discourse. If I may invite you into the study, we can make the proper introductions and attempt to regain some semblance of order for the evening."

The one in red extended a wary smile. Thoughts went 'round in her head. *Perhaps it is best for my evening to end now. My time may be best served by returning to my room. When Alexandra used the name,*

Olivia Smithfield, there was recognition on Mrs. Willard's face. If my stay in Washington is extended, I am certain she will be more than kind enough to welcome me into her home again, especially when she learns more details regarding any connections to Olivia Smithfield. She hesitated to share too much of what she knew as well as the purpose of her visit before her call to the Hargrove's home after tomorrow's sunrise. Thomas had assured her he personally delivered her envelope to Sir Ian Hargrove. She knew its contents would have the Hargroves ready to have an audience with her. Her hope was that their daughter would soon return for there was much to share.

Chapter Twenty-Six

London, England

The inn's down mattress lent little comfort to Morgan's night's sleep. Olivia's skeletal body, like a harbinger of bad news, recurred in her dreams, dragging a ball and chain, barely moving under the weight of it all. Morgan wrestled with her thoughts, tossing and turning, trying to cast aside the image of Olivia while making room for logic to surface. If Olivia's health had been deteriorating as it seemed for several months on end, she may have felt the need to speak, to talk out the knowledge she had kept so close to her vest. She would need a sounding board, a confident. Or, perhaps, in her delirium, she became unrestrained and had set free information that fell on unassuming ears.

Morgan bolted straight up in bed as though struck by lightning. Her dreams may have been fitful, but they had directed her to her next move. *No, I will not proceed to Wales just yet. There is someone who must be questioned, albeit delicately. I found her a curiosity when she defied my previous questions. I shall think of a way to render her willing to communicate what she knows. There must be something that will bring clarity to Miss Smithfield's letter to the Hargroves.*

As a shaft of morning sun peered through the window in Morgan's room, she was already fully and crisply dressed to begin her day. A knock on Agnes' adjoining door stirred Peepers before arousing Agnes.

"Whoa, boy. Whoa, boy. Remain calm. Remain calm," came Peepers command to himself.

"Shhh, you silly bird. Agnes, ready yourself. We must get an early start."

"Off to Wales, are we?"

"Not just yet. Something has come to me and I must pursue it. Secure your notebook. If all goes as I have planned, there will be good reason for our trek this morn."

⸻

Beatrice had just completed Olivia's toilette, gently lifting her limbs when she heard the knock at the door. Olivia was so thin and frail, it seemed the slightest movement might snap her bones in two. She carefully rested Olivia's arm on the mattress and pulled the coverlet up to protect her skin from the morning's chill. As she descended the staircase to the brownstone's entrance, she wondered who would come calling at such an early hour. To her surprise, she beheld the threesome who had left her presence less than twenty-four hours before.

"Good morning, Miss Beatrice. We apologize for arriving unannounced at such an early hour, however, something has come to our attention that must be addressed," Morgan's words surprised Agnes for she was unaware of anything that had come to their attention since they last visited Miss Smithfield's.

"I bid you, please let us in."

"Miss Olivia is truly not up to visitors, mum. It t'would be best fer ye to give 'er a rest. Ye've been 'ere twice and it seems there be little more to gain from, if ye will excuse me mum, badgering 'er further."

Morgan was taken back by Beatrice's accusatory language, yet she appreciated the fact that the girl was protective of her charge. Not to be put off, she looked Beatrice square in the eyes as she stepped through the portal. Agnes and Peepers followed.

"In point of fact, our presence here is not to meet with Miss Smithfield. The audience we seek is with you."

"Me? For whatever reason, mum? I best be tendin' to Miss Olivia."

"Very well. We will join you alongside her bed. She may rest and you may keep a watchful eye on her. Our inquiry will consume very little of your time however, your response may be critical to the progress of our investigation. You see, Miss Beatrice, you are very important."

Agnes was not blind to the velvet glove Morgan employed when she wished to extract information from a witness. Though she had a commanding, stern tone and appeared somewhat unapproachable, people in general fell victim to her style. She could exude charisma when necessary, laced with a determined stubbornness. Ultimately, it seemed, Morgan always got her way.

Beatrice smiled taking Morgan's bait. "Okay then, mum. But only for a wee while. Miss Olivia is likely to need my attention and I must tend to 'er."

Seated around Olivia's bed, even Peepers remained reverent as all eyes rested on the pale, thin form of what had in better years been a robust woman. Agnes reflected on the toll poor health could take on one's body and soul. She wondered what Morgan had up her sleeve. *Why did she want to have a chat with Beatrice?*

"Miss Beatrice, as I have stated, you are very important. Please bear with me. You have been with Miss Smithfield and are more aligned than anyone. You have been privy to her innermost thoughts, albeit they may have been construed as ramblings. We have shared with you the Hargrove name. It is very important that we know anything and everything you have heard from Miss Smithfield in regard to this name. Tell us what she has said. You will be helping more than the two of us. You will be helping Miss Smithfield."

Beatrice listened to Morgan's words. During the weeks she had been called to care for Olivia, she had grown quite fond of her. She knew she was a kind and gentle woman who was very troubled by something from her past. Of late, it seemed her past was ever present. If she could help this kind soul and relieve her of her burdens she knew she would have served her well. But, so many things had been said. What, if any, might be important?

"I dun't know where ye'd want me to begin, mum. Miss Olivia speaks of many things. Sometimes its jest 'bout the butcher, or the color of 'er walls, or a pain she's been havin'."

"Has there been a mention of any names unfamiliar to you? Names that have been mentioned several times?"

"I dun't know. That Maggie Galligan name she told you was one I've 'eard several times. She hasn't used it alone though."

"What do you mean? How has she spoken of Maggie Galligan?"

"Well. I remember one evenin', she was gettin' very tired and called me close to 'ear what she wanted to say. 'Er voice was very weak, nearly in a whisper. She kept repeatin' Maggie, Maggie, and then she kind of rhymed 'er words together."

"Rhymed, in what way?"

"She kept repeatin' Maggie, Maggie, nursin' Annie, Annie."

"Are you familiar with Annie? Do you know of whom she was speaking?"

"No, mum. I dun't even know Maggie. In me weeks 'ere, there's ne'er been a soul named Maggie come by. And that be the same for Annie."

"Well, Miss Beatrice. Does anything else that Miss Smithfield may have said come to mind? Was there anything unusual about her behavior that may not have made sense to you at the time?" Morgan was pleased to once again hear Maggie Galligan's name, but was perplexed about the name Annie being used in conjunction with Galligan's.

"When Miss Olivia needed me to go to market fer 'er, I took a notepad from 'er drawer to make a list of the items she wanted me to purchase. She became very agitated when she saw me with the notepad. She tried to swat it from my 'and and kept pointin' to the drawer. I could see it upset 'er, so I put the paper back. Oh, my, it took 'er quite a bit of time to settle down after that."

"What do you think caused her to act in such a fashion?"

"I was thinkin' she jest didn't want me to leave. That she'd changed 'er mind 'bout my goin' to the market fer 'er. She finally went to sleep and nothin' more ever came of it."

"So, this is all you can recall that she has said in relation to the Hargroves?"

"Yes, mum. That be it." Beatrice felt somewhat guilty but she held her tongue and hoped Morgan would not be able to read anything in her expression to suggest she was hiding something. She knew she knew more but, not about the Hargroves, so, in that respect, she was being completely honest. She had no idea how any other details of Olivia's life would be important to Morgan and decided she had shared enough. She was paid to care for Olivia and would continue to place her loyalty there.

"We appreciate your candor, Miss Beatrice. We said we would take little of your time and will now take our leave. I trust you will welcome us again if the need should arise?"

"By all means, but, there's nothin' more fer me to tell to ye."

As Beatrice led Agnes and Peepers to the door of Olivia's bedchamber, Morgan paused before taking her leave. As the others began their descent to the front portal, Olivia, who had been stoically still during Beatrice's questioning, opened her eyes and rustled her arms under the sheets. Morgan was startled. She had not expected any movement from her. The woman appeared ready to become evanescent yet, here she was rallying with enough strength to convey a message.

Morgan observed her eyes as they shifted side-to-side. Her hand was erratic as she raised her index finger to point in the direction of her bureau only to have her hand come down harsh upon the bed. She tried to move her head side-to-side, but her strength failed her. She moved her mouth, but no words were formed, and she groaned in frustration. Morgan looked in the direction that Olivia's finger had attempted to aim, toward several sepia images in ornate frames that graced the surface of the bureau and nearby lingerie chest.

She took a cursory look at the display not recognizing anyone except Olivia in the images until her eyes froze on one depicting an older gentleman and young girl. The gentleman resembled Olivia. Morgan wondered if he was her brother, the good doctor, Edmond. *But the young girl,* Morgan pondered, *why is there a familiarity?* She lifted the frame from the bureau to study it more closely. *My word. How did Smithfield get this image of Arielle Hargrove? Could the man with the child be Arielle's father?* Morgan put the frame back in its original resting place. *Smithfield is not aware of her actions. I cannot place my focus on the random actions of one in such dire condition. Since the images and Smithfield herself cannot talk, I best be on my way. It's off to Wales we go on the morrow.*

Olivia's shoulders wriggled under the sheets. She once again opened her eyes peering directly into Morgan's stare. She shifted her eyes to her bedside chest with an earnestness in her gaze. Her eyes came upon Morgan with an urgency that forged a connection Morgan could not deny. She knew that Olivia was guiding her to proceed and she willingly followed the path. She pulled open the chest's drawer to find a notebook within. She lifted it up and looked at Olivia who closed her eyelids and reopened them as though sending a distress signal laced with permission.

Sometimes, one holds in her hands something that surpasses the imagination, something that makes little sense but must be pursued, Morgan reasoned. Her hands fondled the cover of Olivia Smithfield's notebook. There was nothing distinguishing about it. It was truly unremarkable though, for Morgan, the notebook spoke to her in Olivia's unspoken words.

A series of sensations filtered through Morgan's mind. She lifted the notebook's cover and set her eyes on the first page. A convolution of words captured her gaze, but what did they mean? Letters forming names appeared in a petite matrix driven diagram. Words unfolded, some familiar, some foreign. Morgan pondered, *What was Olivia trying to convey with her notations?*

And, suddenly, Olivia's prodigious notes came together like a massive jigsaw puzzle whose missing piece had been found. Her genetic map read like a hypnotic braille requiring the senses to decipher its meaning. She utilized letters, drawings, and specific locales as descriptors for Arielle's beginnings, all leading to the same end. Here was the name 'Annie' and the letters 'Ari', for the unfinished name, Arielle. And 'Annie', the name mentioned by Beatrice in association with Maggie Galligan, was in plain view under the word 'mum.'

Over and over, Morgan read through the drawings resulting in the same explanation. The names never differed. Everything led to the same result. If Olivia Smithfield's diagram held merit then Arielle, the adopted child of Sir Ian and Elsbeth Hargrove, was the birth child of a woman named Annie who died soon after giving birth. Her friend, who came to see to her care, was one Maggie Galligan. Morgan noted something odd in the remainder of the diagram. There was a line, an arm so it seemed, drawn to depict something additional, but Morgan could not determine the extension's meaning.

Were these renderings of Olivia's to be held true? Could the recordkeeping of a dying woman be held accountable? Morgan reflected on the earnestness of Olivia's pleadings as she proceeded to exit her bedchamber. Her visual contact and non-verbal conviction lent cause enough to accept her written declarations as fact. Morgan needed to contact Arielle with these revelations. But, first, she must stay on the course that would lead her to Maggie Galligan.

As the brownstone's main door closed emitting the Pennybacker threesome, Olivia rested above. A fractured smile crossed her lips as she drifted to sleep and dreamt of the doors she had at last fully opened.

Chapter Twenty-Seven

Nantymoel, Wales
In South Cymru

A few inquiries in a linen shop had directed Morgan and Agnes
not only to a new resource for materials for Pennybacker's
Stitchery, but also to the modest residence of Maggie Galligan.
She was quite surprised to be confronted by Morgan's entourage
as she opened her front door.

"Miss Galligan. Pray, let us introduce ourselves. I am Morgan
Pennybacker, a businesswoman by trade and private detective by
avocation. This is my assistant, Agnes Fielding. Your name was
offered as important to a case I am investigating. Your diligent
cooperation will be most appreciated."

"Sorry, mum if I appear a bit shaken from me moorings, but
I be quite sure I know not what yer askin' of me. And, what's yer
reason for the bird?"

"Please feel no alarm. This is Peepers. He will cast you no
harm."

"Whoa, boy. That's the truth. That's the truth," cawed Peepers.

Agnes gave his cage a little shake. Maggie shifted her eyes
from Peepers to Morgan.

"Well, 'ow is it ye've come 'bout me name?"

"To be direct with you, Miss Galligan, a woman named Olivia Smithfield spoke of you. She indicated it was important for us to speak with you."

"'Bout what? I ken tell ye I'm confused I am. An' she called me *Miss* Galligan, did she?"

"She, in point of fact, referred to you by your first and last name. Please accept my apology if I have made an error in my delivery. We are inquiring for a Miss Arielle Hargrove."

"I ken be sure I be knowin' no Arielle Hargrove. An' it's Mrs. Galligan, if ye please."

"I stand corrected. I meant no disrespect. In point of fact, we simply need your assistance. Are you sure you know nothing of Miss Hargrove, *Mrs.* Galligan?"

"Oh, I take it back, I do. I didn't know the gel but I know the name. That, I believe, were the name of the colliery owner's child. I did hear 'bout her, but n'er had I seed her."

"Why do you think Miss Smithfield would use your name?"

"I dun't right know, 'cept, I ken tell ye, it's been a very long time since I were with a Smithfield."

"When would you say that was?"

"Oh, a score or more years."

"And, please enlighten us. Why were you together?"

"Oh, we wasn't together but a snitch of time. Olivia Smithfield left as soon as I arrived."

"Arrived where?"

"As soon as I arrived at dear Annie's house."

"Annie?"

"Yes, Annie Hollingsworth."

Morgan felt as though she had hit the jackpot in a friendly poker game to hear the name Annie Hollingsworth surface just as Olivia Smithfield had mumbled to Beatrice in connection with Maggie Galligan.

"Why were you and Smithfield there?"

"Oh, it was a sad, sad day I tell ye. Too sad to think 'bout much."

"Sad in what way?"

"Oh, my dear friend Annie fach. She lost 'er life. I nursed the gel and battled 'er pain as best I could but, in the end, Annie and God won the fight."

"Your friend, Annie Hollingsworth died from what cause?"

"Bringin' her newborn babe into the world. A wee little babe was all she wanted but she n'er lived to give it all the love she stored inside."

"Is her husband nearby and her child?"

"Oh, no. Annie, fach was a good gel she was, but one moment steered 'er off 'er course and she landed with a babby. There were no husband."

"And, what of the child?"

"Ah, now there's where Miss Smithfield do come in. She tell me 'er brother, the good doctor, were takin' care of the babby, findin' it a proper home."

"You and Miss Hollingsworth were very dear friends. Whom did she say fathered her child?"

"I n'er asked the gel' bout the fix she was in. It be best told, we kept to our own dirty laundry."

"Was there nothing additional Miss Hollingsworth shared with you?"

"Muniferni! Is there no stoppin' the words flowin' from your gums?"

"Mrs. Galligan, please understand and bear with me. We have a job to pursue and pursue we must. You are a link in the chain and your importance cannot be diminished. Therefore, with no trepidation or restraint, I must insist that you scour the deepest recesses of your mind and share any minute detail that scrambles forth."

Morgan was clearly losing patience, yet, rather than term the woman daft, she maintained a firm resolve to squeeze every essence of possibility from her. She searched Mrs. Galligan's face, watching her eyes, looking for an illuminating moment when her expression would shift from nondescript to enlightened.

Agnes looked about the four walls of the boxy place Mrs. Galligan called home as the light from the windows reflected off her wire-rimmed glasses, complicating her focus. There was nothing remarkable about the very small-scale cottage. *My, there is barely enough space to cuss a cat without getting fur in your mouth!* Agnes thought to herself.

Morgan noted that every horizontal component of the Galligan residence was laid with piles of papers and articles of clothing. A vast assortment of novelties, figurines and handcrafted ware rested on every shelf of the fireplace's overmantel. *Not the neatest pig in the pen,* she scoffed to herself. Tiny checked curtains of cotton duck, hand-embroidered with rows of daisies, were blowing back and forth, carried by a subtle waft of wind passing through two windows lifted in their sashes.

Maggie was feeling substantially unsettled by the strangers before her. Why had she let them enter her premises? The questions from Miss Pennybacker were making her very nervous and she was not quite sure she felt an ounce of trust where these strangers were concerned. *Why, after all these years since Annie's passin', was the devil stirrin' up the dust?* Maggie pondered. She looked past Morgan and Agnes to Peepers. *Maybe there be a messenger in the bird.* She slowly walked to Peepers' cage and looked him straight in his eyes. She felt a connection with him as though he were a fine-feathered friend sent on the wings of God. Peepers found Maggie's approach curious and delightful. Always pleased to be the center of attention, he softly danced on his perch hoping to gain more of her favor.

"Yer quite a charmer aren't ye little fella?"

"Whoa boy, that's the truth," came Peepers' retort.

"A flirt, I'd say. What is it ye want me ta know? Do ye 'ave a message fer me?"

Morgan and Agnes observed Maggie's behavior. They glanced at each other and at once came to the mutual agreement that she might well not be of sound mind. Perhaps the recounting of Miss Hollingworth's loss had taken its toll on her, or perhaps she was truly daft.

"I ken see ye wonder why I'm talkin' to ye bird here. It's lucky ye are that I'm a wee bit fond o' wildlife. Sometimes I find it easier to 'ave a chat with God's beautiful creatures. They 'ave a natural innocence 'bout 'em, they do, and I find that a refreshin' sight, I do." Maggie looked back at Peepers. *Why is he here? What is he supposed to teach me?*

"Whoa boy. Remain calm. Remain calm. That's the truth. That's the truth." Peepers cocked his head and winked his eye at Maggie's surprised face.

That be it, Maggie thought to herself. *I must remain calm and help seek the truth like the bird said. But, whatever I be knowin' won't be flowin' from my lips to their ears like a swollen river. No, of this I be sure.*

"Miss, that is, *Mrs.* Galligan, if we may continue. We need to know more about your friend."

"I dun't know what more I ken be tellin'. Annie fach was a simple gel. I remember the last day she returned from the pits. 'Er belly was full 'round with the babby. The gel wasn't plannin' to go back to the mines 'til after the babby came. She be quite lookin' forward to bein' a mum. It jest wasn't meant to be I guess, since the babby came fast and God had other plans fer dear Annie fach." Maggie looked at the threesome with saddened eyes.

"We are sorry for your loss," Morgan proffered, feeling she needed to have Maggie gain a level of assurance that they meant her no harm.

"Is there nothing you feel would be of interest to us? Nothing that might help shed light on our investigation? Anything, even the smallest detail might be important. Where did Miss Hollingsworth live? Perhaps we could speak with some residents of the village."

"I ken take ye to 'er cottage. There's been no owner livin' there fer years and only transient folks comin' to live there from time-to-time, just payin' as they go. It's got no folks there now. I don't be knowin' what seein' 'er place will be doin' fer ye, but I ken meet ye there," Maggie suggested, knowing there was something more she could reveal if the mood struck her.

Morgan pondered the offer. She too wondered what would be accomplished by visiting the place of Annie's death. There could be nothing of hers remaining in the place after a score and more years. *But,* Morgan silently queried, *the question remains, what is the importance of Maggie Galligan to Olivia Smithfield that she would evoke her name at the mention of Arielle Hargrove? And, now, Mrs. Galligan connects both of them to the night a woman named Annie Hollingsworth gave birth. Perhaps it behooves us to be present in the place where the lives of the three women intertwined.*

Both Agnes and Morgan busied themselves, jotting notations in their journals. Morgan enjoyed a good curiosity and found Olivia Smithfield's knowledge of Maggie Galligan and Maggie's friendship with Annie Hollingsworth quite curious.

Morgan's head was full with thought and suspicions. *Smithfield's letter to the Hargroves read, 'One such occasion involved the birth of your daughter.' Galligan admits Smithfield's presence at Hollingsworth's the day she gave birth. Could it be that Hollingsworth is indeed Hargrove's mother as Smithfield proclaims in her diagram, and this is the secret she has harbored? There is more to be extracted from Smithfield.* Morgan shook her head. *I hope we do not lose the woman to the great beyond before all is revealed.*

Morgan's latest correspondence to Arielle was cryptic, for she knew the news obtained from Olivia Smithfield, as unenlightening as it first appeared, would best be told to the girl face-to-face. Perhaps Arielle knew of Maggie Galligan and Annie Hollingsworth, but Morgan erred on the side of caution rather than reveal their names in her post to Arielle. She encouraged her to join Agnes and herself in Nantymoel as soon as her health allowed her dispatch. A return post from Arielle indicated she was prepared to travel and would meet them in Wales within the next two weeks. She had been instructed, upon her arrival in

Wales, to retrieve Morgan's instructions from the small postal office located in the heart of the village.

"We accept your offer Mrs. Galligan. Our client should be arriving in Wales within the next few days. We will be in contact with you again shortly and make the arrangements to visit Miss Hollingsworth's residence. On what street did you say she lived?"

"I don't be rememberin' 'at I gave ye a name. But, I'm 'appy to reveal it, I am. Can't be no 'arm in it. Wyndham be the name. Wyndham Street. A sweet little cottage with an odd roof it is. Ye can't miss it."

Maggie was starting to feel a level of comfort with her visitors. They were after all interested in her dear friend. *What harm could come from mentioning Annie's possession? Then I'll 'ave 'em go on their way.*

Morgan observed a slight change in Mrs. Galligan's demeanor.

"Is there something more you would like to add, Mrs. Galligan?"

"Why do ye ask? 'Aven't ye asked enough questions for one visit? My, my, ye could worry the horns off a Billy goat, ye could!"

"Any light you can shed on this mystery will be of great benefit to our client. We will be most appreciative of your cooperation."

Maggie looked at the trio, still considering what she wished to reveal.

"I ken tell ye. I won't be presenting it now, but, I 'ave somethin' 'at might be of interest, but I ken tell ye, I not be quite sure."

"With all due respect, I beg you to please end the suspense. Of what do you speak? Let us be the judge of the relevance of your offer." Morgan nearly had steam flowing from her pores, she was becoming so exasperated with the woman.

"Well, like I said, I won't be revealin' it now, but I will be bringin' it with me to the cottage, I will."

"If you would be so candid, please name of what you speak?"

"Oh, it's jest an old box, older now with the years that 'ave passed. It belonged to Annie, fach. We'll all see it together soon enough."

"Thank you, Mrs. Galligan. Since you appear firm in your resolve to not expose this box, as you call it, at this time, I do request that you bring Miss Hollingsworth's property when we next meet."

"Ye 'ave no need to be bossin' me around. I 'ave said I would and I will. Me word is me word."

Morgan, Agnes and Peepers had barely left the premises when Maggie went to the lower drawer of a heavy oak desk in her parlor. The weight of the drawer dragged against its rails as Maggie gave an extra hefty tug to move it forward. With its contents exposed, she rooted through a pile of documents, tossing some aside as she searched deep into the back of the drawer to put her hands upon the piece of interest. There it was, Annie's box, just as she had left it all these years.

"It's time, Annie. Ye could say, a little bird told me. Yes, it's time, of that I be sure. Ye wanted me to be a safekeeper, Annie fach, and that I 'ave. I 'ave a feelin' it's time this box go back to yer house."

Maggie stroked the surface of the box. She wondered about its contents, if there were any. It had not seen the light of day since Annie's death, but she felt very strongly, now was the proper time for its resurrection.

Chapter Twenty-Eight

Had she a map of the premises, Arielle would be no better guided. Innately, an inexplicable aura directed her to the bedside window. She peered out, casting her eyes on visions that may well have echoed her mother's. Ivy clad cottages greeted her eyes, their simple shutters flung aside, some askew, testing the tenuous hold of their hardware. She stood in reverent reverie as passersby and a garden just beyond the sill gave life to the pedestrian streetscape. Marigolds, daisies and zinnias grew lushly among a cluster of rose bushes that had become weighty with their unharvested bounty.

She lifted the window to clear the small bedchamber's stagnant air. A breeze through its open panes felt fresh against her face. A Thomas Hood verse, often recited to her as a child by Elsbeth, came to mind and she repeated its words out loud, "I remember, I remember, the house where I was born, the little window where the sun came peeping in at morn."

Suddenly, a surge of sensations met her. The need to escape from the ever present and retreat to a distant place of comfort made her feel possessed. *Why, enveloped in my mum's very room, do I feel the need to be in a different place in another time? Enough,* she thought. *Enough.* She shimmied her form to shake away the barnacles of discomfort attempting to encrust her soul in a weighty blanket of fearful despair. She could only attribute her uneasiness to a subconscious sense of impending doom.

I have come so far, I must not retreat. She harkened to Emma's words, 'My dear, you are bound to pursue this to its finish. Nothing can be left to chance, nothing worthwhile, nothing important, nothing about your life.'

Simon Peabody's impish form floated into her mind, his words echoing, 'Check and double-check. Nothing to chance, nothing to chance.' *But, what of chance? How great a risk lay in bringing home the information gathered through Miss Pennybacker's investigation? How on earth will Mum and Father react? How will we face one another? And, William. Oh, we are doomed. Alexandra's precipitous intrusions and accusations will find true merit. He will want nothing to do with me just as she forewarned!* Tears welled in her eyes and trailed downward along the full length of her face with a momentary hesitation before dropping from her chin and landing on her chest, close to her heart.

Another breeze swept across her face. It came as a gentle whisper and calmly floated about her. It was the precise distraction needed to re-direct the processes of her mind. Though Arielle did not exactly know what she was searching for, she knew full well she would know it when she found it. Her greatest hope was that her search would bring her great reward.

Mum was here. My mum. My, mu….Oh, what I would give to have known her. Her look, her voice, her touch. The thought gripped her and tugged at her heart. Her mind dallied away from the loss, but her subconscious brought it back full center. A tingling sensation that seemed to find its origin in her torso, shifted its existence northward through her body, stopping at her lower lip where a numbing vibration resonated across the tender flesh of her mouth. She was instantly reminded all too well of the freshness of the hurt and the loss that left a vacant chamber in her heart. Arielle closed her tear weary eyes as another breeze, blowing its essence from outside in, enveloped her, then lost itself into the space around her. Her mother was not physically here, but her presence was all about her.

A hand came upon Arielle's shoulder. The unexpected touch made her shudder. So deep in thought, she had not heard Maggie Galligan enter.

"Sorry, Miss. I wasn't meanin' to upset ye. It's jest Miss Pennybacker asked me ta join ye."

"Pardon my asking, but who are you?"

"Oh, I'm nobody but an ol' friend of the gel that once lived 'ere, just a simpleton I am. I know Miss Pennybacker will be along soon, but there's somethin' I think ye might as well have now. I'm not quite sure what it's all about, but this old box was in dear Annie's possession and she passed it to me the eve she died. I've taken good care of it, I 'ave, just like she asked of me."

"Of what are you speaking?"

"This, miss. This box. Annie, took 'er last breaths directin' me to this little chest. Its key had gone missin', so it is jest as I found it. I kept it set aside, out of the way of me everyday livin' 'til Miss Pennybacker 'peared on me doorstep. I didn't think much of it, but with all the chatter about Annie and Miss Pennybacker's nosy questions, I thought it might be time to bring the box back to where it belonged. I dun't know, just a feelin' that come over me."

"Has Miss Pennybacker informed you about Miss Hollingsworth or should I say, your friend, Annie, and her relation to me?"

"Oh, no, miss. She was merely askin' me 'bout dear Annie and 'er final moments on this earth. I told 'er that after the babby came, Doc Smithfield's sister called on me to see to Annie. Said there was nothin' more could be done but comfort 'er, that she was in God's 'ands and I was there to comfort 'er."

"Did you see the baby?"

"Oh, no. The babby was gone. Miss Smithfield said 'er brother would see it got a proper home since Annie was an orphan 'erself with no kinfolk known to 'er."

Arielle felt an unusual calm in Maggie's presence. She felt an unexplained kinship that prompted her to tell the news Morgan had uncovered. She imagined she would go insane if she kept the painfully fresh information to herself.

"Well, I will tell you. I am Arielle Hargrove."

"Oh, that name rings a bell, it does. Are ye a relation to the Big House? What a sight it be fer the eyes, I be sure!"

"Yes, Sir Ian Hargrove is my father. I feel calmly assured for some unknown reason that you can be trusted. It seems if my mum trusted you with her possession, then I too shall do the same."

"Your mam? Are ye sayin' dear Annie was your mam fach?"

"Yes. That is precisely what I am saying."

Arielle was caught again by a wave of disbelief. *How could this be happening? How could I be the baby of Annie Hollingsworth? Morgan must be misinformed. Olivia was hallucinating she said, passing in and out of reality. Her words could not be trusted, yet how in the world did she pick my name from so many millions and follow my path to America?* Arielle felt ready to swoon. Her emotions easily bled through. It would take no more than the graze of a cat scratch to draw a crimson line along the surface of her vulnerability. Maggie caught the pasty expression descending like a pulled window shade over Arielle's beautiful face and moved to support her. She rested the box on the bedside table drawing a chair near for Arielle's safe comfort.

The air surrounding Arielle was clear and transparent as a ghost, yet she might as well have been in a dense fog whose borders defied distance or definition. The fog, manifested solely in her mind, was as thick as a preponderance of gauzy cobwebs. She could hear a voice calling to her.

"Miss Hargrove. I say, Miss Hargrove. Are you quite alright?"

This could not be my mum calling to me. She would use an endearment. Something tender, comforting, like 'sweet girl.' She would not call me Miss Hargrove. She would cuddle, stroke and soothe me. The words resonated in Arielle's head. She blinked and blinked to clear the webs of confusion only to see Maggie before her.

Maggie was barely believing what her ears were hearing. She was privy to some news that would have all the teeth in the whole of Ogmore Vale chattering away. But her allegiance was to Annie, and that meant her allegiance would be extended to her issue as well.

"'Ere, miss. This news must be shockin' ta ye as much as it is to meself. In me whole life of days, I never thought I would meet the offspring of me dear gel friend, Annie. Just wait 'til the whole of the vale learns the news," Maggie said as she reached to steady Arielle.

"No. We must keep this to ourselves. There is no need to take this further than the threshold."

"Miss, you don't know the vale, do ye? 'Cause if ye did, ye'd know we's all family. Nantymoel's a mining village and where there's minin' there's the need to know your neighbor's business. Oh, you can best be sure there'll be no one learnin' this from me lips. But, somehow, someday, the truth will surely be known. Everythin' comes 'round eventually, of that ye can be sure."

Arielle felt insulted by this common woman telling her she knew nothing of the vale. Of course she knew mining. Her father may have kept her from its depths, but she had made herself privy to his conversations enough to know the operations of the mine. She knew the business of the mine, the safety concerns, the labor union difficulties, resulting in uprisings that threatened the livelihood of the mine itself and the families who counted every bean put on their tables by the menfolk who worked the dark, dank depths of its shafts and tunnels. She knew. How dare this simple woman challenge her this way.

Arielle stopped herself. This simple woman was her mother's dear friend. Had this strange twist of circumstances not occurred, she would be part of this vale family and kith and kin to all who resided from birth to death under the veil of the mine, her father's mine. She had lived a life of privilege in the 'Big House', or 'tyrn vawr' as the townsfolk called it, high on a hill looking down upon the town from which she was no longer far removed. The cobblestone streets of Nantymoel were her streets, the townsfolk were her people, and all the preconceived notions she held about them were now being shed in rivers of painful, self-inflicted tears.

Maggie watched her face, her pierced brow giving an indication of her distress. *Oh, a beauty she is, despite 'er pain,* thought Maggie. *How proud Annie would be to 'ave such a lovely gel to call 'er own. 'Ow she would have loved to scrape together what she could for the unplanned youngin' who cost 'er 'er life.*

Arielle wiped at her face, then looked straight up into Maggie's caring eyes. "Tell me of her."

"Your mam, gel?"

"Yes. Please. Tell me of her. I need to know her. I must know."

"I ken tell ye first that ye've an eerie resemblance to 'er. Not yer 'air, for Annie's was a rich auburn with brilliant strands o' red like the red-orange blaze of the sun, but it's yer face. Annie, like ye, 'ad the most lovely complexion, creamy smooth, with jest a blush of rose 'igh on 'er cheekbones. But, with ye, it's the eyes. Very few folk ken e'er pride 'emself on the sparkle Annie 'eld in 'er eyes and ye've got it gel, flecks of sparkle that dance in the light. Oh, 'er eyes could capture the attention of perfect strangers to be sure. They could intoxicate a mun as bad as several 'rounds of stout at the 'Double Duchess.' Yeh, Annie was a looker, though 'er daily dress would've fooled a mun or two."

"How do you mean?"

"Did Miss Pennybacker tell ye any part 'bout Annie?"

"Miss Pennybacker told me to meet you here, that she would explain what she knew in person."

"Then maybe it's best if we wait for 'er. She's an odd sort she is, wit that other woman, Agnes, she calls 'er. She said she's 'ere on yer behalf. Is she like a relative settlin' a score? It's rare to see a woman doin' that, is all. And, she's no hired gun, specially with the bird an' all, 'less the bird's a distraction. That's some bird for sure. Every time I answered Miss Pennybacker, the bird chirped, 'Whoa, boy. Whoa, boy,' like an 'ole feathered worry-wart. 'Peepers,' she calls it. Like it has an eye on ye. Or, maybe it's cuz of its way, makin' a peep here and there like it's got ta get a word in. Oh, I dun't know, it's jest unusual is all, to have a bird as a companion. It's a standout, it is, that's fer darn sure!"

"What time is it getting to be? Miss Pennybacker should be here by now. She typically prides herself on her punctuality." Arielle was becoming impatient and felt the need to move things ahead, to get to the matters at hand.

A knock at the door brought closure to Arielle's query. Morgan entered, her demeanor as crisp as the suit she wore. Precise. Everything precise. Agnes made her way through the portal, Peepers' cage forming a buffer between the doorframe and his feathered frame as the cottage's door swiftly closed upon them. Agnes leapt into the room, attempting to keep her balance lest Peepers be flung from swing to sidebars and back.

The assembly stared at one another. A moment of stiff silence was broken by Morgan's cleared throat, "I see Mrs. Galligan has given you the box."

The box. Arielle was shaken into instant awareness of the object of Morgan's focus. She had paid it little attention since Maggie presented it to her, her mind focused on more distant thoughts, more distant times. The box. A simple structure of six-sided oak, well grained and deftly rubbed with wood oil. The box. Very pedestrian in design, ornamented only by a small iron lock with a floral knob centered on top. The flower. A beautifully carved rose poised itself on the box's hinged lid. *Roses,* thought Arielle. *Again roses.* She had admired the fragrant gathering of rose bushes from her mother's bedroom window only to find their form repeated on her mother's possessions. *The rose. A thing of beauty to be admired. A thing of beauty to be cherished. A thing of love.* Arielle ran her fingers across the carving, passing her fingertips along the ridges and valleys defining every petal of the flower's design. Her exploration ended upon Morgan's determined inquiry.

"The box. Has its contents been of any value?"

Value? Arielle was feeling quite exhausted. The emotional heft of the box far surpassed its actual weight. For all she knew, its interior remained as empty as her sorrowful soul. *Oh,* she sighed a deep, deep sigh as though the life might be sucked from her body. She cast her eyes toward Morgan, back at the box and away again. She was so greatly absorbed in self-pity, she might otherwise have been in an empty room, for she had tuned out everyone around her.

"Miss Hargrove, are you quite alright?"

Arielle felt anything but alright. She was for all intents and purposes numb to the core. She shook her head thinking that a good jiggle of her brain might expunge her of these circumstances. But, the box. The box and its contents might well be a precious link to her mother.

"I must…" Arielle hesitated, feeling overcome with rugged despair. She swallowed and paused to collect herself. *How could a benevolent God exist who would cast such a pal over my being?* "I must first know more of this woman you claim is my mum before I endure the opening of this oak coffer and even begin to embrace its contents, be there any."

"As you wish, Miss Hargrove," Morgan acquiesced. Though she preferred to exercise the efficiency of time, she was indeed a hired agent and must take heed of her client's request. "Mrs. Galligan, if you will so indulge us, please tell what you know of Annie Hollingsworth."

Maggie looked at the foursome, including Peepers in her count, feeling reticent. She was unaccustomed to being singled out, much preferring to remain in the mix of the shadows. Public speaking was not her wont. However, it was obvious the heat she felt from Morgan's stare would only be extinguished with her response.

"I ken tell ye, she was a lovely gel who worked 'ard, 'ard as a mun, she did. That be quite right."

"What did she do? What was the nature of her work?" Morgan queried.

"Well, I s'pose since Annie's gone 'n all, 'er secret'll do no 'arm ta 'er now, 'n she'd be forgivin' me for breakin' me silence."

"Please go on," Morgan urged.

"Annie had to keep up her disguise. She was good, as good as a mun, but every inch a woman. She had to make a livin' as she had no kinfolk to support 'er. We looked out fer each other, we did, and I 'ave always 'ad limited funds meself. But, we always got by. Annie was very proud of 'er work. We used to laugh that she couldn't call 'ers 'honest work' since she was foolin' Paul the Overman and Tim the Under-Manager day-by-day. She did a grand job of it, she did. Oh, the gel was smart and a beauty. Ar doriad gwawr, at the cut of dawn, Annie was hard at work. When the first hooter blew at five o'clock, the gel had to change 'er-self to look like a mun, which challenged the gel after she took with babby. Rising daily before the first drop of the morning's dew began to fade, Annie splashed 'er face with an eye-openin' bit o' water from the porcelain basin on 'er oak washstand. The gel would dab 'er face with a cotton cloth, bringin' a ruddy pink blush to 'er tawny skin. She'd gaze in the mirror with 'er emerald eyes half askew and blink 'er dark auburn lashes several times at-temptin' to keep 'er eyelids aloft. She slipped into 'er blackcloth breeches, ran a brush threw 'er tresses, coiled and knotted 'em, then reached for 'er blue cotton bonnet. The gel placed it on 'er head and tied it securely in back so there were no tellin' she be a gel. Then, when the pit hooter began shrieking at five thirty in the mornin', the gel was on 'er way with the rest of the queue of mun, walking silently in the moon's shadows to the top end of the village. Argllwydd mawr, gels. Ye should've seed the look I did give 'er when first I seed 'er in 'er pit-grimed clothes." Maggie smiled with pride as playful images of Annie replayed in her mind's eye.

"This woman, my mum, worked in the pits of the colliery?" Arielle queried, aghast to suppose herself the offspring of a common, coal-dust encrusted, pit brow girl.

She could envision the promenade of workers returning to their homes at the close of day, their faces and clothing black with coal dust. She had, on numerous occasions, observed the workers' raccoon-like eyes, the white circles closest to their eyes forming the only element on their bodies free of dust.

Arielle mused, *How could one be with others and at once feel sad and alone? What was the point of it all?* She began to question her worth, her raison d'etre. Her emotions began to send staggering waves of emptiness, loss and despair across her flesh. The sensations challenged the rational processes of her mind and shook her moorings. At once she sensed there must be nothing more intense or hard to shake off than interminable sadness. It came on gang force like a chronic disease with no end or hope for cure. She was like a ball rolling downhill with nothing in sight to slow her momentum or buffer her ultimate impact. She became quiet, drawn against herself, and wondered how she could miss someone so abundantly whom she never knew.

Arielle felt like escaping, dying, but she was too curious. Too curious about her own life. Too curious about what tomorrow would bring. Too curious about the one life she had been given by birthright and the grace of God to make a difference, to make a mark, to have some distinction on this planet called earth. She must keep going. She must renew herself if she were ever to realize her hopes and dreams. Taking hold of her racing mind, she sought the proper perspective to gain relevance about all that was being placed before her. She knew the events that triggered her fragile emotions were not of her doing yet, her response to them would be. How she would redeem her hold on all that was good and sane and right was not yet within her vision, but she was determined to clear all of the fog-filled webs of confusion and, at present, Maggie Galligan was her most ready source for clarity.

"I apologize, Mrs. Galligan. Events of late have tested the limits of my grace. I beg you, continue."

Maggie hesitated. She was not yet recovered from the verbal slight to her friend, Annie fach. She had before been subjected to the high and mighty refined folks such as the likes of Miss Hargrove and she knew her father's name well. The miners had oft fought with colliery officials, the sods of the powerhouses, about timber shortages and the immense danger to the miners without proper shoring to the pit walls. There was no lack of danger in the mines. *Oh, tut, tut,* she thought to herself. *They think themselves the cat's whiskers because their toilets aren't in the yard. Well, I'll teach 'em a thing or two 'bout the real pit residue of the village!*

"That you do blame your mum for 'er livelihood is most unfortunate. Try to bear up the best ye can for she always thought of others 'fore herself. She was a kind gel and she never be too shamed to raise her head. Yer father, I be too sure, spoke in yer home of the 'splosion at his colliery, the village runnin' to the top edge of the vale as the iron knocker sounded six times signaling death in the pit to all anxiously waitin' above for the cage to rise to the surface. Thee daily vessel of transport to thee coalface became a mobile tomb for e'vry mun burned and charred beyond his famblies recognition. Oh, sad times was these, n'er a dry eye or household free of sighin' for all the butties lost. Muniferni! These were mun reared in the life blood of the colliery. They were its lungs and sensed its spirit and force. Ye could hear a hymn sung o'er and o'er," Maggie related as she quite naturally began to sing:

> Beth sydd ymi yn y byd
> Ond Gorthrymderau mawr ohyd.

> What in this world for me
> But great grief and agony.

"Ye may 'ave been in the Big House, lookin' o'er the valley and the pits, fer from the mun an' their famblies, but I ken tell ye, the pain 'n sufferin' was nearly more then the village could bear. Oh, it were sad times indeed. The mun know the dangers of the mine an' are prepared to die, but that dun't ease the truth of death fer the ones left behind. Yer mam rallied the other gels in the village, gave 'em comfort. Argllwydd mawr, gels. You should have seed the look they did give her. Like there were no hope left on this earth. But, Annie, oh she gave 'em hope of spirit and, once the pits re-opened, worked double shifts to bring some coin to their tables. She told the gels, 'The good Lord brought us through this and he'll bring us through the rest of it.' Ye can think what ye will, but if ye think ill of Annie fach, ye be thinkin' wrong."

The audience of four looked at one another, taking inventory of their facial expressions. Even Peepers was strangely mute. Maggie's words were sobering. Each visage carried the similar sullen look of one duly reprimanded for unbecoming behavior. Maggie was obviously a true friend indeed, dedicated more than most to keeping sacred all memories of Annie's life as she lived it on earth, while protecting her blessed soul that was cast too soon to eternity. *They're a crude bunch, they are,* thought Maggie. *Fancy clothes and fancy words to go 'long with 'em. Well, I dun't fancy 'em much. I've a mind te leave 'em with no more talk of Annie. Oh, Annie fach, how I miss ye gel.* Maggie could see Annie's lovely face, her kind smile encouraging her to continue. *This is yer gel, Annie fach. I know I must do me best fer 'er same as I done me best fer ye.*

"We stand corrected, Mrs. Galligan," Morgan apologized for the assembly. "Please forgive our prejudices, for they hinder our discourse with you. Nothing would please us more than to have you proceed. I pray, please continue."

"Ye know, I be jest thinkin', it can be a burden, bein' with babby with no mun to clean you by marriage. Annie, I be quite sure, would 'ave liked to live the dream and 'ave a proper fambly, but the gel tried to bear up the best she could. I reminded 'er we'd both known gels who'd drove their ducks to muddy water. They'd married the wrong mun and never agen had a happy life. Once she found 'erself with babby, she took great care to protect the babby and 'er secret. Workin' too many hours in the pits were probably wots killed 'er. She went stiff now and agen from stayin' down too long."

"The question begs to be asked who got the gel, I mean girl, with child?" Agnes queried, her sudden outburst promoting a cautioning rise in Morgan's eyebrow, a gasp from Arielle, and 'Whoa, boy,' from Peepers.

"What?" Agnes asked, responding to their shocked reactions. "I'm no more curious than the rest. Surely, we all desire an answer to this for the puzzle's anything but complete. Let's see. We have a mother and a baby, it's only natural to want to know about the father." Agnes held her ground, her sense of purpose giving her an uncommon sense of confidence.

"Agnes, please allow Mrs. Galligan to complete her discourse without a discourteous interruption from you. Remember, all things in good time. In point of fact, Mrs. Galligan, Agnes here is forgetting the importance of your telling us what you know in your own way. Please indulge us some moments more. About the father. What do you know of him?"

Agnes' mouth formed a smirk-like smile as she looked away from Morgan, quite pleased that she had a hand in guiding the telling of Mrs. Galligan's story. Her years with Morgan had always placed her in a subservient position but, like their companion, Peepers, she was on occasion compelled to spread her wings, never knowing if her flight of words would find her at a safe destination in Morgan's world. Having suffered the rise of Morgan's brow for her latest inquiry, Agnes determined it best to remain silent and make not another peep, at least for the time at hand.

Maggie was feeling very worn down by the inquisition that she was barely enduring. It was all taking a nasty personal turn and she was not liking one bit of it.

"I 'ave no idea who the father be. Annie, and me, we was close, close as kin, but the gel only now and agen said he was a verra well set-up mun."

"Well set-up?" Morgan queried, not as familiar with the Welsh language as she would like.

"Well dressed," Maggie answered.

"So, you have little or no idea whether the father was a neighbor in the village or one of the men working in the pits?" Morgan asked hoping to glean some clue.

"No idea. Dim Llawn Llathen! Do ye think me without a full yard? I'm not empty-headed! The gel n'er confided in me 'bout the mun. As I've told ye, I asked 'er no questions 'bout the fix she was in. 'E's as much a mystery to me as the likes of ye. A'I wynt yn ei ddwrn! Ye've got the wind in yer fist! Dun't be in such a hurry. Look at how fer we've got to now. Chwilen yn dei phen! Ye can't have a bettle in y'er head. It's taken more 'an two score of years fer me to 'ave Annie's babby come before me eyes. I hope Annie fach is lookin' down from the 'eavens and knows I did seed 'er."

Arielle's eyes filled again with tears. She was feeling empathy for a woman she never knew as she swathed herself in interminable pity. The road of discovery had come to a halt with seemingly no feed to fuel the rest of the journey. As she readied herself to tell Miss Pennybacker it was time to cease their visit and abandon further investigative pursuits, she turned from the trio only to find her gaze fixed on her visage in the freestanding cheval mirror in the corner of the petite bedchamber. There she was. But for Arielle's raven hair, the ghost of Annie Hollingsworth stood well before her. There, within the dusty haze of the looking glass, emerged an apparition, a spitting image of the young pit brow girl who bore her into the world only to be deprived of the joys of seeing, caressing and knowing her. She nearly gasped as she viewed her reflection, but was suddenly jolted from the phantom stare by Morgan's commanding voice.

"Agnes! Stop fidgeting!" Morgan's ire with her less than successful questioning of Mrs. Galligan came across loud and clear as she lost patience with Agnes' behavior.

Agnes had rested Peepers' cage on the chair next to the bedside table. Her hands free, she began exploring the oak coffer Maggie had placed on the tabletop. Her fascination centered on the beautiful wooden rose set atop the coffer, its elaborate carving giving rich detail to every petal. Her hand was firmly gripping the ornamentation when Morgan's voice gave her an enormous startle causing her hand to jerk so severely she sensed the rose had been plucked from its formidable base. Instead, all stood in amazement as the rose, no longer centered, shifted to the side, revealing a shallow compartment beneath. Agnes looked at the compartment, then to Morgan to take a cue for her next action. None of the others were in a position to see what Agnes saw. Morgan sensed there was more than remorse coming from Agnes' expression for having altered the original condition of the box.

"What is it, Agnes?"

Taking Morgan's query as her entrée to reveal her find, Agnes placed her thumb and forefinger into the shallow reserve of the chest's lid. Using her pincher grasp, she removed an object and held it in the air for all to see. Sunlight through the nearby window danced on and off the gleaming metal piece. A key. A shiny brass key. Could it be the simple device that would unlock a coffer kept sealed more than a score of years? Would it be the device to unlock the history of a family that was never to be? Arielle stared at the box. Could it be that it held secrets to her mother's life and thus her own?

"Whoa, boy. Whoa, boy," Peepers exclaimed as he flitted about his cage.

What to do now? The assembly looked about at one another. Morgan reached for the key in Agnes' hand and offered it to Arielle.

"Would you, Miss Hargrove, like to perform the honors?"

Arielle could not immediately speak, and tears were once again threatening to well in her eyes. With her fingertips, she took the key from Morgan's hand and rubbed her thumb about its surface. She looked at Agnes and reached for the box. She had already been so rattled to the bone, she imagined there was nothing more that could shake her. She would be true to her task and unveil the contents of the coffer that meant so much to her mother. Slowly and methodically, she placed the key into the lock and gave it a simple turn. There was a soft click sound, but the lid remained unmoved. She slipped the key from the lock, placed it back into its reservoir under the carved rose and slowly slid the rose back into place. Her fingers fondled the oak flower, then moved across the top to its front edge. She lifted the lid, squinting her eyes with hesitation as though a serpent might rear its ugly head and take a swipe at her. As her fear dissipated, she set her eyes upon several items comprising the contents. A folded paper, a spoon, and an old daguerreotype with curled edges rested before her.

Arielle lifted the daguerreotype from the box giving it only a furtive glance as tears filled her eyes blurring her sight. Maggie glanced over Arielle's shoulder. The quality of the image left quite a bit to the imagination. Somewhat faded with fingerprint smudges across its surface, it was still remarkably evident to Maggie that it pictured a young woman posed before a fine coach.

"May I have a look at it, gel?" Maggie took the photograph from Arielle and examined it closely, holding it to the light emanating from the window.

"Jest as I thought from a distance. It's me dear Annie."

Morgan glanced at the image. "You are sure this is Annie Hollingsworth?"

"As sure as I am 'bout me own likeness. Oh, a pretty gel she was. Pretty 'til the day she left me face frozen in sorrow."

"May we take this along with us, Miss, um, *Mrs.* Galligan?" Morgan queried.

"That would be quite up to Miss Hargrove, but I say, if it be o' more use to ye then meself, I say yer welcome to it. Annie's forever vividly etched in me mind and me heart with or without that faded piece of paper. But, it's Miss Hargrove ye need to be askin'. I 'ave done me part for Annie, as yer bird there says, 'That's the truth.'"

"I stand corrected. Miss Hargrove, before we depart, do you mind if Agnes and I have this piece? In point of fact, it may be instrumental to any further inquiries we make on your behalf."

"By all means, Miss Pennybacker. I would be most relieved if you would carry the box with you as well. I see no further cause for me to remain abroad. On the morrow, I will begin my return to America. The contents of the box can be further studied at a later date. I fear I am not as strong as I thought. It will best serve my health to gather my strength for the conversations that are inevitable with my family." Arielle turned to acknowledge the group and bid them adieu with her parting words.

"Mrs. Galligan, I thank you for your friendship to Miss Hollingsworth. I am unable to publicly reference her as my mum for I never knew her as such. As the days ahead come before us, perhaps all that has transpired will come into clear view. I thank you as well for your kept promise to her. She was, in your case, a fine judge of character for you have fulfilled her last wish. With the aid of Miss Pennybacker, I will soon pursue the meaning of the items in this box. For now, I will take leave and return to America to collect my thoughts."

Arielle gave a nod and the box to Agnes and exited the cottage. She knew she had come so far with so much farther to go. The next familiar ground she would set foot upon would be in Washington, District of Columbia, yet her home on Vermont Avenue seemed remote and gravely changed. Facing the two who created her world of lies was a daunting thought. Her mother and father were going to have to admit the truth for there to be any hope for the healing process to begin.

The sky immediately above Arielle filled with a mass of birds. The flock swarmed, then spread in perfect, synchronized formation. She watched with admiration, hoping the days ahead would bring such perfect choreography to her life.

Suddenly, an unfamiliar sensation overcame her. *Was it the birds or another winged force?* A welcomed feeling of composure spread through her as she blended her world as she knew it with her mother's world as she imagined it. A universal sense of security washed over her as she realized a common denominator that separation by space, time and secrecy could not negate. Arielle's blood flowed with renewed force. For the moment, she felt free as a bird and willingly cast aside the ashes of her past to receive what she perceived to be her birth mother's promise. She cast her eyes to the heavens, realizing she was being made whole by a power larger than herself, and she gladly surrendered to it.

As Morgan and her entourage took their leave, she realized that in her haste to be on her way she had not inquired about the coach in the daguerreotype. *Surely, a girl of Miss Hollingsworth's standing would not have access to such a handsome park drag. Tomorrow will be soon enough to ask,* thought Morgan. *Perhaps, another visit to Mrs. Galligan's is in order. And, then again, she has no information regarding the sire of Hollingsworth's issue. She is probably as daftly uninformed about the coach. There is someone who knows and I intend to find him.*

Chapter Twenty-Nine

Washington, District of Columbia

Ian observed the letter in quiet contemplation. He sat in an awkward position, as though he was uncomfortable to read the words before him. The initial strokes upon the parchment, plagued with spastic penmanship, made the hand difficult to decipher. Row after row of jagged letter formations challenged his ability to interpret the words comprising the composition. He so wished he could deliver himself from its reading. But, avoidance would not be his guidepost this day. Read it he must and, this time, with Elsbeth close at hand. He had spent time enough without her. He knew his indiscretions full well, and knew he must, without hesitation, bring her onboard before their relationship that gave him anchor, drifted past settled shores to an endless, unretrieveable sea.

He was well aware that Elsbeth could endure little more. He loved her. He loved their companionship. He loved their length of union. He too indeed loved his self-established rules that allowed him to deviate from the covenants of the vows to which he solemnly gave his oath nigh a score and five years before. *Sacred* would remain the full commitment espoused by Elsbeth.

Ian, having created his own tome for the proper deportment of a spouse, would continue to amble his way in and around the dalliances that threatened to usurp the relationship held in bond of marriage by man and wife.

He turned toward the doorway of his study, subconsciously digging the heels of his black leather boots into the receiving fibers of the dense wool carpet, as though such a temporary gesture against the pile would permanently hold him back, allowing him escape from engaging Elsbeth in the turmoil to come.

With little effort, his boots left their shallow entrenchment as his feet made steps into the hallway, past the staircase, to the conservatory at the rear of the manse. There he found Elsbeth, solitarily at work on an intricate needlepoint design. Upon completion, she intended to use it as a new cover for the stool sitting in wait at the piano for anyone of talent to rest awhile and have their musical way with the black and white ivory keys. Her love of nature and birds was evident in the detailed leaf motif of the pattern, prominently featuring a pair of cardinals in its center. The 'love birds', as she was wont to call them, had always been favorites. The vibrant red, particularly of the male, represented for her the heart's great passion and fire of desire. She knew the accent of red in the parlor would add a tasteful burst of color among the hunter green, brown, black and ecru of the room.

Ian kept his eyes affixed to the gentle woman who had accepted his advances and willingly become his bride. How quickly, he mused, the years had passed, days and nights melding into weeks and months, becoming a blend of success and failure, happiness and sorrow, love and loathing. Loathing. He could honestly say he had never felt such emotion toward Elsbeth, nor felt it reciprocated by her. She was his stability, his light and he, at times, felt ridden with self-reproach for having been dishonest in his fidelity. She so wanted to bear children and when that ability was deemed impossible, he agreed that they would make other arrangements so she could feel fulfilled and make the utmost use of the nurturing skills begging to be put to the test of rearing a child. Motherhood suited Elsbeth. Motherhood came quite naturally. She was calm and supportive with a patient, guiding hand. From the moment Arielle entered their lives, Elsbeth was filled with a greater sense of purpose. She kept a pleasant balance between her duties as wife and mother, never neglecting either role, and she drew Ian into his position as father, encouraging outings and gatherings that would highlight their bond as a family.

"Elsbeth." Ian broke the great silence of the space with the simple calling of her name.

She looked up from her needlework, taking a moment for her eyes to focus on the figure of her husband standing in the doorway. He looked quite handsome in his black pinstriped suit with vest to match. His white shirt cuffs extended just enough below the sleeve of his jacket to expose the gold cufflinks she had given him last year for their twenty-fifth wedding anniversary. The gold of the cufflinks picked up the flicker of the flame from the nearby lampolier, enhancing their brilliance. Elsbeth had them engraved with the Hargrove crest rather than Ian's three initials, thinking that a future generation would appreciate the significance of the family heirlooms when Ian's time had passed for the wearing of them. Anticipating Arielle's eventual marriage and offspring, Elsbeth hoped her grandchildren would treasure the cufflinks.

"My dear, I am sorry to take you away from your lady's work, however, the document in my hand was just delivered to us by messenger, and we need to review it together."

"Whom is it from?" Elsbeth queried, assuming it was not a matter of business, for Ian rarely involved her in anything relating to the colliery.

"The messenger said it was from someone in the city. However, the first paragraph of the letter states that the writer is bedridden in London and Olivia Smithfield's signature closes the last page. Unless this document is a forgery, or Miss Smithfield has someone impersonating her, this is clearly written at the hand of someone writing with very limited motion of their digits or under duress. We will assume this letter is indeed penned by the ailing Miss Smithfield. I will make it my business upon the morrow to find out who is acting as her agent in this city."

"So, you have already read the full breadth of the letter?"

"No. I have read only the first paragraph with a quick glance at the closing signature to see it is signed by Olivia Smithfield. The letterhead is inscribed with her monogram and identical to the stationery used for the first letter we received by post from her. She states that she is too ill to travel. Enough of this delay. Let's read the whole bloody thing through." Ian pulled a chair next to Elsbeth, opened the letter and began to read:

Dear Sir Ian and Lady Hargrove,

Please forgive all that requires my discourse with you to be in written form and delivered by other than my own hand. Every desire has been in place for my health to improve to make possible my travel to America. However, significant deterioration in my condition forces me to remain in my London home, in the confines of my bed, with round-the-clock care.

Upon this reading, you will have the information I had so hoped to exchange with you in person. However, that has not been God's will and, I must suffer the additional humiliation of appearing too faint to face you with the truth that I have for so long born. Time and my ill health, dictate that I must reveal the truth that has found its harbor with me. Additionally, of recent days, two women have appeared before me making repeated inquiries about my knowledge of Miss Hargrove and the first letter I penned to you. The woman, who most decidedly was leading the inquiry, identified herself as one Morgan Pennybacker sent, she said, under the authority of Miss Hargrove. She was accompanied by a young, somewhat ill at ease woman, whom she called Agnes, who kept under her care a rather chatty bird. Perhaps you are familiar with the pair. Their visits to me were very strained as I buoyed in and out of consciousness, my delirium more pronounced than not on some days.

If my memory serves me well, there was another female. A young, blond woman with a very direct tone who became relentless in her questions about Miss Hargrove and my association with her. She initially represented herself as Miss Hargrove but, upon my decree that she could not possibly be one and the same, she became indignant and began demanding answers from me. My caregiver, Beatrice, was to be my savior. Her immediate presence drove the blond woman from my bedchamber...

Ian paused in his reading. Looking away from the letter, he turned his eyes to Elsbeth and studied her face to ascertain the toll the words he read aloud collected from her being.

A shield of silent malaise crept across Elsbeth's face as she pondered the full scope of all that would be revealed at the conclusion of the letter. She wondered too, how the women mentioned thus far had come to be involved with her darling, Arielle. Pennybacker was a name familiar to her. She remembered seeing advertisements in the Washington Post and Star for a stitchery store named Pennybacker's, but she knew nothing of a woman named Morgan associated with that business. They were all unknowns and insignificant until now. Her awareness of them created an uneasiness as the unsolicited intruders made an unwelcome entrance into her life. Morgan, Agnes, a young blond. Who were they, and why had they come calling to disrupt her private world?

"Elsbeth, my dear. What are you thinking?"

"At present, Ian, I find myself drifting from a state of conscious awareness to one of hysteria. Trying to find the proper level of endurance is absorbing all skills I have ever known to be at my disposal. These are difficult times and will require, I suppose, difficult measures. My curiosity has been aroused in equal measure to my level of anxiety. Who are these women? This Morgan? This Agnes? And, of the blond woman? How is it that Miss Smithfield was so cocksure that the young blond woman was not Arielle? Why, she has never met Arielle and could have not the slightest conception of her appearance."

"The same questions are most aloft in my mind, as well as the ability of her caregiver to dismiss the blond from Miss Smithfield's residence. I wonder what words were exchanged to that effect?"

"Oh, I just do not know how much more of this my nerves can consume. Please read on. I fear I must hear the complete manuscript Miss Smithfield has penned, down to its denouement and final punctuation mark!"

"Very well, my dear. I shall proceed."

Ian lifted and shifted the multiple-paged communication. The sheets of the fine, watermarked stock easily separated from one another, as though wanting to move along, or expedite the telling of the story.

Miss Hargrove, I knew, would not be blond. Her heritage denied her any claim to flaxen-colored hair. I knew also, that her manor would be one of grace and gentility, which was not the case with the young woman who berated me at my beside. There is another key characteristic that Miss Hargrove must possess that distinguishes her from the blond professing to be her. The blond had unexceptional green eyes without a spark or twinkle to them. Miss Hargrove, by birthright, would have expressive, emerald eyes with brilliant flecks dancing about the iris. Oh, I am sure she is a rare beauty. Her color of hair is my only mystery. Perhaps it is a fiery red like that of the dear lass who never came to know her offspring. Such a pity she succumbed to the rigors of childbirth, but her sacrifice provided immeasurable joy for me and, I am quite certain, yourselves. Oh, this must be painful for you to read and I should not hesitate further to tell you all I know.

"Ian, stop one moment in your reading, if you will. I need a moment to bolster myself for what is to come. What 'immeasurable joy' could Miss Smithfield have garnered from Arielle's birth? Another successful delivery to place on her summation of midwifery experience? To what is she referring?"

"My dear, it would be best for me to read on. I fear the answers will be shortly upon us." Ian once again raised the pages of the letter to a comfortable level, allowing his eyes the most acute image of the words he needed to read and interpret with Elsbeth.

In my first letter to you, I mentioned my presence at Miss Hargrove's birth as assistant to my dear, late brother, Dr. Edmond Smithfield. He was a superior practitioner. We shared a great devotion to one another. I am afraid his great devotion caused him to step over the line of moral conviction on July 7, 1877 when he delivered not one, but two baby girls. He had informed me of the arrangements to be made for the one newborn. She was to go to a wealthy couple who wanted only one child. Noting the look of longing in my eyes, knowing my spinster status, and lost hope to ever have a child of my own, my brother gave me the other baby girl to raise as my own. Her presence with me was easily explained for we had a sister in Manchestershire who passed on just prior to the births, therefore, having none of our Welsh friends familiar with her, it was quite simple for me to tell the story of her recent widowhood, childbirth and death. To all, it made it perfectly feasible that I would raise my sister's child as my own. Dear Edmond was so sympathetic to the loss of our sister and grieving so. His judgment on July 7th declared that his remaining sibling would have what she had always wanted, a child to call her own.

I do not make light of what has transpired. I have erred, and there is no retracting that. It is an indiscretion with which I have had to live and, by the very nature of my act, have forced the resulting outcome upon others. I am most severely apologetic, though no words give proper credence to the thoughts that have consumed me for nigh some twenty years. However, pain and regret shall not fill my final days. For, though at times the pain of my decision has come upon me like the point of the sharpest saber prepared for battle, I shall never regret the little life that beat beside me, filled my days with joy, and grew into a lovely young woman. God, forgive me for the choices I made that found their effect far greater than myself. If retraced, I trust my steps would take the same path, for my guilt has been outweighed with happiness. I feared the newborn would succumb to orphan status and suffer a dreary existence. I merely meant to rescue an innocent child and, yes, I will admit, satisfy a longing, a nagging desire to have a child to call mine that I might love and nurture as my own blood.

Ian ceased his reading. He was shaken by the revelation from Miss Smithfield. He had known Doctor Smithfield for twenty years. The arrangement was clear. As soon as he delivered a child from an unwed mother, he would insist the child be given over to him for proper placement with a family who could give the child all of life's benefits and pleasures. The birth mother would sign an agreement with consent, and Doctor Smithfield would release the baby to them. It was to be simple, 'cut and dried' as the doctor put it.

Elsbeth sat ashen in quiet disbelief. Another child, a twin. *How could Doctor Smithfield have kept such information from them?* She had no idea the young woman who gave birth to their Arielle had perished, or that a second infant was born to her the same day. *What if she had family who would have wanted the newborn as a legacy to the mother?*

Tears welled in Elsbeth's eyes and rushed along the full length of her face, both sides taking on the spillage from a river of emotions held back until now by her eyelids that formed a stoic dam for the salty fluid. She wept and wept and dabbed and dabbed her eyes with the cotton handkerchief Ian passed her way. He, too, brushed away a droplet formed in the corner of his left eye, but stopped the whole process by clearing his throat, shaking his head, raising his shoulders to right himself, and stiffening his back to gain control of the scene before him. He knew it best to let Elsbeth sob herself out. She always appeared the better for it.

"Oh, my goodness, my goodness, Ian," Elsbeth sniffled, as she continued to weep and dab at her tear soiled face.

"I know, I know," Ian comforted, softly rubbing his wife's shoulders to ease her sadness.

"What are we to do?"

"This news is too fresh, and its effect too severe for us to hastily decide how we shall respond. We must stabilize this situation for ourselves and the good of Arielle."

"How can we stabilize something gone so awry and out of our hands?" Elsbeth's words came in choppy spurts among her sobs.

"We must and we will," Ian firmly stated, with more confidence in his delivery than he felt within his being.

"There is one more page, Elsbeth, and it can do us no more harm to hear, to its end, what Miss Smithfield has determined we must know."

Elsbeth suppressed her sobs, the flow of tears ebbing somewhat, having left swollen puffs of skin about her eyes. Since her daughter's absence, Elsbeth had spent time in Arielle's room, sifting through items from her childhood stowed in a small chifferobe. A beloved doll, doll clothing, a tiny bracelet and first drawings were among the treasured keepsakes. *Where has the time gone? Have I given my darling daughter all that is necessary to warrant her continued love?* Elsbeth queried as she held each item in her hand. Her thoughts came back to the present. She readied herself to hear the end of Miss Smithfield's letter.

> And, so, what is done, is done. Before Edmond died, he thought more than once about his decision to give one of the babies to me, separating forever what grew in unison from the same life's blood. He, at their birth, had decided, albeit reluctantly, to give me the family name of the fortunate recipients of the other baby girl, in case there should ever arise a reason to make contact. I, in good conscience, could not have my dear Arianna live the rest of her life without the knowledge that a sister of her own blood, a supreme likeness, exists on this earth. It took me months to locate you as I searched all of Ogmore Vale to determine your whereabouts. Fortunately, your Overman, Paul Nesbitt, gave me your address in America. Please forgive him if he broke a confidence, for I told him it was critically urgent that I speak with you.
>
> There, the truth be told, and with God's good grace, we will all be the better for it. If I may ask, without appearing bold of heart, please take no anger on my Arianna. The doing was not hers. She will have no one upon my expiration. To know she is reunited, as God originally intended, with the flesh and form of her birth, will put to rest years of anguish sustained at the fingertips of secrecy. I respectively plead your forgiveness and remain eternally grateful for the care and understanding you bestow upon this, my final request. May God keep us all in his watchful care.

Sincerely,
Olivia Smithfield

Elsbeth sat quietly stunned. Tears resumed their flow at a steady pace with no sign of relent. Ian, too, appeared undone. He maintained a morbid stillness, his only movement coming from the lowering of the letter to the surface of the Pembroke table positioned next to him.

"The best laid plans," Ian muttered, remembering his mother's proclamation uttered time and again, 'we make plans and God laughs.'

He began to pace about the space, stirring the gas lamp's flame, causing it to wave teasingly across the surface of the palms and ferns placed about the airy conservatory. Air seemed to collect in the room like a giant diaphragm expelling itself into the steeply pitched rotunda-like dome of the welcoming space. Breathe. Just breathe. Ian and Elsbeth, simultaneously, like one valve to another, issued the order to their bodies to take in and expel air in a rhythmic fashion to re-establish their calm and sense of well-being.

This was a day like no other. The proportion of Elsbeth's misery was too intense to comprehend. She knew within the deepest recesses of her mortal being that the words composed by Olivia Smithfield had forever changed her world as she knew it. She would have to make haste to recover order in her life. *Order.* How could she dare think of something so regimented when her world had left its axis? She felt askew. Her mind raced beyond the confines of her form, leaving her body in a wake of vertigo. The dizziness that surrounded her threatened to bring her down, out of her chair, and into a puddle of pity upon the cold, hard floor of the conservatory. She was at one with devastation, despair and disaster.

Miss Smithfield's letter spelled disaster for the future of her relationship with Arielle. Her dear, dear, daughter, Arielle. *Dear Arielle. Born of my heart, Arielle. How will she take this news? Will she ever again hold our trust? Will we forever lose her to the truth that has been detained by secrecy and lies, and not all of our own doing?* Unproductive thoughts of disaster swirled like an impending storm inside Elsbeth's cranium. She began to battle against them, rallying as she heard Ian's voice, albeit sounding as from a far away shore, calling to tow her back to safety and the security that all would be well.

"Elsbeth. Should I get the vapors? You appear very faint, my dear. Perhaps you should lie back on the settee. Let me assist you."

"No, no. Give me a moment. I am overcome, but I feel the worst of the shock has passed."

"You are very pale. Please, I insist. You need to rest..." Ian's words were cut to a quick by Elsbeth's rallied spirit.

"Rest. I can see no decent rest on the horizon for either of us. Only an unthinking fool could rest at a time like this."

"You, my dear woman, have the audacity to cast the aspersion of 'fool' toward me?"

"Sir Ian, please. I am in no spirit to take the English language and mince its words to fancy your ego, nor do I have the strength to provide a defense for the words uttered at such a trying time. Forgive my bold speech, for I am at present, void of the decencies of propriety that would have me speak otherwise."

"We will need to take action on this letter. We must locate the source. We must determine who had this letter delivered to us."

"We must think of the severe consequences of our actions." Elsbeth carefully directed her words to Ian in as limited a challenging tone as she could possibly muster.

"*Potentially* severe my dear, *potentially*," Ian projected his response with so much emphasis on the first letter of the word 'potentially' that the wick's flame before him was nearly extinguished with his pronounced puff.

"We have no assurances otherwise," Elsbeth responded, holding to her resolve that extreme caution should be their guiding force.

"Assurances are impossible. There can be no sure outcome. Assurance is a device of the Devil meant to lure us into complacency. We have no promises or guarantees. We must act on our best judgment, our best authority, our best prayers," Ian stated, becoming much more subdued as he reflected on the need for prayer to bring balance to the ordeal before them.

Meanwhile, words played over and over in Elsbeth's mind. *You do not realize how precious something is until you lose it.* The words circled round and round spinning into a vacuous funnel of despair.

Ian attempted to close his mind's eye, as though doing so would block the words pelting his brain with confusion. *Temptation.* He was reminded of the lure temptation held over him and how, on occasion, he had yielded to it. Could it be that temptation was revisiting him in a way he would never have imagined? *But, I am a risk-taker,* thought Ian, as he worked to clear his newly resurrected conscience. *Has the risk-taking I apply so successfully to my business adversely infiltrated my personal life?* He felt devastated and ashamed. He need only look at Elsbeth to view the toll of Olivia Smithfield's revelations. *Is there more to be learned?*

As he searched his mind and surroundings for a metaphoric silver lining, devastation turned to a determination to face his demons head-on. He would need to work harder than ever for a successful outcome to this news and that work would begin posthaste -- for who knew what might visit his doorstep tomorrow.

Chapter Thirty

Nantymoel, Wales
In South Cymru

Nantymoel's townsfolk took a dim view of the unknown pair walking their streets -- almost as dim as the vale's grassy surfaces closest to the colliery. There was barely a blade of verdant vegetation to be viewed near the coal mine. Thin layers of coal dust sprinkled every living shaft of indigenous foliage. It took a trip into the village to see true color and signs of nature's best.

Suspicious glances were cast toward the two as watchful eyes 'made a go' to place them. Locals searched for some common thread to weave the two into the known fibers of the friends and family comprising their intimate community. In a village as close as Nantymoel, even a flea on a mangy mongrel would be found out. Anonymity was impossible. Decades of living lean and closely knit meant no stranger could go unnoticed. The two resembled none from their village or the nearby Rhondda.

Keeping their chins up and spirits high, Morgan and Agnes braved the disparaging looks as they made their way along the uneven cobblestone streets looking for the prevailing hire, a cab, to take them from the village for their return home. As she,

Agnes and Peepers boarded their hire, the daguerreotype stuck in Morgan's mind. She lifted it from her satchel and rang the driver, halting the carriage in preparation to disembark.

The visit to Annie Hollingsworth's provided closure regarding Miss Hargrove's birth, but there was much more troubling Morgan's mind. She at once reconsidered her final preparations for their return to America. Instantly, she felt the need to ascertain the significance of the photograph obtained from the coffer kept in safe keeping by Maggie Galligan. Extending their stay in Nantymoel might yield her desired result. She knew if she persevered with the right questions, she would be rewarded with the correct answers. She was intent on pursuing the truth.

"Young man, we are in search of a coachman known to drive the coach pictured herewith," Morgan urged as she presented the photograph to the lad driving their cab.

The cabbie squinted as he studied the faded sepia image. He held it away, then close, tilting it back and forth.

"Is this coach familiar to you?"

"Aye, it is, missy."

"Well, speak up young man, and do not address me, sir, in that familiar fashion."

"Now, don't be 'avin' that tone with me. I want ta be quite sure 'bout it fer I give it a go. It's not the finest picture me eyes 'ave ever crossed, but I ken be sure it's the likes of the coach once belongin' to the lord and master of the Big House."

"You mean the owner of the colliery."

"Yes, mum, one and the same. Ye can rely on me."

"You then are referring to Sir Ian Hargrove?"

"No, mum. I am referring to the Prince of Wales!"

"Your sarcasm has no place in this conversation. I simply need your assistance."

"It may well be that's what ye be needin', but yer not goin' 'bout it very well."

"Whoa, boy. Whoa, boy," piped Peepers, his wings full-fledged, as though he would take full flight.

"It seems we have gotten off to a poor start, and for that I apologize. Please do tell us what you know."

"I ken tell ye that the coach's coat of arms is unique, like no other."

"Then you are certain, without a doubt?"

"I say, yer not a trustin' soul, are ye?"

The cabbie was a sprite young fellow. His youth actually bothered Morgan for it rendered her dubious about the merit of his statements. She questioned his possible inexperience and naiveté. However, as he spoke, he seemed to know a fair amount about the colliery. He explained that his brother served a half score of years at Hargrove's, being one of the first to arrive at the crack of each dawn to release canaries into the cavernous tunnels to alert workers of poisonous gases. Rich with black ore, the tunnels brought riches to the master of the colliery in sharp contrast to the limited wages allotted to the workers.

"It's a riskier business for the laborer than the mun at the top. Oh, the mun earn a meager wage, they do. Their monies are like birdseed, so little, and they need to scatter it so many places just to scrape by. When ye think they risk their lives and lungs in them deep, tunnels and treacherous trenches. But, I be sure, little choice is offered a mun with a wife and young ones to feed. 'E either works the mines, footsteps I be sure 'is young sons will soon follow, or falls short on providing a proper sum for 'is wife to clothe and feed them all."

Morgan knew the hardships of mining. Her mother's father met his end in a mining accident in West Virginia. The tragedy so depressed her grandmother, she uprooted her family to Virginia where her mother met Jackson Pennybacker. Mining was an inevitable cycle of the generations, for they knew to follow what they knew, and they had been taught to know the mines. The colliery was the vale's soul, the lungs and lifeblood for its workers whose community was as close as bark on a tree. The dark tunnels were fraught with gaseous and fiery danger. One family's loss was everyone's loss. Joys were communally shared and gossip, or insubordination, toward the colliery's owner was kept under the roof of one's cottage lest you be let go for trying to spread ill will or stir-up trouble.

"The one mun whose name ye 'ear agen and agen is Paul's. Paul the Overman. 'E organized a labor union to establish better wages and safer standards for the mun to work by. 'E insisted that laws barring women from working in the mines be invoked. 'E knew full well that gels under the guise of bein' mun took to the tunnels to earn money for their famblies where no son existed so they could contribute their fair share. They put themselves and others in harms way not 'avin' the stamina or facility to complete the same tasks as the mun. Paul the Overman had seen it all up close. A young worker trapped under a collapsed wall, 'is arm danglin' limp, and fingers splayed with clots of dirt collected in his palm from his last life effort to save his soul, was dug out only to reveal *he* was a *she*. Oh, the poor gel, lost to the earth from whence she came."

"Paul was dead-set on never witnessin' that scene again in 'is lifetime. 'E wanted no more loss of lasses and no chance of distractions to threaten the safety of the miners who had little choice but to return day-by-day to the coal-packed myriad deeply definin' their lives. 'E was dead-set, and 'e knew Sir Ian Hargrove was dead-set, to not challenge 'is cause. Paul the Overman was well respected as a voice for the other workers and a 'ard laborer 'isself. Sir Ian Hargrove knew the union, an arbiter of the times, would remain in force. There, it was best led and negotiated head-on with a mun familiar to 'im. Paul the Overman's job was secure as long as the master of the Big House continued to provide 'is security. Any threatened walk-out 'ad to remain just that, for no one threatened the livelihood of Sir Ian Hargrove without livin' to regret it."

"You have much to tell, indeed, and your information is most insightful, however, in point of fact, we must find the man who drove for Sir Ian Hargrove. Do you know of him?"

"Know of 'im? 'E's me buttie, 'e is. A bit me senior, but me buttie none the same. 'E's not drivin' about no more but 'e keeps 'is arms busy pickin' up pints at the Double Duchess."

"The Double Duchess? To what do you refer?"

"Yer definitely not local gels, if ye 'aven't been knowin' 'bout The Double Duchess. It's the local waterin' hole, it is. And, if ye imbibed of too much *water* you might be seein' double!"

"What is your buttie's, as you call him, name?"

"Oh, I won't be tellin' ya that jest now. You'll 'ave a jolly time findin' 'im out! Ev'ry mun and gel knows 'im at the Duchess."

Morgan was taken back by the young lad's failure to comply with her request. *What difficulty could there be for him to reveal his friend's name?* She shook her head. She had tired of her interaction with him and was more than ready to exit his company.

"Very well, then. Can you, at the very least, drive us there?" Morgan asked, wishing she had phrased her words in a command rather than giving the lad the benefit of a question.

"Oh, no, mum. I 'ave to 'ead 'ome now. Done for the day I am. It won't be a far walk from where I be leavin' ya. Jest 'ead that direction and you'll be ready for a heady pint when ye get there!"

Morgan had heard quite enough. He was fraying her last nerve. His audacity to leave them on the street and not deliver them to his friend was incomprehensible to her. However, evening was setting in and she was set on locating the driver the cabbie mentioned. Morgan took every opportunity to learn all she could at all times from all resources at hand. She watched, listened and queried to her ultimate gain.

Activity on the streets was drawing to a close. She and Agnes had walked several blocks, passing numerous storefronts. One in particular caught her eye. Lights still glowed through the store's bowed front windows. Morgan could see the wares and decided the diversion of stepping within would do her good. The sign read, 'Gwalia House,' or Ty Gwalia to the locals, a popular shop in Cwn Ogwr or Ogmore Vale. In the winter months, the rustic building's hand-hewn brick chimneys attracted patrons who were drawn to the heady smoke they produced from fiery logs used to warm the shop. An enormous variety of wares filled the shelves and aisles, from fabric and clothing, to washtubs and grain. Morgan turned her interests to the needlework section and lifted the linens to feel their hand.

"Agnes, the place. Did you note the name he gave us?" Morgan queried, giving Agnes a look indicating the on-set of her wrath if she failed to deliver the information. Fatigue was overtaking Morgan and with it her sharpness of skills went lacking.

"Yes, yes, just a moment. It was something to do with a Duchess. Just a moment, I have it here."

Agnes put Peepers' cage down and, slipping her eyeglasses into position, rustled through her notebook. She skimmed by pages as she licked her middle finger to grasp the lower right corner of the notebook's paper to locate the source Morgan requested, all the while pleased that Morgan relied on her so.

"Yes. Here. Here it is."

"Well, out with it. We haven't time to dawdle."

"Yes. The Double Duchess. The Double Duchess is what he said."

Morgan sighted a cab discharging its passengers just outside the shop's doorway. "Quickly, Agnes, enough of our walking. We have no idea about the whereabouts of this Duchess place. Let's waste not another minute."

On her words, the threesome exited the shop and stepped upon the ramp-like cobblestone walk alongside the building leading them down to the street and cab below.

"Driver, take us to The Double Duchess forthwith."

"Step-up son!" the cabbie shouted as he commanded his horse to move along. Morgan's and Agnes' bodies jolted back against the padded leather seats of the cabriole, then projected forward as they set their sights on finding the sign -- the sign of The Double Duchess.

"Morgan, if you do not mind my asking, why are you so enamored with this common bloke that you have us off on what might well be a wild goose chase?"

"Agnes, by identifying the crest, and our new awareness of Sir Ian Hargrove's driver, this young man has put flesh on the bones of this investigation. Pursue we must. Soon, Miss Hargrove's wishes will be assuaged."

⟲⟫

A barmaid greeted them at the entry with a nod as she placed a fresh candlestick in an empty wall-mounted sconce next to Morgan's head. The close strike of the flint lit next to her head filled her nostrils with a residual, heady coating of smoky sulfur. It wafted about her, then rested on the lining of her nasal passages. She took several deep breaths to bring fresh air up her nose as she looked about the darkened room. Heavy wrought-iron lanterns with leaded amber glass hung from thick support posts. Several more lanterns adorned the mirrored wall behind the bar.

Morgan and Agnes were among the only women in the pub excluding the barmaids and two girls who were making flirtations with some men in a corner booth. The other tables were anchored by convivial groups of men enjoying the community of one another, several still bearing remnants of their workday with coal dust smudged about their faces. Black beetles scurrying up between the worn, splintered flooring added movement underfoot.

Morgan enjoyed the simple ambience of the pub despite its musty blend of body odor, candle wax, and the essence of old ale spilled on the creaky floorboards. It helped to wash away the effect of the day, providing tasty fare and the opportunity to linger with locals who were equally eager to have a nice chat chased down with freshly brewed ale. She kept focus on her job at hand while casting a glance at the barmaid signaling her desire to be seated.

"What ken I be gettin' fer ye gels? Would you be wantin' a table for three?" The barmaid winked and cocked her head toward the birdcage.

"Seats at the bar will suit us fine," Morgan replied.

"'Ere's a nice little trio right in a row so ye can rest yer little pet atop one. We'll let 'im take a seat, though, I be sure, 'e won't be drinkin' much," the barmaid responded as she took a rag from her apron pocket and began dusting the surface of the barstools.

"Hey, Dolly!' shouted a patron across the room. "What be the occasion? In all me years, I've n'er seen ye prepare a seat like that for me arse!"

"Oh, Bobby McCann. Hush yerself up in front of these ladies before I be tellin' ye where ye can take your arse!" Dolly chided back as the table of men exploded into an uproar of laughter.

McCann put his pint down on the solid oak table with such gusto, a heady slosh lapped over the sides of his glass and puddled onto the tabletop.

"Oh, Dolly, dear gel! Looks like I be needin' yer services o'er here!"

Dolly cast McCann a warning eye. She had heard more than her share of taunting and risqué comments from intoxicated patrons over the years. Most were innocent enough. Bernie the Barkeep handily removed the ones that stepped over the line of propriety.

"Ye don't want to have a meetin' with Bernie now, do ye McCann?"

"Oh, Dolly, gel. I jest be needin' a little something from those lovely hips of yours."

Bernie stepped from the shadows, clearing his throat to gain Dolly's attention. She cast a glance back with a subtle shake of her head. She knew McCann was no threat and his comments were all in good fun. He could be easily sated with another round that would find him finished for the day and on his way back to his wife. McCann leaned back in his chair balancing it on two legs.

"Now don't be gettin' serious there, Bernie the Barkeep. Dolly the Duchess knows I jest be needin' a little wipe with that handy rag she keeps near those lovely hips!"

Morgan, Agnes and Peepers watched the exchange from their perches on the barstools. The scene appeared under control, though Peepers rated it worth one of his, "Whoa, boys."

Bernie smiled at the three, then formed a whistle with his mouth and began to chirp like a bird. Peepers proceeded to flit about his cage, stirring up birdseed and feathers. Bernie promptly ceased his warm-blooded chirp, the shrill sound obviously calling to Peepers' wilder side.

"What will ye be havin' little bird? 'E's a flighty one, 'e is. What be 'is name?"

"Peepers," Agnes happily answered, feeling a proud bond between herself and her charge.

"Peepers, Peepers, Peepers. Ain't that the truth? Ain't that the truth?" retorted Peepers' as he strutted about.

"Oh, Peepers, boy. Bernie the Barkeep jest wants ta be yer friend. Calm down little mun. Bernie won't be makin' anymore bird calls."

"Ain't that the truth? Ain't that the truth?" came Peepers' response as he slowed his movements and gently paced about the floor of his home.

Bernie let out a hearty laugh. "'E's a treasure 'e is! What ken I get fer ye ladies? 'Ere's some ale to start ye off."

"We are in need of your help."

Dolly overheard Morgan's request and moved closer to the threesome.

"What 'elp ken I be to ye ladies?" Bernie asked.

"We need to be directed to the man who drove this coach approximately two score years past," Morgan stated as she drew forth Annie's daguerreotype.

Dolly looked over Morgan's shoulder, catching a glimpse of the faded image. Bernie took the photograph from Morgan and walked to stand under the light of the large gas lantern. Its amber glass cast a brownish-yellow glow across the photograph's sepia surface. Bernie shifted his body weight as he tilted the photograph back and forth.

"Can you identify the coach?" Morgan queried.

"Dolly, 'ave a look. It's not best clear, but I know it be a coat of arms I've seen in Cwn Ogwr."

Morgan gave a look of displeasure to Bernie. She had asked for his opinion and had not sought the judgment of the barmaid. As barkeep, Bernie's exposure to the patrons of Ogmore Vale, their stories, and the local gossip placed him in an omnipotent position. Bernie caught Morgan's expression and read her face well. He was a natural at judging character and knew he had a determined woman before him.

"I ken see miss, that you want an answer from me, I be sure, but Miss Dolly and Nantymoel are longtime kin. Why, she is the Duchess herself, an' if ye stay in these parts long enough, ye will be hearin' tales of Dolly the Duchess an' The Double Duchess, I be sure."

Dolly studied the photograph then gave a curious look to the two. She knew the image on the coach's door but wondered about the girl next to the coach.

"I ken tell ye, if I may, the coat of arms is that of the Hargrove clan. The carriage rarely brought the Lord himself, but his misses would come down from the Big House to shop in the village. The refinements were not to her fancy, but she often shopped for gifts for her house gels and everyday needs. I 'eard they 'ad one child, a gel. I n'er saw 'er I be quite sure. The Hargrove's kept ta 'emselves. I 'eard they left the vale and moved for a time to America. It seems the rich get richer!"

Morgan was pleased to have Dolly concur with the cabbie's identification of the coach. Now, she needed to speak with the Hargrove's driver to learn the full significance of the photograph.

"And you, Bernie, know well as me who drove for 'is Lordship."

"That I do, Dolly. That I do be quite sure," said Bernie with a wink.

"Well, delay no more with your mincing of words. Name the man!" Morgan nearly knocked Agnes from her barstool with her commanding tone.

"'Is name's Wicks." Bernie's face lit up as he revealed the driver's name and went on with more that he knew. "Ye'll know 'im by 'is lame leg and the cap 'e wears bearin' the sign o' the crown.

Poor 'ole Wicks. E'er since 'e gots 'isself stomped on by one o' the Queen's very own 'orses 'es sworn ta wear the cap 'n crown as a decoration o' honor for the one time 'e tried to be somethin' more 'en 'e was an' 'e fell fast an' 'e fell 'ard. Slammed to the ground 'e was by the Queen's household cavalry. Folks ask 'bout the crown and ole Wicks loves ta tell 'em 'bout his fall and 'ow the Queen signaled 'er royal coachmen to come to 'is aid. There's some what doubts 'ole Wicks' story, but that don't stop 'im none from tellin' it just the same. An odd bloke he is -- peculiar and kind 'o fascinatin' in the same swallow."

"Ye won't have ta wait long ta find 'im cuz 'e's been comin' round regular ev'ry night fer years just like the 'ands on ye 'ole grandfather's clock. Ye'll find 'im when the pendulum strikes 'bout eight, headin' straight into the Double Duchess," Dolly added, pleased to be of service.

"'E closes the Duchess down ev'ry evenin' 'elpin' the wenches ta blow the last life out 'o the candles scattered 'round the pub." Bernie nodded in affirmation about Wicks' routine. "They dubbed 'im Wicks, an' the title stuck with 'im. Nobody's asked the likes 'o me, but if'n they did, I'd say Wicks is a hardworkin' mun whose a wee bit off kilter since 'is fall."

"You are suggesting then, the man is not to be believed?" Morgan queried, growing impatient with the length of the answer to her question.

"Oh no, miss! We're merely statin' that Wicks' truth may not be yers! 'Is stories gets better ev'ry time 'e tells 'em! Wicks' is always sayin' he dun't wont the truth to be spoilin' 'is story!" Dolly looked at Bernie and the two threw their heads back in a unified laugh.

Morgan glanced at her timepiece. If Wicks, as they called him, was true to form, she had a solid hour to await his arrival. Wait she would.

"As I measure it by this instrument of time, we have some time ahead before your Mr. Wicks arrives." Morgan turned to Agnes. "Our time will be best served by nourishing body and soul. I know

I am feeling quite hungry and parched. Agnes, what say we dine at the Double Duchess?"

Agnes was in full agreement. She had begun to feel light-headed. It had been hours since they last ate. The mixture of scents abounding in the pub compounded her dizziness. Unbathed bodies, smoke and ale added to the swill-like aroma wafting through the air. She welcomed a meal and the culmination of the day. Sulfur from exhausted candles and pungent platters of food provided her only relief from the noxious smells.

Robust snores from a rotund patron sitting alone in a booth added to Agnes' misery. She watched as he slept, the pressure of his dipped head toward his chest forced his chinbone to disappear into the fatty flesh comprising his neck, making his profile a flabby elongation of itself. His arms rested like anchored bookends on either side of his ballooned belly. His eyelids were closed tight to themselves in contrast to his lips that gaped wide as though his lower lip offered a reservoir for air needed to sustain the lengthy, labored snore resulting from his restricted nasal passages.

Suddenly, he shook himself awake and stared about in a sleepy fog. His arms clutched the edge of the table as he readied his body's forces to launch him from a seated to standing position, an effort made exceedingly more difficult by the devalued length of his legs, both upper and lower. With no ease of effort, he made his way to full stance. He was indeed to be forever challenged by the restrictions diet had placed upon him and he upon himself. Agnes pitied his slovenly soul.

Her focus went to the flame most immediate to her. It invited her into its warm and welcoming trance. A windswept rhythm commenced, as though an invisible wand directed the flame, and its Svengali-like routine captured Agnes in its wake. The sheer exhaustion she felt from the day's efforts, married with the pint of ale she had downed, enticed her to consume the flame's hypnotic aura. She watched it work its way lower and lower in a gradual descent, mimicking her desire to call the day to its close. There remained a momentary glow of golden amber before the wick lost all essence of itself.

Agnes sighed. She felt as fully spent as the candlestick. It would not be in need of Wicks' nightly ritual. No, his services were needed for a more important task, and Agnes was determined to rally her strength. When, and if, Wicks arrived, she and Morgan had to be fully prepared to extract the essence of all he knew.

Chapter Thirty-One

Nantymoel, Wales
In South Cymru

The large pendulum clock anchored to the entry wall gave its quarter hour chime with great gusto. Patrons in the Double Duchess looked about as the single resounding gong momentarily distracted them from their bites and banter. Morgan particularly noted the time. The hour was becoming late, and there had been no sighting of Wicks the Coachman. She was becoming quite annoyed and impatient. She glanced toward the bar to engage Dolly's attention and observed that her gaze had fallen on a roundish, husky chap with a slight limp loping into the pub.

"Well, lest me eyes deceive me, we're receivin' a visit from one of 'er Majesty's gentry!" Dolly exclaimed.

"Oh, dun't go embarrassin' me none now Dolly, fach! An' keep me identity real quiet. We dun't want me arse kidnapped for a King's ransom, I be sure."

"Ye certainly place a high value on yer royal arse. Ye'd do well to have any soul notice you've gone missin'!"

"Oh, my wee feelin's are cut to the quick, and after all I do fer ye, gel."

"Well, we best thought ye'd not be comin' to do yer job this eve. Where may I ask 'ave you been? Has the Queen's entourage run your arse down again?"

"Oh, no gel, today I 'ave no such worthy excuse. But I'm 'ere jest the same."

Morgan surmised, from the royal insignia on the cap atop his head, and the conversation exchanged with Dolly, that this jovial fellow was the much-anticipated Wicks. He wore heavy boots that fell hard upon the wide wood planks of the pub's floor. The pub's low light drew scores of black beetles up and over the crevices between the floorboards. Wicks' left boot smashed the winged invertebrates in his path as the delayed movement of his right leg caused his right boot to drag forward in a sweep, sending clusters of the insects in a scramble to avoid further confrontation with his hardy footwear. Morgan eyed Dolly who caught her impatient stare and gave her an acknowledging nod.

"Oh, Wicks ol' chum. Come and get yerself a pint of the dark ale an' then I 'ave someone I need to make yer acquaintance."

Wicks looked about the pub curious to know whom Dolly intended to introduce to him. The space was lively with chatter and filled with the familiar faces of regular chaps and residual barmaids. Smoke billowed from cigars dispensing clouds of exhaled vapor. The noxious smell of spent tobacco wafted into the air. A heady gathering of smoke dissipated, lifting the screen it formed over a corner table. Wicks thought his mind was playing tricks on him. He saw the outline of a dome-shaped container and what appeared within to be a bird.

"Lawd, does me eyes deceive me? Jesus, Mary and Joseph. A bird's flown into the Double Duchess an' been caught for a tasty supper. Will ye be singin' fer ye supper, little feller?"

Peepers was not pleased. He began to pace about his cage and lifted one wing in a dismissive salute. Wicks took his pint from Dolly and limped closer to the apparition. He marked his path with portions of the potent mix of malt and hops as it sloshed beyond the rim of his mug, dampening the planked floor but not his spirits.

"Oh, it is as me eyes 'ave seen. Muniferni! If it's not the devil's work, sendin' a scrawny little bird to feed the likes o' me!"

Wicks bent low and placed his hand on the door to the cage. His thick digits were quickly throttled by Agnes who slapped his hand and pulled his fingers away.

"I would advise you to mind your manners and keep your distance from that which is of no concern to you!" Agnes' face turned crimson as she boldly faced Wicks who was clearly thrice her size.

"No, no, deary. I wasn't meanin' no 'arm to your birdie," Wicks replied as he looked around noting the eyes of the other patrons fixed on the scene.

"As anyone can see, I didn't intend to do anything today, and so far I'm right on me schedule!"

Rounds of laughter circled the confines of the pub. Wicks knew he was among friends who embraced his humor until he looked back at the pair with the cage. Morgan had taken the liberty to step away from her seat. Placing herself as a barrier to the cage, she sternly stared with piercing intent into Wicks' eyes.

"Aw, me gosh. Me thinks she's 'avin' a spell!" Wicks announced to his audience as he took a hefty draw of ale.

Laughter again rebounded throughout the pub. Wicks was in his element and there was no denying he was receiving the full support of the crowd.

"I may be in a bit of a grump, but I, sir, am not the one fiddling with that which does not belong to me."

"Oh, I was jest havin' a laugh. Ye can't fault a mun for that, now ken ye?"

"I think you should have a look at this," Morgan urged as she placed the daguerreotype within Wicks' reach. "Can you identify this?"

Wicks walked about the room holding the photograph up to catch the light from the candleholder's amber shades. Periodically, he paused at a table and queried a chap or two.

"Can ye identify this?" Wicks asked.

"Sure as me name is Bobby McCann, I can."

"Well, then speak yer mind, mun."

"I be quite sure it's a coach!" Bobby exclaimed with much pleasure.

"Ah, a bright mun you are Bobby. You've always been the sharpest cheese on the loaf! Why, yer so bright, I bet yer father called ye sunny!" The room burst into coarse guffaws.

"Morgan, you would do just as well asking their horses as this sorry lot of old sots!" Agnes blurted, disgusted with Wicks' charade.

"Sir, I see you are having us all on and, in point of fact, I would ask you to bear with me. Dolly has yet to introduce us, and we have an important matter at hand to discuss with you." Morgan searched the faces in the room firmly adding, "The show has ended."

"Oh, mum, ye are not best pleased are ye?"

Morgan needed to turn the tide and put back on course the point of her trip to the Double Duchess. She was not getting on well with Wicks and could see from the expression on Agnes' face that she was disgusted with the sodden souls in her midst.

"There are so many questions Morgan, so many questions and the hour is late."

"Exploration is full of inquiry, Agnes. We must persevere."

"Why not simply review the facts as we have found them to be?"

Morgan's stamina needed a hefty heave as well. She felt Agnes' exhaustion but knew it was infinitely more sensible to strike while the iron was hot. Wicks was here and they must press on with him.

"Bear with me Agnes, for we cannot plan ahead at this juncture in this case. We must let events determine our next action."

Wicks' presence was paramount. If he could provide a missing clue to their puzzle, then they needed to find out at present. Sensing the tension in the pub, Dolly made her way to the corner table that had been garnering so much attention.

"Wicks, ye made yer way o'er 'ere before I could stop ye. This 'ere's Miss Pennybacker, Miss Fielding and, what wun't be served up as yer supper, Peepers the Parakeet. Miss Pennybacker is curious 'bout the photograph yer holdin'. It's serious ta 'er and she needs yer help. Would ya give it a go?"

"Ain't that the truth? Ain't that the truth? Whoa boy, whoa boy," came the flurried liturgy from Peepers.

Peepers' interruption at that moment made Morgan bristle. Her nerves were on edge, she needed to sleep, and Peepers was behaving like an ornithological nightmare. Quite to her pleasure, she saw a smile form over Wicks' face as he shot a look at the bird and back to the image in his hand.

"Mum, what is it ye be needin' fer me to tell ye 'bout this?"

"Can ye, *you*, identify the coach?"

"It may well be that I ken."

"Must I squeeze every syllable from you man? Please speak up and do not offend my sensibilities. Time is of the essence. Your information is pertinent to a case I have been hired to solve. What you tell me will have bearing on a young woman's life."

"Jest, 'ow do ye know it will affect 'er for the better? Sometimes, what we dun't know dun't hurt us."

"No one can know for sure, and that is not mine to judge. I am performing my duties and ask for your cooperative assistance."

Wicks squinted and stared at the photograph. He studied it with thought and purpose. He knew the coach all too well. He had been its coachman for two score and ten years. He was at the coach owner's beckon call, Mr. High and Mighty, as he called him when he was not within earshot. Years of readying the master's horses and his coach at all hours took its toll on his physical form. Cleaning tack, blacksmithing the horses, and maintaining the carriage were full time chores. No, Sir Ian Hargrove was not an easy taskmaster and Wicks would not soon forget the harsh years he toiled for the man in the Big House.

"The coach bears the coat of arms of Sir Ian Hargrove, owner 'e is of Hargrove Colliery. I dun't know the gel, though she worked at the pit."

"Why is she with his carriage?"

"Oh, I dun't know. Too many years and too many carriage rides have passed for this cabbie to remember them all."

"Them all?" Morgan asked.

"Them all. The trips, the gels, the places."

"Please, anything you can tell us will be most useful. Can you remember the location?"

Wicks took another hard stare at the image. Two cottages faded into the background.

"I ken tell ye that one cottage ken start lookin' like the next in this village, but this one is found on Wyndham Street."

"Of that you are certain?"

"I ken be sure. The roof comes down lower on this one than the others. When the butties was buildin' it, it slid a bit off kilter but they left it there all the same. Said it didn't matter as long as there was a roof for over yer 'ead."

Dolly looked at the photograph with renewed interest. She knew the address and with it she knew the face.

"As I thought," Dolly sighed. "The gel in the photograph is Annie Hollingsworth. Oh, the poor gel left us before her time."

"Oh, I remember one thin' more. Paul the Overman, who ye wun't have heard of, was the one asked me to take 'er home," Wicks shared with a satisfied look at the trio before him.

"Was that an unusual request?" Morgan queried. *Wicks should be mindful*, she mused. *There were few who could bury their secrets above Nantymoel soil.*

"No, Mum, not unusual or usual. Jest happened on occasion. Mine wasn't to question. I can tell ye I be sure, I wasn't bein' paid to question the passengers in my fare."

"When would you say this image was captured?"

"From the looks of the trees and the coat the gel is wearin' I ken guess me best guess that the month would be November but, yer askin' me somethin' from a score of years ago I ken tell ye."

"A score of years, you say?"

"Wicks would be right, I'd say," Dolly spoke up ready to corroborate Wicks' timetable. "The gel died a score of years ago, in July, I best be sure."

Morgan and Agnes looked in stunned amazement at one another. They had confirmation about the coach, the cottage, the identity of the girl in the photograph and a tentative calendar. But, the question still remained. What occurred to place Annie Hollingsworth next to Sir Ian Hargrove's coach on Wyndham Street?

"We thank you for your assistance in this matter," Morgan said as she prepared to take her leave.

As they departed the Double Duchess, Morgan turned to Agnes. "I strongly suspect Miss Hargrove's father will find this photograph and the remainder of the contents of Hollingsworth's coffer quite effective in stirring his memory. I further suspect, courtesy of Wicks' utterances and a sneaky suspicion, that there is more Sir Ian Hargrove can reveal." She would soon learn if her intuition served her well.

Chapter Thirty-Two

A rianna's night's rest was fraught with nervous energy. Her mind spun with the remnants of Alexandra's wrath, so vividly displayed at Emma's masquerade. Now the anticipation of meeting face-to-face with the couple that reared the stranger she would call sister felt a daunting task. *How will they receive me?* She pondered, imagined and created numerous stories in her head about how her first encounter with the Hargroves would be. *Arielle.* She thought her mother was becoming demented and simply mispronouncing her name when she uttered Arielle. "Ari..."

On many occasions her mother had begun to speak, only to have the word cut short by fatigue and delirium. In fact, when her mother finally grasped the stamina and presence of mind to share her story, Arianna met the telling of the tale with disbelief. Numbness consumed her being. It was as though, at once, every vital organ ceased its function and time stood silently still. Dead still. Realizing her mother's debilitated state, she shook herself to her senses, asking her to repeat and verify her words. The repeating took away no sting. She was exhausted from her role as caregiver and now was expected to accept a truth that made her entire life a lie. She had little time to drown in self-pity. That indulgence would have to wait for another time. Her mother had given her succinct instructions to hand-carry a letter she penned with Beatrice's assistance to the Hargrove family in America.

Now, here she was, staring at the portal her sister had entered hundreds of times. She closed her eyes and imagined her there. *Mum said we were identical. I wonder if our height, hair color, interests, wants and desires are identical? When we meet, what will we say to one another? What common ground will there be to share and unite us? Oh, this is so confusing. Despite Mum's request, I think I best leave. Surely, the Hargroves have read Mum's letter and know all that is necessary to know. They need not see me, but...I must see my sister. She will be all the family I have when Mum dies. Orphan.* Arianna scoffed. *Once again I return to my status at birth. Orphan. Oh, why did Mum tell me? She could have gone to her grave with this secret and I would be none the wiser. She said she wanted to explain all she knew to me so her flight from this earth would not be met with dissidence or regret. Oh, but for a clear conscience, her secret grows beyond the grave and takes its toll on another family. How can I proceed? I must turn on my heels and flee before I subject myself to strangers who know nothing of me. They assuredly will think me a bastard child now that the truth be out. I should have questioned more. All the early years when Mum talked of her sister whose husband had died soon after my conception. I should have asked more about them both. How did they look? Did I resemble her sister or her husband? My roots were only on the surface. This is my chance to learn more. To meet my sister who grounds me to this earth. Together. Will she want to be together? Oh, perhaps I should not proceed.*

Arianna's sense of dread was nearly overtaking her curious desire to find her sister. If visiting the Hargroves would satisfy her need to know, then proceed she must. Arianna's mind became increasingly muddled. Her thoughts became transfixed with enlightenment and loss. She closed her eyes and searched her thoughts for the most sensible path to pursue, the path that would lead her to her twin, the one person of her own blood with whom she might find comfort, or, at the very least, share a bond of abandonment. *No, I simply cannot.*

The words had barely left her lips when the knob to the main portal of the Hargrove's entrance turned, giving her quite a start. Through the doorframe of the opened-wide door came a small patterned area carpet. It was held tightly on one end by a freckle-faced, strawberry blond who proceeded to flap the floor covering vigorously up and down, shaking its yard residue and pile dust into the open air. The mix created a haze before Arianna. She quickly closed her eyes and her mouth lest she suffocate from the Bridget's cleaning frenzy. She cleared her throat and blinked open her eyes to see if the air had thinned for safe breathing. Fiona stopped her flapping and brought the carpet up against her body as though she had suddenly been found naked and needed to clutch something to cover her form.

"Oh, miss, it's sorry I am. I surely didn't see ye there," Fiona sputtered out her words. "Oh, the lord 'n master will give me a railing for this, he will."

"Think no more of it. There is no need to tell anyone about this. I know I for one shall say not a word."

"Oh, it's kind ye are, miss. Kind ye are." Fiona bowed and bantered as her eyes took on a sense of recognition. There was a familiarity about this visitor.

"I'm sorry, miss. It's as though me eyes are playin' tricks with me. If I didn't know better, I'd be sayin' you was Miss Arielle tryin' to trick me with the color of yer hair. 'Ers is dark like a raven. Is it you Miss Arielle? Are you back so soon and with auburn hair?" Fiona continued to babble as she stared and leaned forward to get a closer look.

"I'm sorry, miss. Me name's Fiona. May I 'ave yer name? I'll need to be announcin' ye to the lord and the missus."

Suddenly, Fiona lost her footing and toppled from the top step to the landing four steps below. To her good fortune, the carpet cushioned her fall as she made her awkward and impromptu descent. Arianna stepped to her aid, helping her up and retrieving the carpet.

"Are you quite all right? You took quite a tumble," Arianna asked as she steadied Fiona.

"Yes, I'm jest embarrassed I am. If'n you was Miss Arielle, ye'd know 'bout me clumsiness. Let's start from the beginnin'."

Arianna interrupted Fiona. "Oh, no, not the beginning! For heavens sake, I prefer not to have carpet remnants flung my way again. I am Arianna Smithfield and I am here to see the Hargroves."

Smithfield. Fiona certainly knew that name. Her incessant eavesdropping had brought that name to her attention on more than one occasion. *But, Arianna was not the first name I had heard. What could she want? What was her business here?* Fiona knew she would make it her business to find out. The doors to Sir Ian Hargrove's library were not foolproof and she was proud to be the fool to prove that so. Arianna and Fiona entered the vestibule then proceeded to the parlor.

"'Ave a seat 'ere Miss Smithfield, it is. I'll be back, jest wait 'ere."

Arianna watched Fiona leave the parlor's wide entry. Mahogany rosettes and routed balustrades formed a stately architectural detail for the opening. The room was tastefully furnished with a large, dense carpet patterned in huge chrysanthemums. The rich cranberry and pink blossoms were striking against the carpet's field of gray enhanced with green leaves and wisps of wild grasses. A conversation grouping of three settees and two channel-back chairs upholstered in cranberry hued cotton velvet was made more colorful with an adornment of assorted needlepoint pillows. Their motifs of birds, butterflies, flowers and foliage brought in the outdoors. Arianna wondered if they were the handiwork of the ladies of the manse. Her attention to the room's décor was cut short as she heard the sound of doors swishing open and voices approaching in whispered shouts. She could sense tension in their tone.

"Wait up, girl. Have you no sense. Lady Hargrove and I will tend to this guest alone. You may go about your other duties. We will ring if we need you." Ian glared at Fiona as he delivered instructions her way.

Fiona reluctantly complied, pausing momentarily to suggest she produce a course of tea, only to run tuck-tailed, like a shamed dog, when Ian's glare spit fire toward her nosy intentions.

Ian and Elsbeth promptly stopped in their tracks. It was as though their regiment had been called to a fast halt. Their feet became planted in place with hasty precision. The vision before them, though they knew it to be real, was not to be immediately believed. In all their years, they had never seen such a likeness of their Arielle. The beautiful young woman sitting in their parlor was nothing imagined. She was no ghost. She was flesh-and-blood-real. They stood in shock.

Arianna was taken back by the sudden appearance and surprised stare of the two. *Someone needs to break this abominable silence. I fear for their fortitude. What best can I say to have them understand?* Arianna reached into the deep recesses of her reserve, gathered her thoughts and emitted a few well-harvested words.

"We have much to discuss and much to share. I thank you for welcoming me on such short notice and under such circumstances. Though strained as we may feel at this onset, I trust our sound minds will prevail and we will all be the better for our meeting."

On her last word, Arianna swept her hand, signaling Ian and Elsbeth to join her in their parlor. The two moved slowly forward in unison, as though in a carefully choreographed sashay. Both felt the numbness trickle through their bodies from top down, leaving their legs feeling like limp limbs. They assumed seats on the settee opposite Arianna, their facial expressions indicating their relief at having made it to their destinations.

"I am Arianna Smithfield. I apologize for any mystery surrounding my visit. My mum's declining health prompted her letters to you. She urgently requested that I come to America and make my introductions before all verification is lost."

Ian and Elsbeth sat dumbfounded. Elsbeth clutched Ian's hand, then looked from him to Arianna. She had not known him to be lost for words. He had even omitted making a stop at his bar before entering the parlor. Perhaps that explained his fervent silence. He was not braced for the reality before him. She gently squeezed his hand, hoping to draw some sensation. She then patted his hand and gazed into his eyes. They were deep, cavernous vessels with much hidden in their darkness. Elsbeth again patted his hand. Ian's body shimmied from his waist up. The final tremor shook out his pent-up tension as he began to speak.

"Miss Smithfield, it is." Ian's words came raspy and slow. "My dear wife, Elsbeth and I welcome you to Washington. We trust your passage from Great Britain was pleasant."

Ian's words were formed with cold pleasantries. Arianna was not surprised to be greeted in such a manner. She was, after all, bringing a reality to their lives that they might choose not to accept. Seeing her made the reality harsh, and one not to be denied. It was a forced gathering of souls who knew not how or why they were being called together. Their lives had entertained routine complexities until the present. Now, all felt fractured and displaced.

"Yes. Thank you, sir. My voyage was unremarkable. I did, of course, have our meeting foremost on my mind. You have read, I do hope, my mum's letter. She wrote her missive to you with only the best of intentions for all parties involved."

"You must understand Miss Smithfield, Lady Hargrove and I are quite taken back by your mother's assertions. Why are we to believe the words of a woman who is nothing but a stranger to us?"

"You first sir, may look at the person before you. I have not seen your daughter, but I may say with unequivocal resolve that those who know her and have been in my presence are at once astounded by our likeness. That others are confused by our uncanny resemblance is a message to us all and should not be summarily dismissed. There are other factors as well."

Ian and Elsbeth were calling on all their reserves to maintain their composure. *Oh, my God,* thought Elsbeth. *She is but the spitting image of my dear Arielle. How will Arielle receive her, for I can barely accept that which is before me. Two wee babes? Born of one on the same day and torn from their mother's bed? Torn from what God himself intended?* A chill came over Elsbeth. She felt more than faint. She felt empty and invisible.

"Lady Hargrove," Arianna's voice softly swept over Elsbeth like the fingers of a finely formed glove.

Arianna went to her, held her hands, and warmed them with her caress. Elsbeth felt a sweet familiarity and was at once comforted. Arianna stroked Elsbeth's hands, soothing them as she said, "All will be well. Trust in what is right and just, Lady Hargrove. We will all be better for what we know. The truth shall set us free from bondages that have held our God-given lives at bay. I am here to help, and to find my way to the sister whose flesh I have not touched since birth."

"Miss Smithfield, our Arielle is to return from abroad shortly. We anxiously await her arrival and, upon assessing her well-being, will be in communication with you. Where may we find you?" Elsbeth held her composure as she gave her word to proceed on Arianna's persistent path.

"I am residing at Mrs. Willard's home on 16th street. Perhaps your daughter could meet me there. I understand they know one another and, according to her resident horticulturalist, Mr. Peabody, Mrs. Willard has served as a mentor to Arielle. Mrs. Willard is a quite capable and amazing woman. I know, in my short acquaintance with her, she has an acute ability to make one feel very safe, secure and able."

Elsbeth looked into Arianna's eyes. The flecks about her irises beheld the truth of all truths. She knew, deep within the recesses of her mind and motherly being, that the person before her was indeed her daughter's sibling, her daughter's twin, her daughter's bond to a legacy that remained as much a mystery as tomorrow's promise.

Chapter Thirty-Three

September1897
Washington, District of Columbia

Arielle's trip abroad left her feeling physically spent and weak of spirit. She had said little of her trip when she returned, feigning fatigue and sequestering herself to her room with visits predominately from Fiona to tend to her needs for sustenance and toilette. Fiona's behavior was drawn in familiar ways, harkening to the curious manner she displayed when Alexandra Whitaker made her first call on the Hargrove home some months ago. Arielle wondered what news Fiona had lent her ears to of late, for the girl had a penchant for snooping around. She was quite surprised her parents were not wise to her spying. But, Fiona kept much of her knowledge to herself. Her fidgeting and odd retorts were usually the only slip in her secrecy. In awake dreams, Arielle relived the halcyon days of her youth. She imagined her life exempt from recent facts, exempt from Fiona's ambiguous bantering and exempt from her world of changes.

"Well, Miss Arielle, ye best be gettin' ready fer this day. It will be an eye-opener for sure."

"Fiona what do you mean by eye-opener. Do you have something more to say?"

"Oh, no, miss. I'm jest lookin' out the window, I am, and seein' all that bright sunshine pouring in."

"Fiona, what pray tell have you done now? If the sun is shining so brightly I would think one would feel the urge to close their eyes rather than find the day an 'eye-opener' as you say."

"Oh, jest forget I said anythin' Miss Arielle. You know me better then anyone. I jest dun't always say what I should."

"You are making me think you mean there are things unsaid by you that should be said."

"I best be gettin' you ready to go downstairs. Ye will be wantin' to look your best ye know, like the only you in the world."

"The only me in the world? Fiona, stop with your riddles. What are you not saying?"

"Yer jest such a beautiful one, the world would be even lovelier if there was a double one of you."

"Thank you for the compliment Fiona but this conservation is going in circles. Let me finish dressing."

Elsbeth and Ian respected Arielle's need for time to herself. So many revelations had presented themselves that they were hesitant to share their newfound knowledge. Identical thoughts swirled around in their heads. *Learning of her adoption, and knowledge of her birth mother was stunning enough. What would be her reaction to a sister who was essentially a stranger?*

They had asked Arianna to remain in Washington until Arielle's return. Emma's home provided the perfect respite for Arianna, and Emma had promised to allow Ian and Elsbeth the opportunity to reveal the details about her to Arielle before she made another visit to Chestnut Heights. Simon had become quite fond of Arielle's sibling. He enjoyed her daily sittings to sketch and paint her interpretations of the season's changing landscape in the gardens he created. He felt a great affinity for her, not only with her mirrored resemblance to Miss Hargrove, but also for her love of flowers. She was particularly skilled with her interpretations of roses, having studied under the tutelage of an elderly student of Redouté's. She took to painting from her first initiation. From wild roses to classic, her illustrations were feasts for the eyes.

Like Redouté's, Arianna's paintings were beautiful. She took great care to ensure the flowers she depicted were as scientifically exacting as possible, and she had developed an enormous portfolio, just waiting for the opportunity to show her work in a gallery. In the acute detail of her paintings, it was as though one could feel the tips of the rose petals as they seemingly curled upon the vellum. She enjoyed painting as a solitary pleasure, but was equally pleased to share her talents with others upon their asking. Arianna could be found with paper and paints in hand whether on the cusp of daylight's dawn or under the flinty light of a pale moon.

Early one morn, she and Simon observed a stunning lemon and lavender sunrise. Arianna captured its striations in one of her paintings.

Simon excitedly exclaimed, "I too am a painter, yes, a painter, yes, a painter!"

Arianna laughed at his unabashed enthusiasm. He seemed years younger when they were together.

"I paint with my flowers! Every shrub and botanical I plant is my brushstroke across the garden's canvas! Yes, indeed it is, indeed it is." Simon stood on his toes and enthusiastically extended his right arm out in a horizontal wave directed at the expansive yard and gardens beyond them.

A boxwood hedge surrounding Simon's rose garden maintained a sense of order. For him, it served as a sense of authority over nature's outpouring. The overgrown appearance he achieved in other areas of the grounds mirrored the traditional English gardens of which Emma was so fond, and provided a whimsical quadrant of chaos with heady mixes of colorful wildflowers. They appeared as if their caretaker had gone on holiday for a time. Simon commonly referred to his carefree style as 'controlled disorder.' In other areas, radiant bouquets of coleus, burst well above their pots, gave an impressive show of their richly variegated, crimson leaves.

Emma stepped through the open French doors into the garden space searching for Arianna. Since her arrival, Emma had lent comfort to her, as her concern grew daily for her mother's health. Arianna knew her mother's time was extremely limited but was determined to see her wishes through. She most earnestly hoped to return to her mother's brownstone in London before her passing to ease the guilt that held her mind captive these many years. If she could reassure her that her honesty, though long in coming, had been worth the telling, her mother could go to her grave with a less blemished conscience and peace of mind. Meeting with Arielle was the next important step to complete her mother's wishes, and Arianna hoped to encourage Arielle to accompany her to Olivia's bedside.

"There you are my dear. What an excellent morning you have to take in all that nature has to offer." Emma observed as she admired Arianna's latest work. "It is a challenge for me to decide which is my favorite, for you have such an ability to make each painting so exquisite in detail."

"And that is my mum's doing. I may have studied under the finest tutelage, but mum was always my greatest teacher. She encouraged me to seek out the most minute details in everything around me. What you see is as much through her eyes as my own. I fear she will not be in my life for many days henceforth. It is my fondest hope that my introduction to Arielle will go well, and she will find it agreeable to travel home with me."

"Having spent this glorious time with you, and knowing Arielle as I do, I feel very confident that you two will be of great comfort to one another." Emma placed her hands softly on Arianna's shoulders to reinforce her convictions.

⌒

Arielle opened the door to her bedchamber and poked her head into the hallway. She was surprised not to find Fiona's nose plastered against the doorframe. The girl seemed to be at her every turn. Since her homecoming, she was unsure whether the tension she felt came solely from within or was duly emanating from her parents. *Her parents. What did that word mean anymore?* She was abundant with mothers. She wondered what her mother's reaction would be to the revelation she would share. She could hear voices coming from her father's study and proceeded down the staircase hoping to find both of her parents there.

As she entered the study, she was pleased to see them both seated. After a cordial welcome and morning pleasantries, she took a seat. All faces lost their luster in preparation for the dreaded dialogue to commence.

"We are so relieved to see you up and well, Arielle. Our most fervent prayer was to have you whole again," Elsbeth said as she realized the significance of the word 'whole' and the fact that she and Ian had concealed so much from their daughter. *When we reveal all the parts of which we are aware, will Arielle feel whole or feel she has been shattered into hundreds of little pieces?*

"I appreciate your good wishes. However, we have something, something very serious to discuss. My trip home was very enlightening. I never did have the opportunity to visit Aunt Leta. I sent word to her that I had been in an accident with a lengthy recovery period and would not be able to see her at this time. However, my time abroad was spent in other ways. Miss Pennybacker, a private investigator, unearthed some details there. Details that will bring new names into our lives. I was referred to Miss Pennybacker by Mrs. Willard and I hired her to assist in my journey toward the truth."

Elsbeth and Ian were puzzled. *Bring new names to our lives?* They wondered how Arielle could know about Arianna and keep that discovery to herself since her return home.

"You hired a private investigator without our knowledge?" Ian was aghast to think his personal life may have been tread upon by a stranger.

"With all due respect, there seems to have been much that has occurred without another's knowledge. You both are fully aware of the letter sent by Olivia Smithfield. You could have told me at that time about my birth but you chose not to do so. Your denial and omission has cost me much in worry. Numerous questions swirled in my mind. I was determined to get to the core of the mystery surrounding my birth."

Elsbeth and Ian sat stunned. Both felt they were surviving on borrowed strength. Arielle had always shown an unwitting self-confidence. Elsbeth thought Arielle's independence obviously served her well for her to embark on such a truth-seeking journey so far from the security of their home in Washington.

"I believe it is time for you to admit the details that are the reality of my birth."

Ian and Elsbeth looked at one another then back at Arielle. *Where to begin? How to smooth the emotions and tension rushing through their veins? What to say?*

"Please speak to me. You alone can explain what you were thinking by not being forthright with me."

"It was never our intent to be devious or, through our omissions, to harm you in any way. I fear we never explored the damage and hurt that the truth revealed would bring on your life." Ian's words were some of the softest Arielle and Elsbeth had ever heard uttered from his mouth. "But, the letter from Smithfield? How on earth did you discover that?"

"I will tell you for I feel it is more than high time we ceased the dangerous game of playing with deceit. However, though I will not term myself the victim here, for I detest the word, I cannot have you challenging me about my sources or actions. Father, your carelessness found the letter in the hands of a young woman named Alexandra Whitaker. You may have heard of her late father, Andrew Whitaker. He was quite wealthy, having built an empire in the textile industry. But, I digress here. I met Miss Whitaker the evening I met William Clay. She stopped by our home to deliver to me one of my gloves that I lost in Mr. Clay's carriage."

As Arielle spoke, Ian's face nearly stung with the memory of that evening and his encounter with her gloves.

"I was wont to read the letter after Miss Whitaker made its contents seem very personal to me, albeit the letter was addressed to you, Father. It slipped from its envelope as I prepared to place it on your desk. Fiona had also acted quite curious about the letter so, though I am reluctant to admit it, my curiosity got the better of me and I read it through to the end. I apologize for failing to respect your privacy however, you left the letter in the public domain."

"My dear, Arielle. There is no need for apology. We are so sorry for all the pain and confusion we have caused you. Please tell us what you learned from Miss Pennybacker." Elsbeth wanted so desperately to hug and comfort her daughter but she restrained herself rather than break the flow of their long-awaited and long-overdo conservation.

Arielle proceeded to relay all of the details of her trip to London and Wales. She told of Miss Pennybacker's visits to Olivia Smithfield and her dire condition. She told of Maggie Galligan. She became emotional as she relived her trip to Wyndham Street. She imagined herself as a newborn. She pictured Annie Hollingsworth and wanted desperately to believe she experienced the joy of giving life and that she held her, her baby girl, close to her heart before passing from the earth. Suddenly, Arielle became aware that she had crossed her arms as she spoke, placing her hands on her upper arms as she hugged her arms to her chest. The self-embrace made her shudder with warmth.

Ian and Elsbeth only periodically interjected a question to gain clarity, for they wanted to listen to Arielle's telling of her journey without further delay or interruption. Both appeared shocked to learn that Annie Hollingsworth was not only Arielle's birth mother but she was also a pit brow girl at Hargrove Colliery. Elsbeth knew the law renounced girls and women from working the depths of the coalpits. She looked to Ian for a reaction, but his expression was benign. *Ian will have to take this matter up with Paul the Overman,* she thought to herself. *Though this woman worked the pits some score of years ago, I will make a point to discuss this with him.*

However, I must dismiss the topic for now. That Arielle knew Annie was her birth mother kept Ian and Elsbeth subdued.

"This, Miss Pennybacker. You trust her information is accurate? I for one would like to meet with her," Ian scoffed as though he could alter the facts before him.

"Oh trust me, Father. You will have your opportunity to have an audience with Miss Pennybacker. She will soon return from her buying trip. In her luggage is a possession of Annie Hollingsworth's given to me by Maggie Galligan. It is a wooden coffer of extreme importance to Annie according to Mrs. Galligan. Most of its contents are a mystery to me, for I could not bear to look through any part of it when I was at Wyndham. I was quite exhausted both physically and emotionally. Miss Pennybacker removed a carte-de-visite depicting a coach and a figure posed beside it. Though faded and smudged with fingerprints, Mrs. Galligan felt certain the figure in the photograph was her friend Annie. I barely gave it a glance."

Barely gave it a glance. For that I am thankful, thought Ian. *There is some measure of good fortune heard this day.* Ian's memory was being jogged and he was wont to understand why. *The girl, the young woman from the colliery. Where had Nesbitt said the coach was sent? Why did the street ring with familiarity?* Ian shook his head, not to clear the cobwebs from his mind, but to shake away memories coming back to haunt him. *Oh, Ogmore Vale is full of coaches. The carte-de-visite was faded, Arielle said. It could be a photograph of any number of coaches.* Ian turned his attention back to Arielle.

"Miss Pennybacker took great interest in the image. She asked permission to carry it with her."

"Has she been in contact with you since your departure? Have you had any correspondence from her?" Ian asked with all the calm he could muster.

"No. Miss Pennybacker said she would contact me upon her return, therefore I have no knowledge of any additional information she may have discovered."

"Arielle, our dear girl. I barely know where to begin with the news your father and I must share. We can hold back not another minute some information that recently came to us. We are so thankful you are even speaking with us, that you have not turned from us and retreated from your life with us."

"I think first, before you proceed, you must know that I forgive you for your poor judgment, though it will take some time for me to recover and adjust to all that has come to light. Mum, as much as I have learned of late about Annie Hollingsworth, I cannot imagine my life without you. I would be incomplete without your presence, your influence, your love. Had you been forthright with me years earlier, who is to say the sting would have been less? Although the wound heals, its scar remains an everlasting mark on the flesh and the soul. What has come before is indelible in its imprint. I, however, am willing to forgive you both and take solace in the love you have shed on me." Arielle's words spilled forth as she extended every ounce of effort to comfort her mother and herself with her oratory.

"Arielle, please know we made what we thought was our best choice at the time and we hope you do not judge us, or the whole human race for our decisions. We Hargroves are a resilient lot because we have to be." Elsbeth words came forth in muffled sobs.

Oh, Arielle thought to herself, *if I could only reverse time. And then, what would I gain? I stand alive and well today and must move on. To dwell on an uncertain past is to my disadvantage. My life as I knew it has changed forever. To hold bitterness and grudges harms no one but myself. I must adjust to what has been presented to me and make the very most of the life God has granted me.*

Her thoughts turned to a conversation she had with Emma Willard. "Remember, my dear. You must not re-visit your wounds, for then they will never heal." Arielle knew, for time to heal her, she must make the most of that time. And perhaps, in due time, she would discover all that she really was.

"I have told all I can at this time. You say you have news that has recently come to you. What can it be?"

"Please sit down, here, near to me," Elsbeth offered pointing to the large winged chair she hoped would envelope Arielle with comfort. "What your father and I have to share with you was something, or I should say, someone, about whom we knew nothing."

"And how did you come to know this information?"

"A messenger sent a letter to us. Another letter from Olivia Smithfield. Your father and I were quite stunned by its contents. We want you to read it through. Please believe us when we say we were unaware that someone else has an important place in your life."

Elsbeth presented Arielle with Olivia's letter. Reluctantly, she unfolded its pages and began to read. The muscles in her torso tightened, she took shallow breaths as she read Olivia Smithfield's words of disclosure. Her eyes welled with tears as she read, 'when he delivered not one, but two baby girls.' She continued her reading. A tiny gulp was emitted as she held back a lump in her throat. The urge to heave came and fortunately quickly passed. She wanted nothing to deter her from reading the letter to its end. And then the name. Her sister's name. 'I, in good conscience, could not have my dear Arianna live the rest of her life without the knowledge that a sister of her own blood, a supreme likeness, exists on this earth.' *My sister. Arianna. My twin.* Arielle could not believe what she was reading. *How could this possibly be true? All these years without any knowledge of a sister. There must be a mistake. This must be a fabrication.* She read the last words of Olivia's missive. Her arm went limp as it dropped to her side and the letter slipped from her fingertips onto the plush carpet. She took a moment and gathered her thoughts.

"How can we possibly believe this? There is no proof that a second baby existed. We have nothing but the words of a dying woman. For all we know she is daft and hallucinating, or perhaps she is a vindictive soul who thinks she will benefit in some way."

"Arielle, a similar response was felt by your mother and myself. We felt ready to dispute the contents of the letter and the mysterious way it came to us until proof found itself at our doorstep."

"Proof? What proof?"

"Please remain seated. This is not easy for us to say to you and again, please remember, we had no knowledge of this until recent days. Arianna Smithfield, your sister, came to visit us. She has remained in Washington so she may meet you. She has verified that Olivia is her mother and that she is very near death. She has confirmed the veracity of everything stated in her mother's letters."

"But, we still cannot be sure she is my sister, my twin."

"When you see her, you can be the judge my dear. Other than her color of hair, she is the spitting image of you. Her eyes are so like yours, the wonderful flecks that bring so much life and expression to your face."

"I feel like I have gone mad, as though we have all gone mad! I cannot believe we are even having this conversation. I must pinch myself to prove this is not a very, very strange dream. In fact, I had such a dream of papers being handed to me. I never knew my dreams would awaken in reality! This is mad! And, you both! You believe this Arianna is my sister!" Arielle was nearly ranting as her voice raised several octaves.

"Arielle, we are so sorry to upset you. You have every right to feel so undone. You have been deceived. Your mother and I have been deceived. There is no way around the truth. Accept it we must, and take one day at a time to heal and accept what we can of the truth."

"Accept this. Of late, you have forced my hand to accept unimaginable things. What a wicked dream this would be if it were a dream. The truth? I must see my own truth." Her words came in gasps as she made every effort to calm her nerves. "You say she has remained in Washington. Where is she staying?"

"You will be interested to know that she has found lodging at Mrs. Willard's. Apparently, as fate would have it, when she arrived in Washington, she was guided to inquire about a room there. Mrs. Willard invited her to remain until your return."

So, the welcoming arms of Chestnut Heights have extended themselves on my behalf once again. Of course, Emma would invite my sister to stay. What better way to keep a watchful eye over her and to know her better. She is protecting me and my sibling. I am once again in her debt for she is a true friend. Tomorrow, I will go to Emma's and meet my sister. Sister. The word was so foreign to her. She had been raised as an only child. She had been given every luxury but that of a sibling. And now, on the morrow, she would come to know her sister, her twin. She knew she must accept all that had come before. *I cannot say goodbye to my past, for it makes every difference for my future.* The last line of Olivia's letter reverberated in Arielle's mind. *'May God keep us all in his watchful care.'*

Chapter Thirty-Four

September 1897
Washington, District of Columbia

Today was Arianna's long-awaited day. She had received a correspondence by messenger that Arielle Hargrove would arrive unaccompanied. Her parents would remain at home, and for that Arianna was thankful. She wanted to greet her newfound sister alone, without the trappings of an entourage. She felt very unsettled, her nerves a twisted montage of things past and present. Emma had been most supportive and had made arrangements for her staff, with the exception of Thomas, to remain at bay to ensure that an atmosphere of peace and privacy would prevail for the two whose unfamiliarity would soon reverse itself.

A knock from the massive doorknocker on the entrance to Chestnut Heights took its toll across the foyer, resonating into the parlor's grand salons. All else was so deathly silent, that the faint whistles from a tufted titmouse, had there been one, could have been heard. Arianna could hear the distant shuffles of Thomas' feet as he moved through the foyer to the main portal. She heard him greet their guest. Her nerves pulsed through her body. This was the moment she had anticipated. She knew her mother would want this moment to go graciously well for them both.

Thomas guided Arielle into the parlor with a presentation by his outswept hand and, as gracefully, he exited into the foyer's shadows, leaving the two young women to fully face one another, alone yet together. Resentments for time lost and truths not told seemed to shed their ugly skins as the two beauties viewed one another. They were awed by their very likenesses to one another and suddenly, conversation began to flow as naturally as their beginnings. It was as though there had been no separation, no distance set by time or the interference of man.

"I am so relieved to meet you, to be in your presence," Arianna said being the first to break any silence.

"And I with you," Arielle responded still not quite believing there was someone in the world with whom she shared so very much in common. *Adopted.* The word stung when she first learned she was adopted. She had felt disparate, so physically unrelated to anyone in the home she had known for her score of years. Now, here, in her very presence, was her blood relation, a physical link to her history, her heritage.

"To have someone related to me, an extension of my family, fills me with elation. We have our very future to find all we have in common," Arianna said and smiled as she admired the form before her.

"Yes, and time enough to establish shared memories." Arielle nearly cooed as her flesh absorbed all the sensations thrust upon her as she accepted this extension of her family, this sister, this twin, this mirror image named Arianna.

The two were so enamored and spellbound by their shared images they were nearly thrown off balance when several loud strikes sounded from the doorknocker at the main portal. Thomas lumbered to the door, pausing only a moment to view the scene unfolding itself in the parlor.

"Oh, Mista Clay, so good to seez ya, sir. Miz Willard will be mighty glad yer here, yez sir, yez indeed. G'won the parlor."

"Thank you Thomas. It is always good to see you. You do such a fine job and I know my aunt sincerely appreciates that."

Arielle heard the voice that continually took a very pleasant toll on her senses. *William. So good that he is here to be a party to this day. How did he know I would need him now? It seems he is always at the ready to come to my rescue.* As William rounded the corner into the parlor from the depths of the foyer, he was taken back by the visions before him. Not one, but two beautiful women stood before him, as alike as any two could be. Separated only by their color of hair, he immediately recognized the one with the rich auburn shade as the stranger who made her debut at his aunt's masquerade party. Flashes of her being thrown to the ground by Alexandra with Simon Peabody embroiled in the fray gravitated through his mind. *How could this be? Aunt Emma told me there was a bond about which I would soon learn.*

"Greetings, ladies," William bowed as he admitted himself into their presence.

Arielle was exceedingly pleased to see him. However, she noted an awareness, a familiarity he seemed to project toward Arianna. William caught her eye and at once set to quell any mis-givings she might have.

"Why, it seems our paths have crossed at Chestnut Heights on another occasion...a rather formidable one at that," William exclaimed as he turned his attention to Arianna.

"You are quite right, sir, and I thank you for coming to my aid at a very precarious moment."

"I again apologize for the behavior of Miss Whitaker. I assure you, she has seen the error of her ways and will not soon be re-peating the rather unfortunate performance she exhibited that eve."

Emma's full skirt preceded her as it swirled into the room. "Oh, my goodness, oh my goodness, oh my goodness and, I must say, I suddenly sound like Simon. I was only just aware that you had arrived William. When Thomas summoned me, I was otherwise engaged. I had so hoped to greet you before you met my guest.

This must be very awkward. I do apologize, for I hoped to spare you any discomfort. As you can plainly see, there is good reason to have these beautiful young women in the same room together. We were unaware at my masquerade party, but within hours, Miss Smithfield shared her identity with me. She, of course, needed to first deliver a message of introduction, so to speak, to the manse of the Hargroves. All felt it best to await Arielle's return from abroad to reveal my guest's identity."

"Miss Smithfield, as in Olivia Smithfield?" William queried.

"William, I introduce to you, Miss Arianna Smithfield. She is the daughter of Olivia Smithfield."

"Your supreme likeness to Arielle, Miss Hargrove is compelling."

William stared at the two, his eyes glancing back and forth like the pendulum on a clock.

"I know Miss Whitaker became quite engaged and actually, quite enraged with your resemblance to Miss Hargrove," William explained as he again turned his full attention to Arielle.

"As it so happened, Arielle, at Aunt Emma's masquerade party, Alexandra mistook Miss Smithfield to be you, and, knowing her as you do, she spiraled out of control. Jealousy is no friend to Alexandra."

"It would seem my presence has had that effect on many I have encountered," Arianna mused.

"William, I would have been very forthcoming with you had I had the authority to do so, however, as you find with your clients, and the trust with which they hold you in such high esteem, I was not at liberty to speak a word of what I have known and, I have known for a very limited period of time. Arielle, I hope I have not overstepped my boundaries."

Arielle could see in Emma's countenance that it was time to bring William into their circle of truth. She hoped he would not find her to be the bastard Alexandra claimed her to be. She hoped he would accept her sister as she was wont to do, and she hoped he would understand that the circumstances of her birth were not of her doing.

"Mr. Clay, William. I am pleased to introduce my sister, Arianna. We have only today come into one another's presence. We have much to learn, much to accept, and much to understand. With your aunt's immeasurable guidance, we will come to know one another. The aura of Chestnut Heights has healed me on more than one occasion. I can think of no better place to not only rest a weary soul, but to revive one's weary spirits. I feel I must speak to the revelations from my trips to London and Wales. The facts gathered there are of extreme pertinence to Arianna and myself. Please bear with me as I do my very best to explain all I know."

Arielle looked at the faces before her and began to retell the information about Morgan Pennybacker, her assistant, Agnes Fielding, and their peculiar tag-along, Peepers. She told of Olivia Smithfield, of Maggie Galligan, and Annie Hollingsworth. Arianna offered her portions to the storytelling, including her mother's grave health, and the letter she had Thomas deliver to the Hargrove manse the afternoon of Emma's masquerade party, confirming that they were indeed twins. Arielle told of the weeks she lay in a hospital bed at Providence under a mistaken identity gathered from assumptions courtesy of a calling card, and how William's visit was a turning point in her recovery providing verification that she was indeed not Olivia Smithfield. And, then came the revelation of the coffer and Annie's request that Mrs. Galligan be her safekeeper. Arielle described the daguerreotype, and noted that its faded and smudged image was something she gave only a glance. She explained that recent correspondence from Miss Pennybacker indicated she would return within the month and had news to share. She stressed that it would be important to have her parents present.

"I will write Miss Pennybacker immediately to apprise her of our meeting. I know she will be most pleased. Arianna, will you remain in Washington until she returns? I so want us to be to-gether to hear her news."

"It will be my great honor to be with you. There is, however, something very pressing that I must do. I have remained far past my intended time here and must return to London posthaste. My mum's caregiver, Beatrice, has urged me to be at Mum's side. I fear this will not be a pleasure trip, for it is only a matter of days before she loses her grip on life. It has been the secret she has kept for all these years that has given her the strength to remain on this earth these past months. I must go to her."

"Is this a trip you wish to make on your own?"

"Are you asking, or suggesting that you accompany me?"

"If that is your wish, I would like to meet my sister's mum. Though frail of body, I am certain the love she has held for you this score of years will be felt by all surrounding her."

"And she will want to see you, Arielle. Of that I am sure."

"Then, let us make our arrangements at once. We can go by rail to New York and book our passage on the White Star's SS Britannic. I had a very pleasant experience on the ship and it will take us directly to the Dock at the Pool just south of London Bridge. There are always a wealth of cabbies to get us into the city."

William listened intently as the sisters enthusiastically made their plans to leave Washington. He hoped there would be no re-currence of the fate that befell Arielle on her first trip to the rail station. A thought occurred to him.

"If I may, ladies, I would like to offer my services as your escort. I know, I for one would feel more comfortable to have a watchful eye on you, particularly upon your arrival. The area in the vicin-ity of the Pool is not the safest, especially for two young women."

Arielle smiled as she watched the concern and sincerity in William's face. She could think of nothing that would comfort her more than to have him present. She looked to Arianna to see if she was in agreement and found the identical expression of ac-cord on her face. Emma had remained silent as she watched the young women who so quickly came to know one another. She listened as they planned their trip together and swelled with pride that William would join them. Arielle and Arianna simultaneously nodded to each other and in unison said, "Yes."

William smiled. "I will go directly from here to the station and secure our tickets. When do you want to leave?"

"I say we leave tomorrow. I can have Fiona pack my things. Mum and Father will understand and, quite frankly, given the circumstances of late, will refrain from holding me back. Is tomorrow too soon for you Arianna?"

"Tomorrow will be quite right for me. The sooner the better to assure I can be with Mum before she passes."

"Aunt Emma, will you be fine in my absence?"

"Oh, yes, my dear, and thank you for asking me. It gives me great joy to see the three of you together," Emma assured the trio. "In the telling of this, your mother has given us a gift. There is a strength among you that is so comforting for me. And, Miss Smithfield, I will especially be thinking of you as you make this trip. I know it will be a difficult and bittersweet time."

"Thank you Mrs. Willard. When I return to America to meet Miss Pennybacker, and once again visit the Hargroves, I hope to see you."

"You know, Miss Smithfield, you are always welcome here. Consider Chestnut Heights your home as well. And, about this Mrs. Willard business. I insist you call me Emma. When Arielle took to calling me by my given name, it brought me great pleasure and I will feel the same delight when you do so."

"Emma it is then, and you must call me Arianna."

Emma stood and, as she walked toward Arianna she stood as well, and the two embraced one another. Arielle and William smiled as they shared the pleasure of her sibling's presence and the warmth being felt throughout the room. William sensed the trip to London would be difficult for Arielle and Arianna. Not the travel itself, but the circumstances of their time there. All indications pointed to Olivia's death being imminent. He had been present when his Uncle Horace succumbed to influenza and he could not think of a sadder day. To witness the breath leave the body and the heart stop, to beat no more, was a gripping scene he wished never to repeat, but knew that the reality of life, and certainty of death would not make that so. With Horace's passing, his aunt had lost the love of her life and was devastated. William took special care to see to her well-being and doted on her as much as she on him. He would be with Arianna and Arielle and provide the same stalwart support he had lent his Aunt Emma. He knew what they would need and he would be there to ease their pain.

Chapter Thirty-Five

Mid-September 1897
London, England

Beatrice opened the door for the threesome. Arianna, Arielle and William reverently stepped inside. Word had been sent by messenger to Olivia's brownstone that Miss Arianna was returning today. Returning she knew to a dismal homecoming.

"She has awaited your arrival, miss." Beatrice's words were solemn at best as she stepped aside and ushered in the visitors, exhibiting a brief curtsy as introductions were made to Arielle and William. Her face had the full imprint of the gravity of the atmosphere soon to encompass them all.

She led them up the staircase to Olivia's chamber, the room that for several months had become her tomb. What remained of her facial muscles made every effort to form a welcoming smile. Olivia's old self, her strong, healthy, vibrant self that now remained no more than a memory, for a moment, regaled itself. It was as though some last bastion struggled with the concept of letting go to a place where her original self would be no more. She signaled Beatrice with the limp wave of her hand toward a carafe of water. Obligingly, Beatrice poured a small amount of water into a waiting glass and gently lifted Olivia's head as she put the liquid to her lips. Several tiny sips were taken, then Olivia ever so slightly shook her head indicating she needed no more. Beatrice was quite relieved her charge had not given up the ghost before her daughter's return.

Olivia explored the faces before her as best she could, her vision having become as weak as the rest of her body. She had longed for this day. The day she would see her Arianna reunited with her sister. And, here they were together in the company of a very handsome gentleman. Arianna bent down and placed a gentle kiss on her mother's forehead and stroked her cheek.

Melancholy washed across Olivia's face as the reality of her fate inched closer and closer. "I do not want to miss anything." The well-enunciated words slipped across her tongue. Her manor was clear, her thoughts were clear, and she was at once a vibrant woman in a decaying shell. She knew that her prognosis was bleak, very bleak, yet she was determined to use every ounce of energy she could rally to offer important details to the sisters before she took her last breath.

"Arianna," Olivia pronounced every syllable in beleaguered syncopated breaths. "The name seemed a rightful choice."

She continued, each word taking an unprecedented toll on her lungs. "I labored a score of days, a poor word choice, I fear, nonetheless, I will go on."

Her speech required the utmost of effort, as her upper body nearly lifted off the bed sheets when she spoke. She maintained her resolve to explain her daughter's beginnings. Her liturgy of words came soft and slow.

"I struggled over a proper name for the baby. Oh, such a pretty little bundle, and so painfully orphaned." Olivia gasped upon each word.

"One day, one of the Hargrove's housemaids, on holiday visiting her elderly grandmum, stopped in at the market to buy the old woman some cubes for her tea, and she raved about the beautiful baby girl her master and missus had. She said everyone was so very happy, for the Hargroves had wanted a child for some time hence. Then, the housemaid spoke close up and softly. I had to strain my ears to hear her say that the missus had been away for an extended holiday and, when she returned, she had a baby in her arms."

"I had to look away so the housemaid would not think I was putting my ears where they should not be. However, I could tell from what she said, that everyone naturally figured with the missus away that her time came without any of them having the slightest awareness of a change in her form. It was the only conclusion they could draw. Why would they think anything else? The shopkeeper appeared uncomfortable talking about Lady Hargrove's being with child and raised her voice to ask the wee one's name," Olivia paused to take a sip of water offered by Arianna and regain her speech.

"The housemaid brought her voice up to a more public level so I no longer needed to strain to hear, and she boasted that the newborn's name was Arielle, a lucky seven letters for a lucky baby, born on the seventh day of the seventh month. It came to me quite easily that to name my baby girl Arianna would serve to honor the memory of her natural mum and give her the lucky seven letters to grow by. She would forever be bound to her twin by a name with similar derivation and the heritage of luck."

Olivia's eyes closed and her breath became more shallow. Like a pair of worn billows, her lungs failed to provide the force of air she needed to continue on.

Arianna leaned forward and kissed Olivia on the cheek as she held close her hand. This woman, who was slowly and painfully slipping away, was the only mother ever known to her. She had been her North Star, her guiding light, and yet no powers of the celestial universe could turn back the course now set. She had sacrificed her secret and, knowing time was no longer her ally, she felt her decision had led her along a righteous path that might serve her well at the gates of the Almighty. Olivia looked from Arianna to Arielle. She sucked in the deepest breath she could muster as her body shuttered from the force of the effort.

"You have lived the life of one without the knowledge of two. Please forgive me for keeping you from your own blood these many years past. My great hope is for you to overcome your separateness and find joy, to know one another as sisters, and realize in your heart of hearts that decisions were made and choices selected, not from a source of ill will, but with the utmost love and desire for your well-being." Olivia suffered with every earnest breath she took to utter the words from her parched lips.

Arianna held her mother's hand as she looked up from her bedside to her sister. Arielle felt absorbed in Arianna's pain. She knew Olivia's time was measured, and that knowledge found her senses splayed raw and open. She could taste the loss. William held sentry over the trio. He could sense the three growing more fragile as Olivia prepared to slip from life and the sisters prepared to witness her departure.

The anticipation of her mother's passing precipitated a swarm of emotions. Loss, death and grieving swirled artfully together like a tearful strain sung by a violin's proficient bow. The imagined refrain sent a resonance of emotions rebounding against the interior walls of Arianna's body, rendering her weak and faint. She nearly swooned. Before her lay a quagmire of emotions. Before her lay visible grief, undying questions, and possibly, requisite renewal. Before her lay the only woman ever known to her as 'Mum' yet, suddenly, she bore the face of a stranger. Her mother's rapid decline was mortifying, but real. Tears streamed from Arianna's face as she considered her soon-to-be twice orphaned status. She wished for more moments with her mother, yet knew they would not be realized.

"Why are you crying?" Olivia's gasped words came with great effort and care. "I love you. Don't worry. Everything is going to be alright. Everything is as it should be now. Fear not for me. I come to Him singing with joy."

Always the mother. Always the comforter, thought Arianna

"As you wish, Mummy. You may go and fear nothing. Go in peace Mummy, and know I love you more than my mortal words can ever express."

Arielle could tolerate little more. Her heart let out a silent roar. Her body barely endured its deafening sound. Though inaudible, William seemed to feel the reverberations passing from her flesh and bones to his. He reached for her and gathered her in the sway that threatened to catapult her to the ground. His able arms held her securely close. They gazed into one another's eyes and, as though transfixed by a power greater than themselves, a sense of oneness filled any vapor of space between them.

Their day had been one of nurturing, separation, loss and reunion, far more than most souls could absorb in such a short space of time. William searched Arielle's face with loving intent, yet knew he could not fully put words to what her eyes were saying. Her deep respect for the life being lost before her kept her in a state of stunned composure. Emotions battered her insides. *Why do I feel the pain of this loss?* She lifted her head and opened her eyes catching Arianna's gaze. It was as though a mirror had presented itself, and the tears in the eyes of the image before her were her tears, the sorrow her sorrow, the loss hers too. William placed his able hands upon Arielle's shoulders. She felt the strength and heat from his touch. She swayed and drew her shoulders up to her neck totally enveloping his caress as she waited to exhale and let all the pain and confusion leave her being.

She turned to look at William. A titillating sensation rushed throughout her torso and into the very tips of her limbs. She was at once swathed in his caring manliness and knew without hesitation that they had become figuratively one with each other. She blushed. The rush she sensed from her loins emanated up to her lips. She searched his face and, sensing the same awareness of spirit, prepared to lift her lips to his. Her shoulder turned into his and, as their eyes grew closer to one another, a sound, the gentle sobs from Arianna reminded them of the moment and the need to postpone, if only for the present, the lust and love they could not deny.

Olivia's breathing became very shallow and she ceased responding in anyway. It was a struggle to live, and she chose to struggle no more. Arianna held tight Olivia's hand until her last breath and all was still. It had been a slow, slow fade and now she was gone. Her mother's life had expired and with it went her ability to reach out and comfort her child forevermore.

Olivia's final journey had begun. The room became soulfully reverent. Arianna became recollective. Slowly, she lifted her eyes with renewed resolve. It was time to better know her flesh and blood, her sister, Arielle. She turned to catch her gaze. Arielle stood with her head bowed. In the same cadence her sister had employed, she raised her eyelids to see the juxtaposed image of herself with dark auburn hair.

"Cry not, my sister, for you know you were holding her hand and that, that is the most important. She slipped away in the comfort of your loving fingertips. Fingertips that gracefully lifted her to the greater beyond."

Arianna listened to the warm, softly spoken words of her sister.

"Arielle, I now know what it is to pass on. It is all but a breath away. God gave us the strength to shelter my mum on her journey. We must make the most of the time we have. We must make every breath count."

The look the two shared lent unspoken confirmation to the bond now formed. William's left arm remained around Arielle's waist as he placed his right hand on Arianna's shoulder. He became a conduit of comfort between the two. As they gained fortitude from their proximity to one another, the trio felt the mutual sensation of an allegiance formed on winged-wishes as an angel carried Olivia's spirit to peace.

"I have oft felt there was no one other than Mummy who was a part of me. This discovery of you, my sister, is a blessing of Mum's passing and the resolve of her conscience to end years of silence. Uncle Edmond once shared with me his observation that death is a reflection of life, that when people die, they die with love or hate, the energy for one or the other is there as it has been while living. Mummy bore no hatred, love remained with her to the end. Her voice is heard on high today. May her life be a blessing for us all, and may we thrive with new strength."

With those words, the two sisters, the twins who had such freshly opened wounds, embraced one another and sobbed and sobbed, not for what was lost, but for what had been found.

Chapter Thirty-Six

Late September 1897
Washington, District of Columbia

Agnes and Morgan's conversation from the moment they turned the key to lock Pennybacker's storefront all the way to the Hargrove's doorstep, was consumed with summarizing the circumstances of the months past. Both reveled at how decisions made at birth and death could be so tightly intertwined into a mysterious mire.

"If you ask me, the man should be horse-whipped."

"Well, Agnes, no one is asking and I suggest you sequester that thought."

"Whoa, boy. Whoa, boy," came Peepers' warning refrain. "Whoa, boy."

"Hush," Agnes reprimanded as she gave his cage a gentle rattle.

They had been summoned by Arielle to bring the oak box and meet at the Hargrove manse to validate their findings. The daguerreotype viewed and identified by Maggie and Wicks had been returned to the coffer for safekeeping just as Annie had placed it over a score of years ago. Morgan had listed for Arielle the other items in Annie's coffer with brief descriptions. When she shared the information with her parents, her father's reaction was most curious and Elsbeth appeared quite taken back. Arielle, in fact, had not seen her father so sullen. It was as though the Grim Reaper stood before him.

The coffer was of grave importance. Today, it would be placed in his hands and she sensed its contents, and her father's words, would prove something she and Miss Pennybacker suspected. Arielle wanted to ensure there would be no room for denial from her father. It was indeed time for him to face his demons. Though losing face among strangers could evoke his ire, it was a risk she deemed worth taking if healing was to begin for her mother, herself, and the sibling new to their lives. For all of her father's failings, she could not find him repugnant. He and Elsbeth were her family and she only had what she had because of their love and care for her.

Arielle had called a cast of witnesses to be present including William and Emma. Though reluctant, for fear of being intrusive in the family's private matters, both understood Arielle's need to be surrounded with their devoted and loving support. Had they not come into her life, she might never have had the wisdom or strength to pursue the course that led her to this day. This she hoped would not be a day of Calvary for her father. Instead, her greatest hope was, that through confession, he would not only find reform from the error of his ways, but mend the fragile relationship he now held with her mother and herself. *No*, Arielle thought. *I must pursue this meeting. It is an important step. Like water seeks its level, I must go this way.* Re-building trust was a journey on which she hoped they would collectively embark. Time, patience, commitment, strength, a will to accept, and a desire to rehabilitate past behaviors would be keynotes of their healing.

Arielle heard conversation in the foyer and assumed her invited audience was beginning to assemble. Her assumptions were confirmed when Fiona, having raced up the staircase, came panting into her room.

"Miss Arielle," Fiona gasped placing her right hand on her chest to slow the pace of her heart. "Miss Arielle, the family will be wanting your presence in the parlor."

"The parlor? And why not the study?"

"Seems Sir Ian Hargrove be wantin' to be in a neutral space, least that's what I heard him whisper to Lady Hargrove."

"Fiona, have you been eavesdropping again?"

"Oh, no miss, I jest have the ability to hear the faintest sounds, I do."

"Very well. I suppose Father is avoiding his study where he conducts business since today is business of a different sort. No matter. Fiona, who has arrived thus far?"

"I 'ave been greetin' 'em I 'ave. Lovely folks they are one an' all."

"Just answer my question. Have Mr. Clay, Mrs. Willard and Miss Smithfield arrived?"

"Oh, my they 'ave and that Mr. Clay, oh my, e's a 'andsome one 'e is. Easy on the eyes 'e is."

"Fiona, please stay focused on my question. And what of Miss Pennybacker and Miss Fielding?"

"Both went to find a seat for 'emselves. They was 'avin' a chat with Mrs. Willard and Mr. Clay stood when they entered. 'E bowed real gentleman like. 'E even gave a bow to the bird Miss Fielding was a carryin'."

"And, Father and Mum, have they come downstairs?"

"'Aven't seen 'em."

"Very well. Please inform my parents that they are needed in the parlor. I will be along shortly."

Arielle took a final glance at herself in the cheval mirror. She threw her shoulders back. From head to toe she exuded a confident stance. *Is it the mirror playing tricks on me, or am I really that sure of myself?* She shook her head trying to release any remnants of doubt from her being. *Will this feeling last, or will my nerves get the better of me?* She lifted one of the petite decanters from the service tray on her vanity and removed its slender crystal stopper. With simplicity of motion, she stroked her wrists, then the nape of her neck, letting the fragrant indulgence dissipate onto her flesh, its essence igniting her senses. She knew the journey down the staircase would find her long in thought for at its end, she would step into a familiar room with an unfamiliar agenda. Fear started to creep under her skin. She turned, taking the necessary steps to exit her bedroom while her legs held the strength of character to move her forward. As she descended the staircase, she could hear the muted voices in the parlor. *At least they are not all in complete silence. Perhaps this will be a cordial gathering.* She knew she was fooling herself. *How could the gathering remain cordial once the questioning of Father begins?*

As Arielle entered the room she wondered, *Why do I feel so undone, so nervous, so ill at ease? I should never have questioned myself in the mirror.* She tried to shake off the feelings, casting them aside before they got the best of her, and caused any remaining confidence to fall away. She had felt this way before, knew the feeling well, and knew too that it would pass. But waiting for its departure was torture. She looked about the room at her invited guests. Immediately upon her entry, William stood and walked to her side, guiding her to the settee next to his aunt. He stood behind the two watching the doorway for the Hargroves to enter.

"I want to thank you all, indeed. That is, Arianna and I want to thank you all for coming today. The day is of great importance to us."

Arielle, with worry beginning to form on her brow, looked to Fiona who was presenting only a sliver of herself as she clung to the draperies swagged over the arched opening to the parlor. She was losing patience with the girl's interminable habit of putting her ears where they did not belong.

"Fiona. Please remove yourself from this space and inform my parents that company has gathered and awaits their appearance."

"Right you are, Miss Arielle."

Fiona climbed the staircase very slowly, taking one step at a time, hoping to miss not a single word emitted from the parlor.

When she arrived at the Hargrove's bedroom suite, she could hear muffled voices through the thick mahogany double doors. She paused. *Oh, my. They's 'avin' a few words, they is.* She strained her ears to catch pieces of their conversation.

"This is a dark chapter in our marriage, indeed, for you know what I suspect," Elsbeth shook her head and closed her eyelids inhaling as she tilted her head low. Her weighty exhale seemed to bear the burden of their years together. Though not all were blemished with deceit, it was the knowledge of this most unchaste episode that threatened to crumble all she had worked stoically to preserve.

"My dear, Elsbeth. I beg your indulgence. We would be hard pressed not to glean the radiance of this day. We have not one, but two beautiful daughters as it so happens. It is a day to rejoice, not one for repentance nor regret." Ian made his declaration with weakness of spirit and voice. He knew deep within his heart he had wronged his beloved Elsbeth and only hoped his proclamation would aid him in retrieving her acceptance and forgiveness.

Slowly, Elsbeth raised her head. Her eyes opened wide and she stared so hard the intensity of her trancelike vision bore through Ian's being. He stumbled backward as though pierced by a dagger then caught himself, though he was none the stronger for it.

Ian knew Elsbeth found his explanations and exclamations untenable. His character was anything but flawless, of which he was well aware, and had always fully accepted himself as such. There were some, Ian among them, who would proclaim his successes to have been aided by his flaws. His attraction to women, and they to him, strengthened his confidence, bolstering his ability to take on risks from which others would shy. His innate charisma made him a force to be reckoned with whether engulfed in meetings with the Trade Council, near the bowels of the colliery, or tending to the needs of a femme fatale. He was a titan of business and commerce and that could not be denied. However, Elsbeth knew his flaws well and elected to not only endure them, but to equally deny them. For her, he was her one true love and, though some might think her foolish or weak, she had vowed to love him through thick or thin. It was a vow she considered sacred, though with it came not only enormous joy, but also excruciating pain.

Elsbeth's reaction was shaking Ian to his core. He was feeling quite undone. *Damnation. What spell has this woman cast upon me?* He was certainly not feeling himself. Nothing had ever transfixed him in such a manner. He held a deep and abiding love for Elsbeth that could not be turned asunder by weaknesses, which, on occasion, overcame his flesh. In his own way, he held an unflinching commitment to her.

The past was the past. His allegiance was to Elsbeth. He knew every effort of his body and soul must be addressed to her wellbeing. She was his rod and staff, and without her, his world was incomplete.

"My dear. I wish I could turn back the clock, but alas, I have no such power. I will not retreat from the pain my actions now inflict upon you. We shall face, full throttle, all that has driven us to this day and correct our course. We will gain strength, and be no less for my misguided behavior."

Elsbeth heard Ian's words, but listening would not make accepting come as easily as the hearing. *Strength. Who was he to speak of strength? How can we be stronger when I feel no stability of foundation?*

"You, sir, have rifled me to my core! And, who knows what effect this will have on Arielle! Has she not endured enough?"

The innermost chasms of Ian's soul reeled with unchained guilt, bouncing within and about him like an echo chamber filled with millions of variant voices, each sounding discordant notes, all painfully aimed at his conscience. He felt weak and without substance, alone and without solace, and removed far, far away. Guilt, an emotion from which he thought he was exempt, had infiltrated his fortress and now pummeled his resources for defense. Guilt. He thought he was immune for he never let it near, but here it was, bold, daring and in his face.

Bastard. Elsbeth thought to herself but would not let her mind remain there. "Sir Ian, I am speaking to you! Why have you been so careless and thoughtless?" Elsbeth's voice seemed a faint vapor of sound with no essence of her words reaching him. Her voice became more pronounced, waking him from his stupor. "Were you bored with me? Am I not an able wife? What were you thinking to take on a consort?" Her face felt solely on fire. Her husband's secret was fanning the flames of a burn that came over her and would not easily be soothed.

Ian looked at Elsbeth. She did not have to be heard to be heard. Her face, reddened by anger, was frozen with a pained expression of betrayal. Her silence surpassed any economy of words needed to convey her mood. He knew well enough that boredom with their relationship did not cause him to stray, for he loved Elsbeth and would not imagine himself without her. At the very minimum, he owed her full disclosure and only hoped she would sense the genuine sadness and tremendous remorse he felt for placing their marriage in such jeopardy.

The knock at their door startled them both. Regaining their composure, Ian opened the door to find Fiona so plastered against it that she was flung into the room.

"What in the blazes are you about? You are a clumsy buffoon. Why we have you in our charge escapes me. What is it Fiona? What brings you to our door?"

"It's Miss Arielle, it is. She sent me ta get ye. The others be waitin' fer ye in the parlor and she asked that ye come downstairs."

"Very well. Elsbeth my dear, let us face the wolves."

"You, sir are the one to fear the wolves. I have only the outcome of *your* acceptance of your actions to fear. You, and you alone, can dictate our future course."

"I love you, Elsbeth. I cannot pretend myself to be otherwise. I know I have behaved in a ghastly fashion."

He had always imagined himself to be a bigger than life force, yet now, at this very moment, he was small, smaller than anything surrounding him, smaller than the space he occupied, and smaller than the air that seemed to suck the lifeblood from him. Yes, he knew it was true. He had diminished himself by his actions.

As Ian and Elsbeth entered the parlor, all present stood in unison as though someone on the highest pulpit directed them to do so. Ian looked into each of their eyes, realizing he was among many strangers. None looked like wolves, but a carnivorous expression beheld their faces, and Ian felt he was about to be devoured.

"Father, we will appreciate your candor today and know this is to be an unenviable position for you. However, it is far time we heard the truth from your lips. I want first to introduce you and mother to Miss Morgan Pennybacker and her assistant, Miss Agnes Fielding. They have been instrumental in bringing to the forefront many facts needed to bring clarity to the circumstances before us. I also am pleased to introduce Mrs. Emma Willard and her nephew whom Mum has met, Mr. William Clay. Both have been most kind to both Arianna and myself. Their presence today is of great importance to us."

Elsbeth moved her gaze to Arielle and Arianna. The proof and products of Ian's infidelity stood not only before her, but one had been provided a safe and loving harbor for a score of years in their home. Her heart welled with despair. Ian stood solemnly silent for he could not disavow his actions. He knew the Devil's fingers had touched him. He hoped the imprints of Satan's digits would not forever sear him with scars. Arielle observed her mother and could see her elder's face begin to crumble.

"No worries, Mummy," Arielle attempted to claim calm, reverting to the endearing moniker she bestowed as a child on her mother.

Arielle recalled Emma's comforting words when first she learned of Olivia Smithfield's letter. *My dear, Arielle, we cannot know what the future holds nor would I choose to know. Such knowledge would take the spontaneity from our step and leave us depleted like children stripped of their sense of wonder. We must confront that which has been given to us, making adjustments as necessary, continually moving forward in anticipation of what the next day brings. Most shadows disappear by the light of day giving us renewed energies and clearness of thought. You will see this to be true my dear, in the not too distant future.* Emma's wise soothsaying lent a careful hand to settle Arielle. Emma was Arielle's confidant and guide, she had been touched by Emma's grace and generous heart, and for that she would be forever grateful.

"Our damn insecurities bring us to this," Ian blurted as he moved across the room to load a tumbler with scotch. "May I pour anyone else a drink?"

"*Our.* What do you mean, *our.* You, sir, are trying to put out a fire with matches!"

Elsbeth longed for what was, for not knowing, for sweet denial. But, that was yesterday, and that was gone from her grasp. They could not return to before. She hoped their daughter would love them equally well and not, after Ian's disclosure, favor one over the other, or at the very worst, deny them any relationship with her. *All I can do is deal with what I have been given. Some things never change and it seems my husband is one of those things.* Her mind pounded with thoughts. It was the loudest silence she had ever experienced.

"At the very best, Sir Ian, we can attempt to regain a modicum of mutual respect, though my spirit is weak. Oh, God help us. God help us."

"Dear Elsbeth, there is usually a way to work things through, if one is so inclined. I beg you to give me the opportunity to redeem those qualities that first met your attraction."

"This is no simple matter. You have for years been intentionally ambiguous about your actions, your behavior, and your whereabouts."

"Oh, I am certain you have heard, a lie well told and stuck to is better than the truth. I am not telling you more than I can tell you. I too am surrounded by darkness and will not dignify any claims made here through repetition or denial! And, Arielle, what influenced you to turn to Miss Pennybacker in the first place? On whose evaluation did you depend to seek her out on your behalf?"

"She came to me on the recommendation of Mrs. Willard and…"

"Sir Ian, Arielle need say no more. Why, Mrs. Willard's merit rates among the best. No one would ever question her authority nor her intent."

"But…"

"You will pardon my candor, sir, but Mrs. Willard is beyond reproach."

William stood at the ready to defend his aunt and take down Ian if the need arose. He held his silence, but was more than prepared to speak if needed.

"Father, Mum's declaration is correct. There is no further need to question or deny the validity of Miss Pennybacker's disclosures that bring us to this day. We ask that you be forthright in your discourse with us."

"And, Sir Ian, you speak of lie's well told, well, the truth be told, your lies have come home to roost!"

"Oh, El, can you not put this more charitably, dear? Do you not see these are unintended consequences of my actions?"

Elsbeth appreciated the diminutive he used and realized she was succumbing to his charm. Quickly, she rose to her senses.

"Do not mistake my good nature for stupidity. I too have honor and pride to uphold and you are making my task extremely taxing. All I can ask is that God give me the strength to use the capacity I possess to forgive. And, to refer to these lovely young women as 'unintended consequences of your actions' is thoughtless, I might add."

"With no harm or disrespect intended, Mum, your common sense appears to be compromised by your pride for you to suggest forgiveness with such ease." Arielle could not grasp, nor ignore the blind eye her mother was wont to use to view her father. "Mum, I find it unfathomable to believe you have elected to condone Father's infidelities."

"Arielle, I forbid that you speak of your father in such a way. We must stand strongly together. I must temper my protest against your father's indiscretions for I see before me two beautiful young women who would not grace this earth without the transgressions of his past and, you know I love you dearly. There is not a prosaic bone in your father's body. Dull has never been his forte. His gregarious style has made him the patrician he is today and all of us who live under this roof have benefited. If I must consign to the past his blatant forsaking of our vows, I will do so with his declaration to never again stray from our commitment to one another. Love does not come without risk or sacrifice. When we accept love, we accept everything that comes with it."

Elsbeth's next words came slowly and deep from within her throat. "Ian, do you think me a fool? Do you think, over our years together, I have not, on more than one occasion, been most aware of the nature of your absence from our home, from our bedchamber? Your 'misguided behavior' as you so term it, cannot be so easily disclaimed and cast aside. It is time, full well, for you to stand before us all and repent. The ugly mire to which you have drawn us will not begin to be abated lest you truly cleanse your heart and soul. The time for truth has arrived. We all await your turn toward forthrightness and the purity of spirit that will bring us to a common bond of understanding. My eyes are awake full-wide, yet I find myself in the midst of a nightmare. Speak now, but choose your words wisely for they most possibly will be some of the most important words your tongue has ever yet to form."

Ian searched the faces of the beauties before him. Suddenly, three women who stood before him were connected to his life and one another in a way he had never envisioned nor planned. He was a creature of agendas, of plans, of minute details. But, alas, that was his business world, his preparation for committee meetings, not the regimen he assigned to his personal life.

"It is time to speak the truth," Elsbeth admonished, still holding her words deep in the bowels of her throat. "Let it be the real, honest truth, *not* the truth you want us to believe."

Elsbeth was not blind to the vast permutations of love. She loved Ian. For her, standing by him was not a sacrifice. It was her choice. *Ian tests my every nerve and the limits to which they can go. He has however, always made me feel as though I was his core, and for that I am grateful and satisfied. Arielle must understand, I am not duty bound. Her father and I remain together by the graces of the bond of love.* Elsbeth was quite prepared to hear her husband speak.

"I must implore, that as greatly as I too seek the blessing of God, it is the blessing of my dear Elsbeth that is paramount at this juncture." Ian's word seemed to bubble in a nervous froth from his mouth.

Peepers paced erratically in his wired home sensing the tension in the room. "Whoa boy, whoa boy. What's the point of it all? What's the point?"

As Agnes moved to hush Peepers' outburst, Morgan's quick glance his way virtually stopped him in mid-prance. She could see the path Ian and Elsbeth's tones were taking with one another without the bird's prompting. She sensed a twin cue from Arielle and Arianna to present the coffer to Ian for his review. Arielle had expressed the need to hear the truth from his lips. Perhaps the contents of the treasured box, so important to Annie Hollingsworth, would stir his memory and provide a much-needed recipe for healing. The eternal struggle between right and wrong was rearing its ugly head for all to view.

Chapter Thirty-Seven

Late September 1897
Washington, District of Columbia

I an stood to receive the coffer from Miss Pennybacker. He held the box staring down at the wood's grain, its veins running in parallel position to one another, parted only by the keystone of a carved rose. The wavy route of the wood grain across the surface of the lid forced his eyes closed for a moment as he reflected on the irregular path he had taken that brought him before this jury of his peers. He opened his eyes praying all he had run asunder could be made smooth like the finely sanded finish the box's creator had applied to its carpentry. Slowly, he walked to a large wingback chair near Elsbeth and sat. A nearby table provided a comfortable resting place for the box. He looked up at his accusers, those who had found him out, and saw an earnest need in each of their eyes to hear his explanation, his apology, to have his conscience cleansed.

Had it not been for Olivia Smithfield's letter, he would have gone to his grave without the knowledge of his daughter's birth mother and his status as the one who sired not only her, but her twin as well. The weight of the moment brought a sobering rush to his upper torso and, for the first time in her lifetime, Arielle witnessed her father's lips and cheeks tremble as a wave of remorse rolled along the shores of his face. His upper body was caught in the motion. His shoulders shook and then quickly regained composure as the tide of emotions receded. He was not going to be washed away by the vestiges of his past. He would weather the repercussions of his actions and restore all that had been good in his life and that of his wife and child. But, the scene had changed and he had another child to consider. He looked up at Elsbeth, then Arielle, then Arianna. A hazy glaze of tears, as soft as the brush strokes defining the lithe body of a Degas ballerina, gathered across his eyes.

"I hope this will not become the lead paragraph in my biography." Ian broke the room's silence with his voice. His attempt at levity was as much for himself as for the tempo of the room. He knew full well any words of sentiment would weaken his resolve to face this chapter in his life head-on.

"So, please enlighten me. What is the purpose of this box? This object is foreign to me. What is to be achieved by my perusing its contents? From where did it come?"

"Father," Arielle found herself the first to speak, "The box was the property of Miss Annie Hollingsworth. She worked at your colliery. Upon her death, the box was transferred to the care of Miss Hollingsworth's dear friend, Maggie Galligan. It remained an unopened keepsake until Miss Pennybacker and Miss Fielding became aware of its existence when interviewing Miss Galligan. It is imperative for us all that you look at the contents and provide a voice for the items there. They were of significant importance to Miss Hollingsworth. Since her voice has been silenced by death, you are perhaps the only living soul who had a hand in their presence, and that hand must now deliver much awaited answers."

"Yes, Sir Ian. I too am curious. The contents of this box may help bring to closure what now seems like a lifetime of disbelief. The time for delay has ceased," Elsbeth made her plea with ease, though weighted by a heavy heart.

Morgan handed over the metal instrument perfectly formed to fit the lock facing Ian. He inserted the key, then gave it a turn, all the while wondering if it would afford entrance into a past he had long since forgotten. He lifted the lid, and though by magic, a daguerreotype sprang into view. He removed it from the box, and adjusting his eyeglasses, gave the photograph a turn in the light. There she was, the one whose name had become synonymous with his Arielle. There she was as plain as day before his coach. He knew his coat of arms anywhere and, though the image before him was faded and without the proper focus, there was no question it was his park drag.

The Hargrove coat of arms was distinctive to no one other than Sir Ian Hargrove. He held no direct descent of ancestry to be heir to another's sign of heraldry, but he felt every knight was entitled to display his coat of arms, and he was no less deserving. Each component born on and about the shield was designed to his specifications to promote his social standing and add an element of pageantry to his coach, while drawing the attention he quite enjoyed receiving. The shield's background was as black as the interiors of his mineshafts, with crisscrossed silver arms formed of links resembling coal buckets.

In the past, some townsfolk had remarked the shield was too dark, but Ian quite liked the stark contrast it provided for the crest that featured three bright yellow canaries sharing one neck. Their feathers spread onto the side of the shield forming its mantle. The universal use by others of a rampant lion or an eagle's head held no appeal for Ian. He rather preferred to display the canaries clinging to a wreath of gilded black laurel. He felt the trinity lent an assurance from God that all would remain safe and well in the Hargrove colliery. For Ian, the canaries represented three attributes he appreciated but on occasion failed to exemplify: freedom from fear and harm, the intelligence to know and do better, and the ability for the unconditional sacrifice of self. At the shield's top, just above the crest, was a banner with his motto in Latin: Carpe Diem. "Seize the day." The words never held more meaning than at this time when the photograph in his hand portrayed a picture that found him wrought with self-loathing and regret for the damage his lack of self-control, over a score of years ago, had brought to this day. He must right his wrongs, and right them he would today and all days henceforth.

So, here she stood beside his fancy park drag, her pit brow girl threads standing in dingy contrast to the clean lines and brilliant paint finish of his fine turnout. His concentration was shaken by Elsbeth's voice.

"Sir Ian. Please share what you have found with us all," Elsbeth politely requested.

Ian passed the photograph first to Elsbeth who reviewed it with discerning recognition of the coach she had so often been transported in throughout the vale.

"Who is this in the photograph? Clearly, she is not known to me and, by all appearances, is not dressed to warrant transport in our coach. She is but a common pit worker. My goodness, Sir Ian. Please explain. You appear to have knowledge of her."

The gathering seemed to collectively hold their breaths as they awaited Ian's reply. He was taking some time to respond, as though the wheels in his head were trying to recall the circumstances surrounding the day the photograph was taken. His mustache appeared to twitch as the muscles around his mouth moved side-to-side and he continued to focus on the face before him.

He remembered seeing her early each morning at the colliery and again in the fading daylight hours before the final whistle blew ending the coal pit's day. He thought she was one of the young men who toiled in the coal mine to earn what little they could to help feed and shelter their families. When he learned he was a she, he turned a blind eye to her existence. Her dedication and hard work made her a valuable asset to the colliery. As long as the authorities were unaware of her gender, she remained a necessary worker on his payroll. Paul the Overman voiced his concern, but Ian paid him no mind. He was the boss, the owner, the one to whom all answered. He was all-powerful and no one, not even a trusted manager, could sway his decision.

Ian knew the name Annie Hollingsworth triggered something from a time far ago. He had not been able to place her name until now. All these years had come and gone, yet her face remained with him. A beautiful face behind the coal dust, wearing a large work hat that held her identity secure until Ian removed it late one afternoon and a coif of lush auburn hair billowed forth. How could he have known about her condition. She worked, never missing a day, until the heat of July forced her away. He wondered what had become of her, having asked Paul the Overman who simply stated she had taken ill and might not be back in the mine for some days. No one ever suspicioned her fate would be to succumb to the rigors of childbirth. Curiously, several years after Annie's passing, no one knew what triggered Ian to reverse his opinion of girls in the mines. He vigorously instituted regulations to ensure there would be no risk with girls. There had been accidents grim enough, and he wished to witness them no more.

Arielle was the spitting image of her mother. Her raven locks being the only feature to betray the likeness. *Of course,* Ian thought, *the product of my loins would share something of mine. Her hair color and brilliant mind for business have provided my bond with Arielle. And, now, Arianna with the visage of Arielle and the auburn hair of her mum. All these years, and I have not been privy to the results of my actions. Oh, God help me that there be no others.*

"Sir Ian, I beg you answer."

Ian appeared to suffer a crisis of confidence as his voice became hushed to a whisper and he began to share words of his past, revealing truths that would remain secrets no more.

"My dear Elsbeth, I cannot justify what you are about to hear. There was a day, late day actually, when I was inspecting the facilities at the colliery. This worker, a young man, or so I thought, fancied my coach and wanted to have a look. Seeing no harm in his request, I invited him to step inside. There are times when it is necessary to fraternize with the working class who, after all, bring the bread and butter to our table. Once inside, he asked details about the coach, especially about the leather seats and velvet walls. I stepped inside to answer his questions. He was running his hand along the edges of the seats, feeling the tufts. I reached to make particular note of the embroidered monogram above the windows and in so doing, brushed my hand across his hat, causing it to fall to the floor of the coach. At that moment, a cascade of auburn tresses fell to his shoulders and the realization that he was not a he became blatantly clear. She had quite a way about her. Her eyes searched mine to discern my reaction to her gender. She knew full well her job was in jeopardy depending upon my reaction. I know I appeared stunned. She began to coax me to keep her secret. She said she needed the work and could not survive without it. Her eyes were most captivating. Flecks about the irises, just like Arielle's and Arianna's. I can tell you, I could not have predicted that day. But, what happened next led, it would seem, to the inevitability of this day. I had my driver carry her home in the coach, never imaging a photograph would be taken to document our assignation."

"The day of our conception you mean," Arianna offered with a tear beginning to form in her eye.

She was stunned to learn this man before her was her natural father. She had forever longed to have a man in her life, a father like her schoolmates had. Now, here he was, all of a sudden thrust into her midst. Could she accept him as a father, or would he remain no more than a stranger? Arielle's mind was spinning with similar emotion. Though suspected, hearing her father admit the truth of his ways was overwhelming. For her entire life she had believed these two were her natural parents. *Adoption. Conception. Redemption.* Arielle wondered if she could accept all that these words embodied as they circled in rapid pace about her mind.

"I was solely unaware. There was never another meeting. She kept her job and I went about the business of the colliery. Had I known the girl was with child, I would have assisted her in some way, I suppose."

"You suppose? Oh, Sir Ian, on what scale do you rate your conscience? You have much to repent. I can hardly believe my ears. And, our coach of all places. To think I rode in the very bucket of iniquity you used for such dalliances. How many others soiled the interior of my vessel for travel? I am outraged!" Elsbeth could hear herself shouting. A wave of vertigo passed over her and she gulped to catch her breath.

"There were no others in our coach, I assure you," Ian said, moving his hand to Elsbeth's shoulder to steady her emotion, at once accepting the chastisement.

Elsbeth knew how to interpret his candor. There may have been no others taken in the coach however, that did not extricate Ian from having taken others in a host of other settings. She was trying so diligently to accept this man, her husband, for his shortcomings, his infidelities. Her convictions and her pride were rising up to protect her from his darker side. Though Ian had never taken a hand to her, his emotional detachment on occasion had rendered her without confidence and fully enveloped her in self-doubt. Protection and strength were shields she needed in great measure if she were to forgive his actions and move forward with their lives. Lives that now encompassed not one, but two daughters. The truth be told, Elsbeth enjoyed her life the way she lived it and could only hope the addition of Arianna would provide sorely needed balance.

"The coffer, Sir Ian. Is there more within?" Elsbeth asked with reticence as though hoping no more pain would be extracted from the box's interior.

Ian reached his hand inside as though he were searching a mystery bag whose contents needed to be removed before any true identity was revealed. He held forth a sterling silver serving spoon. He rubbed its bowl, moving his fingers up the length of the handle where his digits rested on the monogram etched into the end of the handle. A capital 'H.' He rubbed his thumb over the engraving.

"Hargrove," he spoke aloud. "I had no idea she would keep this piece in her possession."

Elsbeth and Arielle looked at the piece with immediate recognition. Elsbeth recalled the day Ian presented her with a full service of the very flatware he held in his hand. It was a wedding gift he bestowed upon her the evening after they took their vows. The flatware had been a staple at every evening meal. She had taken its significance for granted until this moment. Ian passed the spoon to her. She held the implement in her hand. In times past, it had served delectable dishes of sustenance. She stared at its empty bowl and its tarnished surface. Like her spirit, it suffered from a lack of care and attention. Time had truly passed. Objects and human beings had been sacrificed. Elsbeth wondered if she could muster enough courage and strength to freshly polish her life with Ian.

"How did Miss Hollingsworth come to have this? Was this a payment of sorts for services rendered?"

"Do you remember, Elsbeth? You asked that this piece, this berry spoon, go to Samuel the Silversmith for a proper buffing. It was in the carriage. I thought it would not be noticed if it went missing from our silver chest since we had several similar pieces. The girl, I felt, could sell it and make use of the funds for her well-being. As I said, I had no clue she would keep the piece in her possession."

Arielle looked about the room. Emma and William remained silent. The two were sympathetic bystanders to an unfolding drama cast with characters to whom they felt a great kinship. William tilted his head her way, a warm glow of concern and care evident on his face. Emma's eyes spoke in similar fashion. Arielle knew they held her best interest at heart. Their steadfastness would sustain her. Miss Pennybacker maintained her silence in contrast to Peepers who needed to periodically be quietly hushed by Miss Fielding after an exasperated, "Whoa boy, whoa boy" burst from his throat.

Miss Pennybacker, having been in courts of law on many occasions, appeared to relish Ian's flow of testimony. She had reason to suspect the contents of the coffer would stir his memory and bring clarity for all. His revelations did not disappoint.

Ian reached inside the coffer and withdrew a folded piece of stationery. Its edges, yellowed and curled, had become somewhat brittle. Carefully, he unfolded the paper and was confronted by a poem written in a flowing cursive style. He looked up at his wife and daughters, then to the others surrounding him. This would either become his circle of forgiveness or a noose by which they would lasso him to render the punishment he deserved. He read over the words without a sound. His eyes welled with tears that he choked back.

"What is it, Sir Ian? What does the paper convey?" Elsbeth queried, taking a deep breath to prepare herself for the next assault to her senses.

"I am not prepared to read this aloud. Perhaps we can forego…"

"We have come this far, Father. If I may, I will share the contents of the paper with everyone. To begin anew, we must forego nothing. All must be relinquished so we may step beyond this quagmire in which we have found ourselves," Arielle implored.

"Very well. I must first say, dear Elsbeth, I had no knowledge of the girl's feelings nor, I must reiterate, her condition. This news is very painful and I wish I could reverse the clock."

"*'Oh, bid time return. Call back yesterday'* are words my husband would quote from Shakespeare's Hamlet if, bless his soul, he were with us today. Hindsight is a valuable resource to help turn the tide of the future. Forgive me for speaking, sir, but I have become very fond of your daughters. As difficult as these proceedings are for all involved, it behooves us to remain of open mind. Some things may have changed, but there is great room for adjustment in the human spirit. I have seen it time and again. I pray for healing insight for all."

Emma placed one of her hands on Arielle's hand and the other on Arianna's. William placed his hand on his aunt's shoulder in affirmation, connecting each of them to the other. The warmth of his contact seemed to travel through her to the sisters. The foursome felt a sudden sensation come over them, like an angel testing its wings had just brushed them with grace. Was there indeed a strong power in the room transmitting the reverberations, or was it a bad case of nerves descending upon them?

"Sir, without being presumptuous, if I may, unless one of the ladies would like to do so, I can read the paper aloud for you." William's words gave Arielle a sense of relief. She was certain she would not be able to read through the entire piece without some ill effect.

"By all means, Mr. Clay," Ian said as he handed over the paper for William's reading, noting the non-verbal exchange between his daughter and the lawyer. Mr. Clay was indeed totally besotted with Arielle.

William cleared his throat and silently read through the first two lines before proceeding to read aloud. As he read the words to himself, he felt as though he were privy to someone's innermost thoughts, that he was the outsider who had not yet been ushered in. Though uncomfortable, he determined himself to do this for Arielle and would see the reading through for her. He began:

Sharon Allen Gilder

Comfort Evermore

He had some care for me I know
Though 'twas not born of love
He had some passion once bestowed
Whispered on wings of doves

A moment quiet yet bold
A remembrance left behind
Voices echoing through the years
"Cherish the secret, forgive the lie."

When of a time all is set free
As truth comes from the dust
When of a time one withers in grief
Songs of angels you must trust

For I am but a simple soul
Whose fate the wind has cast
The bounty of our union
Shall be for everlast

Though my time here may have ceased
I have a wish, a plea
Let the gentle tunes of angels
Softly sing comfort evermore to thee

Signed: Anna Hollingsworth

Annie's audience was silent. Only the rustle of paper could be heard as William folded and passed the poem back to Arielle. Before returning it to the box, she rubbed her hand over the lid's carved rose, her fingertips riding the intricate peaks and valleys of the carving. A simple thing of beauty, nature's perfect fragrant gift to life and love, had come to represent her natural mother in a way she would never have imagined. A single tear, as solitary as the coffer's rose, fell from her eye to be caught by a waiting petal. It glistened in the room's light, making the flower appear kissed by the renewing powers of morning dew. In moments, the tear was absorbed into the thirsty wood. It, as Arielle, had become one with her past.

Elsbeth closed her eyes and prayed. She prayed Ian would never again reprise the ways of his past. Slowly opening her eyelids, she broke the room's silence directing her carefully selected words to her husband.

"Sir Ian, it is my sole desire to render trust in your direction however, you must help me justify this trust."

"You may rest assured there will be no repetition. I have been fully confronted with the force of my actions." Ian sucked in a deep breath, which he emitted in a slow, rolling exhale as though the telling of the incredulous news of late had provided his absolution.

"Then, sir, I will exit this day with a heart much lighter than when I entered," Elsbeth sighed. As difficult as some changes could be, she understood a life well lived was a masterful composition of changes. She found herself a willing victim of interminable faith.

Suddenly, the vast cadre of clocks in the Hargrove manse stirred the gathering as each made note of the passing of time. Signaling the arrival of noon in a miscued chorus of tenors, basses, altos and sopranos, the timepieces chimed away in a slightly staggered refrain. For Ian it was an awakening. Quite possibly, it seems, his darkest hour had become his finest. Only time would tell.

Chapter Thirty-Eight

Late September 1897
Washington, District of Columbia

"Arianna, tell me more of your mother, of Miss Smithfield I mean. I was in her presence for such a short, short time. She seemed very dear and quite devoted to you. It would help us all I believe, for you to speak of her so we may know her better," Arielle queried, feeling her sister's loss was still fresh and needed to be acknowledged.

"Mum was my friend and teacher. We had few others in our lives, and I now understand why. I always thought her part recluse but, now see she was merely protecting me, keeping me safe. She protected me like a treasured jewel she feared she would lose. Uncle Edmond was the only father figure I ever knew. His visits brought laughter to our days. Mum always delighted in his stories. She would often say he brought life into our home. I never knew how true those words would be. Now that I have learned of his part in my birth, I fear I question his judgment. Perhaps, he knew best. Perhaps he knew I would have become one of many orphans. Perhaps I would never have had the loving home and privileges that came to me under Mum's guidance and care. He is gone, Mum is gone. I loved her immensely and will miss her with the same intensity. As you know, Arielle, William, she was able to utter few words at the very end. She told me she loved me. Those words were all I needed to hear and will remain with me always. I will forever feel the loss, however, there is no turning back the clock, so I will have to continue with the strength of spirit Mum instilled in me. She always encouraged me to persevere and be of good faith. There seems no better time than now."

Arianna found herself poised between joy and sorrow. *My greatest sadness is that Mum is not here to witness the ultimate joy her revelations have brought.* She took Arielle's hand in hers.

"I am blessed to have a sister, to meet my father, and be surrounded by this room full of loving care. We all have much to understand and accept. Together we will accomplish what to some might seem insurmountable. Mum would want me to do no differently. I will honor her memory by living a life of victory against all odds."

Ian absorbed Arianna's words. Arianna. His daughter's twin. Arianna, his daughter. He shook his head in disbelief. The news was so fresh, he felt raw inside. Olivia Smithfield coming into his life was his greatest blessing and his biggest curse. Her correspondence had caused his most blatant indiscretion to be ferreted out while it simultaneously yielded amazing revelations that products of his loins existed in the world. A fact he could not repudiate. Now, here he was preparing to celebrate the woman with his daughters. *If they will accept me with warts and all I will be a most grateful man and, for Elsbeth, this will bring calm and make her home complete.*

"About those drinks, sir. I think a round for all is in order."

"My yes, where are my manners. Mr. Clay, if you would be so kind, would you do the honors?"

Ian pointed to the crystal carafe on the server. The mirror on the back of the buffet reflected the rich crimson liquid within the large vessel. A sterling gallery tray held heavy, cut crystal stemware. William filled the glasses with claret, handing one to each in the gathering. Ian declined the Bordeaux and instead reached for the bottle of Macallan, his favorite 12 year old single malt Scotch whiskey.

"Would you like a splash of water to accompany your drink?" William inquired.

"Thank you sir, but no. It has been in the bottle long enough. There's no need to enhance it."

"Point well made," William said as he concurred with Ian's explanation.

Emma raised her sparkling crystal glass and turned to address Arielle and Arianna. "I extend my hand in lasting friendship with a toast and wish for you dear girls. If one keeps revisiting old wounds, they never heal. So here is to casting the past aside. Time passes, and with it withers youth but, hope always lingers. May you live long, healthy lives to remember Olivia, for the spirit never dies. Life may end, but relationships do not. You shall be forever joined in your beautiful hearts and minds."

"Here, here," came the collective voices joined in unison of spirit and resolve to make amends and appreciate the bonds of life.

"I would like to add an addendum to Mrs. Willard's beautiful toast. We know not what tomorrow brings. We must embrace today and praise God for it no matter the circumstances of the moment. The tide has changed and on the morn we shall rise renewed. As Lady Wilson so eloquently stated, 'We are but birds of passage…and must build our nests out of what materials we can find." Elsbeth took a deep, long sip of claret -- the richness of its bouquet left a silky coating as it channeled along her throat.

"Here, here!" Laced with the soothing tonic, the gathering exploded in a rousing cheer spun from the melded force of frayed nerves and the long-awaited feeling of relief provided by the open airing of the events of late. They had become a group of kindred spirits and kindred souls unfettered by differences of judgment or moral character.

Arielle and Arianna's love and devotion for the other transcended love of self. In such a few short weeks, the twins had mastered the art of sharing a life with another. In unison, the two looked at one another and shared a heartfelt smile.

The group's cheer was fragmented by a loud knock at the front portal. Fiona scurried forward to answer the caller's peal. Before her stood a very agitated flaxen-haired woman she recalled greeting on another occasion. Fiona pursed her lips together and shifted her eyes side-to-side as she considered whether she should provide entry to the one before her. She knew she had been less than welcome on her previous visit. Fiona's hesitation was no match for the visitor as Alexandra burst past her and swept into Ian's study with as much gusto as the earthquake that befell the city months earlier. Alexandra's tremor could be felt by all before her. Emma cast her a look of disappointment. She had hoped Alexandra was finished with her railings about Arielle. Her performance at the masquerade was sufficiently deplorable. She hoped the girl had learned her lesson and would allow good breeding and decorum to prevail.

"Oh my goodness, William. Hopefully, I have arrived in time," Alexandra exhaled, her words coming forth in exhausted puffs.

"In time for what?" William queried as he moved closer to Arielle in a protective stance.

"Oh my word! Do not tell me that you have believed a single thing that woman has had to say! How can you be so taken in by her pathetic story? She does not deserve your sympathy, William. Please tell me you have not fallen victim to her scam!"

William looked at Ian and Elsbeth. He knew there were few in the gathering who could withstand any further emotional upheaval. He moved from Arielle to Alexandra to silence her and remove her from the room.

"Alexandra. It would be best for you to take your leave now. This is a private gathering and one you have entered without invitation. Here, let me escort you to your carriage."

"Unhand me, William. You treat me like a stranger. You know how I feel about you. You must know. Have I misread your intentions? Am I nothing to you but a commitment you made to my father? I cannot believe you are treating me so. Here, have a look at this." Alexandra's voice cracked as she attempted to cry, but even her tear ducts failed to find any sincerity in her plea and became as hardened as her demeanor. She could barely endure William's disdain. She twisted her arm away from him and looked glaringly at Arielle. From her purse, she withdrew a small frame and tossed it toward William which he adeptly caught in mid-air.

"Where on earth did you get this?" William queried.

Arielle caught sight of the frame's contents. The image of a young girl, a child identical to herself at the same age, was posed on a settee. Had she not known better she would have mistaken it for herself though the color of hair was of a different hue and the frame was foreign to her.

"Do you not see, William? Are you so blind that you will not see? Lies, they are filling your mind with lies. Miss Hargrove is not whom she claims to be. She is an imposter on a mission to ruin your good name and claim you for your riches."

"I ask again, Alexandra, where did you get this?"

Then she noticed the one from the masquerade. *Oh my God! Here she is. But for the color of hair, she is the spitting image of sweetie, sweet, Arielle Hargrove.* A sound like a hiss came from Alexandra's mouth. Her serpent's tongue was in full force. She saw defeat before her. She was no match for the one, much less two. Her shoulders began to slump down as she felt consumed with failure and then her shoulders rose. She stood erect. Filled with venom and ready to strike, she held her head high and slowly looked each of those before her in the eye.

"You missy, had best learn that this man you hold in such high regard had promised his heart to me. Now, it appears, he has taken another path, a path of which you should be wary. I warn you to take leave of him before you too are treated in a despicable way such as myself. And, as for the photograph, it found its way into my position on a visit abroad."

"This explains the information shared by Miss Pennybacker that my mum expressed the presence of a flaxen-haired visitor who failed to reveal her name. We thought Mum was hallucinating and, for her sake, I wish she had been, for to think you stood before her, in her weakened state, and tormented her with your very presence. The thought sends chills through me." Arianna looked at those gathered in stunned silence, their faces echoing her distress as William handed over her mother's stolen property.

Arielle felt enormous pain for William. She knew he was a fine man and Alexandra's behavior was taking a significant toll on him. She wanted her to disappear. Her life was on the cusp of making sense. She had a sister to embrace and know better. She had much to look forward to putting into place. It was time for Alexandra to go. She would be denigrated by her no more. *If I never see her again, it will be quite soon enough.* She had no patience for her bellicose behavior yet hesitated to further incite her. She could abide her presence no longer, but she was determined to hold her poise. Witnessing Alexandra getting her comeuppance was wont to bring a hidden smile to Arielle's face.

"So, you have taken to theft? You, my poor dear, have gotten it all wrong. Your ignorance of the facts, and desire to smear the reputation of Miss Hargrove is misplaced and intolerable. Your nefarious practices are not your best servant." William maintained his deportment as he delivered verbal blows to Alexandra's ego.

"Alexandra, I beg you to exit now. We have all been through so many trials these past months. Please allow William to accompany you to your coach."

Emma was quite weary of Alexandra and had held her silence long enough. A life of affluence and doting had not served Alexandra well. Emma had hoped to spend more time with her to guide her in the grace and courtesy lessons she so lacked. She knew their ill-fated visit to Purdy Court was a setback that would take some time to remedy.

"You have much for which to be thankful, my dear. Having William as a loving friend is merit enough for your relationship, which at its core must harbor mutual respect. Now, let him see you out. Life's lessons can be difficult and unpalatable. Love can be stronger for one than for another and cannot be forced. I am certain if you search your soul you will come to this same conclusion."

William grasped Alexandra by the elbow as she tried to twist from his hold. He held his body against her back to control her as she fought his guidance. He continued to direct her toward the main portal. Their movement became a forced shuffle as she resisted his efforts to expel her from the Hargrove's home. Her behavior ever since his first encounter with Arielle had left a deleterious effect on all in her wake. It was due time for her ship to sail a new course.

"You have not heard the last from me," Alexandra railed. "William and I have much to discuss. He cares for me, I know."

Her exclamations and avowals of love became weaker as she questioned her own words. She was filled with torment as reality took hold. She felt a sudden squeeze in her chest as any hopes of a spark being kindled between herself and William summarily expired. She looked back into his eyes and knew from the expression on his face that the reservation for his affection did not hold her name, it had been reserved for another. As he moved forward, she fell to the floor and crawled desperately across the carpet to capture his attention.

"I apologize for any discomfiture Miss Whitaker may have caused." *William, always the gentleman,* Arielle mused as she listened to his words.

Alexandra grabbed William's leg and attempted to hold him back with all her might. "Please, please, William," she pleaded, tears streaming down her face as she delivered her well-rehearsed line. "Please, do not forsake me. I love you and you know you love me."

William bent low to lift her from the fog of doom rapidly enveloping her. In Alexandra's zeal to keep him, she was willing to deny the humiliation she suffered. As the others looked on in stunned silence, William, and a very reluctant Alexandra, exited the front portal. Her journey home would find her very far removed from William, not only physically, but also a great distance from his heartstrings. *No, I will not be easily rejected, and certainly not for some wimpy snippet like Arielle Hargrove. If they think putting me in my carriage sends me on my way, they had best remember with whom they are dealing. It may take some time, but I will conquer William in the end, of that I am most sure.* She was determined their shared history would not be left to the past.

Alexandra stared through the windows of her carriage. *Focus, focus. I must focus.* The horse's hooves picked up pace, causing the scenery outside the coach to blur. Alexandra blinked her eyes to clear the dust and webs of confusion. She would not be put off without a fight. She had revealed herself and thus made herself more vulnerable. She would however not retreat. Her eyes suddenly overflowed with tears. She could feel the teardrops on her heart like little daggers causing her wincing pain. *Everyone needs someone to love,* Alexandra thought to herself and tightly closed her tear-swept eyes, forever oblivious to the fact that her primary love would always be herself.

Chapter Thirty-Nine

Late September 1897
Washington, District of Columbia

I n pursuit of fresh air, and a momentary escape from the day's
revelations, William, Arielle and Arianna stepped through the
conservatory's side door into the garden. The scent of autumn's
approach wafted toward the trio, invigorating them as they inhaled its cleansing freshness with welcomed gusto.

Evidence of fall was tapping deciduous trees whose leaves
were beginning to change in hue. Annuals were attempting to
hold their zest, though their fate was doomed with the fast approaching drop in temperatures. The unseasonably early, and
cold fall, left rose bushes scantily clad. Most were shed of their
blooms and ready to hold themselves dormant for the frigid
months ahead. Fortunately, the gardener's careful placement of
boxwoods around the perimeter of the Hargrove's rose garden
provided year-round color and structure.

Washington's winters could be robust. Temperatures below
freezing, patches of ice, and blankets of snow often paralyzed the
city. Arielle was least fond of extreme weather conditions, much
preferring the moderate cycles of spring and fall.

She looked about the outdoor space before her and was reminded of a pleasant January morning the year past when she awoke to a patch of sunlight casting its path into her bedchamber through the branches of a stately maple tree. The bitter cold night had left remnants of decorative ice crystals on the upper casements of her bedroom windows, forming bursts of fern-like feathers on the panes. Individual crystals were clustered in poufs resembling frosty confetti with shaggy crystalline fringes outlining their boarders. They appeared as flattened flakes etched firmly upon the pane and, as the sun lit them, they looked like the cut edges of crystal prisms. Their beauty had mesmerized Arielle.

Her mind traveled back to today. A crisp fall day. A day to shed summer's heat, rejuvenate and harvest all the good in her life. Though the hues and shades of summer were now no more than a memory, the sylvan setting did much to enrich Arielle's soul. She observed the rich texture of the evergreens, those with variegations on their leaves appeared splashed and splotched by Mother Nature's hands. *With William and Arianna, I have everything I ever wanted and, yet somehow, never knew I did.* Arielle's thoughts brought a smile to her face as the words took hold in her mind.

"If you do not take exception, I would like to venture this direction to see what lays beyond the hedge. Please do not feel you must accompany me, for I am fine with a bit of time alone in the garden." Arianna smiled as she waited for her companions to set their course. She sensed they would find no objection to their threesome becoming a twosome. Arielle looked to William who stood waiting for her to signal the direction they would take.

"Sister, enjoy your time here. We will join you again. I can see you are prepared to use your talents and would not want to delay such creativity. So, off you go to the east as we saunter to the west." Arielle took William's arm and proceeded along a stone path to the outer edges of the property.

Arianna looked about the outdoor space. She found the gardens at the Hargrove's brownstone charming. They were defined with benches and a mix of boxwoods and hollies that established a lush framework for the remainder of the garden to rebound. A large statue of Diana, the Roman goddess of the hunt, held vigil over the flora, as if keeping it safe from the ravages of ravenous wildlife.

The basin of a concrete birdbath was an aquatic aviary, attracting the bathing attention of blue jays, cardinals and tiny sparrows that lighted on its rim to dip their beaks in a repetitive pecking fashion. Upon consuming their faces in the cool liquid, they gyrated their bodies in vigorous shakedowns that seemed to propel the refreshing wet substance throughout their plumage, doubling their girth at least half again. Arianna's presence sent them on their way as she proceeded along a pebbled path past a hedge where a small bed of rose bushes awaited pruning. Only a handful of mature flowers remained. Their prime had long passed. Withered, burnished edges in tired reds, pinks, and yellows greeted Arianna but did not discourage her from her quest. With art box in hand, she was determined to record this milestone day in her life in the way that most naturally came to her.

She removed her supplies, laying them beside her on a garden bench, and uncapped a vile of water sufficient for the paints necessary for her artistic expression. Propping a pad of heavy paper on her lap, supported by her left hand, she began to moisten the paints with her wet brush and softly applied paint, layer upon layer, to reach the depth of intensity she wanted to achieve. As time progressed, leaves and imagined blossoms developed on the paper, some as fresh as a summer rose and some replicating the remnants of fall's touch. The blend created a lovely bouquet to the past and present. Arianna held the painting away from her and squinted her eyes to view her work. She added a few finishing strokes of her brush and determined the composition complete.

William and Arielle met their destination at a large stone-wall along the west side of the manse's property. They felt far enough removed from the house to privately enjoy one another's company while maintaining the propriety expected by their elders. Arielle paused and took in a deep breath of the crisp air. She looked to the base of the wall where a lone rose bush held its place among much hardier shrubs. The climbing rose bush's vines trailed their way up and along the knobby surface of the cold, heavily shaded stonewall, wedging their way among the stones wherever the timeworn mortar had gone missing. Thorny tendrils of stems stretched and branched their way along, over and through, retreating to the other side of the wall where the stems, spent from both their buds and blossoms, appeared to find new freedom to stretch and expand anew. A band of sunlight could be seen, shedding its radiant warmth on the opposing face of the wall that provided division from the garden and the path shared by the neighboring yard.

"I will be forever grateful to your Aunt Emma."

"You may speak of her as your aunt as well, my dear. I know she would want that to be so."

William's words sent a chill of excitement through Arielle's body. All she had hoped for was coming to be. She felt more like herself than she had ever felt before. Throughout her accident, recovery, and the answers to her earliest beginnings, William had not been far from her side. She had oft questioned whether she would see this day, but she need question no more.

"You are quite right, and I gratefully acquiesce to that knowledge. She is one among few who have come before me and spoken life into my dreams. She has my undying gratitude. As I look before me and gaze into your eyes, I have truly found heaven on earth that, but for her guidance, might never have come to be."

"Look here, Arielle. It is curious how nature finds her way among the most formidable foes to renew and redeem herself. Against all odds, this delicate rose vine has taken the challenge of mastering a structure far stronger than itself to pursue its course.

There is a lesson to be garnered here or, perhaps, the journey ends at the wall and only appears to continue to another realm," William surmised as he lent his best effort to bring comfort to Arielle by discussing the flower about which she and her sister were most passionate.

"Will. Oh, do you mind if I call you so, or do you prefer the formality of your full given name? I do not know what has come over me for the word 'Will' simply slipped from my tongue."

"From you this is an endearment which I wholeheartedly accept. Will or William, you may call me either and I will gladly respond."

"I know when first we met, my heart leapt. I must say, once again it seems my heart cannot contain itself with you in its midst. You exceed any expectation I might ever have had about caring and devotion. My heart sings with the mere thought of you and when you are near, it knows abundant joy. I am forever blessed with you in my life," Arielle's voice cooed with emotion.

William's eyes met hers, causing a subtle reverberation to course through his facial muscles. He was in deep love with the woman before him and she with him.

"You know my fondness for this flower," Arielle said as she lifted the bloom and gave it a sniff to see if any fragrance could be inhaled from its petals. "From my most recollected and earliest beginnings, it has contributed hope, inspiration, and beauty to my life."

"There is no greater beauty than yourself, my darling. Even this glorious gift of nature must sense competition with you in its presence. I know your heart is heavy and your mind is weighted with the news that has come your way. Feel comfort in what we have and in what we have yet to experience as we build our lives together."

"Years from now, how will we look back on these days?"

"There will be no regrets."

"Of that you are sure?"

"Of that I am most certain."

"And, why so?"

"For, I am with you and you with me, and for that I shall be forever grateful. Until the last rose blooms and its essence leaves this earth, I shall love you all my days."

"And I you."

Arielle took William's hand and gazed into the deep blue sea of his eyes that held her afloat and buoyed her spirits.

"Do you ever wonder if the vines have really advanced to the other side or lay at the end of their road on this side of the wall?"

"Will, why don't we go back to the house? The others will wonder what has kept us so long."

"What, and not find an answer to the question I have posed?"

"Come, Will. We can save that for another day."

"Another day might see the opportunity passed. The weather grows only colder and this vine we witness today may be nothing more than a memory tomorrow."

With one swift motion of foot, William stepped on the long stone bench that provided contemplative seating for garden respites and he hoisted himself atop the wall. Arielle watched with amusement as his lengthy form dangled against the wall while he gripped its uppermost cap and peered over its firm surface.

"Arielle, you must come and see."

"Will, of what do you speak?"

"Why, you will not believe me unless you see this thing for yourself. Come, I will lift you to the top of the wall."

William slipped back to the surface of the bench, firmly planting his feet so he could reach for Arielle and raise her sufficiently high enough to peer over the wall. Her body stiffened as she readied herself to be lifted. William's hands came up about her waist as she raised her hands to grip and look over the top of the wall. He was cautious in his movement, stabilizing his stance so the two would not be thrown off balance and bring down the very vine that consumed their conversation. Arielle grunted as her fingertips slipped on first attempt and William realized he needed to raise her higher so she could latch onto the uppermost portion of the wall. At last, success arrived and, with his strong hands securely holding her in place, Arielle cast her eyes over and down the other side of the wall.

Her eyes welled with tears of joy as she spotted the single red rose that William had witnessed before her.

"Will, it is a sign. It is here as a sign, it must be. As Maggie Galligan relayed to Miss Pennybacker, when my mum passed, this graced her bedside."

"What, my darling."

"The rose. The rose beyond."

"Yes, my darling, the rose."

"You see, Will. The rose grows. The rose grows beyond the wall."

Only the heart knows how to find what is precious. Fyodor Dostoyevsky's words came to Arielle's mind. She slid down the side of the wall into William's very capable arms. The two rested their feet on the sturdy stone bench. Her arms were raised with her hands on his broad shoulders. His hands kept their grip on her petite waist as their eyes met, and a nervous shiver coursed through their bodies. They drank in the sweet nectar of the moment, their eyes begging for more, and their minds imploring them to follow their hearts. William felt ready to devour her with his lips. She was all he had ever wanted, and he had known no greater joy than when in her presence. Arielle felt ready to burst. She so wanted to lean into and partake of every facet of him. They held their stance as William answered her call and gently brought her closer to him. He bent down and placed his lips on hers with reserved passion. He wanted to savor every moment of their intimacy. Looking into her eyes and holding her was reward enough. But, the kiss. The kiss brought them together in a way both had only dreamed. It awakened all of Arielle's senses as she closed her eyes and kissed him back, wanting their encounter to last a lifetime. Their lips released. They gazed into one another's eyes and went back for more.

"I love you." The words came spontaneously and in unison, as though the two had been rehearsing for this most important performance of their lives. The stage was properly set, and the curtain had risen on their scene. All of a sudden, a bolt of green flew through the air. Peepers had escaped his incarceration. He rested his feet on William's shoulder.

"Whoa, pretty boy. Whoa, pretty boy. I love you. I love you," Peepers repeated as he cocked his head back-and-forth looking from William to Arielle.

The two threw their heads back and laughed.

"It appears, Fiona is not the only one bent on eavesdropping," Arielle mused.

"Ain't that the truth? Ain't that the truth?" Peepers squawked as proud as a peacock with his newfound freedom.

William and Arielle heard the French doors open and close as someone exited the manse onto the patio. Morgan's voice could be heard calling for the bird between reprimands to Agnes for letting him escape his cage.

"Peepers, make yourself known boy," Morgan implored.

"I can tell you, Morgan, you will have to bribe him to get him back. He is a stubborn old bird," Agnes shook her head as she proceeded to find Peepers.

"In point of fact, most old birds are," Morgan chided.

"Well, Will. It looks as though we have solved a mystery for Miss Pennybacker," Arielle smiled as she gathered Peepers from William's shoulders and held him securely in her hands.

"Indeed. Here is to life's mysteries," William smiled as he placed his arm around her waist and escorted her back with their feathered captive to join the others.

Emma beamed from the doorway of the conservatory. She could not be more pleased to see her beloved nephew resplendent with joy. Morgan and Agnes led the way to recover Peepers from his escapades as Arielle caught Emma's gaze and shared a smile that radiated through their eyes.

Arielle reached into her dress pocket and handed an envelope to Morgan. "I cannot thank you enough for your fine work on my behalf. Enclosed, please find payment for your services. I hope our relationship does not end here. Though I never want to be in need of your skills for anything of the sort we have experienced these past months, I am quite fond of handwork and I am especially pleased to know of your exquisite store. I am sure you will find me there on many occasions as I undertake new projects. Perhaps I will be able to tempt Arianna to slip away from her watercolors long enough to try her hand at needlework."

"It has been our pleasure to assist you. We are glad for the resolution of your inquiry," Morgan said as she turned her head toward Emma. "And, Mrs. Willard, we thank you for your referral and the opportunity to be in your company."

"The pleasure dear is mine. I had heard you were the best in the city. Your reputation not only precedes you, it stands firm. I will not hesitate to recommend you in the future."

Morgan began a modified bow in Emma's direction, only to be stopped midway by Emma's approach. "Oh, let me give you a big hug dear, you have done so well. I just have to hug you."

Agnes thought she would have a stroke. She knew Morgan's style was to remain aloof, and could only imagine what Morgan's reaction would be.

Peepers stopped pacing on his perch, cocked his head forward and nearly popped his eyeballs staring at the embrace as he chirped, "Whoa boy, whoa boy, ain't that the truth, ain't that the truth."

Morgan, in stiff fashion, accepted Emma's embrace, backing away slowly and smoothing her overcoat as she gathered her composure. She was like a wild stallion not easily soothed by one attempt to tame her free spirit.

"Well...well...thank you again, Mrs. Willard. We will be on our way."

William moved to Arielle's side and walked to the front portal as the Pennybacker entourage made their exit to the street.

"Well, another superior job, Morgan. An open and closed coffer so to speak, to be sure," Agnes snickered, taking great delight in her sense of humor.

"Whoa boy, what's the point of it all?" chirped Peepers.

"Oh hush, you silly bird," Morgan admonished. "The point is, we have met with success. Our attention to detail has gotten us to the heart of the matter." Morgan knew the morning and the claret had taken its effect on her for she was now answering the inquiry of a bird.

Agnes looked over her shoulder at the couple in the doorway of the Hargrove manse. "I should say, if you ask me, the heart of the matter is right behind us. Indeed, those two hearts have found one another."

"So, you now consider yourself a soothsayer is that it?"

"It is just my intuition working away. I have a good feeling about this. I like that Mr. Clay and, what a handsome couple they make. Mark my word, he is carrying a torch for Miss Hargrove. She would be wise to snatch him up."

"Agnes, I do not think I have ever heard such talk from you. We had best be getting back to open the store. There is a storm coming and, in point of fact, my intuition tells me we have much new work on our horizon. Just wait and see."

Arianna emerged from a garden path to join Emma, William and Arielle at the door as Morgan, Agnes and Peepers took leave. As their carriage pulled away, Emma turned to William and Arielle.

"I hope you will join me for dinner this eve. You know my home is more than open to you, and Simon will be most pleased to have you within its walls. I have asked Arianna to join us as well. This is a night for celebration and we must not let it escape us."

Arielle gently tugged on William's coat sleeve and looked to the darkening skies.

"Oh, Will. It appears we are in for a downpour."

"As I recall, we have weathered many a storm before, my love."

He placed his fingers on her chin and lifted her face to his. She soaked in his handsome face and felt a radiant tingle throughout her body. She had never known such happiness and at once wanted to be his in every sense of the way. It was time to take leave and revel in all that lay ahead.

Arielle stepped beyond the portal where nature's elements began to fall. Slowly, splashes of rainwater put drop upon drop of precipitation against her face. William gathered her in his arms and momentarily lifted her from the pavement. He placed soft kisses on her cheeks drying the raindrops away. Arielle felt like cooing as she looked into his eyes.

"Emma, or, may I call you, Aunt Emma? Your dear nephew and I met on a same such stormy night," Arielle said as she kept her vision focused solely on William's face and the tantalizing muscle pulsating in his right cheek.

"My dear, he is your dear now, and yes, of course, you may call me Aunt Emma. I will be most honored to have such an endearment bestowed upon me by you."

William signaled Emma to reach her arm into his and Arianna followed as the foursome descended the stairs to his waiting carriage while the rain ensued in force. An air of déjà vu whispered past Arielle for, on an eve in the not so distant past, William had rescued her with great finesse from the ravages of the elements and the burdens of inevitability. Though this storm would soon abate, others were certain to arise. But for now, the warm, welcoming doors of Chestnut Heights awaited their arrival.

Photo: Stone Photography

Sharon Allen Gilder is a native Washingtonian. She resides in Maryland and South Carolina with her husband.

For more information, please visit
www.sharonallengilder.com

Made in the USA
Charleston, SC
17 June 2014